The
Listener

The
Listener

Robert McCammon

CEMETERY DANCE PUBLICATIONS
BALTIMORE
2018

The Listener
Copyright © 2018
by Robert McCammon

Cemetery Dance Publications
132B Industry Lane, Unit #7
Forest Hill, MD 21050
www.cemeterydance.com

The characters and events in this book are fictitious.
Any similarity to real persons, living or dead,
is coincidental and not intended by the author.

First Edition

ISBN: 978-1-58767-613-0

ONE.

Someone's Angel

One.

The Devil can be a man or a woman. The Devil can be a hard spring in the seat of a car, a gnat in the eye, or the whack of a wooden baton on the iron bars of a jail cell. The Devil can be a flash of lightning, a swallow of bad whiskey, or a rotten apple slowly decaying a basketful of good ones. The Devil can be a belt across the back of a child, or a cardboard box of cheap paperback Bibles swelling up in the hot rear seat of an eight-year-old faded green Oakland two-door sedan held together by rust and wires.

Which, today, the Devil was.

The man behind the sedan's wheel looked to be someone's angel. He was thirty-two years old and handsome in the way of a lost cherub, with two lines of sadness bracketing the corners of his mouth. He had curly blond hair, cut short, and eyes the color of summer smoke. He wore the pressed trousers of a white suit and a white shirt with a new collar and pleats down the front. His thin black tie was held in place by a silver clip of two hands clasped in prayer. A straw fedora with a black band sat on the cracked leather seat beside him, along with the folded white suit coat. His hands upon the wheel were soft. He was not a man who lived by physical labor, in a time when so many others dug ditches for their dollar-a-day. As he had an aversion to the fierce summer sun of southeastern Texas that burned men and women into withered and leathery sticks, he depended on his intelligence and wit to see him through the tough times.

Trouble was, he'd never seen a time that wasn't tough.

He guided his tired car along a rutted and dusty backroad that cut through spiny pinewoods. Just below his right elbow was a hand-drawn map of the country he now travelled, with an inked-in "x" here and there along this track leading to many small towns and farms that dotted the scorched landscape. He had not far to go to this one, but many miles to cover today.

His shirt was damp with sweat. The air that blew into the car seemed to steal the breath, and smelled faintly of rotten peaches. The aroma stirred a memory in him but he wasn't quite sure what it was so he didn't try to draw it up. Whatever it was, it belonged to the past. He was a man of the future, which was becoming the present second-by-second. He figured that in this tough old world if a man wanted to live he had to learn to shed his skin like a snake and move from the shadow of one rock to the shadow of another—*move, move, always move*—because the other snakes were on the move too, and they were always hungry.

It was the first week of July in the year 1934. Less than five years ago on that black Tuesday in October the bottom had dropped out of the nation's economy. On that day the stock market had collapsed, and one bank after another had begun to fail across the nation. The windows over Wall Street had opened, allowing rich men who found themselves suddenly reduced to paupers to follow their fortunes down to the hard pavement of reality. Businesses went under by the hundreds, as the flow of cash had stopped at the shuttered tellers' cages. Debt and foreclosures boomed. In the aftermath of the stocks and banking bust, winters had never seemed colder nor summers so brutally hot. The Great Plains was hit by high winds that blew topsoil off the drought-stricken farms to scour the tortured land into churning dust storms. Breadlines grew in once-dynamic American cities. Many thousands of vagabonds rode the rails in search of work, and many more thousands roamed the land on foot or in cars and trucks that were a broken axle or blown gasket away from their last mile.

It was a time of misery from which there seemed no end nor respite. The cheer from such radio shows as *The Major Bowes Amateur Hour*, *The*

National Barn Dance, Amos 'n' Andy, The Lone Ranger and *Buck Rogers In The 25th Century* was welcome, but was only a passing moment. Beyond the entertainment of disembodied voices and the merry golden glow of the radio tubes the harsh world remained, a fact that President Franklin Roosevelt's measured and earnest "fireside chats" could not overcome. America—and indeed most of the world—had been shattered, and even now the pieces of the future were being gathered and reassembled by Stalin in Russia and a puffed-up mug in Germany named Hitler.

But today, though it was hot enough to fry an egg on the hood of his car, the man in the faded green Oakland was on velvet, as the saying went. He'd had a good day yesterday and made nearly thirty dollars. He'd enjoyed a steak and fries last night at a cafe in Houston. There he'd gotten into a conversation with a travelling shirt salesman about whether the Feds were ever going to find out who'd kidnapped and killed the Lindbergh baby. It was called the Crime Of The Century and everybody who could listen to a radio or read a newspaper had kept up with it since the child's corpse had been found, its skull smashed, a year ago last May.

The man who looked like someone's angel didn't care if they ever found out who'd killed the baby. Such things happened, it was the way of the world. The Lindberghs were richer than Midas, they'd be okay and they'd already had another kid since that one died. These were desperate times and people did desperate things.

The car's tires jubbled over railroad tracks. He passed a roadsign pocked with rust-edged bullet holes. FREEHOLD, he noted the sign said. He drove on from blinding sun into pine shadow and back again.

The sight of the bullet holes drew him to an area he thought more interesting and surely more entertaining than the matter of Lindbergh's kid. He'd been following the exploits of Bonnie Parker and Clyde Barrow since the pictures of the two of them clowning around with pistols and shotguns had been found in a camera they'd left behind up in Missouri and had gone out to all the read-rags. Too bad Bonnie and Clyde had been shot to death by a posse of six lawmen on a backroad in Louisiana not two months ago.

He'd read that there were so many holes in the bodies the embalmer had trouble getting the fluid not to leak out, and that the cops who'd done the shooting had gone deaf from all the blasting.

He hated that because he was going to miss hearing news about the Barrow gang, who all they'd robbed and killed and so forth. Sure they'd been living on their rabbit's foot, but there was something to be said for making your own way in what the country had become even if that meant using the noisemakers. The odds were against the regular joe, it was you against the big blue, and what was a joker going to do but find a way to blast out of that gray concrete vault they were always trying to wall you up in?

Well, there was always John Dillinger to follow. They hadn't gotten that rowdy bastard yet, and he'd been lying low since April but he was bound to show up somewhere soon. His shootouts were always arousing news.

The man drove his raspy Oakland into the little town of Freehold, which came up from the pinewoods just beyond a red stone church and a small cemetery with a statue of an armspread Jesus at its center. He was approaching a little forlorn-looking Texaco gasoline station coming up on the right. Though he needed no fuel because he'd filled up in Houston and he always carried a spare can of gas in the trunk, he turned into the station. He pulled his car up beside the Ethyl pump and waited with the engine running. In another few seconds a young man with one leg shorter than the other and wearing a built-up shoe on the foot of his afflicted limb came out of the hut wiping his hands on an oily rag.

"Mornin'. Need to cut your motor, sir. How much you need?" the young man asked through the toothpick in his mouth. He added, "We just got some of that new Fire Chief gas in."

"No gas," said the driver in a soft, quiet voice. It was a voice carrying a nearly-musical Southern accent that had been called both *refined* and *aristocratic*. "I am needin' some information. Do you know how I can get to the Edson place?"

"Toby Edson's?"

"That would be it."

"Well...yessir. It's on along Front Street, past Wahouma Street and take a right at the next one, which would be State Road Sixty. You go out about another mile...mile and a quarter, I reckon, and you'll see the mailbox on the left says Edson on it."

"Thank you kindly. And for your trouble." The man brought a shiny nickel from his trouser pocket and placed it into the oily palm.

"Much thanks," the young man answered. He frowned. "If you got business with Mr. Edson, I have to tell you he passed away last week. Buried him on Thursday. His heart give out."

"*Oh.*" Now it was the driver's turn to frown. "I am sorry to hear that. Still...I do have business at the Edson house, and possibly I can be of a comfort. Good day to you." He gave the young man a nod, put the car into gear and started off again.

Freehold was a dusty town with several shuttered storefronts. He passed a farmer driving a watermelon wagon on Front Street. A couple of old cars and a battered Model A with an iron pick-up box welded to the back were parked in front of a place whose sign proclaimed it as *Betsy's Cafe*. Nearby, two elderly gents wearing overalls and straw hats sat on a bench watching the man in the faded green Oakland glide past; he waved at them, just being neighborly, and of course they waved back.

He turned right on State Road Sixty and picked up some speed after he'd left the town limits. The mile and a quarter passed. He saw the Edson mailbox on the left. He pulled off onto a dirt road that threw whorls of dust up behind his tires. Pine trees and underbrush grew on either side of the road. In another moment he came out upon a clearing where stood a small white-painted house under the spreading limbs of a huge oak tree. A few cows were grazing in a fenced-in pasture, and about fifty yards distant from the house was a weather-beaten barn. He stopped in front of the house, cut the engine, retrieved his white coat and his fedora, unstuck his sweat-damp back from the seat's leather, got out and put on both coat and hat. He smoothed his tie and adjusted his collar so that the coat hung as perfectly as he could manage. He noted a tire swing hanging from one of the oak tree's lower branches and briefly envisioned Toby Edson's two kids, Jess and Jody, playing there in the sweet shade.

The screened front door groaned open. "Mornin'," said the woman. She sounded both weary and wary. "Help you?"

"Yes ma'am, I believe so. This is the Edson residence, if I am correct?"

"It is."

He was already walking around to the other side of the car. Dust from the road drifted in the air and sparkled golden in the sunlight. "I have somethin' here for you and the children," he said.

"Pardon?"

"Somethin' for you and the children," he repeated. He opened the passenger door, pulled the seat up and reached back to get one of the Bibles from its box. The proper one was marked with a yellow tag with the number One on it, meaning it was the first delivery of the day. Moving quickly and deftly, he removed the tag, dropped it onto the floorboard, and slid the Bible into a white cardboard box designed to fit it snugly and made to look like leather. The words *Holy Bible* were tooled across its front in gold-colored ink. Then he closed the door and turned toward the widow Edson, summoning up the proper expression of both regret and expectation.

"I am sorry for your recent loss, ma'am," he offered, with a slight bow of his head. "I learned at the gas station in town that your husband has only recently passed away."

"Buried Toby last Thursday," she said. She was blonde-haired, had a pale long-jawed face, a sharp nose and eyes that looked drowned. The man from the Oakland noted that she held the door open with her right hand while her left hand was out of view in the house, and he wondered if she might be gripping onto either a pistol or a shotgun. "What're you wantin'?" she asked, ready for the stranger to clear out.

He paused for a few seconds before he answered. "Well...this is a difficult time for you, I know, but—"

He was interrupted by two children who came out of the house and stood around their mother's skirt. They were both blonde and fair, like the woman; the boy, Jess, was maybe eight and the girl, Jody, was about eleven or so. They were clean and cleanly-dressed, but they had the rawboned look of kids who'd been hit hard by life. They both stared at him as if he'd just dropped down from another planet.

"May I approach you, ma'am?" he asked.

"What do you have there? I've paid what I needed to pay this month, I'm all square with the bank."

"I am sure. And you are square with Jesus and the Holy Father, too."

She blinked. "*What?*"

"Allow me." He lifted the Bible in its white presentation box and waited for her to motion him forward. As he reached the woman and her children, he heard a dog half-barking and half-baying from the direction of the barn.

"Dottie wants her pups back," the woman said to her kids, though her eyes never left the white box that the stranger carried. "Go on and take 'em."

"Ma, we just brought 'em—" the little boy started, but the woman shushed him. The man smiled politely, waiting for this small family drama to pass. It was then he saw that both the boy and girl were holding a puppy cupped in their hands, the one dark brown and the other a lighter shade with a cream-colored spot between its eyes.

"Newborns," said the man, maintaining his soft smile. "Nice lookin' pups."

"We got six of 'em." Jess held his up closer for the man to see. "Fresh-baked."

"Hush that," the widow Edson said sharply, and the man from the Oakland thought it was probably an expression her husband had used. "Go on, do like I told you."

The boy started off, though reluctantly. Jody said, "Jess, take Dolly with you too." She gave the pup a quick kiss on the nose and then handed Dolly to her brother, and with one puppy cupped in each hand the boy trudged on toward the barn while the mama dog continued to bay forlornly. Then the little girl stood at her mother's side, her face expressionless but her jaw set, and her blue eyes seemed to cut right through the skull of the man who looked like someone's angel.

"You have somethin' for us?" the woman prompted.

"Most certainly I do." He offered a smile to the little girl, but she wasn't having any so he turned the full force of his gilded charm upon the widow. "First, ma'am, let me show you my business card." He reached into his inside coat pocket and brought it out, a clean white card fresh-baked, as Toby Edson might have said, last night in the hotel room. When he offered the card, the woman seemed to pull back a space and the little girl took it.

"Says his name is John Partner, mama," said Jody after looking it over. "Says he's the president of the Holy Partner Bible Company in Houston."

"That I am." John Partner retrieved the card and put it away. He thought *the woman can not read and she depends on the child. Well, that is interesting.* "As I say, I know this is a difficult time for you, but possibly my visit will be some comfort to you today. I have the Golden Edition Bible your husband ordered last month."

"The *what*?"

"Oh...pardon. You weren't aware of this?"

"You need to speak plain English, Mr. Partner," said the woman, near exasperation. "I'm awful wrung out right now."

"Your husband," said John Partner, "placed an order last month with my company for a Golden Edition Bible. He sent one dollar pre-payment, as I specified. The inscription was done, as he asked, and I responded that I would personally deliver the item." He pushed back the brim of his fedora, brought a white handkerchief from his pocket and mopped his forehead because the heat was truly fierce even here at just after nine o'clock. "I... suppose he didn't tell you any of this?"

"A Golden Edition Bible," she said. Her eyes had reddened. "No. No, he didn't say a thing. You mean...he sent you a whole *dollar*? By mail?"

"Yes, ma'am. He must've seen my advertisements in the county news-paper." His gut tightened. If Toby Edson was also unable to read, the game might well be up. But the woman remained silent though her stricken expression spoke volumes, and John Partner plowed ahead on the fertile field of human suffering. "My guess, Mrs. Edson...is that your husband meant it to be a surprise. Maybe a gift for a birthday, or an anniversary?" She didn't respond, so he used another tool from his well-used box of sentiments and softened his voice to deliver it.

"Or possibly...he had a premonition that his time was short. Many people do. It is the voice of God speakin' to them. Or at least that is what *I* believe. But it all comes down to love, Mrs. Edson. The love of God to let someone gently know that their days are numbered, and the love of a husband—and father—for his wife and children. Would you like to see the inscription he asked me to make?"

"I don't..." She had to stop and take a long breath, as if she'd been stunned by a belly-punch from the blue. "I don't read so well, sir. Would you read it for me?"

"Surely." He was aware that the dog had stopped baying from the barn, content that her puppies had been returned, but Jess evidently had decided to stay in there for awhile. The little girl's solid, no-nonsense stare made John Partner a shade uneasy, and he wished she too had gone to the barn but it was part of his craft and gift to show no crack in his calm demeanor. He withdrew the Bible from its box, turned to the inscription page where the receipt was folded, and began to read with appropriate gravity: "*To my dear family, my wife Edith, my children Jody and Jess, your loving husband and father.*" He offered her the bit of paper. "This is the receipt, one dollar paid by Toby Edson of Freehold, Texas. You will note the date was the 12th of June, but I believe my secretary made a mistake and that date is incorrect by a few days, give or take."

The widow Edson accepted the receipt, unfolded it and looked at it with blank eyes; then she gave it to her daughter, who read it with the attention that John Partner thought a canny lawyer would give to a foreclosure notice.

"I'm just...I'm not knowin' what to say," the woman told him.

"I understand." He made a show of examining the house with a wandering but careful gaze, as if he were the banker set on foreclosing. "Well," he said, "usually it would be five more dollars, cash on delivery, but—"

"*Five* more dollars?" The way she said that, it sounded like five hundred.

"Six dollars is our rate for the Golden Edition. You understand, ma'am, it is a family keepsake meant to last for generations. On the receipt, it says five dollars due."

"Oh...yes sir, but...that's a terrible lot of money."

"Mister?" said the little girl. "Can I see the inscription?"

"Certainly. Bear in mind, it is not in your father's handwriting. It is printed there by our special process and with ink blessed by Reverend Winston Carter of the First Baptist Church of Houston." He gave her the Bible and turned his focus again on the distraught woman. "Now, Mrs. Edson, do not fret," he said gently. "I am not a mercenary man, and our dear Jesus and Father in Heaven would not wish you to be deprived of your late husband's gift to you. There *are* costs to consider, though. It is the penalty for living in Caesar's world. But let me offer you this: the Holy Partner Bible Company will take four dollars for this special edition, and we can call it—"

"Mama," Jody interrupted, "don't give this man no money."

John Partner stopped speaking, but his mouth remained open.

"*What?*" the woman said. "Don't be rude to—"

"The words written here," the child went on. "They're what he said they were, but...Mama...it's got my name spelled wrong."

A piece of hard rock seemed caught for a few seconds in John Partner's throat. When he got his voice out, it sounded thin and shrill in the quiet. "Spelled *wrong*? *How?*"

"My name," said the little girl, with her defiant blue eyes burning into his skull, "is spelled with an 'i', not a 'y'. Daddy wouldn't have made no mistake like that."

Somewhere out over the pasture, a crow cawed and another answered from the trees at John Partner's back. Otherwise the world seemed to him to have stopped all other motion and noise, except for the roaring that was beginning to rise in volume in his ears. It came to him to wonder if that sound was what the deputies heard after all the shooting had gunned down Bonnie and Clyde.

"Her name *is* spelled J-o-d-i," said Edith Edson. Her eyes narrowed. "Surely Toby couldn't have told you any different."

It took only three seconds for him to regain his composure. He restrained himself from snatching the Bible out of the child's hands because he knew full well how he'd spelled it, the name had been spelled that way in the goddamned obituary in the county newsrag. He squared his shoulders and answered, adamantly, "If we have indeed made an error in the spelling, we will be glad to correct it."

"My name's spelled wrong," said the girl, and she showed him. "See? Right there it is."

Her index finger pointed to the offending 'y'. Then she showed her mother, who if she could not read much else could at least make out the names of her children.

"Four dollars," Mrs. Edson said, "is still an awful lot of money, sir. How are we gonna correct this?"

Before John Partner could reply, the child said, "I think he ought to give us the Good Book for free, mama. Let that be the end of it. Daddy would likely think it was funny. I can see him laughin' about it right now."

"Yep." The woman nodded, and maybe a small shadow of a smile slipped across her mouth. "I can too." She took the Bible from her daughter and ran the fingers of one hand over the front cover, which had begun to buckle in the heat. "Seems like this was a nice gift to us from Toby, but my man wasn't one to throw money away on somebody's mistake. He'd appreciate the effort you made and all, and he'd say this is a real pretty Bible, but... he'd tell me to pay you one dollar and let that be the end of it, like Jodi says. Does that suit you?" When John Partner didn't immediately respond, she went one step further. "Don't think you can sell this one to anybody else, can you?"

His face felt paralyzed. It seemed a long while until he heard himself say, as if from a great distance, "All right. One dollar."

She took from him the white cardboard presentation box made up to look like leather and slid the Golden Edition Bible into it, and then she went inside to get the money. He was left staring at the little girl, who simply stared back at him in silence, yet her accusing eyes seemed to send to him the message *I know what you are.*

When he had the dollar in his fist he gave the woman a cold smile and wished her good day. Then he turned his back on her and the child, went to his car, took off his coat and fedora with regal grace as the mother and daughter watched him, and climbed in. The engine started with a bone-shaking rattle and a harsh bark. Going out he passed the little boy coming from the barn, who waved to him in a neighborly way but John Partner did not wave back.

He drove away, leaving in his wake roiling clouds of dust.

Continuing his route by following the "x" marks of recently deceased people in the small towns on his roadmap, he had a mixed day. He sold two Golden Edition Bibles for six dollars and one for three because it was all the old lady could get out of her cookie jar. He stopped alongside someone's muddy lake near noon, ate some crackers and drank a Nehi orange soda. His next stop was aborted because there was a Texas trooper car parked in front of the house, and the stop after that was to an empty house with a foreclosure sign nailed to the door.

But all during the day, he thought of how that little girl had stared at him, and how her voice had stung when she'd said *Don't give this man no money.*

It had long been his feeling that people had no idea how hard he worked for his dollars. As hard as any ditch-digger, it seemed to him. Poring over the obituaries in the different county rags, getting the names and the addresses and whatever other information he could, then using his small rubber-stamping machine that allowed him to change the lettering and stamp in gold-colored ink what needed to be on the page. The Bibles and the presentation boxes combined cost him only a quarter from the company in Fort Worth, but the ink was damned expensive at seventy-five cents a bottle and it had to come all the way from New Orleans.

He thought that he was selling a valuable commodity, and people didn't realize it. The *law* didn't realize it. He was selling a lasting memory. A dream, of sorts. He was selling golden thread to tie up all the loose ends of a life. He was doing society and the grieving families a good service.

Don't give this man no money.

It just didn't sit right with him. It gnawed at his guts and made the crackers and Nehi orange soda boil in his belly. A few miles outside the town of Wharton he had to pull the Oakland over and throw up on the side of the road.

After that he felt cooler and calmer and he knew what he had to do. He sat in his car, rolled a cigarette and lit it with his silver lighter that had a pair of praying hands on it just like his tieclip. Then he rolled on into Wharton and in the five-and-dime there bought a baseball bat sized for a child.

He was surprised to find that Wharton had a movie theater and an afternoon showing of *King Kong*, which he'd seen last year when it came out, but he had enjoyed the movie and thought it was worth seeing again. When he emerged from the theater dark was beginning to fall, and as he had time to kill he had a plate of pork sausage, creamed corn and turnip greens in a little cafe a block down from the theater. He smoked another cigarette, nursed a cup of coffee down to the last drop and flirted a little with the red-haired waitress who brought him a piece of pecan pie on the sly. Then he paid his bill and left.

At the next junction of state roads, under the stars and the faint glow of a half-moon, he turned his car's headlamps in the direction of Freehold.

Don't give this man no money.

The injustice of it made him want to cry. But his face bore no expression but resolve, and his eyes remained as dry as prairie rock.

It was after nine o'clock by his wristwatch when John Partner pulled his car off State Road Sixty about thirty yards short of the dirt road that led to the Edson house. He figured he had to work fast, in case any troopers were on the prowl, but he'd already seen today that this road didn't carry a lot of traffic. The next house was probably a quarter of a mile west. He took the child-sized baseball bat and his can full of gasoline and started walking.

There were a few lights on in the Edson house. Lantern lights, they looked to be, and burning low. No electricity there. John Partner went to the barn. The door was already open a crack, so much the better.

When he stepped inside he flicked his lighter. Instantly the mother dog on her red-and-black plaid blanket in the hay almost at his feet started growling and tried to struggle up but the six puppies were feeding and they dragged on her. Before the dog could let loose a bark, John Partner clubbed her in the head with the bat.

He hit her a second blow, all his strength behind it, just to make sure.

Then he surveyed what he had done and went on to finish the rest of it. He covered the puppies with handfuls of straw. He poured the gasoline.

His lighter flared.

In the red glare of the flame, John Partner no longer resembled someone's angel. For an instant it was as if the flame revealed the face behind the face, and it was not something that John Partner wished to have on public view.

He picked up a final handful of straw and touched it with fire.

"J-o-d-i," he said quietly. His eyes were dead.

He dropped the burning straw upon the gas-soaked puppies on their gas-soaked blanket beside the body of their mother. They went up with a hot little *whoosh* that almost took his eyebrows and some of his curly blond hair before he could step back.

As much as he would have liked to have stayed to watch them burn, it was time to get out.

But he left the baseball bat. Jess might get some use from it.

John Partner returned to his car feeling as if a heavy burden had been lifted from him, or a terrible wrong set right. He put away the gasoline can, and with his load of Golden Edition Bibles he drove away into the night, into the dark, away and long gone.

Two.

"How long you figure on stayin' with us, Mr. Partlow?"

"I am not sure yet. I may get lucky."

"Oh? How would that be?"

John Partlow looked into the gray eyes behind the glasses. The old man had a heavily-lined face, a spatter of age spots on his forehead and gray eyebrows as thick as broomcorn. "The mechanic at the garage—Henry by name—tells me he will get the necessary part for my car from Shreveport as soon as possible, within three days if all goes well."

"I know Henry Bullard. Does good work but he tends to underestimate. I'd say you'd be settlin' in for a goodly stay, dependin' on what kinda part you're needin'."

"A new carburetor, unfortunately. I broke down about five miles out and had to be towed in. If I had not flagged down a haytruck I might still be out there."

"Hm," said the boarding-house keeper, whose name was Grover Nevins and whose wife Hilda was standing just beside him, both of them behind the black-lacquered waist-high desk where John Partlow had just signed the register. "Carburetor ain't good," he went on, with a rise of the mighty eyebrows. "Bet you'll be with us goin' on a week."

"That may be so, but I hope you don't mind that I pay on a day-by-day basis?"

"Don't mind at all, we ain't ones to put the squeeze on nobody."

"As long as you pay by ten a.m. sharp," said the woman, whose crimped mouth hardly moved as she spoke. She had large, owlish eyes and swirls of gray that swept back through her dark brown hair from the temples. "*Sharp*," she repeated. "We're kindly folks but we don't suffer no freeloaders." Her eyes had already seen the praying hands tieclip. "'Course," she added, "I figure you're all right."

"I appreciate your trust, ma'am. I would never intend for anyone to suffer on my account," came the reply, with a soft and cherubic smile to accompany his most musical voice. "I will be at an uncomfortable disadvantage if I have to stay here any length of time, as I have not even a change of underwear with me." He said that directly to her face, so he could watch her sallow cheeks bloom some color. He turned his considerable focus upon the man again. "This seems to be a quiet little town. I hope there's a place to find some supper? Or does my money buy at least a sandwich and a cup of coffee from your kitchen?"

"I don't cook for the boarders, Mr. Partlow," said the woman, with a lift of her sagging chin. "Groceries are too expensive nowadays."

"Stonefield Cafe is two blocks south," Nevins offered. "They stay open 'til eight. Good fried chicken over there."

"Thank you." Upon entering the boarding house at the corner of Second and Third streets in Stonefield, Louisiana as Bullard the mechanic had directed, John Partlow—alias Partner, but all those business cards and that identity had been destroyed a couple of weeks ago—had taken stock of the place with its dark-panelled walls, its rather threadbare carpet and on the shelves the collections of little ceramic bells, thimbles, figurines of horses and other such knick-knacks and decided these two would be easy touches, no matter how canny a judge of character the woman thought herself to be. The sense of order in here made him want to start shattering things. He wanted to seize their pitiful sense of control and wring all the blood out of it right in front of their faces. They knew nothing of the world, whereas he knew it all too well. He could imagine taking one of the ceramic horses and jamming its hooves into Hilda Nevins' eyeballs.

He heard what sounded like a woman's shout from upstairs. Quick and then gone. A curse word, it had sounded like, but it was over too soon for him to register exactly what it had been.

In any case, it had been nearly a snarl.

"Ah," he said, with a reappearance of the soft smile. "I thought I would be alone here tonight."

"Don't mind those two," said the woman, who had no idea her eyes were bloody holes in the imagination of the man she spoke to. She lowered her voice to a conspiratorial whisper. "A Dr. Honeycutt and his...well...I don't know what she is, but she ain't his wife."

"Interestin'," he remarked, with a tilt of his head and purse of his lips that said *tell me more*.

"When they got here yesterday afternoon, he wanted just the one room. But she said she wasn't havin' any of that and she wanted her own."

"Hilda," said Nevins, "I don't think we ought to be—"

"Givin' a talk at the Elks Lodge Hall tonight, in the auditorium," she went on, and John Partlow thought she was obviously gratified to find a willing ear to dish her swill into. "Know what the talk's about?"

"No ma'am, I don't."

"They've been puttin' up broadsheets all over town. Grover brought one to show me, but I wouldn't have it nowhere but the garbage can."

"Hilda!" The man's face was starting to cloud over. "Come on now, let's—"

"A *sex* talk," she said, with a quick glance at the staircase to make sure nobody else was listening. "It's called *'Better Understandin' Of The Facts Of Life'*, but it's a sex talk all right. How they got a permit to spew such trash I don't know, and there ain't time to get my church group together to run 'em out."

"We don't *want* 'em run out," said Nevins with a long sigh, and this sounded to John Partlow like a statement that had been made many times today, as the man seemed weary of saying it. "We need the money, and I reckon the Elks Lodge don't want to turn down a night's rent. Likely givin' Eugene a cut too."

"Eugene?"

"Our good-for-nothin' *sheriff.*" The lady of the house was now running full steam ahead on the fuel of stored-up indignity. "He got his job years back on the money of bootleggers and he ain't give it up yet."

"*Hilda,*" said Nevins, who actually sounded near tears. "Please *stop.*"

"All right," she answered curtly. "All right, I'll stop. For now. I'm just sayin', we're in a fix here." Her gaze returned to John Partlow's tieclip. "Are you a preacher, sir?"

"No, but I do try to spread blessin's wherever I go. I appreciate the compliment."

"You look like a preacher. You have a very kind face."

He bowed his head slightly, as if this were a humbling observation. "Now...I suppose I should get on to the cafe, shouldn't I?" He was hoping she would invite him into the kitchen, but the biddy's charity obviously ended at compliments.

"Good fried chicken there," Nevins repeated. "Tell Ollie you're stayin' with us, he'll take some off your bill. Room Four." He handed the key over. "We lock the front door at ten thirty."

"Sharp," the woman added.

John Partlow took the key, put it in the pocket of his white suit jacket and thanked his hosts for their hospitality. Then he left the boarding house, visualizing in his mind what the faces of Grover and Hilda Nevins would look like if they were half eaten away by cancer. He set off in a southerly direction through the streets of a small town that like most had been hit hard by the Depression. He doubted that Stonefield had been much of a boomer even before the banks had started shutting down, but added to the setting sun there was a glow in the sky to the southwest that indicated some kind of mill or plant was in operation. He had passed much farmland, many pastures and cotton-fields on the road before his Oakland had choked and died, so he figured this area might indeed be a fertile field for Dr. Honeycutt and the doctor's rather sharp-tongued female to be plowing, with all the farmboys around. *A sex talk.* Indeed, he thought. A nice little moneymaker, if it was handled right.

The streets were quiet as evening came on. Most of the meager little downtown area had closed up except for a barbershop on the next block. The cicadas of early August were shrilling in the trees, the air still and humid. As John Partlow approached the barbershop and its spill of light upon the sidewalk he saw taped to the front window a poster for Honeycutt's extravaganza. It bore a rather crude drawing of Cupid about to let fly an arrow into a Valentine's Day heart. Above the drawing was the statement of subject matter as Hilda Nevins had already told him: *A Better Understanding Of The Facts Of Life.* Below the drawing was printed *A Lecture Given By Dr. William Honeycutt With His Able Assistant Ginger LaFrance, No Man Should Miss It.* Then at the very bottom, stamped in red by the same kind of portable rubber stamping device that he himself knew so well was *Eight O'Clock, Thursday August 2nd, Elks Lodge Auditorium, Admission Twenty-Five Cents.*

John Partlow allowed himself a faint smile. *His Able Assistant, Ginger LaFrance.* Yes, that would bring the farmboys in from miles around. But twenty-five cents? Damn, they thought highly of themselves!

He walked on south toward the Stonefield Cafe and found it housed inside an old red caboose sitting alongside railroad tracks that cut across the center of town. He pushed in through the batwing doors past the sign that said *Whites Only*, settled himself in a booth on a hard slab of a wooden seat, and studied a chalkboard on the wall to decide between the main dishes of fried chicken, chicken-fried steak and something called Minnie's Meatloaf. His arrival brought forth a few curious glances from the six men and two women who were already being served by a chunky, curly-haired waitress, but they were used to seeing travelling salesmen even though his white suit and straw fedora marked him as a cut above the usual.

He took off his hat, ordered the fifty-cent special—fried chicken, black-eyed peas, collard greens, a piece of cornbread and a glass of iced-tea ("as sweet as you can make it, darlin'," he said to the waitress)—and found himself looking at his own reflection in a mirror that hung behind the counter.

He had realized several weeks ago that he'd done a rash thing by returning to the Edson place. The action had meant he'd lost an entire county to operate in. If the Edson woman had gone to the law, they might be looking for him thereabouts and they would know his car right off. So scratch that whole county off the list, and to hell with it. Then, toward the middle of July, he'd gotten rough treatment that had cemented his decision to find new territory. When he'd driven to the farmhouse of a recently deceased man in Burleson County and presented the Golden Edition Bible ordered by old dead Jonah, he had received the business end of a shotgun pointed in his face by a wizened widow who informed him that he must be a damned flimflam man because she'd already bought the Angel-Touched Good Book Jonah had made out to her from the Sacred Heart Bible Company of Houston.

So...with everything to consider, it was time for him to pack up his operation and move.

East or west? A coin flip determined it. Hello, Shreveport and the Dixie Garden Hotel.

As he ate his supper, he kept checking the clock on the wall next to the mirror. One more glass of sweet iced-tea and a cigarette or two, and then... maybe it would be interesting to take a little stroll around town, what there was of it.

When he asked the waitress where the Elks Lodge was, she gave him a knowing look that made him want to slap her so hard her big front teeth would shatter. The place was just over on the next block to the east, she said, past a small park and the statue of the local Confederate hero Samuel Petrie Blankenship, whose eyes—she was proud to say—wept bloody tears whenever a nigger walked past.

He told the waitress to inform Ollie that he was staying with the Nevins, and therefore did get a dime taken off his bill. He left the dime for the waitress in a wet puddle on the table where he'd spilled out a little tea, and then he put his hat on, straightened his tie and stood up. He felt the floor trembling under his shoes and heard the wail of an airhorn that shook the windows in their frames. As he went through the batwing doors the freight train that was rumbling through the town in a clattering cater-waul of thunks, bellrings, whistleblows, hisses and metallic clanks was just passing the cafe, stirring up whirlwinds of dust and grit that danced back and forth along the street. A few dogs chased the engine with their teeth bared and their barking swallowed up by the cacophony.

In the train's wake, John Partlow brushed away a few specks of grit that had settled upon his lapels and aimed his chin in the direction of the Elks Lodge.

The moment he entered the brownstone building on Fourth Street he was struck by the sight of a blonde woman sitting behind a table next to what he assumed was the door to the auditorium. She was selling tickets and putting the money in a cigar box, and taped to the white cloth that draped the table were several of the Honeycutt *Facts Of Life* posters. She had a knot of five men of various shapes, sizes and ages before her in the process of spending their hard-earned coins for a little racy education. What struck John Partlow about the scene was that the woman wore a white long-sleeved hospital coat buttoned up to the neck, the demurity of which did not exactly match the amount of thick makeup on her face and the slash of crimson lipstick across her mouth. Indeed, she appeared to be wearing a doll-like mask that allowed absolutely no expression, which intrigued John Partlow because the idea of hiding one's true self—or one's true face—was never far from his motivations. He put himself behind the gaggle of local men. They talked and laughed too loud and jerked with nervous anticipation before the woman's cool gaze, as if she were a female from a far distant and more worldly world, which of course she was. When John Partlow reached her his first glance was into the cigar box to see how the team was doing tonight, and it appeared from his quick estimation that they'd sold between twenty-five and thirty tickets.

"My, my," he said, and he looked into the woman's eyes.

They were the color of champagne, he thought. Just that suddenly he felt as though he'd downed a glassful of the bubbly—or several, enough to make his head spin. The champagne-colored eyes, which were a little almond-shaped like those of a feline, seemed to scan him up and down. No expression registered on her face. She had a pug nose, a broad mouth and a forehead that was an inch too high and a chin that was an inch too wide; she was no raving beauty, but in her own way she was to John Partlow very— and maybe disturbingly—attractive. There was something in her face both sophisticated and crude. He thought that she was champagne at the top and rot-gut down deep. Hiding her real self from the world, just as he did. Her hair, obviously dyed blonde because dark brown was showing at the roots, was a mass of curls at the front and pulled back tight along the skull with black-and-red lacquered combs. He inhaled a whiff of her perfume, which smelled to him of a sweetly-musky and beguiling scent that he could only describe as charred roses.

Neither one of them spoke for a few seconds. Finally he gave a crooked grin and said, "What're you lookin' at?"

"A little too much sugar for a dime," she answered, again with no expression. She had a Southern accent, but it was high-brow. It was from the mistress of the plantation rather than from the backwoods Bertha. Her eyes narrowed just a fraction as her gaze moved across the praying hands tieclip, the pleated white shirt and the vanilla-cream suit coat. "What're you dressed up so pearly for?"

"For *you*," he said, regaining his balance on this slippery dancefloor. "I wouldn't want to hear all about the facts of life dressed like a tramp, would I?"

Her face remained immobile. "A quarter gets you in, same as the tramps." She tapped the edge of the cigar box with a forefinger, the polished nail glistening blood-red.

"I am from Shreveport, stayin' with the Nevins."

"Good for you. No free rides, pearly." Her gaze shifted from him because two more men, both of them farmers in their best overalls, had just entered the Elks Lodge. She dismissed him with, "In or out, as you please."

A little piece of coal had begun to heat up in John Partlow's stove; he was not used to being dismissed, surely not by a bleached-blonde thirtyish housewife who thought herself such a smooth piece of leather. Ordinarily he might have shrugged his shoulders and turned on his heel, but this setup interested him from a professional point-of-view. He dropped a quarter into the box and took the ticket she offered. Then he walked on into the auditorium and left her smiling silkily at the rubes.

It wasn't a large auditorium, maybe room for fifty people on wooden church-pew seats facing a stage shrouded by wine-red curtains. Glass globes at the ceiling lit up the place with a slightly yellowish hue. Just above the stage, fixed to the wall, was the cast-iron head of an huge-antlered elk blackened by time. A fog of cigarette smoke was already rising to the roof, its ascent bothered only marginally by a single fan that sought vainly to clear the air. John Partlow saw that indeed he was the twenty-seventh attendee to this gathering of overalls, bowties and snuffboxes, and including the two farmers who'd come in behind him that would be seven dollars and twenty-five cents, which was a pretty paltry haul in anybody's racket.

He figured there had to be more to this than met the eye. He sat down over on the left side where there were only four other men. He took off his hat, placed it beside him on the pew, and waited for the show to begin.

Five more men drifted in, bringing the audience count up to thirty four. About fifteen minutes after John Partlow had taken his seat, the blonde huckster in her white hospital coat walked down the aisle without looking to right nor left but with a slow and enticing roll of her ample hips. She went through a door on the right side of the stage. Then everybody sat and waited some more while the cigarettes burned down, tobacco was spit into tin cans or inhaled from snuffboxes, and one of the older men had a coughing fit that sounded like his lungs were clogged with Louisiana mud.

Without fanfare the curtains were opened. A few men clapped with anticipation and John Partlow looked around at the grinning faces and wished them all dead.

Blondie stood at center stage behind a podium. A haze of cigarette smoke drifted around her. On her right was a table with a cardboard box atop it, and on her left was a small blackboard on wheels. She was holding an honest-to-God pointer, the kind a grade school teacher would use to show the dumbfool students how two and two made four and how "cat" wasn't spelled with a "k". Except John Partlow thought that the way she held it and looked at the audience with a little curl to her upper lip said she wished it were a bullwhip. Abruptly her face altered itself into a smile, which John Partlow noted did not exactly register in the cautious eyes. She said, "Good evenin', gentlemen," and a third of the audience good-eveninged her back with a couple of them hollering out their "howdies" that sounded liquor-laced. "We're waitin' for Doctor Honeycutt," she announced. "He should be here any minute."

"We don't need no doctor in *this* house!" somebody shouted, followed by a burst of nervous laughter.

John Partlow folded his hands in his lap. This was going to be an interesting entertainment for a summer's eve, and totally unexpected in a rube berg like this.

"Dance for us, darlin'!" urged a black-bearded and overall-wearing man who sat two rows in front of the visitor from Shreveport.

"Oh, I don't dance for *strangers*," she answered, keeping her smile fixed in place. "But…I imagine we'll all be good friends by the end of the doctor's lecture. In the meantime, I ought to make myself more comfortable." Then, moving as smoothly as a snake through wet grass, she came out from behind the podium and unbuttoned her prim hospital coat. The sight of the flame-red dress underneath it caused all chuckling and jibes in the audience to immediately cease. She took the coat off, folded it and put it on the table beside the cardboard box, and John Partlow wondered how it was that a woman could pour herself into a dress. The coat's stiff starch had hidden Blondie's curves, which were breathtakingly dramatic. Up on the stage now stood a red-hot sexbomb, who used her hands to smooth the dress and so slowly moved along the fleshy territory it barely concealed. In an instant the ownership of the Elks Lodge auditorium changed from its audience to the woman onstage, and in the silence that ensued the smoky air was heavy with what John Partlow could only describe as wanton desire coupled with a little plain shock. He doubted the local wives and womenfolk in this town had ever dared to show so much leg and breast in public. But here was the dish, all dished out.

She's got them, he thought. Nobody would be asking for their money back now, no matter what.

"Here's our Doctor Honeycutt!" she said brightly, but there was a grind of hard grit in her voice.

The man who advanced along the center aisle was staggering more than walking; he was two sheets to the wind, and John Partlow watched with increasing amusement as the silver-bearded so-called doctor in his gray suit, vest and black bowtie stumbled over his own two-tone shoes. The inebriated educator of the evening went to the door on the right side and had as much trouble with the handle as if it had been a live catfish coated in motor oil.

"Come on up, *Doctor!*" Blondie urged, and now it really did sound as if her teeth were clenched. "Just open the door and come right on up! Pardon the doc, y'all," she told the audience. "He just got out of a major operation, had to drain the fluid out of a whiskey bottle." That brought a few chuckles. She pressed on: "Kinda looks like he might've got the cork stuck up his ass, too. William, honey? Just turn that little ol' handle like you're bendin' your elbow for another snort! Come on now, do it for Ginger!"

Somebody stood up to help the doc, but then Honeycutt by trial-and-error got the door open and started through. He turned to give a theatrical bow to the onlookers who were enjoying this spectacle as much as a hound dog enjoyed a coon hunt, and John Partlow recognized the man for what he was: a broken-down ruin of the sharpie he'd likely been in his youth forty years ago, maybe a flimflammer with some acting experience and stage presence because even shit-faced he wore his costume and his bard's beard well. John Partlow mused that it was the ultimate fate of all confidence men: the loss of wit and quickness, the slide into a bottle because only there the Big Dream lived on, and without the Big Dream the confidence man had nothing to live for. It looked to John Partlow as if Doc Honeycutt's days were fast running out, because this Facts Of Life lecture idea was as broken-down as the man.

Still…he thought that Ginger LaFrance had potential. She knew what she was doing, how to use her body to command attention, and he imagined that she'd been Honeycutt's valuable commodity for a long time...long enough, it seemed, for her to get sick and tired of him.

Honeycutt was on stage now, pulling himself up to his full height though it appeared his legs wanted to sag out from under him. His full head of gray hair needed combing and the wild weeds of his eyebrows needed mowing. He nodded at Ginger as he took his place behind the podium, she gave him the pointer and sashayed over to the blackboard, and Honeycutt addressed the assembly in a voice slurred by devil whiskey but still strong enough to boom amid the rafters: "Gentlemen! You intelligent and brave men of—" There was a little pause here, as it seemed he'd forgotten where they were. "—Stonefield!" he went on. "I say intelligent because you are here wishing to gain more knowledge of the facts of life, and brave because you are here likely in *spite* of forces that may have tried to detain you! Yet with the knowledge you will gain here, you may bravely return to your homes and—may I say—earn the everlasting gratitude of your wives for having come here this evening! In truth you will thrill your wives with renewed vigor and performance, and if twenty-five pennies seemed a great expense to some of you tonight, rest assured you will leave here feeling as enriched as kings, which you will certainly be to your wives in your bedrooms forever more. Now let us first of all..." He seemed to blank out again for a few seconds; his mouth moved but made no noise and a shine of panic jumped into his eyes. Then he caught up to himself again and the moment of distress passed. He said, "Let us show our appreciation to my lovely assistant Miss Ginger LaFrance, and I'm sure you boys would like to give her a nice big hand."

John Partlow joined in the applause, but much of it was for Honeycutt's performance. Even as high as a kite, the old doc was still able to stick to his spiel. Likely he'd spilled it so often on stage to rubes like these that every phrase and pause came out on automatic. After the applause the real show began, and John Partlow watched with professional interest as the two grifters went to work. The show consisted of Honeycutt blathering on about "marital practices" in high-falutin' lingo while Ginger took the low road and with yellow chalk drew dirty pictures on the blackboard.

Honeycutt's exposition was only so much noise to the depictions of penis, breasts and vagina that the woman sketched out, erased and then drew again with rather tantalizing movements of her hips. John Partlow noted that every new drawing made the penis and ladybumpers larger and the vagina more accommodating, and the abject silence from the house of yokels made it clear her messages were hitting below the belts. This went on for maybe twenty fascinating minutes. The doctor's delivery stalled several times and he seemed to have gone mingo but the woman played it easy and in four or five seconds the doc drifted back to where he'd left off. Then Doc Honeycutt shifted gears and started the real low-down, which involved painting a mental picture of what went on in Tijuana, Mexico, with the help of the Spanish Fly you could buy from the sex doctors in that notorious town while Ginger drew increasingly larger and more rampant members on the blackboard.

By the end of this, John Partlow himself could hardly cross his legs and if he didn't know better he would have thought Spanish Fly was the greatest invention for men since Eve. It came as no surprise to him when Ginger opened the cardboard box and with a sexy flair and knowing smile showed the yokels the bottles of Tijuana Joy Juice for sale at one dollar a throw.

John Partlow sat and watched the men swarm to the stage with their money in hand.

They were going not only to get lit up by the juice—a questionable result, since the brown liquid in the bottles was likely only stale cola flamed with a little dash of cocaine—but to get the woman to look them in the eyes with that slow fever-burn she was exhibiting, or to breathe a whiff of her scent or get a touch of Ginger-flesh. Anyway, not all the rubes could afford a buck for a bottle but most coughed it up, and John Partlow figured Ginger and the doc were going to clear another thirty skins, which was not a bad haul.

Then came the most difficult part for the team: getting the marks out of the auditorium so they could pack up and scat. Ginger had done her job so well a knot of overall-clad farmboys with bottles of Tijuana Joy Juice in their paws thought they were one tobacco spit away from an easy score with a red-dressed wanton. They were grinning like little boys and slurping on the lollipops of their dirty imaginations. Several of them kept calling to Ginger as she was taping up the cardboard box for transit and the doc was trying to focus on counting the cash. Therefore John Partlow saw his opportunity, and he quickly walked up to the stage and said loudly, "Ginger, darlin'? You need some help with that? Seems like a husband ought to lend a hand instead of just sittin' out here watchin' his wife work."

She didn't miss a beat.

"Yeah, babe," she answered, with just a fast appraisal done by a sidelong glance. "You want to carry this to the car, that would be trim."

John Partlow nodded. *Trim*, he thought. Slang in the con game for sliding one past the suckers. "You got it," he said, and he reached up and took the box as she handed it down.

Around him the knot of men burst asunder and they went on their way, for it was apparent that even their own countrified good looks and so many bottles of joy juice could not compete with a white-suited city dude who looked like somebody's angel...and, obviously, was.

"Car's around back," she told him when she and the doc came down from the stage.

Honeycutt was holding onto her arm for balance, and he looked at John Partlow through bloodshot eyes and rasped, "Who are *you*?"

"That's my new husband Pearly," Ginger said. "Didn't you know I got hitched up in Knoxville?"

"*What?*" The doc staggered a step.

"I'm funnin' you. He's a charmer, that's all. Come on now, watch where you walk."

They went past the Negro man who'd come in to sweep up. Full dark had fallen and the only lights were the shine of a few streetlamps and the glow against the night from the mill to the southwest. John Partlow followed Ginger and Honeycutt around back of the Elks Lodge, carrying the box of unsold joy juice bottles. In a small dirt parking lot was a metallic blue Packard sedan that had a few dents and knocks on it but otherwise looked to be a pretty fine automobile, quite a few steps up from the old tired Oakland.

"You walk from the Nevins' place?" Ginger asked.

"I did."

"Keys," she said to the doc.

"I'm drivin'," Honeycutt answered, with a defiant lift of his sagging chin. "Feel fine enough to—"

"*Keys*," she said again, more firmly. She held her hand out in front of his face. "The car and the room keys both." She paused a beat. "Remember what happened in Little Rock."

He started to protest, but then the keys came out of his pocket and into her hand. She unlocked the trunk, put her shapeless white hospital coat inside it and took from the interior her plain black purse. She motioned for John Partlow to put the box in the trunk and he did as she indicated, noting that inside was a second cardboard box, a folded brown blanket and a gasoline can. As Ginger closed the trunk's lid a hip and a shoulder pressed against John Partlow's side, and he couldn't help but feel a hot jolt of electricity pass through his body and seemingly crackle between his teeth.

"Climb in the back," she told him, and Honeycutt looked at him with a dazed expression and asked, "Who are *you*?"

When they were in the car, with Ginger at the wheel, Honeycutt reached under the seat and brought out a silver flask which he immediately uncapped and began guzzling from. The smell of strong whiskey pricked John Partlow's nostrils. He said, "You've got a smooth pitch, Doc."

"Hm," the doctor grunted, and kept drinking.

"What do you sell?" Ginger asked, as she fired up the Packard's motor.

"Myself," said John Partlow. "And a few Bibles on the side."

"Hearse-chaser?"

He took his time in answering. "Maybe."

"Hearse-chaser," she said with certainty, and she gave a small and brittle laugh.

They passed the boarding house. Ginger did not slow down a half mile-per-hour. "Hey!" John Partlow said. "We just—"

"Settle down, Pearly. We're goin' for a little ride."

His heart had started beating harder and his mouth had gone dry but he kept his calm, at least on the outside. "Listen, Ginger…I'm not worth the trouble. You want to rob me, you're gonna find that—"

"You talk too much," she said, and with one hand she took the flask away from Honeycutt's mouth and gave it back to John Partlow. "Have a drink and relax, Pearly. This is not a robbery."

"Pearly?" Honeycutt scowled and tried to find his flask, as if it had just disappeared by an act of Houdini. "Who the *fuck* is Pearly?"

"The man who's gonna kill you," said Ginger LaFrance, as the Packard followed its headlamps into the Louisiana dark.

Three.

After making this statement Ginger let out another sharp little laugh, and the drunk doctor gurgled and laughed too, but in the backseat the man who wore the name of John Partlow as one of his many disguises squirmed uncomfortably because he had heard the hard edge of truth in the woman's voice.

They'd passed Henry Bullard's garage where the sick Oakland was kept, and they were outside the limits of Stonefield on the winding country road that led in from the west. All was dark but the occasional glint of lamplight through a farmhouse window and the sparkle of stars above the summer tree-tops. "You can pull over and let me out here," said the hearse-chaser, who suddenly wanted nothing to do with either hearses or chasing. "I'll walk back."

"That wouldn't do," the woman said. "A wife to ditch her fancy hubby on the side of the road? No, it wouldn't do."

"What's the game?"

"Drivin'," she replied. "Just drivin', that's all."

"Where's my drink?" Honeycutt asked, and leaned down to find it under the seat again. "My drink! Where's my drink?"

John Partlow reached over and tapped him on the shoulder with the flask. It took the doc a few seconds for him to register what was tapping him, and then a few seconds more for his hand to curl around it. He drank again from it, noisily. John Partlow figured Honeycutt was only good for one thing anymore, and that was standing up on a stage reciting the sex talk he knew so well by memory; the rest of the man's brain was shot to hell either by whiskey, old age or just plain hard living, and maybe all those put together.

"Stella?" Honeycutt said after another swig and a wipe of his mouth with the back of his hand. "Where are we?"

"I'm not Stella. I'm Ginger."

"*Who?*"

"See what I have to put up with, Pearly? By day I have to feed him like a baby and by night I give him his bottle to suck on 'til he passes out. You say he's got a smooth pitch? Sure he does. Only it's been gettin' ragged 'round the edges for quite a time now."

"Uh huh. Well, you can let me out anywhere."

"Sellin' Bibles as you do," she said as the Packard negotiated a long curve between stands of forest. "You make a livin' off that?"

"It's hard work and it can go wrong in one shake of a pig's tail. Listen… Ginger…wherever you're goin' and whatever you're wantin' to do, I don't have any part in this. Hear me?"

"I like your company. We both do. Don't we, Willie?"

"*What*? Fuck I know what you're talkin' about."

"There you go," she said to John Partlow, as if that explained it all. "I'm lookin' for a road we passed on the way in. Should be comin' up on the left in a minute."

"I've gotta pee," said the doc. "Aren't we back at that damn place yet?"

"Soon," she answered. "Real soon now."

John Partlow sat frozen; he didn't like how this show was moving along yet he could do nothing to stop its progress. Whatever was ahead, he realized that all control had been taken from him and it awakened old horrors in his soul.

"Here's the road," Ginger said, and she slowed the car and turned it off to the left, onto a narrow dirt track with dark forest on either side that seemed as impenetrable as granite walls. She kept driving, as curtains of dust churned up behind the tires. "Let's just see where this goes," she said brightly.

"You get a flat out here, it's snake-eyes," John Partlow said, and was shamed to hear the nervous quaver in his voice.

"Oh, I like to gamble. I'm a good gambler. Isn't that right, Willie?"

He made a grunting noise around the lip of his flask.

In another minute or so the Packard's headlamps brushed across the remains of what had been a farmhouse that was now falling to pieces and overtaken by brush and weeds, its roof collapsed. Ginger slowed the car to a crawl. Past the equally-decrepit hulk of a barn the woods boiled up again, and the dirt road petered out.

She stopped the car, turned the engine off, and they sat without speaking while the hot engine ticked.

"I guess," she said, "this is as far as we go."

"Let me out, I'm walkin' back," said John Partlow.

"Finish your drink, Willie," she said. "Then we're gonna take a little walk ourselves."

The doc lowered his flask. He asked in a bewildered voice, "Where's our place?"

"We have no place," she answered. "Said you had to pee. Get out and do that, we'll get on the road."

"Listen," said John Partlow, but he didn't know what to add to that. "*Listen*," he said again.

"Get out and go pee," she told Honeycutt. "Those woods over there. Go on, darlin'."

"Awful dark," he said. "Where the fuck are we?"

"Lord have mercy," she replied, as if to a frightened child with whom she had lost patience. "Okay, I'll come around and hold your hand but I'm not aimin' your dick for you." She removed the key from the ignition but left the headlights burning. When she got out of the car she took her purse with her, and John Partlow saw her place it atop the hood. Then she came around to the door that Honeycutt was struggling to open, opened it for him and said, "Come on, let's get this done. Pearly, I'll need your help."

"No, ma'am," he said, and he pushed the seat forward that Honeycutt had just vacated so he could get out the passenger side. He stood beside the car and looked back along the dark road, his heart pounding. The insects of the night were putting up a symphony of *chirrs* and *chirrups*.

"Go on, then," Ginger said. She was holding onto Honeycutt's left hand with her right. John Partlow saw her reach into her purse with her left hand. It emerged holding a small but ugly .38 revolver. "Come on, Willie," she urged, "let's find us a place."

"I can pee right here," he said, his voice muffled and somehow faraway. He started fumbling with his zipper, but she pulled at him and got him walking toward the woods to the right of the car.

"What the—" John Partlow had to try again because the words had logjammed in his throat. "What the hell are you *doin'*?" He had the crazy sense that this was some kind of con game aimed at him, and he was supposed to react in a certain way to step into the sucker trap, and he should turn and run along the dirt track until he got to the paved road and he could wave down a car—if one ever came along—unless the dame shot him in the back before he could take two steps.

"I'm all right, Stella," said Honeycutt, who had staggered and had to catch himself against a treetrunk. Then he said, painfully, "Somethin' scratched me. I can't see where I am."

"Just pull it out and pee, then we'll get on about our business," she told him, and she let go of his hand and stepped back.

"Last time I go to Georgia," he said as he unzipped and pulled himself out. He looked around, dazedly, and in the wash of the headlights John Partlow thought Honeycutt had a profile like the actor Barrymore and likely had been a handsome young man. "Where are we?" the doc asked, looking up as if questioning the stars.

Ginger didn't answer. When the pistol fired with a sharp *crack* all the night insects went silent and John Partlow nearly let loose a cup of piss into his own trousers. But even as Honeycutt cried out, clutched at his side and fell into the underbrush John Partlow thought sure this must be a con rigged to snare him up in something, but what the game was he could not see.

As the fallen doctor tried to crawl through the brush, Ginger walked back to the car with the smoking gun in her hand. She went to the trunk, unlocked it and reached around until she found what she was looking for. She turned the flashlight's beam on and held it out to John Partlow. "Take it," she said. "Come on and hold it on him."

"I'm not here," he answered, shakily.

"Really?" Her champagne-colored eyes fixed upon him. "Well, I was gonna give you the car if you want it, but if you're not here I guess that won't wash."

"The *car*? Why would I want the car?"

"Because it's a nice car, nearly new, and the papers are in the glovebox." She paused, glancing back at Honeycutt as he gave a terrible moan, then she returned her focus to the hearse-chaser. "I figure you're a smart man with the resources to get your own name on those papers. What *is* your real name?"

"John Partlow."

"I can smell an alias. Try again."

"John Partner."

"Ha," she said quietly. "That's even more made-up than the first. Try again?"

"John Parr."

She studied him in silence for a moment. "I think," she said, "that you've got even more names than me. I'll just call you Pearly, how about that? You can put what you like on the papers. Come on, hold this light and let's get his wallet before there's too much blood on it."

"Are you *crazy*? Absolutely fuckin' out of your *mind*? You just shot a man! Likely he's gonna lie there and die!"

She nodded. "Yeah, that's the picture."

"The police will take your goddamned picture after you fry in the hot chair! You've got to be nuts, doin' somethin' like this!"

She rested the barrel of the .38 against her chin. "Listen, Pearly, here's the scoop: I've been with the doc for the last two years, travellin' around doin' these shows. I took over from the last girl, Stella by name. She told me how bad off he was gettin', that he was on his last legs even then. I stuck with him, though, 'til I figured out I wasn't meant to be a nursemaid to a sixty-eight-year-old man losin' his marbles. Oh yeah, he could throw the pitch, sure he could. But otherwise he's got so many bats in his fuckin' belfry it would scare the shit out of Dracula. Now—you bein' a man of the road as I'm gamblin' on you to be—how do *you* want to end up? You want to fade away sittin' in a room droolin' in your soup? Peein' in your bed and not knowin' you're lyin' in it 'til somebody tells you? You want to go out simperin' and stupid, not knowin' what day it is but just that the hands on the clock don't hardly ever move? Or you want to go out fast...like..." She thought for a few seconds. "Like Bonnie and Clyde," she said. "Leavin' a trail of fire. Bein' *remembered*," she said. She motioned with the gun toward the man in the weeds. "He's got no family. Well, a daughter in California but she's married and on her own, he never hears from her. So if he was in his right mind he would be the first to say he wanted to be cut loose from this goddamned world. Cut *free*, if you believe anything the preachers say. And you bein' a Bible seller and wearin' a tieclip like you've got on, you've got to see in the eyes of the people you sell to that they believe there's some-thin' better than..." She looked around at the woods. Honeycutt had begun to quietly sob. "*This*," Ginger finished, with a hint of a sneer.

"Oh, *yeah*," Pearly said, returning the sneer. "Tell the cops it was a mercy murder, they'll fall down on their knees and make you a saint."

Incredibly, she gave him the slightest smile and her eyes seemed to shine. "What do the *cops* know about any damned thing?" she asked.

It was a warm night. Pearly felt the sweat trickling down under his arms. He felt a damp sheen on his forehead beneath the brim of his white straw fedora. The insects were starting to whisper and thrum again, and it sounded to him as if the night were asking him a question: *What are you going to do...to do...to do...to do...?*

"Help me," Ginger said, and pressed the flashlight against his right hand.

Did he remember taking it? Or did he just remember how her face looked in that moment, as if she already knew everything about him, everything he tried to hide, all the secrets? When she looked at him with those champagne-colored cat eyes he thought she could see right to his beginnings of being the baby that everybody hears about but nobody knows, the kid left in a basket on the church steps a couple of hours before early Sunday service, and then on into the maelstrom of foster families, one after the other and none of them worth a damn, on into the never-ending storm of being a beautiful boychild that some people wanted to use and some people wanted to use others with, and on and on into the early and terrible realization that no one was on your side in this world, nobody gave a shit about you and nobody was going to feed you when you were hungry or hold your hand when you walked where the angels feared to tread, so *mama don't give this man no money* because no one was to be trusted and *mama don't give this man no money* because the only value of a name was as a disguise and so he had gone through many of them, many disguises and many masks, and down deep where the ashes lay ever-smouldering in the burnt-out cellar of his soul he had the satisfaction of being smart and quick, a survivor to the core.

When he took the flashlight from Ginger into his own hand and followed her to where the doc lay dying it was just a natural progression of the survival instinct that had been doubling and redoubling itself since he'd been old enough to steal a box of stogies and sell them to other kids for twice their value, earning money to get out of that house in Waycross, Georgia, where the old man with the white beard and the old woman with the constant cough dressed him up as a cripple with two small crutches and paraded him from country church to country church to beg for donations to their non-existent Poor Orphans' Home. And at night the old woman came upon his bed with her toothless mouth and her crazed eyes and the old man rasped with whiskied breath that if you didn't act your part and do it right two broken legs were the least you're gonna get.

And he meant it, which was why on that last night the boy whose name then was simply Sonny hit the man in the head with a clothes iron while he was sleeping and when the woman woke up and started to shriek he threw a handful of salt in her eyes because he'd known she would awaken, and then he bashed her in the forehead and got out before he knew they were dead or not but there was no time for that, no time, no time at all…

"Sixty-two dollars, two quarters, three dimes, three nickels and sixteen cents," said Ginger, after she'd gone through Honeycutt's wallet and his pockets. "Not bad." On the ground the doc was still trying to crawl away, but his efforts were as weak as if he were attempting a mile-long swim through mud.

The man who had accepted the name of Pearly heard himself say, "I want half of that. *And* the car."

"Do tell. He's owed me for the last four shows, ten bucks each."

"I don't care. I said I want half of that and the car."

She cocked her head at him. Her tongue came out along her lower lip as if she were tasting something surprisingly tangy. "You do know *I'm* the one holdin' the gun, right?"

"Wouldn't dare forget. But this is business after an act of mercy by one of God's true saints, isn't it? So share your manna with the heathen, half-and-half."

She smiled. The light glinted off her front teeth. "Earn it," she said, and she offered him the pistol grip-first.

He hesitated, staring at the gun.

"Lady Nevins says they lock up at ten-thirty sharp," Ginger said. "I believe her. We don't have time to dawdle, with the things that have to be done. We don't want to wake anybody up to get into that house, do we? And sure as hell we can't walk in together."

"You're crazy! I'm not shootin' anybody."

"Can't just leave him here alive, Pearly. You know that."

"Why didn't you shoot him in the head? Christ A'mighty, he might get a second breath and walk out of here!"

"Doubtful, but possible. And I didn't shoot him in the head," she said, "because I told him *you* were gonna kill him. And you are, Pearly. You're gonna finish the job and you're gonna do it quick and earn your split, so we can get back to that house within an hour and we don't get locked out."

"But…why even go *back* there?"

"Because I want to see the Nevins before they turn in, and I want to tell 'em that Doctor Honeycutt got real drunk and real sick and it's best he sleep in the backseat of his car tonight because he's already puked once. They won't be askin' where he is, and they won't be amblin' out to the car either." She glanced down at her victim. "Somebody'll find him, by and by. I just want it to be later than sooner. Got it?"

Pearly didn't answer. He did get it, but he realized he had just stepped into a swamp that could very well suck him under...though, strangely, he enjoyed the weight of the gun in his hand, and the sight of the helpless man on the ground and the enticing woman in the red dress standing next to him, whose perfume smelled like charred roses.

"I'm goin' to get somethin' out of the trunk. Just hold off a minute," she said, and she walked away.

When Ginger came back she had the blanket and the gas can. She put the can on the ground, folded up the blanket and put it over Honeycutt's head. "There you go. One shot through the nuthouse. Don't want to get anything on that nice white suit."

"Have you done this before?"

"I read *The Police Gazette*. One shot only. More than that, any farmer around here might come lookin'."

"This is...it's *crazy*..."

"It's necessary. The car and half the money. Doin' Willie a favor, really. He's been gone a long time."

"*Crazy*," Pearly repeated, and he had the thought that this must be a scam, it must be a variation of the old blackmail dodge, where you lured somebody into doing something that you could hold over them for the rest of their lives, and in this case the bullets in the gun were blanks and Honeycutt had squeezed a red dye capsule all over his side and the next shot would be a blank too, and afterward Honeycutt and Ginger would meet up and laugh over how that sucker had fallen into the trap, and now they had him on the hook and he would never ever get away from—

Pearly fired one shot into the blanket over the doctor's head.

Smoke spooled up from the hole in the blanket. Honeycutt's legs jerked a few times, as if running against his onrushing death. Then the movement ceased, and as smoke curled from the pistol's barrel up into Pearly's face the sound of the night insects rushed in to fill the silence.

He stepped back as Ginger took the flashlight from him and leaned down to lift the blanket.

"That got him," she said with a sudden release of the breath she'd been holding, and he looked over her shoulder at the dark hole in the back of Honeycutt's head that was oozing red in the light's cold beam. His heart was pounding so hard he feared it would burst through his chest; his stomach pitched and rolled, and he had to walk away a few paces and make a couple of circles before he realized the sickness had passed and he was all right.

"We've got some work to do," Ginger told him. "Better take your hat and suit coat off, put 'em in the car. We've got to strip the body."

"*What?*"

"Get his clothes off him. Bundle 'em up, put 'em in the trunk and dump 'em somewhere a couple of miles away. Make sure we don't get blood on our hands or on the car. Then…you got a lighter? If not, there are matches in the glovebox."

"I've got a lighter. Why?"

"We need to put the blanket on his face, pour some gas on it and light it up."

"Light it up? What for?"

She parked the flashlight's beam somewhere between them. A dog was barking but it was in the distance, way off through the woods. "We have to burn his face," she said, as calmly as if talking about setting fire to a pile of trash. "You know what I'm sayin'," she went on, when he didn't respond. "*Melt* his face, I mean. So when they find the body they can't figure out who it was."

Pearly was staring down at the dead man. He had the quick mental image of puppies burning on a gas-soaked blanket, making the point that he was no longer a helpless child tottering on crutches he didn't need. He said, "Thought all this through pretty well, huh? How'd you know I'd go along? I could've been anybody."

"But you're not just *anybody*. One of my gifts is bein' able to read people. I can size 'em up real quick. Know what they want, what they'll do and not do. Know their price, too. You fit the bill and the time was right."

With a grunt, he said, "Lucky me."

"Come on, we've got to strip him first and you don't want to get any blood on that suit. Don't want the fire to get too big, either, in these dry woods." She motioned toward the car. "Get your hat and coat off."

"Okay," he said, but still he stood staring at the body. The gun in his hand felt natural to him, though it had been years since he'd held one and he'd never fired a bullet at a human being before. It was a powerful feeling. He understood why Clyde Barrow and Bonnie Parker played around with guns, to get and keep that feeling of power. To be able to take a person out of the world, or aim a gun at a person and then decide to let them live…it was nothing short of the power of God.

"Time's tickin'," Ginger said. "We got to get a move on."

We? Pearly thought. She kept saying that: *we*. Never before had he thought of himself and anyone else as a *we*. He lived alone, ate alone, slept alone…and, had always worked alone.

Before now.

We, she said.

He shuddered. It was not because of the body laid out before him in the brush—and he could imagine it days hence, when the animals of the woods followed the smell and got to work on the meat that the flies and swarms of insects would have by then started breaking down into mush— but because of the moment. Something had changed; something new had come, and as yet he did not understand exactly what it was but his shudder was like the first motion of a reptile shedding old skin, getting ready for the journey ahead.

"Go on," Ginger said, but it was a gentle urging. "Better roll those sleeves up too."

"Yes," he answered. He walked to his new Packard with the gun in his hand. He had a strangely serene feeling in his heart and a new focus in his mind, the feeling that he was indeed lucky and the focus that from here on out—starting real soon and maybe this single minute—there was a whole lot of very profitable work to be done.

Four.

He was lying on his back in the bed, staring up at the cracked ceiling and smoking a cigarette. A single low lamp burned on the bedside table; he usually didn't mind the dark, but tonight the dark seemed darker. The time was a little past midnight. He couldn't sleep. The sound of the pistol shot that had sent the bullet into Honeycutt's skull was a constant echo.

He thought also of the conversation he'd had with Ginger—or whatever her name was—in the Packard on the way back from the murder scene. For such a hot looker she was all ice.

He'd never met a woman like her before—one who was so in control of her emotions, and could make murder sound like what the victim really wanted as an escape from his frail and fading frame. He had killed a man for her, and he'd barely known her thirty minutes or so before the deed.

But then again, he didn't know her and he thought no one did.

When they figure out who he was, Pearly had said on the drive back with the Packard's steering wheel firmly in hand, *they're gonna come lookin' for you. It's your name on all those posters.*

It's the name of Ginger LaFrance, she'd answered. *They won't be lookin' for Lana Kay Riley.*

That's your real name?

No, but it'll do.

What is your real name?

She'd made a sound that could have been a small laugh but it was hard to tell. She had the window rolled down and one elbow stuck out to jab the ribs of the world. *What's a name, Pearly? It's somethin' hung on you, so people think they got a handle. You and me are alike in that way, aren't we?*

What way?

We don't want handles on us, she'd said, and to him that made the most sense of just about anything he'd ever heard in his life.

So, she'd continued as he had digested this morsel of truth, *when we get there park around back, there's a grassy lot. You walk in, I'll be behind you by about ten minutes.*

Cuttin' it close.

It'll work out. In the mornin' just give me a ride to Shreveport, let me out on the corner of Texas and Edwards streets and we're quits.

He had allowed a few seconds to slide past. Then: *That easy, huh?*

Yep. Just easy-breezy, she'd replied, her voice as light and carefree as if in the last half-hour she'd shrugged the weight of the world off her shoulders.

But in his small room, lying on the bed with the cigarette burning down between his fingers and through the haze a canary-yellow sticker on the inside of the door that had No Smoking printed on it, Pearly felt anything but light. He had the key to the Packard sitting atop the dresser next to his wallet. In his wallet was his newfound split of the take. All he had to do in the morning was tell the Nevins he was getting a ride back to Shreveport with Honeycutt and the woman, and then at the garage tell Henry Bullard he'd return for the Oakland in a couple of days but in the meantime there was a box of Bibles he had to retrieve from the trunk. Then on to Shreveport with the woman, in his new Packard.

Easy-breezy. Or was it?

He tapped the ashes into a waterglass on the bedside table. The old lady would likely raise hell at him for smoking up the joint, but who gave a damn? Anyway, Hilda Nevins would be as glad to see him leave as she would be to see the doc and the woman in red sway their asses out of Stonefield. Pearly—he liked that monicker, thought he'd stick with it awhile—intended never to come this way again; Bullard could have the Oakland, for the two bits it was worth.

But damn it all, he couldn't find a wink of sleep. It wasn't the killing; that was like putting a sick dog out of its misery, and there was a lot of truth in what Ginger had said about the confidence man's life being snuffed before the brain went mushy. What did the con man live on but the sharpness of his wits? When those were age-riddled and full of holes, what more was there to living? No, it was a slow fall to oblivion—to nothingness—and Pearly hoped that when—*if*—he got too old to think straight somebody would put a bullet in his head as cleanly as it had been done to Doc Honeycutt. Well...the shot in the side hadn't been too clean, and maybe that was what bothered Pearly; Ginger could've just whacked the doc in the head with the gun and laid him low that way instead of the rib-buster. She had been mighty fast to push things past the point of no return, so there would be little use—and time—to argue over the execution.

On the way back from the road where they'd left the body, Ginger had told him to slow down because they needed to find a place to dump the clothes. A little cart track off to the left had led them into more woods and no lights around, so the clothes had gone into the brush. A pour of gasoline had been used to burn the clothes, both of them careful not to get any gas on their hands or their own clothes. Before the fire got too high Ginger had told him to stomp the flames out and he had done so. Then it was on into Stonefield and on with the plan, and Pearly lay in bed thinking that if he let Ginger out on the corner of Texas and Edwards streets in Shreveport tomorrow morning she would be just a few blocks from his own hideaway at the Dixie Garden Hotel on Cotton Street. It would be a kick in the head if she were living at the Dixie Garden too, but she didn't want him to know where she was living so that's why she wanted out on Texas and Edwards. He hadn't lived very long in Shreveport and for sure had never seen her there, unless she'd been wearing a wig and was dressed down like a farmer's wife, which he couldn't really discount.

An owl hooted in the distance outside his window, a forlorn yet haunting sound that for some reason had always made him feel a kinship to the hunters of the night. The dark belonged to them. It was not a happy place but a place of need and necessity, and he knew it very well.

Came a soft tapping at his door.

Tap tap. Tap tap. Then her voice, hardly a whisper enough to be heard: "Open up."

He was still mostly dressed, had only taken off his shirt and his shoes before getting into bed and lighting up the fag. He went to the door and paused only a heartbeat before flicking back the latch. Then he peered into her face in the ruddy light that came from a red-tinged glass globe at the hallway's ceiling. She looked tired, her eyes swollen as if she too had been wrestling with the elusive demon called sleep; her dyed-blonde hair had been released from its tight bondage of combs and the loose curls had boiled down over her forehead to the plucked brows. She wore a lavender-colored gown with a red satin rose embroidered just above the left breast.

"You gonna just stand there?" she asked, keeping her voice quiet. She lifted her right hand and there in it was the dear dead doctor's silver flask.

Pearly stepped back to let her in. She was carrying her purse in her left hand. She put both the purse and the flask atop the dresser. Then she turned around, went past him to the door and pushed the latch firmly home, and after that she looked at him as if she were true to her feline nature and he was a mouse who'd just taken a bath in catnip.

"Can't sleep?" he asked.

"Smoky as hell in here," she answered. "Smell it in the hall."

"I needed a cigarette."

"Need a drink too? Got a few swigs left."

He nodded. "Sure, I can use a drink."

"Who but a fool would ever turn one down?" Ginger asked, and as she retrieved the flask and unscrewed the cap Pearly knew exactly why she had come to his room, and that she was priming the pump. It was a mechanism that didn't need much priming, if any at all, because even though he had the memory of the killing shot echoing in his brain his body was deaf to the murmurs of the past, and with the woman here in her filmy gown and offering herself to him nothing much mattered anymore about the passing death of a senile con man.

He took the flask from her fingers and drank. She reached out, covered his hand with her own; he gave the flask up, she drank and stared into his eyes and gave a crooked little smile and said, "What's on your mind?"

He shrugged. He was sure she knew, but he wasn't going to give it up without a little coy dancing. "Just thinkin'," he said.

"Wastin' time, just thinkin'," she told him.

Then she was on him, not like a cat upon a mouse but more like a tidal wave upon an unguarded shore; he thought that if she could've plunged through his skin into his very heart, arteries and nerves she might have done so. Even with the barrier of flesh between them he was overcome for a few seconds by the tremendous heat and passion of her energy, her hands latched to his body, her mouth suctioned to his and her tongue lashing his own. Her tidal wave, which seemed more lava than water, flowed into and through him and carried them both onto the bed where clothing was unbuttoned and unsnapped, opened and discarded as if she also were mistress to the whirlwinds. Beneath them the bedsprings yowled like Cab Calloway's horn section on nose candy. It seemed to Pearly that the noise was loud enough not only to wake up the Nevins and all of sleeping Stonefield but also to stir Samuel Petrie Blankenship from his eternal grave.

There was no gentleness in her mouth upon him, and no gentleness either in the way she pressed herself upon his mouth. Instantly she seemed to break a sweat. Her aroma of burned-up roses became more of an acrid bonfire. It was all Pearly could do to keep from ending their escapade with a premature explosion, and then in the midst of their contortions and exertions Ginger came up for air and said breathlessly, "Wait...wait..."

She got up off him and lunged for her purse on the dresser.

From it she withdrew the ugly little .38 revolver.

Pearly watched, transfixed, as Ginger also took from her purse a cartridge box. She removed one bullet, put it into the cylinder, spun the cylinder and cocked the pistol. Then she came back to the bed in nearly a leap, her face shiny with perspiration and her eyes ashine with need.

"*Hold it,*" he said in a croak. "What're you—"

"Take it." She pressed the gun upon his right hand. "Come on! Put it to my head and fuck me!"

"*What?*"

She grabbed a handful of his hair and got astride him. With her other hand she gripped his right wrist and guided the revolver to the side of her head. "I said fuck me! *Right now!*"

"I can't—"

"Put your finger on the trigger! Do it! *Hurry!*" She sounded near crying out in her desperation.

Pearly obeyed before she could force his finger on the trigger and maybe make the gun go off, because even as she was telling him to do it she was trying to work his hand into the proper form. Then she was holding his gunhand with the barrel at her left temple and she was pounding herself up and down on him like a battering ram, and by all reason and sense his flagpole should have withered and melted away but he was whipped up in this crazy frenzy too. Knowing he was screwing her in a mad game of Russian Roulette—that he was inside a woman whose head might be blown away by any errant twitch of inflamed nerves to his index finger—made him harder, and the sensation of death being so close was an unexpected thrill. He'd never experienced anything like this; the most off-beat sex he'd ever had had been with a prostitute in a Houston whorehouse who'd insisted on chewing Tootsie Rolls while she sucked him to orgasm. But a loaded pistol to the head, and maybe one jerk of his finger to send the bullet into her brain?

This was a new one on him, and one that fired him up as nothing had ever fired him before.

And for sure the woman was fired up too. Any more fire and Pearly thought her hair would burst into flame. She was crashing down on him with fevered abandon, the bedsprings were shrieking and the pistol's black grip was slippery in his damp hand. A convulsion of the trigger finger, and there was one chance in six that the brains of Ginger LaFrance would be spattered across the wall; and that, Pearly realized in this frenzied blur, was the meat of the matter and what was driving the woman to the heights of ecstasy.

He heard what sounded like a low moan that issued from the center of the earth, as if the gates of Hell were grinding open. There was another noise like the banging of a distant gong, getting louder. It took him a few seconds to register that a train was passing through the middle of Stonefield, only a couple of blocks away. Glass rattled in the windows and the tired timbers groaned. The entire house seemed to be shaking itself to pieces in the throes of its own mad moment. In this maelstrom of movement and noise the man who held the revolver had a vision of voluntarily firing the weapon because he was so close to it anyway, so very close, and with a blast of additional noise and a spurt of flame Ginger LaFrance's head exploded and that was the end of a fancy lady who thought herself so hot and so icy. The thought and the image was so intense that it suddenly pushed him over the edge and lifted his hips off the bed with a shout caught between his teeth. Above him the woman shuddered, her back arched as if it were about to break, her eyes squeezed tightly shut and the sweat gleamed on her face, and the train clattered its way through Stonefield like a storm made up of a hundred whirling iron pots and pans.

In the aftermath of the train's thrumming passage, Ginger sat atop Pearly and quickly pushed the pistol away from her head.

Pearly managed to speak though his chest was heaving and it took him a few seconds to find his breath. "Don't have much sex, do you?"

"Nope. But when I do, it's a doozy." She accepted the gun from his hand and emptied the cylinder of its single bullet. Then she eased off him, took the gun and the bullet to her purse and put them away, after which she returned to the bed and lay down beside him, not with her head on his shoulder but upon the second pillow.

They lay there listening to each other breathing for a little while. Then Ginger said, "How old are you?"

"Thirty-two," he answered. And though it might be an indelicate question, he asked it anyway: "You?"

"Thirty-four," she said without hesitation. "You married?"

"No, never been. How about you?"

"Not *now*. I *was*. Twice."

"Kids?"

"*No*." She'd said it as if the very idea had stricken her with an intestinal pain. And she emphasized it: "*Lord*, no."

Pearly waited a few heartbeats before he ventured any further. Then: "What was that with the gun? You get a thrill out of that?"

"Sure. Didn't *you*?"

"Maybe," he had to admit. He added gravely, "Wouldn't have been such a thrill if my finger had slipped on that trigger."

"But it didn't," she said. "See, that's what it's about, Pearly: settin' the gamble, and winnin' it. And about somethin' else, too: keepin' some part of yourself in control, no matter what you're doin' or thinkin', no matter where you are, no matter who your cock's in or whose cock's in you…always there's some part of yourself that stays…well, *distant*, I guess it would be. Like you're watchin' from another place, instead of bein' right there. You had a taste of that tonight…or this *mornin'*, I ought to say. It's good for you, Pearly. Toughens you up."

"Toughens me up for *what*?" he asked.

"For whatever," she answered. "You never can tell what's around the corner."

"Sunrise, I suppose."

"Yep," she said. "Sunrise. And I'll be wantin' to slip this burg early, too." She got out of bed, and Pearly watched as she retrieved her gown and put it on, covering up her voluptuous body. "Need some sleep," she told him. "My own room. Meet me downstairs at six-thirty. That suit you?"

"Yeah, that's fine."

"Okay, then." She went to the dresser and picked up her purse. "Get some sleep too, you may need to be rested tomorrow."

"I'll do that."

She paused at the door and gave him a long, steady look. "How long you plan to be chasin' hearses?"

"It's a passin' thing, I figure."

"What else you got cookin'?"

"Nothin' right now," he admitted. He shrugged. "I'm doin' all right, most weeks. But somethin' else will come along. I just have to find it."

"It may find *you*," she said, and then she gave him a smile. "Sleep tight." She pushed the latch back, opened the door, closed it behind her, and she was gone.

He lay in bed for awhile longer, lingering over the afterglow, and then he got up to lock the door. Ginger's violent exertions had made him feel as if some of his bones had slipped from their sockets. He returned to bed, nearly walking with a limp, settled himself into it and as he fell into sleep heard only the faintest echo of a gunshot.

At quarter to six by his wristwatch, Pearly in the pink light of morning discovered two things: first, that the key to his Packard was gone from atop the dresser, and second, that as he hurriedly dressed he found two blotches of blood on the right leg of his white trousers just above the shoe. One was small, about the size of a thumbnail, but the other was larger and shaped like a seahorse.

In his hurry, with his own blood pounding in his face and his teeth clenched behind grim lips, he misbuttoned his shirt twice. He figured Ginger had put the key in her purse either when she'd removed the pistol or put it back in. He checked his wallet and found all his money there; he was surprised the bitch hadn't copped that too, but then again he might have instantly noticed it was gone from the dresser after she left.

He got himself dressed except for his tie and hat, and he was still lacing up his left shoe as he threw back the latch on his door and nearly ran to the stairs. Then he checked his rush, because even though he figured he'd been stung he still had to be careful, had to keep himself in order.

He straightened his coat and his shoulders and forced his legs to carry him down the stairs at a stately pace.

"Mornin'," said Hilda Nevins as Pearly reached the bottom of the stairs. There was no expression, good or ill, in the greeting. The severe-looking woman, dressed in a brown-checked robe that was buttoned to her throat and nearly swallowed her up, had been using a featherduster on her shelf of ceramic bells. "Up early," she observed.

"Yes ma'am." He gave her his soft smile while behind the mask of his face his braingears were going ninety miles a second. His eyes scanned the room, looking for any trace of Ginger LaFrance…her bags, a hat, anything. Nothing there.

"Servin' breakfast at the cafe," she said, as she returned to her dusting with the great care an empress would give to her collection of priceless diamonds and emeralds.

"Um…well ma'am…I'm somewhat confused." How to put this? Just go ahead fullsteam, he told himself. "I was thinkin' I was gonna get a ride to Shreveport with Doctor Honeycutt and Miss LaFrance." The woman stopped dusting and turned to face him, and Pearly felt like backing away a few steps because she seemed to be looking right through him at a murder in the woods but he stood his ground. "Are they still here?"

"That *lady*," Hilda Nevins said with the sarcasm dripping from the edges of her lips, "woke us up about four o'clock. Seems she needed to go out and check on the doctor, he was sick last night and slept in his car. Seems he wasn't no better than when she'd left him, so she was gonna pay their bill and head on. Grover offered to help carry the bags out but she said there was only two and she had 'em. So she paid and they're gone and that's that." She shrugged. "Fine with me, that perfume she wore gave me a headache."

"Ah," Pearly said. Had his voice cracked? He imagined he felt sweat gathering at his temples.

"*And*," Hilda Nevins continued, with her dark and owlish eyes condemning him, "I'm gonna have to charge you an extra dollar for what went on in your room last night."

"*Ma'am?*"

"You smoked a cigarette," she said, as if she were saying *I know you shot somebody last night.* "At least one," she added. "Smelled it in the hall when I went up to check their rooms. So I'm addin' a dollar to your bill, and it'll be another dollar tomorrow if you do it again."

"Fine." It had come out as a mumble, so he tried it once more. "*Fine.*"

"Henry's at work by now, if you want to give him a call." She motioned with the featherduster to the telephone on the black lacquered desk. "Phone book's in the top drawer."

Then she turned her back on him and began earnestly dusting her collection of little ceramic horses.

Bullard answered on the fourth ring. *Nope, Mr. Partlow, I'm waitin' to hear from my supplier in Shreveport. Could be today, could be tomorrow. I'll let you know when I'm gettin' started. That oke with you?*

"Oh sure," Pearly replied grimly, as he found himself staring at the seahorse-shaped bloodblotch on his trouser leg. "Oh yeah, that's just peachy."

"Cafe's servin' breakfast," Hilda told him again, after he'd returned the receiver to its cradle. "Good for a fella to start his day with a hearty breakfast."

Shit, Pearly thought, but he gave her a tight smile and answered, "Thank you kindly." The idea that he'd been hoodooed by a murderous slut was a burning blade that kept driving itself into the base of his neck. No way could he live with this; if he ever hoped to draw another breath as a man he was going to have to find that woman, get his Packard back, and exact some kind of revenge. He could track her down somehow...somehow, he would get on her trail no matter where she was hiding.

This he vowed, both to himself and to any God who happened to be listening.

A sudden realization struck him hard, right at the gut.

"Mrs. Nevins," he said, at the same time shifting his balance and moving his body so his trouser leg with the offending bloodstains was hidden. The woman paused in her horse-dusting and turned to look at him, her eyebrows raised in question. Pearly went on: "I do believe I'm going to need some clothes." He gave her a smile and a shrug that said he was just a poor and honest traveller hit by the misfortune of having a shitty automobile. "I'm hoping there's a store not far from here?"

"Surely," she answered. "You likely passed it on your way to the cafe last night. Two doors down from the barbershop. Opens at ten-thirty." Her gaze swept over his suit. "Nothin' like *that* in there, though. Mostly dungarees, workshirts and such for the men."

"I have nothing against clothes made for men who are the salt of the earth," he said.

"Well, you can get yourself fixed up there, then." Her frown returned and for an instant Pearly thought she'd seen the stains but then his fear passed because she was looking straight into his eyes. "Word of warnin'," she cautioned. "Watch your wallet in there and make sure Vincent Lee don't overcharge you. You walk in wearin' that getup, he'll see you as a slicker ready to throw your money into his pocket."

"Thank you for the advice."

"Vincent Lee's as bad as his brother the sheriff," said Hilda Nevins as she returned again to her chore. "Two peas from a rotten pod."

Pearly had started ascending the stairs when it very quickly dawned upon him that going into a clothing store run by the sheriff's brother and wearing white pants with bloodstains on one leg was not going to hit the bull's-eye on the smart target. He could not explain to Mrs. Nevins why he was unable to walk into that store like any normal customer, yet neither could he parade around town as he was, for though the stains were small they might catch somebody's attention...in the cafe, maybe, where he would have to go if he wanted any food until that hick Bullard got his car working again and he could blow this fleabag town.

In three seconds he decided there was only one thing he could do to get out of this jam, and with no further hesitation he did it.

Five.

There was the door he was seeking. On it were the tarnished metal numerals three and seven.

Thirty-seven, go to Heaven he thought as he stood before the door and balled up his fist.

But he didn't doubt that Hell wouldn't claim Ginger LaFrance before the count got to a mere three. For the moment, though, he had first dibs on her. And boy, did he mean to get his Satan's share of payback.

He knocked. One…two…three. *Bust your knee.* He waited a few seconds and then he said with his face pressed toward the door, "Shreveport Police, Miss Wiley. Open up." And he added, "We have a man at the bottom of the fire escape, just for your—"

The door was unlatched and swung open in one smooth motion.

And there she stood, all five feet six inches of her, but if he hadn't known that Ginger LaFrance was now going by the name of Lana Rae Wiley he might never have recognized her.

She had darkened her hair to a dull shade of russet, she wore a sensible and conservative gray dress with a dark blue trim, and her champagne-colored eyes—very hard to disguise those, of course—regarded him with cool composure from behind the horn-rimmed glasses any stern librarian might choose. Her makeup was minimal, no lipstick at all, no nail polish, the swell of her breasts confined under a bra that must've been made of steel bands. She lifted her chin a few degrees, she put a hand on one hip, and she said quietly, "Took you long enough to find me."

"Yeah? Well, I—"

"Come in," she told him. "Voices carry."

Thus it was that thirty seconds after finding the woman who'd left him high-and-dry in Stonefield eight days ago, Pearly was standing in her apartment at the Hotel Clementine on Texas Street near the working docks and warehouses on the mud-colored Red River. It was the hot and humid afternoon of August 11th, stifling outside; an electric fan atop a table stirred the air, its back-and-forth motion sending a breeze past Pearly's cheek like the caress of a soft and invisible hand.

Ginger LaFrance—for that was the name Pearly decided suited her best, being so theatrical and damned arrogant—latched the door. She turned toward him, her back against the door and her hands behind her, and she stared at him in silence. A clock ticked somewhere and a tug's horn hooted on the river. Pearly stood at the center of the room. A pulse beat hard at his temple. He had come to rough her up and get the key to his Packard; he had envisioned coming in here—breaking in, if he'd had to—and then seizing her by the hair and maybe busting her lip, enough to let her know he meant business. It would've been fine with him if she cried and begged for mercy, and then he was going to make her kneel at his feet and repeat *I am a lying bitch and I am not worth a shit*. After that they would be all evened up, as far as he was concerned.

She spoke.

"I was about to make myself a bologna sandwich. You want one?"

He was amazed at her composure. If she'd been a man her balls would have been dragging the floor. "I've had all the baloney I can stomach from you," he said.

She shrugged. "I need some lunch." She walked past him, as brazen as if there had been no murder between them and no betrayal; she was headed for the little kitchenette and stove over in the corner, and her air of nonchalance was more than he could stand. His face flamed. He reached out to grab a handful of her hair and bring her to heel, and then she abruptly stopped and looked at his hand and her eyes seemed to freeze it before it got to her.

"I see you dressed like Dick Tracy," she said, referring to his dark blue suit, the white shirt and the thin black tie, his sedate outfit topped with a black fedora. "But I knew your voice right off. How'd you get past Teddy?" When he was slow to respond, she prodded him. "The clerk downstairs. He's pretty good at guardin' the place. So how?"

He wanted to hit her in the face. He wanted to see her lower lip burst open and the blood spew out, and for those piercing eyes behind the specs to look shattered for a second, and then when she staggered he would throw her to the floor and stand over her to show her who was the boss around here.

But instead, to show her what he'd gone through to find her, he used his hand to produce his wallet, flip it open and display the bright shiny Shreveport Police detective's badge, number five-one-one.

She gave a low and appreciative whistle. "How much that set you back?"

"One hundred bucks from a guy in the backroom of a Bossier pawn-shop. I had to approach him *very* carefully."

"Nice. So…you want a bologna sandwich or not?"

"What I want is to beat your lyin' ass. Then I'll take my Packard, thank you."

Ginger's short, sharp little laugh was almost paid for with her teeth. She turned away and walked the few steps to the icebox. She opened it and brought out a piece of bologna wrapped up in brown paper. "About the Packard," she said as she struck a match and lit a burner on the gas stove. "I saved your tail on that one."

"Really? I'll bet."

"Sure." She opened a drawer, took out a knife and began slicing the meat with a steady hand. "I started thinkin'…maybe it wouldn't be so smart for you to be drivin' around in the dead doc's car. If anything happened, I mean." She glanced over at him. "How many slices you want?"

"Can the bullshit," he said.

"Three slices for me, three slices for you. Oh…and go pick up that envelope on the bookcase over there. See it?"

He did. It was a small dark brown-painted bookcase, flush against the wall. A book was lying flat on top of it, and on top of that was the envelope.

"Go on, it won't bite." She put the bologna slices in a frying pan and started frying them up.

He went to the bookcase but he didn't put his back to her. The envelope had the name *Pearly* written on it in small but precise handwriting. When he picked it up he noted that the book's title underneath it was *The Mystery Of Human Psychology* by Dr. Morris Fonaroy.

"Open it," she urged, and then she began rummaging in the icebox as if she were totally alone in the room.

He tore the envelope open. In it were twenties and tens…three hundred dollars in all. Counterfeit? No, his fingers told him the paper felt right and the color was government-issue.

"Like I said…three slices for me, three slices for you," she offered. "I sold the Packard for six hundred. I've been keepin' it safe for you."

He didn't know what to say. His voice came out with, "I ought to beat you bloody for the hundred I spent on that goddamned badge."

"You're two hundred skins ahead of the game, Pearly. And you got a good deal on the badge. No tellin' when you might be able to use it again. I like spicy mustard. That suit you?"

"I think you're fuckin' crazy," he said.

"Why?" She turned toward him and gave him a withering smile with a little glint of teeth behind it. "A lot of people like spicy mustard."

He was stumped for a reply and almost thoroughly floored by the dough in the envelope. As Ginger returned her attention to the frying of bologna slices, Pearly took a look around the place. It was basically one room but spacious enough, with a Murphy bed in its upright position behind a pair of doors; there was another narrow door that must be a closet, and the door to the small but tidy-looking bathroom was open to show its black-and-white tiled walls. Pearly wished he had his own private bathroom, but the Dixie

Garden was one to a floor. He saw pretty quickly how neat and orderly the place was; the furniture wasn't new but it wasn't ratty, she had a nice console radio and the crimson rug on the floor wasn't worn to the weave. All in all, Ginger LaFrance or Lana Rae Wiley or whoever the hell she really was, she wasn't rich but she lived okay and though he himself was neat in his habits she appeared to be a few rungs higher than him in that department.

"You need the specs?" he asked as he watched her at the stove.

"Clear glass," she said. "I'm doin' some research."

"On what? Connin' a secretarial school?"

"Nope," she answered, but offered nothing more. The slices in the pan were sizzling.

"I've got a pitcher of sweet tea in the icebox," she said after a pause. "Make yourself useful and pour us a couple of glasses. The glasses are in the cupboard up over there on the right."

He had a moment of nearly bursting out laughing, but he swallowed the laugh down. He had come to beat her ass and here he was being invited to a late lunch…and craziest of all, he was okay with that no matter how much his gut twisted at the thought. He wished he could at least give her a punch for having to fall down on the Nevins' staircase that day and pretend to have sprained his ankle. *Oh no, I don't think it's broken, ma'am, but it does hurt a smack. Don't think I can walk very far today. Lord…I do need at least one pair of trousers…what a fix this is! Do you think…maybe…and it would be awful helpful…that if I gave your husband my size and some money he could go to the store and get me a pair? I'd be glad to pay him an extra dollar…and I swear too, no more smokin' in the room. No need to call a doc, I'll be fine just restin' it awhile.…believe I can make it back to my room all right, thank you kindly.*

He'd just as soon kicked Hilda Nevins in her teeth as looked at her. But Grover did go to the store and buy him a pair of ill-fitting dungarees, and later that day the Nevins had brought him some beef stew and crackers from the cafe, so all was right with the damned world.

"I've been through a shitmess because of you," he told the woman at the stove. "I was in that fleatrap for four more days. And guess what? The last night I was there, they were talkin' at the cafe about how somebody's huntin' dog found some burned-up clothes in the woods and it was mighty peculiar because it looked like it used to be a nice suit with a *vest* and all."

"Hm," she answered. "Did you hear me about the tea and the glasses?"

He felt deflated. In fact the air seemed to leave his lungs with a little whistle like a distant steam train. Still he maintained his stance of defiance at the center of the room...until she gave him a glance and a quick wicked pursing of her lips and said, "Does baby feel better now, gettin' all that ol' nasty out of his system?"

"*Jesus*," he said.

"Chop chop. If you're stayin' for lunch, take off your hat and coat. I'm not sharin' my bologna with Dick fuckin' Tracy today."

Incredibly, he did what she said. He thought she must have the power to bend his mind. He found himself going to the cupboard to get the glasses, and then it fully dawned on him that she had been expecting him to find her all along. "How'd you know I'd track you down?" he asked as he stared at the back of her head.

"I didn't. But I gave you enough clues to get you started lookin', didn't I? I even gave you the name I'd be usin'. Maybe not *quite* the name, but near enough. I had to make it a challenge for you. Right?"

"This doesn't figure," he said. "What's the angle?"

"Want yours on a plate, or will a paper napkin do?"

"Napkin's fine. I asked you a question...what's the angle?"

"Ice in the icebox," she answered, in nearly a musical sing-song. "Bread's in the breadbox. Mind on the moment, Pearly." Then she took off her glasses and turned toward him with a dazzling smile that had not a shade of malice in it, and for a few seconds Pearly thought he was looking at someone else entirely; he could imagine her as a shopgirl innocent to the world, and he her beau equally innocent waiting for her outside the shop with a bouquet he'd picked up on the walk over. It was nearly a shock to him, to see how quickly she could transform herself, as if the smile had altered the bones in her face and made her look so soft she couldn't bite through a marshmallow. He felt a little tremor pass through him, and it came to him that he was standing on the edge of not the summer garden she wished him to see, but a quicksand swamp. In that moment he nearly turned and walked out the door, and to hell with the Packard and the revenge-beating and every other damn thing, but maybe she saw that in his face because as she focused her attention on the frying pan once more she said quietly, in a voice like silk being drawn across satin, "How'd you like a split of two hundred thousand dollars?"

Get out, he thought.

But he did not move.

"You heard me," she repeated over the noise of sizzling meat.

It was another few seconds before he got his tongue working. "I'm not up to robbin' the United States Federal Bank."

"Well, they're broke as hell anyway," she said. "We're ready here. Where's the bread?"

They ate their sandwiches at a little round table set near the window that gave a view of the river. Pearly kept waiting for her to speak again about this two hundred thousand buck deal, but she did not. Instead, she began talking about New Orleans, how'd she visited there several times and it seemed like a place she might like to live in at some point, with all the fancy old architecture and the wrought-iron balconies...and, of course, the Mississippi would be so much more interesting to watch than the Red, because there was a whole hell of a lot more river traffic to—

"Did you test me?" he asked suddenly. "That about givin' me clues to find you. All that crap you were spewin'. You were testin' me to see if I'd come through?"

She took a sip of iced tea and lifted her chin into the fan's breeze. "Yep," she said.

"And killin' the doc too? That was a test?"

"That," she said, "was a necessity. Had to get him out of the way. Not safe to have him out there somewhere, prattlin' on about whoever and what-ever." She clinked the ice in her glass and tilted her head toward the sound, as if it had stirred some pleasant memory. "But yeah, I guess you could call it a test, if you want to. See, when you walked into that place and presented yourself, I thought, 'Boy, here's a square peg who thinks he's a rounder'. I knew you were a grifter right off…it's a little too obvious for anybody but a total idiot, and you ought to be glad so many soft touches out there *are* idiots. But then…when you stepped up and helped clear us out as smooth as you did, I thought, 'Hmmmm. Now maybe this fella has some potential. *Maybe.*' Figured I ought to give you a chance to show your stuff."

"See if I could kill a man, you mean?"

"See if you appreciated *logic*," she corrected. "And as I said, I like to gamble. So…I took a gamble on *you*."

"What's the payoff?"

Ginger finished her sandwich and licked spicy mustard off a forefinger before she replied. "You asked what the angle was. Look out that window at an angle of about…oh…twenty degrees."

He had to get up from the table to do so. He peered out into the bright sunlight across the street at the wharves, workshops and warehouses along the sluggishly-moving river. "Okay," he said. "What am I lookin' at?"

"There's a name painted in red on one of the warehouse walls. See it? Read it."

"*Ludenmere*," he said. "So what?"

"You never heard of Jack Ludenmere?"

Pearly turned from the window, his eyes stung by the glare. "Sounds to me like a cough drop."

"Ha," she said without humor. She sat staring at him for a few seconds and he felt the intense scrutiny nearly crawling under his skin to inspect the foundation of his innards; he figured the champagne-colored eyes were sending the last signals to her brain whether the gamble had paid off or not. Then she got up, went to the narrow-doored closet, opened it and from the top shelf brought out a small metal lockbox. She set it on the table between their sweating glasses of iced tea. She flicked open the latch, lifted the lid, and Pearly saw that inside was a collection of newspaper clippings.

"Jack Ludenmere," she said, "started his shipping company here in Shreveport about fifteen years ago. He did pretty well, but he was limited by the river. So he keeps his warehouse and some of his barges here, but he pulled up stakes, took some cash and went to New Orleans to build his business there." She chose one of the clippings, unfolded it and showed it to Pearly. The headline read *Ludenmere Wins Coveted Contract.* "He just got a shipping contract from the government to move building materials up and down the Mississippi for the CCC," she said. "Worth upwards of a million dollars, is what both *Fortune* and *Forbes* magazines say. And a certain private secretary for the Randolph Construction Company of Tulsa, Oklahoma, can find out a lot by smilin' real nice and shakin' her tail for the businessmen around here."

"Oh," he said. "That's the get-up, huh? Okay, so this Ludenmere gent is loaded. Good for him, but like I asked before, what's the game?"

She smiled faintly, refolded the clipping that announced the bargeman's triumph and returned it to the lockbox. "Ludenmere's wife is named Jane," Ginger said. "They have two kids: Little Jack, eight, and Nilla, ten. Think each kid would be worth a hundred thousand, if they were to get…shall we say…*borrowed* for a time?"

There was a silence but for the stuttering of the fan as that sank into Pearly's brain.

"I've got some ideas," Ginger went on, in a voice that was both eerily quiet but as firm as reinforced concrete. "Just some things to think about. But I believe it could be done. You ever read the *New York Times?*"

"Above my paycheck," he heard himself say, like a ghost in another room.

"I read it at the library," she said. "Every so often they run on the front page a little box that tells you what kidnapped kid—or whoever, it's not always a kid—gets returned to their family. Swear to God. Sometimes they list five or six names. It's a fuckin' epidemic." She shrugged. "But…what they don't report in those little boxes is how much dough got paid out. They don't want you to know that. Gives people ideas."

"That's where you got this one from?"

"I've been chewin' on this ever since I got here, four months ago. I saw that big name in red letters and I wondered who that was and if there might be a score to be made. So I started readin', and I found out about his business, his wife and his kids. Found out they'd moved to New Orleans just before the girl was born. Then this news about the CCC contract came up a few days before I went on the road with Honeycutt." She tilted her head as if to look at him from a different perspective. Her eyes gleamed in the hot light. "The first ransom note for the Lindbergh kid asked for fifty thousand and then it got upped to seventy. A hundred grand ought to pay for each Ludenmere brat…he'll make that back in six months, no skin off his ass."

"Sure," Pearly said, with a slight sneer. "He and his security men'll just step aside and let 'em be snatched, right off the street. You don't think he hasn't got three or four bodyguards watchin' those kids?"

"Maybe, maybe not," she answered. "Hey, I know there are things to work out. We may move along and figure it can't be done. Then we can scratch it and scram. But just think of the money, Pearly. Think of figurin' a way to get those kids, gettin' all that money, then dumpin' 'em on the side of the road somewhere and headin' straight to Mexico. Think of it, let it get in your head."

"Dumpin' 'em?" he asked. "Like you dumped the doc?"

"No! Hell, no! We get the dough, we put the kids out. *Alive*. But somewhere they can't get to a phone or help so easy. That's just common sense. Then…*Mexico*."

She came upon him quickly and put both hands flat on his chest. Her eyes seemed to him to be ablaze with an inner fire…no…more than that… what they called a *conflagration*.

"I *did* test you," she said, softly, as if she were whispering it in his ear. "I tested you by leavin' you in a fix in Stonefield. Wanted to see how you'd react. I knew you'd find me…I mean…I *hoped* you would. I figure you could've hired a private dick to hunt me down, but you didn't want to involve anybody else and have to explain why you were lookin' for me. Oh yeah, I know you could've made up a good enough story, but I know too you came to bust me up. So that's why you hustled the badge. You went to a lot of trouble, Pearly...but you *found* me. You passed the test. See?" Her hands smoothed the front of his shirt. Her eyes never left his. "I needed to find somebody I could count on...to help me think...to figure things out. Sure there's a lot to work through...but you and me...we can do it, if we put our minds and our wits to it. Two hundred thousand skins, Pearly. You'll never have another chance in your life to get a score like that. Never *ever.* And you know what? You need me just as much as I need you. Yes." She nodded. "You *do.*"

He said, "I don't need to spend the next twenty years of my life in pri—"

She pressed an index finger against his lips, sealing his mouth. "Other people," she said firmly, "figure it out and get away with it. Plenty of other people. And people who aren't nearly as smart as you and me. All you have to do is read a few of those newspapers to see that. Now...I can't do this alone...and I can't imagine that you want to spend the next twenty years of your life chasin' hearses. Do you?"

He didn't answer; he didn't have to, for her to see in his face that he knew full well he didn't have a bright future in following the trail of obituaries to sell heat-swollen Bibles in white cardboard boxes. Those damned boxes had more than once made him think of his own coffin, and how when they locked you away in one of those and sank you six feet under it was all she wrote, brother.

"This could be the answer," Ginger said, and it seemed her face had come closer to his. "*Could* be, if everything feels right. You and me...we'll know if it's worth a go or not when we get deeper into it."

"I think you already are."

"Not yet. I need *you* to help me cook the plan."

He stared at the floor because he didn't know where to set his eyes. He could hear her breathing, again as if she were up right next to his ear.

"Let's see that badge," she said, and he dug his wallet out and showed her. She took it over to the window, where the light was brightest, and spent a few long seconds examining it from every angle. "This on the level?"

"Supposed to be real, yeah."

"Got a story behind it?"

"Nope. Just a hundred bucks worth of city dick badge, that's all I know."

"Hm. Looks real enough." Ginger closed the wallet and gave it back. "So," she said, with a slight upward lilt to her voice, "what do you think?"

It was a moment before he could answer, but the gears had begun turning in his own brain. Did he dare to move in a direction like this? Still…she was right. They could scotch the deal and scram if it looked like a dead end. Two hundred thousand dollars. Was it worth even going forward just a little ways? He said, "It wouldn't be like nabbin' the Lindbergh kid at midnight. That was a baby. Here you've got two brats with loud voices."

"Sure. So we figure out how to take 'em in broad daylight, and in a way that they won't be hollerin' for Daddy."

"Good luck with that."

"Has to be a good *plan*," she corrected. "But it's a hell of a gamble, sure it is. I don't know about you, but I'm a little weary of livin' from hand to mouth. Tired of the grind, and I know you must be too. You and me… we've got talent that we ought to put together. Seems a shame to let this go…sooner or later, things bein' as they are, somebody not near as talented as you and me are gonna try for those kids." She paused for a moment and Pearly could see she was coming up with something from the shine of her eyes. "You know, *that* could be the angle."

"What could be?"

"Put on your thinkin' cap, mack! Maybe…if somebody *else* was plannin' a snatch…" She left that hanging with one of her small and deadly smiles. When it faded away, she was all hard bricks-and-mortar. "Are you in or out?"

"Gonna kill me if I say I'm out?"

"What would you do in my place?"

"*Crazy*," he muttered, but he had already sent his mind to Mexico. A hundred grand could buy an awful lot of good living south of the border. There were places a man—alone, or with a woman—could disappear into, enjoy the fruits of his labor and never look back. *A hundred grand.* Who ever saw that kind of money but the crooked bankers, the top-cat businessmen who were themselves as crooked as Shandy's mile, and…well, yeah…the gamblers, like himself and Ginger LaFrance. He was standing on a beach… white sand…blue water…a fishing boat in the distance…maybe a nice stone villa up in the hills behind him…and money in a cashbox, ready to be spent on whatever else the hell he decided to buy. Then he was aware again of this room at the Hotel Clementine, the chugging of the fan as it sprayed the room with a breeze, and the woman before him who was offering him the chance at a life he had never dared to imagine. He said, "I'm in until we run against a wall…then I'm walkin'."

"I'm real good findin' a way either around a wall or through one," she answered.

"That remains to be seen."

Her eyebrows went up. "So…we're partners in this, right? For the time bein'?"

"For the time bein'," he echoed, still uneasily, though the sultry shores of Mexico did beckon his imagination.

She nodded. She took the metal lockbox back to the closet and put it up on the high shelf.

She rummaged under what appeared to be a blanket, and when she turned back to him again she was holding the ugly little .38 revolver that had dispatched Doctor Honeycutt from this world.

She spun the cylinder.

"Let's celebrate," she said.

Six.

She lied.

It had been on his mind ever since she'd told him, two days ago, and it had nearly eaten him up on the four-hundred-mile drive from Shreveport to New Orleans. He was sitting now with Ginger on one of the long wooden pew-style benches in the huge Union Station on South Rampart Street, the place smelling of cigar and cigarette smoke, the sweetish tang of the solution that was used to mop the black-and-white marble tiles on the floor, and another aroma that Pearly likened to the ozone of a passing lightning storm, which he figured might have something to do with the hustle-and-bustle of train travel or the metallic smell of the trains themselves, which pulled up on four tracks outside and sat there breathing steam like sullen bears. Two large fans stirred air up at the ceiling, voices were turned into murmurs and echoes, and metal things bumped and clanged beyond the archway that led to the tracks. Redcaps—the Negro men who helped passengers with their baggage—moved smartly back and forth in service to their job; they wore neatly-pressed dark blue uniforms with gold buttons and of course the scarlet caps on their heads, and Pearly smoked a cigarette down and thought that the Redcaps could've made good soldiers because they all looked like they probably slept at attention, even the one who looked old enough to have been a grandpa during the Civil War.

A speaker crackled and a man's singsong voice announced the arrival of the Illinois Central train from Memphis, but that was not the train Pearly and Ginger waited for, so at the end of his cigarette he crushed it out in a dark brown ashtray that stood next to his knees and lit another. Something in his movements must have either irritated Ginger or brought her out of the silent reverie she'd been wearing like a shroud since they'd reached the station. She said, "You still sulkin'?"

He took his own damn time in answering. He watched a young Redcap pushing a cart stacked with half-a-dozen suitcases and behind him trailed the white gentlemen in their summer suits and their straw boaters, and the nicely-groomed silky women following behind all giggly-wiggly about travelling somewhere. Pearly considered that the economy might be in the ditch and as of yet the ditch was made of gluey mud, but thems that had dough didn't mind heading north to cooler climes. He hoped the ones passing by and leaving the crisp scent of money in their wake died under tons of scalding iron when their trains went off the tracks, and for a moment he luxuriated in those mental images.

It was mid-August and the days were miserably hot. Pearly thought that there could be no hotter and more hellish place on earth than New Orleans when the heat locked in, the air sweltered and thickened and the Mississippi looked like it was made of a gritty brown soup that reflected the sun back in a dull glare, and to touch that liquid you might expect not to be cooled but to have the skin burned off your bones. It hadn't been too pleasant of an experience driving in the blistering heat from Shreveport to New Orleans, not even in the black Ford Model A fourdoor Town Sedan he and Ginger had gone in together to buy with a hundred bucks of the Packard moolah. She'd explained to him that a new car—not so new, it was a 1930 model with three thousand miles on the 4-cylinder—was essential to whatever plan they came up with, and the Oakland had earned an amazing twenty bucks on trade-in so it hadn't been a bad deal. The Ford was dent-free and looked good, and Ginger had said people judged you by the car you drove, which Pearly agreed made plenty of sense.

He shifted his position on the bench, blew a Chesterfield smoke ring into the Union's sparkling space, and said testily, "Yeah, maybe I am."

"Well snap out of it," she told him after she'd looked around to see that other people weren't sitting close enough to hear. "How old are you, not out of your diapers yet?"

"*Listen*," he said into her face, and he saw the ferocity of his voice make her draw her lips back as if a hard wind had hit her cheeks. "You didn't say anythin' about a *share*. You said it was gonna be a *split*."

"It won't be a share, a split or a *shit* without help," she fired back.

"I don't know this punk! You're just loadin' him in here like this, what am I supposed to think?"

"You're supposed to *know* that I'm doin' what's right for the job." Ginger stopped speaking and waited while an older couple walked past the bench, following the reed-thin Redcap who deftly pushed a cartful of baggage. She returned her focus to Pearly and leaned toward him, into his cigarette smoke. "We need six hands. You and me, we can't do it alone."

"Nice that you didn't tell me you'd wired your damn nephew before you got me into this."

"My nephew is a reliable *force*," she said. "He's got the muscle we need. And I didn't wire him until after I talked to you…after I'd figured out the angle. Okay, you can squawk about shares and splits all you damn please, but the plan needs Donnie."

"My *ass*," Pearly sneered.

"He'll be a good mule," she said, and then she reached out, plucked the Chesterfield from his fingers, inhaled and blew streams of smoke through her nostrils. "We'll negotiate the money with him later, after everything's settled in. Just relax, Pearly. There'll be a time you're glad Donnie's here to help out, I guaran-damn-tee it."

"I guess you spelled the whole idea out in the wire so Western Union got a fuckin' eyeful?"

"You know better than that. Donnie was told I had an employment opportunity for him. That's all he needed. He'll tell my sister he's comin' to New Orleans for whatever reason he makes up, but he'll make it stick."

"Sounds like you've used him before."

"'Course I have, otherwise why would I be wantin' him here? Like I said, he'll be a good mule." She took another draw off the cigarette and handed it back to him with one of her stony little smiles.

"Your sister in the game too?"

"Maybe. What she doesn't know won't hurt her. Anyway, leave my sister out of this, she's got her own row to hoe."

"You must come from a fucked-up family," he said, as he pushed the cigarette between his teeth.

"And *you* didn't?" In an instant her voice and demeanor changed; she stroked his cheek with the back of her hand and she sounded like a little girl burbling to her beau in the neighborhood ice cream soda parlor. "Ohhhhh, baby waby's got his li'l ole feelin's hurt 'cause big bad Ginger figured out the job needed a *third*…and now baby waby's just firin' his mouth all over the place without thinkin' that Ginger has got *his* best interest in mind, too. Isn't that the ticket, lovey dove?"

"*Stop it.*" He brushed her hand away, and when she returned it to stroking his cheek she giggled as if viewing his discomfort was the most entertaining comedy since the Marx Brothers stormed Freedonia in *Duck Soup*.

What might have turned into an ugly scene as Pearly's blood began to boil was averted as the man with the microphone and the speaker switch announced the Yazoo & Mississippi Valley railroad train from Jackson was pulling in on track number two.

"There's our boy," Ginger said, and she gave Pearly's cheek a final light tap. She stood up, and he did too. She put a hand on his shoulder. "You wait here while I go fetch him."

"Why? So you can remind him not to use your real name in front of me?"

"I knew you had brains. Save 'em for later use." She turned away from him and walked purposefully toward the archway to the tracks. Pearly started to take a step after her, but he decided not to push it; he sat down again to finish his cigarette, and he pondered the fact that anyone looking at Ginger LaFrance today, with her dulled-down hair, her lack of seductive makeup and hip sway and her conservative dark purple dress with a trim of lighter lavender, might've taken her for a school teacher or a librarian come to the train station to meet her elderly grandfather.

She's good, he thought. He smoked his cigarette down and watched people moving around in the station and occasionally threw a glance over toward the archway where a hint of steam wafted into the terminal like a wandering ghost.

In another moment he saw Ginger come through alongside a young man in his early-to-mid twenties who carried a single battered brown suitcase. She was talking quietly to him, with an expression on her face of smug self-satisfaction that all was well in Ginger World. As they approached, Pearly crushed his cigarette out and stood up. The young man, who bore the name of Donnie Baines according to Ginger but that was open to question too, had a raw look about him, a sort of primitive craggy Neanderthal set to his large jutting lower jaw and the low forehead topped with a shock of reddish hair allowed to grow long while the sides of his head were shaved to the skin. He stood about five-eight, had wide shoulders and narrow hips and looked like he could brawl with the best of them; in fact his deep-set eyes under the protruding brow were already shifting left and right as if searching for a fight to throw himself into. He was certainly no dandy in his dress; he was wearing a pair of brown boots, tan trousers with darker brown patches on both knees, and a plain blue work-shirt with the sleeves rolled up to display his thick, corded forearms. As the pair came nearer, Pearly saw the boy's eyes fix on him and for an instant the message was transmitted as if through telepathy: *I'll beat your damn ass if I want to.*

Pearly put a smile on his face. "So," he said easily as they got within hearing distance, "this is Donnie!"

Donnie did not smile. He looked at Pearly's offered hand for a second or two longer than necessary before he shook it, and then Donnie's dark brown—nearly black—eyes bored into Pearly's face as the grip strengthened to the point where Pearly thought his knuckles might crack, but he kept the smile fixed in place.

"How do," said Donnie, in a voice like the Mississippi river full of grit and grime and tough old mud might've had, if the river could speak. In speaking he revealed a silver tooth in the front of his mouth, and Pearly thought all the other teeth looked darkened and worn down by gnawing on the thorny flesh of the other cavemen he'd fought.

"Good trip?" Ginger asked.

He shrugged, showing himself to be a man of few words.

"Hungry?"

"I can eat."

Pearly thought all horses in the area should beware; he figured this punk could chew a nag down to the bones, and maybe chewing on bones had done the number on his teeth.

"We'll find us a place to grab somethin' before we head back."

Donnie nodded. He took a long gaze up and down Ginger. "I swear you look so *different*," he said. "Never would've recognized you." He blinked a couple of times, as if trying to reason something out. "Okay, if you're goin' by *Ginger*, and this fella's goin' by *Pearly*, what am I goin' by?"

"*Donnie* will do just fine," she assured him.

There passed a few seconds of silence, as Donnie Baines turned his appraisal to Pearly. Then, abruptly, Donnie swung toward the exit to South Rampart Street and in the violence of his motion his suitcase collided with a passing Redcap who was pushing an empty cart across the floor. The Redcap staggered, the cart's wheels went sideways and skreeched across the flooring, and Donnie Baines snarled, "Watch it, nigger!"

It was the thin young Redcap Pearly had seen a little while before; the kid couldn't be much over twenty, and it would've only taken a hard breath from Donnie to knock his gangly frame to the floor. But the kid did something he shouldn't; when he recovered his balance he lifted his gaze to Donnie, and though the boy's ebony eyes were both startled and bewildered it was the wrong thing at the wrong time to the wrong person.

Instantly Donnie's face bloomed nearly blood-red starting from the neck and rapidly ascending to the fiery hairline, the color seeming to set his hair hotter ablaze.

"Drop them eyes, nigger!" Donnie stormed. He balled up a fist and took a step toward what Pearly realized could bust this game before it even got started.

"Settle down, Heinz," said Ginger, in a quiet and soothing voice, and she laid a hand not on his shoulder but across his heart as if to calm its mad progression. She stepped between him and the Redcap. "Easy, *easy*," she said.

"Drop them goddamned eyes!" Donnie rasped, the old dirty river speaking. His own eyes, fierce as hell's flames, were locked upon the hapless Redcap and he trembled as if about to brush Ginger aside and launch himself like a bullet.

And then the Redcap cast his gaze down at the floor and said in a hushed and reverential voice, "Yes suh." He went to his cart, which had skidded a few feet away. His narrow shoulders hunched up as if expecting a blow to his back, he righted on his head the red cap that had gone a half-inch askew and pushed the cart away across the floor.

"Easy," Ginger said, nearly whispering. "It's over. Let it go."

"Nigger was darin' me to hit him!" Donnie said, way too loudly. Flecks of foam clung to his lower lip. "Knock the black shit outta that bastard!"

"It's over," Ginger repeated. She rubbed her hand slowly back and forth over his heart as if regulating its beating. "People are staring at us, Donnie. We don't want that, because we don't want any undue attention. Do we?"

Donnie didn't answer; his body shivered, the violence within him still straining to break out.

"I think I need another fag," Pearly said, reaching for his pack of Chesterfields. Just that comment and movement was enough to make Donnie advance a step on him with teeth gritted and the silver fang glinting because it seemed the boy needed a fight like anybody else needed to breathe. "Whoa there, Max Baer," he said with a tight smile. "Fuck with me and I'll blow your head off."

Either the reference to the current heavyweight boxing champ or the mild manner in which Pearly had spoken the last part of that—and the business-like way that said he meant it—seemed to cool Donnie's flames. As Ginger took Donnie's arm to both restrain him and lead him out of the terminal station under guard, the blood of anger began to drain from the boy's face.

Heinz, she'd called him, Pearly thought as he lit up. *Heinz ketchup. Suits him. Likely she'd seen this thing happen way too many times.* He blew smoke toward the ceiling. As he followed along behind them he said with a little laugh in his voice, "Hope you know what you're doin', Ginger baby."

"Shut up," she said tersely, and they went out of the station into the blinding light.

TWO.

The Son of Orchid
and Ironhead Joe

Seven.

Here came Ol' Crab, just as Curtis had known he would come.

Curtis heard the clacking of Ol' Crab's polished shoes upon the marble and then Ol' Crab got beside him, nearly elbow-to-elbow, and Curtis kept pushing his cart and walking but he knew it wouldn't be a few more seconds before—

"Stop y'self right there, young man," said Ol' Crab, and that hard old voice from the grave of time that was still strong enough to stop the ticking of a pocket watch could sure enough stop the progress of Curtis Waterford Mayhew. "Now look at me," said Ol' Crab, and when Curtis did the wizened face that might have been formed under pressure from the blackest earth of the Dark Continent loomed huge even though Ol' Crab was even leaner than Curtis and stood two inches shorter. "You run into that gent over there," he said. "Hell of a commotion you done."

"Suh, I was jus'—"

"You run *into* that gent," Ol' Crab interrupted, and Curtis saw the ancient eyes with their yellow whites tick slightly upward and to the left, up toward the office on the second floor where the bossman behind his green-tinted glass was surely watching the floor with his hands on his broad hips and his bald head cocked to one side as if catching every whisper in the realm below.

"Caused *dis*-tress," Ol' Crab went on, his voice quiet but as severe as his expression. "Don't like no *dis*-tress in my house."

Curtis knew he had no out but to say, "No suh."

"Say you're sorry."

"I'm—"

"Not to me," said Ol' Crab. "To my *house*."

Curtis lifted his face toward the ceiling fans. "I'm sorry," he apologized to the great and grand Union Railroad Station.

Ol' Crab nodded. He put a wrinkled paw behind one ear. "Hear her? She say, 'Watch your step so no heedless white man run into you again and make you look like a dancin' fool'." The eyes ticked upward once more and Curtis saw the face relax; the bossman was no longer at his window, satisfied that a stern warning had been doled out by the head Redcap to one of his charges, and life could go on.

"Laughin' my ass off," said Brightboy, as he strode past lugging two suitcases for a man in a blue-striped seersucker suit.

Ol' Crab motioned for Curtis to walk alongside him again, and they crossed the marble tiles under the fans that cooled the passengers waiting on their trains. "How you did today?" Ol' Crab asked.

"Dollar and twenty cents. One fella tipped me thirty."

"Well, that's a nice pickup. Don't be spendin' it all tonight in them juke joints."

"No suh." It was Ol' Crab—Mr. Wendell Crable—who had taught Curtis the ropes of being a good Redcap, and of softening the "sir" to "suh" so no white traveller could mistake the word for anything but agreement and respect. *Always speak soft*, Ol' Crab had told him. *Be quick and mind your business, and anybody throws bad words at you, let 'em roll off your back, hear?*

Yes suh, yes suh, I hear.

"Don't mind what happen'," Ol' Crab said as they walked. He looked up to the right at the big clock on the wall over the ticket desk. Next Illinois Central train wasn't due in for another hour and forty-seven minutes, but both he and Curtis knew that without having to look at clocks or pocket watches. After two years of working here, Curtis knew the schedules by heart and since Ol' Crab had started out first as a janitor here in March of 1911, to him was known every grain in every oak panel, every crack in the concrete platforms and every gray piece of gravel the rails ran over between the station and where the tracks intersected South Rampart. The white managers came and went, janitors and ticket sellers and Redcaps were hired and dismissed or passed away, but Ol' Crab seemed eternal and if anyone could claim the station as his "house" it was surely Mister Crable.

Where the cantankerous gent had collided with Curtis—a suitcase to the ribcage on the lower left side—felt like it had left a bruise that might bother him later on, but on this Saturday afternoon he thought that all was right with the world, and he was happy when Ol' Crab asked:

"Got plans tonight?"

"Oh, yes suh I do!"

"Excited, sound like."

Curtis was amazed. Usually Ol' Crab showed no desire to know anything about his charges outside the station except telling them to stay out of juke joints and to go to church on Sunday morning, and here he was opening the door to hear what Curtis was excited about. It was a relief too, because all day Curtis had been wanting to tell the other Redcaps—Brightboy, Cricket, Rainy and Prentiss, the new man who had not yet earned a nickname—but it had been busy and no one had had the time or, it seemed, the interest to listen. And now that the door was open, Curtis jumped right through it.

"Goin' to a birthday party as soon as I get off," he said. "Ava Gordon's turnin' eighteen."

"Oh, Curtis has got hisself a girl?"

"Not exactly, but…I've been *tryin'*." He smiled, which lit his face up like two dozen candles. "See, she's *awful* pretty, and I think she kinda—"

"That's good to know," said Ol' Crab. He laid a firm hand upon Curtis's shoulder, and with that touch Curtis realized the door quickly opened was just as quickly shut. "You mind these white bucks with dangerous satchels now, hear?" Then Ol' Crab's gaze shifted toward the station's street entrance and Curtis saw him grimace. The eyes that had seen so much narrowed. "Oh, oh…here comes trouble. Friend of yours, I believe."

Curtis turned around. Who had just entered the station but Rowdy Patterson, in his tan-colored pegged trousers and his orange-striped shirt, his thin black necktie and on his feet his two-toned shoes with toes that looked so sharp they could slice the hot pavement as if it were made of soft butter. Rowdy saw he'd been spotted, and instantly he smiled broadly and took off his straw fedora that had a dyed-orange feather sticking up from the hatband. He came on with his loping gait and his bright grin and his eyes were on Curtis and Curtis thought *oh no, not again* because there was only one reason Rowdy would come here and it was not for a train trip.

"Fella's reputation walks ten paces in front of him," said Ol' Crab, with a distasteful twist of his mouth. "Tryin' to shake him loose, I reckon."

"Howdy there, Longlegs," Rowdy said to Curtis. And then, in a quieter voice, "'lo, Mr. Crable. Can I have a few minutes with your boy?"

"The young man's druthers, not mine." Ol' Crab stared at the two-tones. "Lordy, nigger," he said. "What pimp you chase down to grab them blades?"

"Everythin' *old*," said Rowdy with a touch of injured pride in the lift of his dimpled chin, "is just plain *old*. I'm the new breed, don'cha see?"

"I hear breedin' is what you do best. You start workin' for a livin' you won't have so much time to get y'self and so many girlies in trouble."

"Takes two to tango, Mr. Crable."

"Get y'self shot on that dance floor one of these nights, and mark I said it." Ol' Crab realized he had come to the end of his usefulness here, because Rowdy Patterson's business with Curtis was not something he wanted to overhear. "Five minutes," he said to Rowdy, and he stuck five fingers up and wriggled them before Rowdy's amber-colored eyes. "We're runnin' a train station, not no tango hall. Mind y'self, Curtis…and 'member to go to church tomorrow mornin', you might need a li'l extra Bible verse." He fired a final look of utter disdain at the playboy of the Treme District, and then he seemed to spin on his heel and move away not at a walk but at a stately glide suitable to the commander of the American Army.

"Won't stain his soul too much!" Rowdy announced with wicked glee, but Ol' Crab was done with him and that was that. Then as Rowdy turned the full focus of his considerable presence upon Curtis, his handsome face became warped and stricken and his eyes seemed about to bleed tears. "Longlegs," he said in a raspy whisper, "I have got myself in one hell of a hole this time."

"One of many," said Curtis, with a quiet sigh. "Both hells and holes."

"No, I'm *meanin'* it this time! Ellie has thrown me out good and proper, changed the lock on the door, everythin' she can do to toss me away, Curtis… and I swear to God I love that girl and I cain't do nothin' without her!"

"You should've thought of that before…who is it, anyway?"

"Sadie Monette at the Ten Spot…but that don't make no matter, Curtis. Ellie *knows* me. She knows I cat around. Hell's bells, everybody's cattin'!"

"No," said Curtis. "They're *not*. You just want to believe they are for your own sake, like that gives you the sayso to do it."

Rowdy made a little noise that sounded somewhere between a grunt and a sniffle. He put a hand over his mouth as if to stifle any further emotional sounds, and the silver rings on his fingers glittered in the smoky light that streamed from the upper windows. "Swear to the Lord Almighty," he said when he'd lowered the muzzle, "I want to marry Ellie and make everythin' right. But it's my *nature*, Curtis. Hell, when the women come after me, prancin' and smilin'…what am I supposed to do?"

"You're supposed to be faithful to one woman. Maybe you haven't found her yet."

"Oh yes I have, and it's Ellie! That girl makes me glow and I know I make her shine too. Never found one like her and I know I never will again, but…but…I'm in some deep trouble, friend Curtis. That damn Bayard told tales on me and got me in the shithouse. Please…please, and I'm beggin' like I never have before…please go talk to Ellie and smooth it out. Won't you do it for your ol' friend?"

Old friend of about three months since Rowdy had sauntered down here from St. Louis, Curtis thought. And in those three months he had been tasked twice already to get Rowdy out of his hells and holes with Eleanor Caldwell, who lived a few houses away from Curtis in the Treme District. "She won't listen to me this time," Curtis said.

"Ohhhhh, that's where you're mighty wrong about y'self." Rowdy began to straighten Curtis's necktie, though it already hung straight down the front of his crisp white shirt with help of the small metal tieclip shaped in the profile of a steam engine, the same one all the Redcaps wore. "Folks pay heed to you, Curtis. They just naturally do. Somethin' about you... somethin' I ain't got, but you got plenty of. Able to turn that sour water into sweet wine. Take that old mud nobody thinks is worth nothin' and make gold bricks out of it."

"That's goin' a little far, better back your wagon up."

"You know what I'm sayin'. Look what you done for me already—"

"*Twice* already," Curtis said.

"All right, twice already. Look what you done, goin' in there and smoothin' things over with Ellie like it was all Chinese silk. And you know, when she's got her dander up she is hard to handle. But *you*..." Rowdy smiled and shook his head with either pure or pretend admiration; he was so good at puffery that Curtis wasn't sure which was true. "You can have her chewin' on rocks and thinkin' it's rock candy. And she ain't the only one either! I know what you do for folks in need, it's all over the Treme."

"I don't do anything."

"Like you didn't do nothin' for them Watters brothers last month, when they had that fallin' out over the hardware store? And their mama come runnin' to you to patch it up? That's what I'm talkin' about."

Curtis shrugged. "I just help when I can, that's all."

"You got a *talent* in that way, boy. People come to you for help 'cause they know you got that talent, to fix up quarrels and misunderstandin's 'fore they turn into worse. See, it's just so natural to you that you don't think nothin' of it."

"You can drop me in the skillet now," Curtis said.

"*Huh?*"

"I've been rolled in enough butter to soak a dozen crawdads, so go ahead and cook me up."

Rowdy laughed; the explosive sound of it was nearly as loud as a gun-shot and the noise echoed back and forth between the station's walls, which caused several of the waiting passengers to look askance at the Redcap and his friend. Curtis figured the bossman might be peering through the green-tinted glass again, and he expected Ol' Crab to come scuttling over any second now to lecture them both about *dis*-tress in his house.

"I'll go talk to Ellie," he said, if only to get Rowdy out of his way. "How do you want me to plead you this time?"

"Innocent, a victim of Jip Bayard's lyin' mouth."

"She'll know there's truth in it. Best admit to the worst and go from there."

Rowdy's laugh had gone and his smile along with it. When he frowned, two deep lines surfaced where the bridge of his nose met his forehead; the party boy didn't like what he'd just heard.

"Trust me," said Curtis, and he realized that if he had a nickel for every time he'd repeated that to calm someone who came to him for help or advice he would no longer need to be a Redcap.

Rowdy's frown faded. "Sure thing. 'Course I will. Always do."

"I'll go see her tomorrow. Got plans for tonight."

"Oh, you *do*? Woman plans?"

"Well…I'm goin' to Ava Gordon's birthday party. She invited me when I saw her on Wednesday. I'm tickled pink to go, I didn't think she—"

"You have yourself a good ol' time, Longlegs," said Rowdy, and he clapped Curtis on the shoulder. Then he was already moving toward the exit. "Don't do nothin' I wouldn't do!" He stopped and gave a sly grin. "Or maybe you shouldn't do anythin' I *would* do! Thanks for listenin'!" With that, Rowdy Patterson put on his fedora with the orange feather flying high and he walked out of Union Station as if the train he needed to catch were gathering steam at the Rampart Street curb.

"Bags waitin' outside, boy," said a young man who'd strode up so quickly that Curtis feared he was going to be run over beneath his two-toned oxfords. The man wore a blue suit that looked to Curtis like the coolest pond of water this side of Eden. The slinky woman who'd followed him into the station gazed around languidly, her cigarette fixed to a mother-of-pearl holder.

"Yes suh, right away," said the listener, and he pushed his cart toward the work.

Eight.

Trust me.

Astride his silver-painted bicycle with black rubber grips on the handlebars, Curtis Mayhew pedalled steadily through the deepening twilight toward the birthday party. He had tried to let the excitement of the event fully take him over, but he could not and the fault was his own.

Trust me. Those two words he'd spoken to Rowdy Patterson at the station that afternoon.

How was it, he asked himself, that he could offer trust to Rowdy but none to Ellie Caldwell? After all, he'd known Miss Eleanor far longer than he'd known Rowdy, and he knew also that she was a fine and upright young woman…so why was it that he had talked himself into convincing her to give Rowdy another chance when he knew full well that…well, Rowdy might be right for some other lady, but he was not right for Miss Eleanor and no words out of anybody's mouth was going to change that fact of life.

So…what to do?

He pedaled east along Rampart Street, not going too fast but not dawdling either. The Saturday evening carnival of cars was building up to its usual stop-and-go parade. Because some people still drove horse-drawn carts or rode on bicycles like himself, the thoroughfare was not the easiest to negotiate, but this was his usual route and he was sticking to it until he crossed Canal Street, after which he would skirt above the *Vieux Carre* and take a left at the corner of North Rampart and Governor Nicholls Street into the

Faubourg Treme. The city's streetlights were coming on, the bigger buildings of midtown held lights in their multitudes of square eyes, and here and there the liquid fire of red, blue and green neon had begun to flame against the falling dusk. The air was sultry, and in the breeze that swept past Curtis he smelled the mélange of aromas that he knew so well to be the perfumed breath of New Orleans: the odor of roses and other fragrant flowers from Simonetti's open-air florist shop near the corner of Rampart and Gravier; a little further on the sweet warm smells of the cookies, frosted cakes and sugared beignets from Mrs. Delafosse's bakery where he often stopped on the way home to get his mama something (though today there was certainly no time); the aroma of strong coffee being roasted and served at the Central Cafe where he crossed Canal Street and the *thump-thump* eight times across the four streetcar tracks; then the dusty bittersweet incense of the *Vieux Carre* and all the spices of life that went into it, and mingled within all these the metal-and-exhaust smells of the cars and the few buses that rumbled about, and as finishing notes the more earthy aromas of the horse manure that was a natural part of transportation and a workaday chore for the cleanup crews and lastly from the river a muddy, swampy smell which in the heat of August seemed to bloat itself up into a yellow cloud and drift into the hundred-year oaks where it hung like the glistening threads of gilded spiderwebs.

That was his city and his world, and Curtis knew and appreciated every block between the Union Station on South Rampart and his house on North Debigny Street because he had a sense of all the life and history that had built them, and how he fit into it. He considered himself an important part of N'awlins, just as the other Redcaps were; he helped people travel from here to there and back again, he kept the baggage moving and in a way the wheels of the trains rolling, and what could be a higher calling than to be of service in such a way as that?

Behind his bicycle he pulled a small wooden cart on three rubber wheels. In the cart was his dark blue suit coat, carefully folded and wrapped up in brown paper so as not to attract a speck of dust, and atop that package an equally carefully-wrapped little gift box done up in white paper with a gold-colored ribbon, which he'd wrapped himself. In it was his birthday present for Ava Gordon.

In the Union Station's locker room where the Redcaps kept their uniforms under the tight supervision of Ol' Crab, Curtis had taken a shower to remove the train grit and then dressed himself in the nice clothes he'd brought, the pressed dark blue trousers and freshly-starched white shirt and the new blue-and-white bowtie he'd bought on Thursday. His shoes were black and shiny, like himself. He had regarded his face in the big square mirror over the wash-basin as he'd tied the bowtie—and thank goodness his neighbor Harmon Utley had helped him figure out the mechanics of this, because his mama had thrown up her hands at the intricacy and gone back to bed.

Curtis in the mirror had seen a young man fresh of twenty who was, in truth, not nearly as handsome as Rowdy Patterson but then again his face would not stop a clock like that of "Toothless" Bigjaw Coombs. He was on the average side, he figured, though it had been said he had large and luminous eyes and a nice smile. He had good teeth, again unlike the other fellow that had come to mind. Well, he was used to being average and what was so bad about that? His mama always said it was important to let your personality shine through your face, and then she said she could sometimes see his daddy in there looking back at her and that made her sad so she went back to bed again.

He had put small clips on his trouser legs so no cloth could be caught up in or dirtied by the bicycle chain. He pedalled smoothly onward. A blare of jazz music came at him like an assault from a club's open doorway. Hot red and blue neon painted the street. He realized his heart was beating harder, not from the exertion of pedalling because that was no trouble, but from his anticipation of the evening. To be asked to go to Ava Gordon's birthday party! And he'd thought she hardly knew he was alive, even though he slowed down every day as he passed her house after that one time she had been out walking and he had dared with a cold sweat on the back of his neck to pull up beside her, stop and say hello. He recalled that she'd been a little chilly at first, but then he'd told her his name and she'd gotten an interested look in her eyes and she'd said, *Curtis Mayhew? I think I've heard of you. Are you somebody important?* And he'd smiled and shrugged and said, *No, I'm just me.*

She was so *pretty*. So fresh-faced and she smelled pretty too, like cinnamon and cloves mixed together in a Mason jar and put out in a sunny place to warm up. And she wore pretty hats and he had never seen her without her white gloves, though really he hadn't seen much of her since that one day, just glimpses of her through the wrought-iron gate as she sat on the front porch swing or at the little table in the garden drinking lemonade and talking with two other young ladies. But on that Wednesday morning as he'd been pedalling past she'd called to him from behind the gate because she must've been waiting for him, and it pleased him no end to realize that she had taken note of his morning passage, and right then and there she'd asked him to come to her birthday party starting at seven o'clock on Saturday night.

Sure I'll be there, Ava. Wouldn't miss it for the world!

And it was easy figuring out what to get her as a present, too. That first day of their meeting a yellow butterfly had flown around and around them like some kind of creature from an enchanted tale, as if encircling them with invisible cords to draw them closer and closer, and the butterfly had landed first on her hat and then on his shoulder and she had given a little laugh like the gurgling of the garden fountain when he'd said *Oh me, who sent you to listen in on a private conversation?* So it was an easy thing to figure out he needed to find some kind of butterfly brooch for her to wear, and after work on Thursday he had pedalled up and down the wide expanse of Canal Street searching the shops, at last finding at the Kress store a small yellow enamel butterfly pin with gold-colored rhinestones set in the wings, and that was just perfect. A little expensive, yes, but perfect.

He was nearing his turnoff onto Governor Nicholls Street, and maybe he had begun working the pedals a few ticks faster. When he took the turn to the left off Rampart he was nearly flying, and he had to dodge between two cars whose drivers both hit their horns with indignation. Then he was pedaling north toward his destination, on both sides of the street the larger houses and small farms of the Faubourg Treme gentry, all of them protected by brick walls or wrought-iron gates. Ava Gordon's daddy owned two grocery stores in the district. Everybody knew that Mr. Gordon was a fair man when it came to prices on such staples as turnip greens, black-eyed peas and hog jowls. His business smarts had brought him up in the world, and so ahead Curtis saw the big black cars of other high-collared families pulling up to the Gordon manse; for an instant Curtis thought this part of the Treme world was too far above his head, but then again he had an invite directly from Ava so he pushed that little bit of unsurety down and got off his bicycle to unwrap his coat, shrug into it, remove the clips from his trouser legs and walk the last few yards like a gentleman should, pushing his bike ahead of him.

Purple, orange and green paper lanterns were strung above the garden and candles burned in lamps along the porch railing that went nearly all around the two-storied house, which itself seemed ablaze with light. At the open gate Curtis joined a group of young swells who were dressed to the nines. He didn't recognize any of them. They were showing their engraved invitations to a butler in a tuxedo who stood beside the gate and then they were going in one-by-one. When Curtis reached the man, the butler looked at his bicycle as if it might be a big stinky catfish hauled out of the Mississippi mud.

"Invitation?" the butler asked, his thick white eyebrows rising toward the furrowed forehead.

"Uh...no suh, but I was invited by Miss Ava herself."

"Name?"

"Curtis Mayhew."

"Ah," said the butler after a couple of seconds' deliberation. "Go 'round to the kitchen entrance, please. That way." He pointed a white-gloved finger toward a flagstone pathway that disappeared between some shrubbery. Then he turned his attention to the next two people coming in who already were pushing their invitations forward.

Kitchen entrance? Curtis wanted to ask, but the tide behind him was rising and shoving him on, so he guided his bicycle onto the path and went around toward the back of the house. Beyond the shrubbery there was another gate, also open, and he heard voices and young laughter and had the glimpse of other guests in a circular courtyard also lit up by the multi-colored paper lanterns, and there the light gleamed off the brass instruments of a band that was setting itself up on a bandstand festooned with purple and green ribbons and balloons. He was about to go onto the courtyard when a slim octaroon woman in a red dress came out of a door just short of the open gate; she wore a jewelled tiara in her hair, her makeup was perfect and her eyes seized upon first Curtis's bicycle and then himself.

"Are you part of the entertainment?" she asked.

"Well…ma'am…I'm Curtis Mayhew. I was—"

"Leave your vehicle over there by that tree and go right in." She motioned toward the door and swept past him leaving the scent of lemony perfume and a business attitude.

He parked his bike, removed the gift box from the cart, straightened his bowtie and smoothed the front of his shirt. Then he went through the door into a busy kitchen where the steam rose up from a multitude of pots on the mile-long stove and three male cooks were laboring while a rotund female wearing a white apron and a seagreen headwrap was watching over them and barking orders like a military sergeant. Instantly Curtis felt himself sweating and wilting in the barrage of noise and steam. The woman's eyes went to him and her face scowled up as if he were the last thing in the world she wanted to be bothered with.

"Who're *you?*" she asked.

"Curtis Mayhew."

"Oh…you're the…" She saw the gift box. "What's that?"

"It's my present for Miss Ava."

"Wasn't necessary," she said. But she reached out and took it from him anyway. "I'll see she gets it. Your table's set up in the courtyard." Some clatter or hiss or sizzle caught her attention. "Mister *Rufus*!" she growled. "Is that gonna be gumbo or dried-up mudbottom?"

"My *table*?" Curtis asked. "I don't think I—"

"Listen here, sonny!" The woman looked as if she might advance on him like a battleship and run him under. "I don't have time to be jawin'! Got sixty people soon gonna be hollerin' for more gumbo, crawdads, fried chicken, and Eyetalian meatballs! Get on out!"

Curtis backed away. Something was mighty wrong but he couldn't figure out what it was. The woman turned from him and Curtis saw her put the gift box with the butterfly brooch up on a high shelf out of the way of kitchen work. He was about to open his mouth again—though to say what he didn't know—but he thought better of it and he reasoned he could settle this situation once he got onto the courtyard and found Ava. So he went, as behind him the woman began to tongue-lash one of the other cooks about letting the hush-puppies fry up too hard.

In the courtyard where the dandies and the damsels in their finery were assembling around tables that held platters of the food that was being prepared in the kitchen for their second and third go-rounds, Curtis saw first a dappled pony tied to a post with a purple ribbon wrapped around its neck. Then he laid eyes on the biggest birthday cake he'd ever seen in his life or ever thought could be made by human hands. The thing was three tall layers of purple and green icing, like a cathedral of cake, and arranged upon it were eighteen white candles, yet to be lighted. The cake was positioned on a platform in the center of several large metal buckets of ice bricks, and two servants in tuxedos were keeping it further cool and fly-free with big fans made of woven reeds. There was a crystal punchbowl with foamy green liquid in it, and another servant was filling crystal cups for the guests. The band was getting itself ready; on the front of the bass drum was printed the name *The Vanguards*. The drummer let loose a few beats on the snare and the bass, and the trumpet player licked his lips and wiped his mouthpiece with a handkerchief.

And there, between the band and the pony, was a small table with one chair behind it and two chairs before it. The table was covered with a white cloth. At the center of the table was a crystal ball, and a handprinted sign set up next to the ball said *Have Your Fortune Told*.

Was that for him? he wondered. What kind of craziness was this? A mistake had been made…wires crossed…something…

In a daze he crossed the courtyard toward the table. The guests who were busy eating and drinking and merrily prattling let him go through their groups as if he were a ghost at the party. He was nearly to the table when a face appeared before him. She was smiling, she was radiant in her gold-colored gown and her own jewelled tiara, and she was still so pretty.

"Hi, Curtis," she said. "You're all set up."

"Hello," he said. His mouth was very dry. He had to struggle to focus on her, because he could hear and feel a pulse beating in his head like its own bass drum. "Listen," he said.

"Yes?" But she was already looking around, looking elsewhere, with places to go and guests to see, and though her eyes sparkled Curtis knew the sparkle was not for him.

"I think—"

"Oh, there's Preston! Go on, Curtis, I bet you'll have somebody real quick."

She started to move away, and for a terrible instant he was paralyzed but he knew he could not sit at that table and pretend to do what that sign said he could do, not even to be at this birthday party for Ava Gordon, not with the dappled and ribboned pony and the Vanguards nearly ready to play and the ice-cooled cake that was impossible for human hands to bake.

"Miss Ava!" he said, and it came out nearly as a forlorn cry amid the happy voices.

When she turned back to him, she did not look to be so pretty after all.

"What is it?" she asked, and there something in her voice that stabbed him.

"I'm…not a fortune-teller. I mean to say…I think…you've got me mixed up with somebody else." He stared at her as she gave him a slow blink, and she was still smiling but it was a mindless thing that had no meaning. "I don't tell fortunes," he said.

She just continued to smile vacantly at him.

"I don't," he repeated. "That's not me."

"Oh," she said. The smile faded. She touched her throat with her slender fingers, as if she had swallowed something that did not taste good and maybe would not go down right. "Well…I thought…I mean, I *heard*…that you were sort of…you know…that you could *tell* things about people."

"No, miss. I'm just ordinary Curtis."

"*Oh*." When she said that again, there was a finality to the expression. Her eyes had seemed to go darker though they were already midnight black, but for sure their sparkle had gone. "All right then," she said, and she looked quickly to her left at a young man approaching her and she switched her smile back on like an electric light. "Preston, I'm so glad you got here, we're about to start the dance!" She touched his shoulder and he put his hand on her shoulder and then they whirled away from Curtis as if they had been hoovered into the throng. He was left staring at the turbulent air where they had been, and the guests moved back and forth in his vision like shadows of shadows.

How long he stood there being jostled by laughing strangers who gave him not a glance, he did not know. He did know that he was not a part of this party, and no part of him would ever be. Suddenly the band gave an explosive warm-up noise and a long-limbed leader in a silver-spangled suit and Brilliantined hair stepped forward, lifted a megaphone to his mouth and said he wanted to lead the group in singing Happy Birthday to that gracious and beautiful Miss Ava Gordon, the suggestion of which raised a whoop and holler from the swells.

Before they could start the song, a hand clasped Curtis's left arm just above the elbow and there stood the severe-looking butler from the front gate. "I am instructed," he said as the bandleader counted to three with his baton, "to return you to the kitchen."

Curtis walked ahead of the man as the first brass notes from the Vanguards rang out and the voices—most of them unable to carry a tune in a gold-plated spitoon—reared up to frighten the overhanging oaks, which in the colored lantern light appeared to Curtis to have been recoiling from the Gordon manse for a number of years.

He was left in the kitchen to the mercy of the female battleship, who was still firing her guns at the hapless and harried cooks over the pots of steaming misery. A few words had been passed between her and Curtis's escort but she'd given Curtis not a glance. Now, as Curtis stood there both dumbly and numbly not knowing which way to move, the woman's gaze settled on him like an anvil and she asked, "You want your present back, sonny?"

"No," he mumbled, and instantly corrected himself with a stronger voice: "No, ma'am."

She gave no reply. She walked up and down the line of pots to check their progress, and then she regarded Curtis again and hooked a finger at him. "Come on back here and get a piece a' birthday cake," she said.

He crossed the checkerboard-tiled floor to a little square table the woman led him to, and she motioned for him to sit at one of the cane-backed chairs. In another moment she placed before him a yellow saucer bearing a piece of snow-white cake adorned with the purple and green icing. A cup of the green-colored punch cooled with an ice cube followed it. Curtis took the fork she offered. She stood close to him, smelling of all the kitchen odors of gumbo, crawdads, fried chicken, Italian meatballs and hush-puppies her coalblack flesh had absorbed.

"This is from the first cake we made this mornin'," she said, to a question he had considering asking. "Thing collapsed and sat there lookin' fatter'n a cow turd after a summer rain. In a manner of speakin', I mean. So this one's for the help."

He thanked her and began to eat, but he couldn't taste very much other than sweet velvet on the tongue.

"*Mayhew*," the woman said. "I knew a Mayhew one time. Name of Joe."

"That's my daddy."

"Ohhhhhh, is that right? You don't look none like him, though. Your mama ever feed you, boy? There's slim, skinny, and frail, and you is *south* of those."

"I take after my mama."

"I recall Joe was a big fella. Mighty big 'round the shoulders and had that big barn of a back. Oh yeah, I 'member him. I used to work at the Cotton Ball down near the docks on Harmony Street. Place burned down, long gone. But I recall them wild niggers comin' in there after daylong movin' that freight, and how they laughed and hollered and raised such a ruckus. Your daddy was one of 'em."

"I didn't know him too well," said Curtis, as he worked on turning the cake into crumbs.

"Hm," she said. "Bad thing that happened to him. Pitiful."

"This is good cake," said Curtis. He took a long drink of the punch, which tasted like sugary lime juice with a little fizzy soda water in it. "That's good too," he added.

"Yep," said the woman, and whether she was replying to her own statement about the fate of Joe Mayhew or to Curtis's compliments he didn't know. She stood there for another moment, watching him eat but with eyes that had turned maybe to another time and another place. Then she said, "See yourself out when you're done. And tell your mama to put some pole beans and corn bread in your belly 'fore a stiff wind blows you away." With that, she was done with him and she returned to the labors of the kitchen. And Curtis figured she probably ran the house too; he could feel it poised heavily over his head, and it was not a place he wanted to linger in very much longer.

He wheeled his bicycle out the gate when the butler, who was standing guard there, unlocked it for him. He took his suit jacket off, folded it up and returned it to the cart. He put the clips on his trouser legs. He did not glance back again at the Gordon house; he mounted his bike and pedalled off toward Marais Street, away from the sounds of laughter and merriment, a lone figure moving slowly through the night.

Nine.

It had always fascinated Curtis that a world could be so different in the distance of a right turn and two blocks, but so it was. As he neared Esplanade Avenue on his bicycle, his head still heavy with the confusion and disappointment of Ava Gordon's party, the fine big houses protected by walls and gates suddenly stopped as if by order of the law, and he pedalled into the rougher territory of the eastern Treme. Here stood the row upon row of shotgun shacks. Among the tight-packed houses some had small porches and some were close up upon the street, some were garishly painted in the manner of fever dreams and some had shaken their paint off year by year to take on the colors of heat-bleached bones. An occasional vacant lot was piled with rubble where a dwelling had burned down and been left to molder over the humid days and nights, growing green and leafy as if being pulled back into the earth by its jealous hand. What there was of the street pavement had buckled and broken and the dirt ground was climbing through.

Curtis had a ways to go yet. But as he neared the lighted little island of Prince Purdy's barbershop—the sign in the front window among the placards for Wildroot Cream Oil, Brylcreem and Talbot's Bay Rum Shaving Lotion read *Come In And Get Purdy*—he slowed his pedalling and stopped his bike, because he wasn't yet ready to consign himself to home.

Inside the barbershop, the usual Saturday night poker game was in full swing. When Curtis went through the front door into the fog of cigar, pipe and cigarette smoke that hung above the four men at their poker table, only Prince Purdy looked up from his cards.

"Hey there, Curtis!" he said, his big oval face with its halo of white hair breaking from rapt concentration to a quick smile of welcome. "Come on and get y'self a Co'-Cola!"

Curtis did, taking a bottle from the bucket that held them in ice—mostly melted now—at the back of the shop. He popped the cap using the opener tied to the bucket's handle with a length of twine, took a long drink and settled himself in one of the red vinyl chairs where the customers usually sat, the better to watch the game between Prince Purdy, Sam Rasco, Regis Mullahenny and Phillip LeSavan. In a couple of the other chairs were Gerald Gattis and Turk Tomlinson, both of them smoking their cigars and jawing over some important thing that nobody else gave a care about.

"Raise you ten cents," Regis announced.

"See that raise and I will raise another ten cents," said Sam.

"You boys ain't got nothin'," Prince said, but he shifted heavily in his chair. "Curtis, why you all so dressed up tonight?" he asked, mostly to stall his decision.

Curtis had his own decision to make. He wanted to tell somebody about what had happened but he was downright ashamed of it. Ashamed because he'd let himself—or made himself—believe that Ava Gordon maybe liked him as a beau, or maybe could get to like him in time, if she gave him that chance. He knew he should've known better; those rich folks who lived along Governor Nicholls Street were apart from the people in the eastern part of the Treme, across Esplanade, and it was foolish to think that things could ever be any different.

"I just had someplace to go," he said, lamely.

"Where was that?"

It seemed that Prince Purdy was inviting him to tell the story, and Curtis figured it might be a good thing to unburden himself of it. So he backed up on his decision and he said, "I *thought* I was invited to—"

"All right, twenty cents!" said Prince, and he pushed two dimes forward into the center of the table with an exasperated growl. "Well, Curtis," he added as Phillip studied his own cards, "you do look mighty nice tonight, wherever it was you went. Good thing for a young man like y'self to get out and about on a Saturday night. Phillip, you want some salt'n pepper on them cards so you can eat 'em?"

"Eat my doggone biscuits," Phillip replied haughtily, but his nerve had abandoned him. He slapped his cards down upon the table in momentary surrender.

Curtis sat back and sipped at his drink, and the game went on.

"Hey, Prince!" said Turk, who had taken the stub of his cigar out of his mouth and rested it in the ashtray at his elbow. "What color is you?"

"What *color*? What kind of a fool's question is that?"

"You know Dinah Fontaine's workin' as a maid over in the Garden District. Well she told Ermine Yancey a comical thing happened couple of days ago...little boy in that family come up to her while she was makin' a bed and asked if she was made out of *chocolate*."

"Do tell."

"Yessir! Oh, the lady of the house got all upset and shivery, said she hoped Dinah didn't take offense but Dinah jus' laughed, she didn't mind. But y'know...I started thinkin' about color. Being called *colored* and such, by white folks. Gerald and me been talkin' this over. Look in that mirror and say what color you see y'self to be."

"Hm," said Prince as he peered into the big gilt-edged mirror. "Dusky, I suppose. A little red in there, too, seems to be."

"Dusty and *rusty*, more like it," said Phillip, and everybody gave a hoot of laughter but Curtis, who was listening to this exchange but part of him was still at the party going over and over what had happened and dissecting it from every angle.

"That's what I'm sayin'," Turk said.

"Sayin' exactly *what*?" Regis asked. "'Cause you ain't makin' a lick a' sense."

"Look at me, then." Turk leaned forward in his chair and a spring in the seat yowled, but politely. "I'm what you might call a high yella. Regis, you're a high brown but you got some olive in you. Phillip, you got a little slate gray in you, looks to me like. Sam, you're—"

"*Seal* brown, I've been told," Sam announced.

"Yeah, all right, I'll agree with that, whatever that is. Gerald is near tan as a nice Sunday suit and Curtis over there looks like a strong cup a' mornin' coffee. Not one of us is *exactly* the same color, and the differences can be mighty much, too." Turk paused to draw on his cigar and blow smoke toward the light fixture above. "Not one of us here is really *black*, what I'm sayin'. Yet we all know folks like Weston Weaver, and he's so black you can see *blue* in him when the sun's hittin' him right. Same with Stovepipe, and he has got to be the inkiest fella I ever did see. So I was thinkin'…just consider how many colors we got in us, all us *coloreds*. Every brown you can think of, from cream-and-coffee to sable, and light brown to high brown, and all the yellas and the olives and the reds, and then you get into the real solid blacks, and the glossy shades and the dull shades, and it jus' goes on and on."

"Like your mouth," said Regis, but not in an ugly way. "What're you drivin' at?"

Turk sat back in his chair and smoked his cigar with leisure, as if he'd decided to keep a secret to himself. Then he smiled slyly at the group and he said, "Describe to me a *white* skin."

There was a moment of silence. Regis scratched his head and Sam scratched his graying beard. Curtis drank some more of his Coca-Cola and watched the group. Prince at last cleared his throat and spoke up. "They can be kinda *pink*, I reckon."

"Seen some so white they make you go blind for awhile," said Phillip.

"Seen some near red," Sam offered. "Those who've been in the sun too long. Oh, that must be a sufferin'!"

"That's what I'm gettin' at," Turk said.

"Excuse my ignorance, then," Prince answered. "*What* are you gettin' at?"

Turk grinned widely. "How *pretty* we is," he said. "All them colors to speak of, and what's to speak of 'bout white skin? Can you imagine lookin' down at your own arms and seein' that blood flowin' through your veins like some can, they so white? Give me the shivers thinkin' 'bout that. And some got to flee the sun and cling to the shade, 'cause they can't take it? Naw, naw...have to be feel sorry for 'em sometimes."

"I'll cry tomorrow," said Regis. "Listen, I'm down seventy cents. Can we go on with this game, if you please?"

"All I'm sayin'," Turk continued, with another pull from his cigar, "is thank the Lord for all them colors in that word *colored*."

There was a pause as Prince shuffled the cards for the next hand. Then he said quietly, "Thank the Lord for all the chocolate ladies, too."

"Yessir!" Sam's voice had been a little too fervent. He seemed to slink down in his chair a few inches. "Jude'll hear me say that and there'll be one seal-brown skin nailed up on the wall."

The others laughed and their attention returned to the cards. Curtis had come to the bottom of the Coca-Cola bottle, and it was time to move on. He stood up and replaced the empty bottle among the others in their wooden case just past the ice bucket. "Gotta go home," he said. "Thank you, Mr. Purdy."

"Sure thing. Get that chin up off the ground now, Curtis. Can't be so bad as all that."

"Yessir."

"Say hello to your mama for me."

"I will."

"Hope everythin' else is good with you," said Gerald, with just a quick but meaningful glance at Curtis, who knew that Gerald didn't want it to be common knowledge that Curtis had gotten him off the hook last week with Miles Wilson, who owned a fix-it shop further up Esplanade. Miles made a habit of sending very large men out to visit those who did not pay back in time for using the loan service in the back of the shop. He'd worked with Curtis's daddy at one point on the docks, years ago, and so had agreed on Curtis's word to give Gerald one more week to pay back the five dollars.

"Hope you're not burnin' up too many ten-cent cigars," Curtis said pointedly, and added, "Good night, gentlemen." He walked out before anyone could comment on what might have sounded to be a rude remark, but just so Gerald remembered that by Sunday afternoon he had to pony up five George Washingtons or get his fingers burned not by a cigar stub but by the kiss of a hot iron.

Curtis got on his bicycle, pedalled the short length of Marais Street to Esplanade Avenue and turned to the left, going deeper into the Treme.

Under the old oaks that lined Esplanade he passed Mandy's Kitchen Cafe, still open at this time of night and a few customers sitting at the tables within. Further along he heard the brassy blare of hot jazz music and he came upon the small stretch of real estate that his mama warned him not to dawdle in and so did every mama in the Treme give the same warning to their sons. On the left side of the avenue stood The Fancy Acre, though the blue bulb-lit club was more rough than fancy and it didn't take up anywhere near an acre even counting the oyster shell parking lot; on the right side, almost directly across, was the Ten Spot lit up with red bulbs and sporting a similar arrogance, and from its open doorway came the sound of a woman singing to the howl of a fiery saxophone. Past a shoe repair shop and a used-clothing store on Curtis's side of the street was the third club in this section of Esplanade, the Done Didit, and as Curtis pedalled toward the low, blocky brick structure with its glare of yellow and green lights that seemed to throb with the music and bass drumbeat barely contained within, the front door burst open and out spilled a knot of people who looked like they'd been tossed around in a cement mixer. The dishevelled and staggery group came out hollering and laughing and holding each other up against the force of gravity. As Curtis swerved around them to avoid collision he caught sight of Rowdy Patterson at the center of the throng with Geneva Barracone hanging onto him and giving him the gaze of love, and Rowdy was grinning with drunken glee and shouting at heaven as he lifted a flask of rotgut toward the unforgiving oaks.

Curtis pedaled on, but he had decided that Eleanor Caldwell was through being played by Rowdy Patterson. He meant to tell her—and make her understand, before he was done—that she could do a whole lot better and both her time and heart were being wasted on a man who slinked from woman to woman in the heat of the night. Of course he knew that some people never wanted to see the truth even when it was written on their foreheads, backwards, for them to read in the mirror, but he felt he had to give it a try. That *trust me* he'd said to Rowdy cut both ways.

He made his left turn onto North Derbigny Street from Esplanade, leaving the noise of the jukejoints behind, and entered the quiet familiarity of the shotgun shacks pressed close together, where an occasional lantern glowed on a front porch, candlelight flickered in some of the windows and those who could pay for electricity enjoyed a little brighter and more steady light. He veered his bicycle up toward a cream-colored house with dark brown trim that stood about at the center of the block between Dumaine and St. Ann. He was home. The meager glow of a single electric lamp peeked between the curtains of a front window. Curtis pulled his bike and the cart up onto the narrow porch and chained and locked his vehicle to the brown-painted railing. He took his suit jacket out of the cart and folded it over his arm, then he started to use another key to open the front door but the handle turned in his grip and he knew his mama was waiting up for him.

"There he is," she said from her soft corduroy chair, as if she were speaking with a sigh of relief to someone else in the room.

Curtis closed the door behind him and pushed the latch home.

"You look so nice," she said. "That tie and all."

He nodded. "Thank you."

"Been waitin' to hear."

He answered with a shrug of his thin shoulders. The lampshade was dark green and seemed to trap light rather than let it free; what light that escaped was scrawled upon the flower-and-vines garden print of the wallpaper.

"I don't think it must've gone too well," she said, in her tired and fluttery voice that made her sound as if she were perpetually out of breath. "I see it in your face."

"It was all right," he said.

Orchid Mayhew was quiet for awhile, just watching him. Though a boxfan gave a muted rumble from the other side of the room, the heat was just being pushed around. Even so, Orchid was wrapped up in the threadbare blanket that was her favorite, only her oval brown face and her thin hands showing, her hair covered with a gray scarf, her feet hidden beneath the folds of the blanket but Curtis knew she would be wearing the scuffed and well-worn leather slippers, the same as always.

"I told you not to give her anythin' with a pin on it," she said.

"Ma'am?"

"A *pin*," she repeated. Then she gave a small gasp for air as if speaking the word had depleted her lungs. "Bad luck to give a girl anythin' with a pin on it. I told you so."

"No, mama," Curtis said. "You didn't."

"Well," she said, "you should've known it. *Ever'body* knows it. When I saw that pin you were givin' her, I figured you must've *wanted* it to go bad." She made a grimace. The deep lines in her face deepened still more. She was small and frail, her cheekbones were like little blades wanting to cut through the tight flesh of her face, her eye sockets were hollowed down and like the lampshade seemed to trap any gleam of light that might try to escape. She was thirty-seven years old but very easily could've been taken for forty-seven. Many did. "Mercy me," she said. "My back is hurtin' so much tonight. Mercy, mercy. Hold onto your youth, Curtis. It goes so fast."

"Yes'm." He'd heard those statements a hundred times a hundred; he had answered the same way, a hundred times a hundred.

"You eat?"

"I had some birthday cake."

"Must not have gone too *very* bad, then, you gettin' some rich daughter's cake."

He took in a long breath of heated air. The words jumped out of him before he could stop them. "When I got there...I was thinkin' I was a guest, but—"

"You don't belong over there," Orchid said. "You know it and I know it." A hand as slim as a shadow moved at the end of a skinny arm to massage the back of her neck. "Long past my bedtime, waitin' up for you to come home."

Curtis's mouth closed. He nodded again, and that was all he could say.

"Help me up," she said, but she was already trying to stand on her own. "I'm goin' to my bed. A tired lady here...waitin' up worryin'."

Curtis helped her. She was like a little bundle of firewood that would crackle and crisp away with the first hot flame. The faded pink robe she wore beneath the blanket floated around her like smoke. Her scuffed leather slippers sought purchase on the weary brown rug. When she took a forward step she trembled and winced as if the pain of the world had shot through her bones. "Easy does it," she said, and she leaned her slight weight on him for support. As usual, he found himself nearly carrying her to her room, which was lit by another single lamp but seemed to be a chamber of shadows.

He helped her into bed, propping her up on the assembly of pillows. "Left over chicken gizzards and some tea in the kitchen," she said, as she arranged herself beneath the bedclothes. "Get y'self fed."

"Yes'm."

"Give us a kiss," she told him, and he kissed her cheek. She ran a hand across his hair and patted his shoulder, and she gave a sigh and stared up at the cracks in the ceiling as if seeing there the stars of eternity.

"G'night, mama," Curtis said as he retreated.

"Aren't you sorry you went?" she asked just before he closed the door.

"It was good cake," he answered, with a slim smile.

"There's your daddy again. Ironheaded, just like he was. If a rattlesnake was to bite you, you wouldn't say it hurt."

"G'night," he said again, but she wasn't done with him yet and he knew it.

"I don't know if I can go to church tomorrow. My back is hurtin' so bad."

"It'd be good for you to get out some."

"In this heat? I feel like I would melt away. But you go on, and tell ever'body I'll be there next Sunday rain or shine."

Once more, this was a ritual many times repeated. Curtis said, "I will, mama," and as he closed the door she reached over and turned out the lamp on the bedside table and there was a deep silence in the room.

In his room, behind the closed door, he flicked on the overhead bulb and then turned on his own bedside lamp, which gave the space a warmer glow. He used a brush on his suit jacket before he hung it up in the closet. His room was immaculate, the bed made—done every morning before he left for work—and everything in its own proper place, *spic'n span* as Ol' Crab might've said. He started to undress for bed and then something seemed to give way in him, like a flaw in the floor of an otherwise carefully-constructed house cracking open and collapsing. He eased down in a chair by the single window, and he felt that if he ever could move again it would take another Curtis Mayhew—a stronger one, one with much more energy than he had tonight—to help him to his feet.

He listened to the night. A dog was barking somewhere near. That dog named Topper, from the Aubrey house across the way. And music was out there too…the snippets of someone playing a trumpet, fading in and fading out as if heard on a defective radio, but Curtis knew it was George Mason who still worked at the docks that had ambushed his daddy back in the year 1920 when Curtis was six years old. You could tell how Mister Mason was feeling, by the wail of that trumpet, and tonight it sounded like the music was just as wounded as Curtis felt.

He put a hand to his face. How could he have been so stupid? To think that…yes…to think that he belonged there. How could he have let himself possibly think he would be welcome in that world?

He needed a listener. Oh, how badly he needed a listener this night of all nights.

He formed the word in his head, formed it strong and clear, and he sent it out on his own wavelength as mysterious to him as any radio frequency travelling through wires in the air could ever be, but it was his and he owned it.

:*Hello*:, he said in his mind.

He waited, but nothing came back.

:*Hello*:, he tried again, a little stronger this time.

Again, nothing. Well, she might be asleep by now. Sometimes he called and she didn't answer, so—

:*Hello*:, she came back, and even though it was his own voice in his head it sounded different...some inflection, some emphasis different...and he knew she was on the line.

:*You trying to sleep?*: he asked.

After a little pause she said, :*Just lying here.*:

:*Oh. I didn't want to bother you.*:

:*I'm not real sleepy,*: she answered.

:*Me neither. Everything good with you today?*:

There was another short pause, and then she said, :*My little brother got a whipping today. He ran across the street to go see the ice cream man.*:

:*What street would that be?*:

No answer returned for awhile. Curtis smiled a little. He knew of course that *she* was a girl—she'd told him so—and that she was ten years old, also told to him, but she wouldn't give away her name or where she lived. He figured she lived somewhere in the city because he didn't think he could hear anyone for many miles away, otherwise he might be hearing other voices night and day and they might be people who had no idea they were speaking to anyone else. His own ability had started to show up, little by little, when he was nine, so he thought maybe it was the same with her, whoever she was. They'd been speaking like this for about four months, off and on; certainly not every night, but once or twice a week, just talking at night like two people on the cusp of sleep but not quite ready to let the world go. Sometimes during the day he heard her, but it was like an *Ouch* or a *Darn it* or an *Oh no* as if she'd stumped her toe or dropped her school books or some such small calamity that made her speak out stronger. In respect to her he never replied unless she said *Hello* first and he didn't press if she didn't answer after two of his own.

:*Just that street,*: the ten-year-old mystery girl replied, and Curtis knew she was smart not to reveal any more because she was still figuring out and exploring her own ability and she probably yet couldn't get a firm handle on it.

:You do know that I'm a real person, don't you?: he asked.

:My daddy says you're not. He says I'm making you up and there's no Curtis.:

:My mama's name is in the telephone book. I told you that already. He could—:

:Daddy says I'm not to do this anymore,: she said.

Her voice, even reflected in his own that he heard in his head, was strong. He thought hers was probably stronger than his had been at that age and she was just learning it. He recalled his own confusions when he was a little boy, and at one point hearing words in his head that sounded like the language Mr. Chlebowski used when he talked to himself behind the counter at the butcher shop. It had been a long road to figure out that he wasn't crazy—hearing strange words and people speaking in his head that he knew were not simply his own thoughts—but he'd made it through, and with luck and guidance this little girl would too.

A *lot* of luck and guidance, he figured. Otherwise a person could lose their mind over something like this.

:You can't help it,: he replied. *:It's just the way you are, same as this is me.:*

:I don't want this,: she said, and he heard the words quaver as if she might be thinking of it as a disease or a curse that was going to plague her the rest of her life.

Which might be true, depending on how she handled it.

Curtis waited awhile for her to settle down, and then he said, *:I kinda got a whippin' myself today.:*

There was no answer.

He waited. She's gone, he thought, but he was able to keep those private thoughts guarded from her and he didn't know how that worked though he realized that when he sent his thoughts he used a different place in his mind to project them, sort of a different station on his personal radio set. *Telepathy*, was what that book at the library had called it, and that really did sound like some kind of dread bone-warping disease.

He didn't want to bother her again. She was gone for tonight, and maybe for a good long while. He started to get out of the chair. It was time for him to undress and turn in for the night because Sunday morning came—

:*What happened today?*: she asked suddenly. And then, :*Who whipped you?*:

Curtis paused and then let himself relax in his chair, all his energy focused toward sending the words out on their strange journey from mind to mind. :*I think I whipped myself, mostly. I thought I was invited to a birthday party by a girl I kinda like.* Liked, *I mean. Turned out she only wanted me there to play the fool. So I didn't stay too very long.*:

:*Oh. Did you take her a present?*:

:*I did.*:

:*Was it nice?*:

:*Nice as I could afford.*:

:*You didn't leave it with her, did you?*: When Curtis didn't answer at once, she said, :*You* did *leave it.*:

:*Yes, I did.*:

:*I went to Ryan Buckner's party and I took him a nice present and he was so mean to me at school that next week I told him if he didn't behave himself I was going to take it back. I didn't want to go to that stupid party anyway. Just goes to show you.*:

:*Show you what?*: Curtis asked.

:*Not all people deserve to have nice presents,*: she answered. :*When they get them they don't even know what they've got.*:

Curtis gave a slow smile to the wall. He said, :*I do believe you're right about that.*:

She was quiet for about fifteen or twenty seconds, and then she came back with :*I'm sorry you had a bad time.*:

:*It's a passin' thing, and matter of fact, it's already passed. But I thank you.*:

:*I'd better get on to sleep now, Curtis.*:

:*Yep. Headin' that way myself, directly.*:

He started to unlace his shoes. She stopped him by saying, :*Is there something wrong with us? I mean...this thing.*:

She had asked him that question several times before, and he answered as he always did.

:*We're different. Nothin'* wrong *with us…just different. Now…if you'd let me visit your daddy and mama, and tell 'em what I know to be true it'd be a great help for you.*:

:*No,*: she said as she always did. :*I can't do that. Maybe sometime, but…I can't right now.*:

:*All right. If and when you get ready, I will be.*:

:*Goodnight,*: she offered.

He answered, :*Goodnight,*: and this time he felt an almost physical disconnect from her mind, a blankness where there had been the electric buzz of energy, again a sign to him that she was getting stronger and was likely much stronger now than he'd been at her age.

He figured she was going to have a hard road ahead if she didn't let him help her, but Lord only knew what her daddy and mama thought about this. Just like his own mama, who'd reckoned he was smack out of his mind until they'd gone to see Lady and Mister Moon.

He couldn't do anything right now, so he let it go.

Curtis undressed, put on the skivvies he wore as his nightclothes and got under the sheet. Off the bedtable he picked up the book that he read from nearly every night, even though he'd already read it cover-to-cover several times. He could never get enough of Sir Thomas Malory's *Le Morte D'Arthur*, and even though he didn't know how to pronounce the title or some of the words in the book that little problem mattered to him not a whit. It was the tale of the noble knights and their magnificent adventures that counted.

He read awhile, until he was too sleepy to go on, and then he switched the lamp off and gave himself up.

Ten.

"Mr. Ludenmere, pardon me but there's a man here to see you. I told him you were busy."

Jack Ludenmere, the forty-four-year-old owner of the steamship freight line that bore his name, reached across his oak desk and pressed the Talk button on his intercom. "Alice," he said tersely, "Victor and I are *real* busy. I said I didn't want to be disturbed. Is that clear?"

There was no response. Ludenmere looked at his company's attorney, Victor Edwards, and shrugged. Suddenly the office's door opened, without the customary knock and invitation. Alice Trevelyan entered with a brown manila envelope in her hand. She said, "I'm sorry, sir, but he's insisting I give you this." She set the envelope down on the dark green blotter before him, next to the contract papers he and the attorney had been going over. "I told him you were with someone. He said—" Here she paused, because Jack Ludenmere was a fair boss and paid good wages but when he gave an order he expected it to be followed and now she saw in his light blue eyes a little flash of the lightning that could strike at any second to burn to ashes anyone who got on his bad side. But she had no choice, she had to continue. "He said he wasn't going to leave until he saw you personally, if that took all day, and he needs to see you in private."

"Who the *hell* does he think he is, Huey damn *Long*? How'd he get past Roger?"

"Mr. Delacroix called to tell me the man was very forceful, to say the least. He told me he was sending him up and for me to decide what to do with him."

"I don't have time for this crap!" Ludenmere pushed the envelope away, but his fingers felt something hard within it. Something metallic, it felt to be. His curiosity jumped up and bit him. "Jesus Henry Christ!" he said, and he tore the envelope open to get a gander at what was inside.

In another few seconds, he said in a subdued voice, "Vic...let's take a break, shall we?"

"What's in there?"

"We'll talk later," Ludenmere replied firmly, and that was Victor's cue to get up from his chair and skedaddle. The attorney, who was pushing sixty and had the dignified air of an elder statesman, capped his white Parker fountain pen, stood up and left through the door that adjoined his office to Ludenmere's. As soon as Victor had closed his door, Ludenmere said to Alice, "What's his name?"

"He wouldn't give it."

"Well, *damn*. All right, tell him I'll spare him ten minutes. And the next time you come in here without knockin' I'll have to kick your tail." When Alice had gone, Ludenmere emptied from the torn envelope the Shreveport Police Detective's badge onto his blotter and stared at it to make sure he was seeing straight. Though he still did business there on a limited scale, he was nearly eleven years out of Shreveport; what could this possibly be about?

Within a few seconds, the detective came striding in like he owned the place. The man was of medium size, not very imposing and about four inches shorter than Ludenmere's six-two. He wore a dark blue suit, white shirt, black tie and a black fedora. Dressed for serious business, Ludenmere thought. The man was handsome in sort of a soft way, like an aging choirboy, but his eyes were hard. In fact, there was a deadness about them that Ludenmere found to be unsettling, and at once Ludenmere felt an ominous prickling at the back of his neck.

"Thank you," the detective said to Alice, but she stood there and looked at her boss until he waved her away. "Close the door, please ma'am," the detective instructed, and she had been about to anyway so she closed it a little harder than usual.

Ludenmere did not stand nor did he offer to shake the man's hand, and the detective didn't offer his hand either. Neither man smiled.

"My name is John Parr," the detective said. "Here's my card." He slid it from his wallet and placed it down on the blotter alongside the badge.

Ludenmere spent a few seconds inspecting it. Printed in black letters on the small white card was John Austin Parr, Shreveport Police Detective, Badge Number 511, and below that the name of the Chief Of Police, Dennie Deere Bazer, the address of the police department and the telephone number OR7-1572.

The detective picked up his badge and put it into his inside coat pocket. When the coat opened, Ludenmere saw he was wearing a shoulder holster with what appeared to be a .38 revolver lodged in it.

"I drove from Shreveport all night to get here this mornin'," the man said. "I'm hot and tired and I'm not in the best of moods. I understand it's difficult to get in to see you and I had to nearly threaten that fellow downstairs, but this is of the utmost importance. I didn't show anybody else my badge or tell them who I was, and I think you'll appreciate that in a few minutes."

"What's this about?"

"It's about a kidnappin' plot, sir," said the man known to Ginger LaFrance as Pearly, who was keeping himself focused though he was mightily impressed by the large picture window behind Ludenmere's desk that gave a panoramic view of the Mississippi river and the docks where the company's steamships were either unloading or taking on freight. "Your children are in danger."

"My *children*? *What*?"

"We have word," Pearly went on, "that someone is plannin' to kidnap both your children. You have a daughter, aged ten, and a son aged eight. Isn't that correct?"

"Wait a minute! Hold on!" Ludenmere held up a hand as if to grip and stall time itself. The detective's hard dead eyes stared at him impassionately. "What do you mean, you have *word*?"

Pearly took his hat off and walked to the free-standing bamboo cane hat rack where Ludenmere had hung up his own seersucker suit coat. He placed the hat on a hook and stood looking out the magnificent window onto the grand vista of Ludenmere's holdings.

Make it good, Ginger had told him before he'd left Shreveport. *It's up to you to make him believe. We'll do our parts, but you've got to have the right attitude and say the right things.*

Listen, he'd answered back. *I've been practicin' up for this all my life. If it goes wrong, I'm out of there…but I'll know what to say and how to act when the time comes.*

"Detective Parr." Ludenmere's voice was strained. "I asked you a question."

This scheme had been born less than a week ago, after Donnie had arrived at the Union Station. It was Ginger's brainstorm, but Pearly had added his own elements. *I'll make sure he sees the gun*, Pearly had said. *That'll go a long way with him.*

Was he scared at all? He was sweating under his arms and it was more than the heat, but he was energized more than afraid. When he'd first caught sight of the big graystone building with its huge sign that proclaimed it to be the Ludenmere Shipping Company, he'd realized the gargantuan size of the fish they were angling for. It was a whopper, and it had to be pulled in just right or either it would get away or it would turn upon him and snap him in two like a bait shrimp.

Scared, no…but the stakes were mighty high here. Maybe his gut jerked now and again but he dared not let any hint of anxiety slip into his voice. He was Detective John Parr, a hard case who carried a .38 and knew how to use it—*had* used it, on several occasions. If he could make himself believe it, making this long lean drink of water named Jack Ludenmere—who put on his trousers one leg at a time the same as any hobo who ever rode the rails—believe it was a piece of grandma's puddin' cake.

"Last Monday," Pearly said as he stared out upon the river that seemed plated with brown armor, under a morning sky dappled with fleecy clouds, "we arrested a local man on a charge of breakin' and enterin'. He has a prior conviction, served some short time. This time he'd be going up for about fifteen years in Angola Prison. When that sank in, he started singin'. Seems he wants to make a deal with the district attorney...cut his sentence for help in bustin' up an attempt to kidnap your kids." Pearly turned his intense focus upon Ludenmere, who at forty-four looked like he could still be the basketball athlete he'd been at LSU; Ludenmere's hair was reddish-blonde and neatly-trimmed, with slight hints of gray at his temples. His angular face was lined by the concerns that came from running a business such as this, but he seemed physically fit and of a keen mind. He wore a light blue shirt with the sleeves rolled up on forearms that showed knots of muscle and corded veins. His necktie was red-and-blue striped, the knot loosened as if he followed the businessman's habit of wearing a tie but he didn't much care for it.

"This *felon*," Pearly went on, congratulating himself on his spur-of-the-moment use of that word, "operates in a circle of others equally as fucked-up as he is, and I hope you'll excuse the term but that's how I describe him."

Ludenmere nodded.

I've got him, Pearly thought. Ginger had done her homework on him well...the ex-LSU basketball athlete was known to curse a blue streak when it pleased him, and now man-to-man they were on the same earthy level of communication.

"So this bastard wants a deal," said Pearly. "What he's heard on the grapevine about the plot to take your children, for a reduced sentence."

"What's he heard?"

"Right now he's playin' it tight-lipped."

"So you don't know if he's tellin' the truth or not?"

"Not for sure." Pearly paused for effect, and then he said, "Would you want to take the chance he's lyin'?"

Ludenmere gave no reply. He looked at his hands before him on the blotter, the fingers working his knuckles almost as if they were moving without effort or accord from their owner.

"The reason we're so up in arms on this," Pearly said, in a quieter voice, "is that this piece of shit could've chosen anybody to *lie* about. There are plenty of public figures in Shreveport he could've said were targets of a kidnappin' plot…or their children were. If he was lyin', why did he choose *your* family to lie about?"

"Because I'm goddamned *rich,* that's why. And sometimes it's a burden, I'll tell you that right now. But Jesus Christ, is that all you have to go on? This sonofabitch tryin' to stay out of Angola?"

"Not all. He's mentioned some names we know. One of them we believe was an accomplice in the kidnappin' of a doctor's wife last year in Arkansas. Also, he's told us some interestin' facts about other burglaries in the area… helpin' us nail a few fellas we've been lookin' for before somebody got hurt. He says he'll tell us more when the D.A. agrees to a deal, and that's where it stands right now."

"These names you know. Why don't you pick 'em up and grill the hell out of 'em?"

"We're lookin', sir. Just a matter of time, we'll run 'em to ground."

Ludenmere sat back in his chair. "My God," he said softly, as if the enormity of this had just dawned on him. "Kidnap my *children*?"

"Such things happen, this day and age," Pearly said, and looking at the fresh lines of concern on the man's face and his dazed expression made Pearly wish he could take out his gun and blow this shining example of Louisiana businessman into the next world. How stupid Ludenmere was, to think he was so smart! This was like setting up a blind man to walk off a cliff believing he was going to get new eyes if he just stepped down a little.

In the next instant Ludenmere returned to his senses and the powerful force of his personality rushed back. His voice was harsh when he spoke. "You've got the police here workin' with you, correct?"

"Ah," said Pearly. "Here's the problem with that." He took hold of the empty chair in front of Ludenmere's desk, turned it around so the backrest was facing Ludenmere, and sat down. Now came the moment where everything was riding on Pearly's talents. Ginger had also supplied this story, but it was up to Pearly to make it work. If it didn't, he figured he could still get out of the building with his skin on. He said calmly and quietly, "We don't want to involve the police here."

"*What?*"

"Same reason I didn't show my badge to anybody. We want to keep this quiet." Pearly continued on before Ludenmere could open his mouth again. "Chief Bazer has given this over to Captain Arlen, Chief of Detectives. Captain Arlen gave it to me to come here, make contact and to be in charge on this end. The one thing we do *not* want, sir, is for this to get into any newspaper."

He had to pause for a few seconds, in which his mind shook the framework of the assembly he and Ginger had constructed and found it to be sound. He crossed his arms before himself on the backrest. "We can control the reporters in Shreveport," he said, "but we can't control 'em here. I doubt if you could either, and this is the kind of story that could get blown up and on the wires real quick."

"Is that a bad thing?"

"It *might* be. Say this bastard's spinnin' a lie. Okay. But somebody out there reads about it and gets the idea he might try for your kids himself. Or somebody else somewhere who's never given a thought about kidnappin' anybody decides maybe he wants to give it a shot. That's how these things happen. One copycats another, especially if their mark is so...so goddamned *rich,*" Pearly said, and added a thin smile. "But these days the mark doesn't have to be so rich," he said. "Anybody who's got a family could be taken off the street at any time, and I'm here to tell you it's done—or tried—nearly every day."

From Ludenmere there was no reaction. For an instant Pearly thought he hadn't been convincing enough and he tensed up...and then Ludenmere gave the slightest nod, and Pearly relaxed again.

"Our department," he went on, "doesn't want to be responsible for plantin' the seed of any more kidnappin's. Not in this state or any other. So, like I say, we can control the penpushers in Shreveport, but not here. We just don't want this thing to *escalate*, especially before we get the names we need." He checked his wristwatch; it was time now to start what might be the most dangerous part of his visit today. "I need to check in with the captain," he said. "Mind if I get a long-distance operator?" He nodded toward the telephone on the desktop beside Ludenmere's left hand.

Ludenmere pressed a button on his intercom. "Alice, connect my line with long-distance."

In about fifteen seconds the secretary came back with, "On the line, sir."

Pearly picked up the receiver. His palms were damp. If this didn't work, the jig was up. "Operator," he said, "give me Shreveport, Orchard 7-1572." He waited, listening to the various clicks as the circuits were connected. His heart was beating harder. The phone started ringing.

Once...twice...*pick up, damn it*, he thought, and then she answered: "Shreveport Police Department. Do you have an emergency?"

That had been in case Ludenmere had wanted to make the call himself. Pearly said, "Ruth, this is John Parr. Let me speak to Captain Arlen, please."

"One minute, John," she replied, playing her part very well indeed.

There was a short pause. When Donnie came on the line, it was with a single, "Yeah?"

"Captain, I'm here with Jack Ludenmere. I've explained the situation. Did you have anything you wanted to tell him?" Even though Donnie was silent, Pearly said, "Yes sir," and handed the receiver to the man behind the desk.

Now, Pearly knew, it was up to that damned young hothead. Less than an hour after Donnie had arrived at the train station, he and Ginger had been snarling back and forth at each other in the car on the drive back to Shreveport because the kid was supposed to bring a hundred bucks to add to the pot and had only brought thirty-two dollars and seventy-four cents, all he could steal from his mother's shoebox. If Donnie didn't handle this right—even with Ginger standing behind him in the hallway of the Hotel

Clementine with the kid speaking into the payphone's receiver—the whole thing could go down in flames, and Pearly realized he might not know it until he sensed that Ludenmere had smelled the smoke.

But for the moment, Ludenmere was listening. Then he said, "Thank you, captain. This thing has thrown me for a damned loop. Yes, I appreciate it. Right, I will."

Pearly knew what the spiel was supposed to be, if Donnie stuck to the script. *Sorry to spring this on you. It's serious business. Detective Parr is a good man, he'll do his best. We all will, you can count on it.*

Suddenly Ludenmere threw a wrench into the machine: "Mind if I ask what happened to Ray Culley?"

Pearly felt his hard-beating heart go up into his throat; he had the sensation of being in a car that had very abruptly lost both its steering and its brakes going sixty miles an hour on a rainslick road.

"I ask because Chief Culley was my scoutmaster when I was a kid," Ludenmere said into the phone. "I guess he retired a few years back?"

Pearly waited through a silence. He hoped Donnie was saying something on the other end.

Then Ludenmere said, "I figured he might go south, because he enjoyed his fishin'. Sure, sure. Thanks for lookin' into this thing. I hope nothing comes of it." He offered the receiver to Pearly. "He wants to speak to you again."

"Yes sir?" Pearly asked into the phone.

"I'm sweatin' fuckin' bullets," Donnie said.

"I will, sir. Thank you."

"Kiss my ass," Donnie replied, and he hung up.

Pearly returned the receiver to its cradle. He was going to have to throw a fit when he got back to Shreveport, and he figured Ginger was already scalding Donnie's butt. What if an operator had been listening in? You never knew.

"He sounds like a tough bird," said Ludenmere.

"He is." Pearly wanted to probe a little, to make sure the man hadn't smelled any whiff of smoke. "You say Chief Culley was your scoutmaster? He was gone when I signed up."

"How long've *you* been there?"

"Goin' on three years. I was on that Butterfly Man case in April. After that, I figure I can take anything."

"Yeah, I read about it. Damn gruesome." Ludenmere frowned at the telephone. "I meant to ask your captain if I could tell anybody about this. My family or anybody. Christ…my wife—Jane—she's nervous anyway and she would worry herself to death. I can't tell *her*, for sure. My lawyer was in here just awhile ago. Can I tell *him*?"

Pearly realized he had to be definitive, because he didn't want Ludenmere dialing that number on the card, and the card had to be left with him. That damn card represented eight passes through Pearly's printer before Ginger had said she thought it looked clean enough to show anybody with good eyes and good sense. "Word I got from the captain yesterday," he said, "was that the more people who know about this, the more likely the paper'll get hold of it. It's up to you, of course, but my suggestion is that you keep it to yourself for at least a few days." He decided to quickly switch gears. "Do you have a bodyguard on the payroll?"

"My chauffeur. His name's Clay Hartley, he was a police officer in Houston a few years back. He's trained in firearms and he keeps a pistol in the glovebox."

"Does he live on your premises?"

"Got an apartment above the garage. He takes the kids and Jane wherever they need to go."

"That's good," Pearly said, but he was thinking the opposite. Still, it was to be expected and at least there weren't multiple bodyguards to worry about. It was time for him to get a move on; it was pressing his luck to stick around here much longer. He stood up. "Borrow a pen?" he asked, and Ludenmere gave him one.

Pearly turned his identification card over, uncapped the fountain pen, and began to write.

"I'm at the King Louis Hotel on Broad Street. Room Sixteen." *King Louis, Rm 16*, he wrote. "No phone in the room, but you can reach me through the front desk." He slid the card across the blotter toward Ludenmere. "I'm to stick here until Captain Arlen orders me back to Shreveport, and I'm to check in with him every few hours. Somethin' might break, one way or the other, in the next day or two."

"The King Louis is a *dump*, isn't it?" Ludenmere asked. "Let me pay for a hotel with a phone in the room."

"Thank you, sir, but no. Policy forbids that...and, anyway, if my fiancee found out I was livin' high in New Orleans with her in Bossier City, I'd never hear the end of it." Pearly offered a disarming smile, but just with his mouth. The money that was pooled between himself, Ginger and Donnie for this job could only go so far, and a fancy hotel would be unseemly anyway for a Shreveport dick. He took his hat off the rack and gave the vista of the docks and the steamships another appraisal. Two hundred thousand dollars? Looking at this chump's setup, it might not be nearly enough.

Ludenmere stood up. "What're you doin' for supper?"

The question threw him for a couple of seconds. "I hadn't thought about it."

"If you can't—or won't—let me pay for your hotel, then at least come to my house for supper tonight. It's 1419 First Street, in the Garden District. Come on over about six-thirty and ring at the gate. You can meet my wife and the children."

"Ah," Pearly said; he hadn't anticipated this, but it was a good step forward. "Well...okay, but surely you're not gonna introduce me as a Shreveport detective?"

"You'll be a business associate. That's all that needs to be said."

"Fine." Pearly shook the man's outstretched hand. "I'll see you at six-thirty. I may have more news by then."

"Um...you probably shouldn't bring your gun," Ludenmere said.

"Don't fret," Pearly answered. "I'll just be there to enjoy the meal." *And*, he thought, to take stock of the brats, the ex-cop-turned-chauffeur, the nervous wife, the house and the whole shebang. Plus he'd be getting a decent meal instead of eating from cans and having the occasional bologna sandwich. So, as Ginger might've said, *Enjoy the ride, Pearly, and while you're at it put yourself in the driver's seat.*

"Thanks again, John," Ludenmere said.

Detective John Parr nodded, put his hat on and left the office.

Ludenmere sat down. He stared for a moment at the opposite wall. A pulse beat at his right temple and his eyes were hooded. He turned Parr's card over and ran his fingers across the lettering. Then he pressed the TALK button on his intercom and told Alice to get him the long-distance operator.

Eleven.

As a man calling himself Detective Parr was getting into his black Ford sedan parked on Washington Avenue after his meeting at Ludenmere's office, Curtis was pedalling his bicycle toward Congo Square in the Treme on an urgent mission.

When he'd gotten to work this morning, he'd been collared by both Cricket and Brightboy on his way to the locker room. *Bossman wantin' to see you soon as you got in*, Cricket said in his deep-throated rumble, punctuated by the clickings of his false teeth. *Said not to change your street-clothes, just go on up.*

So it was that barely three minutes after stowing his bicycle and cart in the locker room, he was standing within the upstairs office with the green-tinted glass, and the heavy-hipped and bald-headed boss of the whole Union Station asked him around the stub of a cigar if he knew where Wendell Crable lived, over on St. Ann Street just past Congo Square. Curtis had said he did, he'd passed the house many times.

Wendell didn't come in this mornin', the bossman had said. *He don't answer his telephone, neither. Get on over there and find out what's wrong.*

It was shocking news. As far as Curtis knew, Ol' Crab had never missed a day. Therefore as Curtis—wearing his street clothes of tan trousers and a blue-and-green-checked shirt—pedalled as furiously as his legs could handle along his usual route, he was sure that something was very wrong with Ol' Crab. Just yesterday Mr. Crable had complained of indigestion, saying that he thought a pork chop he'd eaten the night before at Mandy's Kitchen Cafe had come back to kick him in the gut. Curtis hoped it was just indigestion, but he'd read that heart attacks could sneak up on a person in that kind of disguise.

He diverted from his route to aim toward Ol' Crab's house, and crossing St. Peter Street he entered the nearly sacred ground of Congo Square. Some of it was grassy, but in most places the grass had been stomped flat to the dirt by the feet of generations of the slaves and their children and their children's children. They had thronged here by their thousands since the early 1800s to hold markets, meet together, play music, dance and sometimes by the flame of torches and the light of the moon offer frenzies to the voodoo gods. Now, as Curtis pedalled across the Square and squirrels darted out of his way to get back to their nests in the overhanging oaks, he heard the beat of drums and the crash of cymbals. He saw that a lone drummer had set his kit up in the shade to pound out a rhythm while nearby an old woman sold apples and oranges from a cart, and beside the cart was a lounge chair she'd put out to recline in under the leafy branches.

Congo Square was indeed nearly sacred to the residents of the Treme, and particularly so for Curtis…but not for any reason the others might share.

His mind drifted back in an instant to an evening in May of 1923, the sun just sinking to the west and the blue shadows beginning to crawl across the Square, and here and there a lamp burning as if to mark a path for his eleven-year-old self and his mama, who had hold of his hand and was pulling him along to a place he did not wish to go.

On that evening, too, a drum was beating but at a distance; it was a low thumping sound off on the other side of the Square, and over there the younger Curtis could see torches burning and the shapes of figures moving about…but slowly, as if seen in the thickness of a fever dream. Orchid pulled him on toward their destination. It was where she'd been told to go by the young woman in the bright red headwrap who'd come to the house that past Sunday afternoon.

Curtis was a child, but he surely knew what this was about.

I want to know, his mama had said to the young woman who came to visit, *if my boy is crazy in the head or not.*

He don't look crazy, the young woman had said after a brief inspection.

He hears voices, Orchid had answered. *Sometimes they ain't even in English, and he cain't understand 'em. Other times he hears 'em clear enough. This has been goin' on for two years now, and it ain't gettin' no better. Mercy, mercy, I'm already a sick woman and this thing is puttin' me in my grave.*

On that May evening in 1923, Orchid had pulled Curtis toward the eastern side of Congo Square, where the oaks stood tall with gnarled intertwining limbs that must've been old when the first slave touched a drum and dreamed of the green hills of Africa. In the deepening twilight Curtis could make out three figures beneath one of the trees; they were illuminated by the ruddy glow of a pair of oil lamps set upon a small card table. Two of the figures were sitting in canvas chairs and one was standing, and in another moment Curtis saw who they were and his legs froze up. His heart pounded and his heels dug into the earth but at that time—nine long years ago—his mama still had some strength and determination, and she hauled him along like a flopping catfish on the end of a five-fingered hook.

He had known they were going to see someone who could help him, according to Orchid, and he'd thought maybe it was another doctor but now he realized she was pulling him toward a reckoning with two of the most powerful and strangest characters who had ever cast their shadows in the Treme.

Lady and her husband, Mister Moon. As a matter of fact, he had never seen them out by the light of full day, and so they likely only cast their shadows by the pale of the moon and the dance of red flame that spat sparks in the wicks of their lamps.

But there they were. Standing behind them was the young woman with the red headwrap, and she came forward to meet Orchid and Curtis as they approached, one hauling and the other near bawling.

"Comes Mister Curtis," he heard Lady say, in a soft voice that for some reason made him think of cool water, but he was shocked because never in his life had anyone called him *mister* and he wasn't sure he liked being so high in this voodoo woman's regard.

The other mister on the scene stood up from his chair and gave Orchid and Curtis a little bow. "Pleased," he said nicely, but Curtis thought his voice was like the rattle of dry bones in a haunted house.

"I've brought my boy," Orchid said, as if they needed to be reminded, and she shoved Curtis forward like giving up an offering.

When Curtis had regained his balance he stood like a statue and stared at the two of them. In the lamplight that could have resembled the flickering of crimson-eyed ghosts in St. Louis Cemetery Number One, Lady and Mister Moon might have been dapper phantasms, only they were all too real.

It was said that Lady was born in the year 1858, which made her sixty-five years old. In this low light and with the wide-brimmed violet-colored hat she wore, her face was a mystery of shadows. Curtis had never seen her up close before, so he had no idea what she looked like. He had heard plenty, though: about her being a slave, and running away from the plantation with her mama into the swamp before the Civil War, and growing up in a colony of lepers, escaped convicts and other slaves in the bayou below New Orleans, and down there was where the voodoo gods and goddesses had found her and annointed her to be one of their own. He had heard *more* than plenty, and more than he'd wanted to hear: about the cottonmouth snake she kept in her house on St. Louis Street and called "Sister" for all the secrets it told her; about the trunk she kept full of shrunken heads of young'uns just his age who had stupidly wandered up behind the green wall of Giant Salvia, umbrella plants and huge Devil's Trumpets that bloomed like tropical furies in her front yard; about the glowing purple orbs that constantly circled over and around her house as spectral watchmen, and sometimes at night it was said those orbs could be seen crawling spiderlike across the roof.

There were other frightening things too, and Curtis kept them firmly in mind when he stared at what deceptively appeared to be a thin human woman in her violet-colored hat and dress and violet-colored gloves on slim-fingered hands at the end of spindly arms. She was the blue-black color of deepest Africa, untouched by the white explorer.

As scary as Lady was, Curtis found Mister Moon to be downright spine-shiveringly creepy, no matter that he was a polite gentleman. It was certainly not Mister Moon's fault that he'd been born with or been afflicted by a condition that had turned one side of his face pale yellow while the other side remained ebony, the two halves merging in a war of splotches down his forehead, the bridge of his elegant nose and his gray-tufted chin, but it was not easy to look upon. He too was a long tall drink of arsenic, dressed to kill in a trim-fitting black suit, a thin black tie decorated with red squares, a black top hat and black gloves, and on each wrist glinted the faces of two wristwatches. On a chain around his neck hung a gilded crucifix the size of the biggest pig's foot ever cooked in a Treme stewpot.

"Come closer, young man," Lady said.

Curtis didn't move until Orchid pushed him forward some more, and even then his shoes dug up near-sacred earth.

"I understand," Lady said from beneath her hat, "you say you hear voices in your belfry. The ringin' of other bells not your own, let's say." Her head cocked slightly to one side. "That true?"

"*Tell her*," Orchid said before Curtis could even think how to answer. "Go on, this ain't the time to be all stitch-lipped!" When Curtis again hesitated, Orchid said to the voodoo woman, "He don't know how he's killin' me with this, ma'am! My back…somethin' ain't right…I'm weak all the time…can't think straight, with all this weighin' on my—"

"Mrs. Mayhew," Lady interrupted, but softly. "Why don't you go over yonder where Mrs. DeLeon is cookin' up a pot full of gumbo. See her over there at the fire?" She waited until Orchid nodded. "Go tell her I said the word 'Biddystick', and she'll laugh and give you a free bowl." She glanced at the young woman in the red headwrap and then at Mister Moon. "Both y'all go on with her, leave Mister Curtis with me. Scoot, now." She waved her gloved fingers toward Orchid as if brushing crumbs off a table.

The young woman moved silkily forward and hooked Orchid's arm with her own, while Mister Moon plucked up an ebony walking-stick that had been resting beside his chair.

"Tell her true, Curtis," Orchid said; it had come out as a demand. She turned her sad eyes upon Lady once more, the corners of her mouth down-turned. "You know my husband left me," she said. "It happened six years ago. The accident at the dock, I'm sayin'."

"I know all 'bout that," returned the reply. "I was sorry for you then, and I'm sorry for you now. Go on, get y'self a bowl of gumbo and be a little piece happy."

Orchid started to speak again but the young woman was gently pulling at her, and so Orchid gave Curtis a last look that had a pinch of urgency in it and then she allowed herself to be moved. Mister Moon swept past Curtis with his walking-stick, leaving in the air the scent of sandalwood and lemons.

When the three had gone on toward Mrs. DeLeon's gumbo pot, Lady drew in a long breath and let it out. "Now we can talk," she said, with some relief in there. She lifted her face toward Curtis. He saw the light catch the sharp bones of her cheeks, the formidable ridge of her nose and the intense emerald-green of her eyes, which startled Curtis because they looked like spirit-lamps glowing with a fierce energy that could burn something to destruction if she allowed.

"I imagine," she said, "you've heard all kinds a'things about m'self. Things that give young'uns bad dreams. You know what I'm sayin'."

Curtis forced himself to nod.

"We ain't here to go over all that..." She paused, searching for the correct word. Then: "*Description*," she said. "I want to know 'bout the voices. Your mama's awful worried, and you know she loves you. If she didn't, you wouldn't be standin' here. Oh, listen...ain't that pretty?"

The crickets had started up, and from the oaks came the *shurrah...shurrah* of the night's insects awakening from their daily slumber.

Curtis felt himself shiver, though the air was warm and humid. He pushed whatever fear he had down, because now was the moment to speak and there was no point in holding back any longer. "I don't...exactly hear voices," he said. She was silent, and he went on. "I hear my own voice. But... it's hard to explain, kinda...I know that what I'm hearin' are other people speakin'. In *my* voice, I mean. That's the voice I know. It's just that...the way things are said...it's not me talkin' to myself. I know that for sure."

"For *sure*?" she asked, and it sounded like a challenge.

"As sure as I can be without the Good Father steppin' down and tellin' me," he answered, and thinking it had been spoken too impudently he added, "Beg pardon, ma'am."

"And how can you be so almighty sure? Your mama says it started after your daddy left home, and she thinks that made your head go bad. Says she took you to see two doctors but both of 'em said it was your imagination and a passin' thing. Says she's at her wit's end tryin' to figure how to help you, and it's breakin' her down day after day. So how can you be so almighty sure?"

Curtis couldn't help it; the way the voodoo woman had spoken, with more than a dash of hot pepper in her voice, made his own pepperpot start to boil. "I heard somebody talkin' in a different tongue," he said. "I think it was what Mr. Danelli at the market speaks. Eyetalian."

"The word is *Italian*. Say it like that. The other makes you sound like you don't have any learnin'."

"Yes'm," he replied. He shrugged. "I couldn't understand any of it. It was just there, and I didn't hear it again."

"But there've been others?"

"Sometimes. One of 'em sounded real far away...somebody yellin' at somebody else, it sounded like. He used some bad words."

"How'd you know it was a *he*?"

Curtis shrugged again, but she was waiting for an answer so he gave it to her. "He said somebody should bite his pecker."

"Oh." Did she smile a little? It was hard to tell, under that hat.

"But I can tell if it's a he or a she," he went on. "I don't know how, it's just somethin' in the way it's said."

"And you can tell the distance?"

"Some are stronger than others. I mean…I don't hear a whole lot of 'em. They come and go." He squared his shoulders and looked directly at her. "It didn't start when my daddy left. I was eight when that happened. I started hearin' the voices when I was nine."

"Can you answer 'em?"

"I don't know, ma'am, I've never tried."

"Could you try now? By sayin' somethin' in your head and seein' if I can hear it?"

"Yes'm," he said, and he closed his eyes and thought :*Hello*:. He saw not the word but the blur of a faintly golden iridescence moving out of his head and picking up speed, faster and faster away until it seemed to take wings and fly like a quick bird through the trees and gone.

"Nothin'," Lady said. "Try again. Stronger, if you can."

He did, and this time he squeezed his eyes shut and gritted his teeth and thought of the word as a shout through space, and there it went—:*Hello*:—flying away in its luminous blur.

"Nope," Lady said.

"That's about the best I can do," he admitted.

Lady was silent but the oaks in the Square were thrumming with life, which Lady seemed to be listening to as if the small creatures were telling her secrets the same as her snake "Sister." "They called your daddy 'Ironhead', didn't they?" she asked.

"Yes'm."

"You know why?"

"No'm."

"That accident. As I heard it, the tar barrel fell off that platform and hit him in the head before it busted his shoulder and his ribs. But his head was like to be made out of iron, didn't even leave a mark. Yessir, he must've had a mighty hard head."

"I guess," Curtis said.

"Come right up to me," she told him, though he thought he was standing too close already.

She started taking off her gloves. When he obeyed—however reluctantly—she put her hands on his head and started feeling around on his skull. "You have headaches?" she asked.

"No'm."

"You know what's gonna happen tomorrow, or the next day?"

"No'm," he replied, and he nearly smiled at that one because if he'd known about this yesterday he would've played he had a stomachache and stayed in bed.

She kept running her hands over his head. Her fingers felt like bands of metal. "I'm gonna tell you somethin'. I'm havin' some trouble with somebody here. Another woman. She don't like me very much. I'm gonna think her name and you tell me if you hear it. Go ahead."

He listened, but all he heard were the trees speaking. "No'm, I don't."

"All right, then. I'm ponderin' over leavin' N'awlins right soon. Got three places in mind to settle in. Nice quiet places where nothin' much ever happens. I'm thinkin' the names of those places. Can you tell me one of 'em?"

"No'm," he said, "I can't do that."

"*Huh*," she replied, a sound of both consternation and maybe confirmation. She ran a hand across his forehead, the fingertips pressing into the flesh, and then the examination seemed to be ended. "You ever see double?"

He shook his head. "Just single, like everybody else I guess."

"No," she said. "I don't really think you're like ever'body else. Run over there to Mrs. DeLeon and fetch your mama back here. Bring me a cup a' gumbo while you're at it."

When Curtis had done so and Orchid, Mister Moon and the young woman in the red headwrap had returned to where Lady was sitting, Lady took the offered gumbo cup and Mister Moon settled himself back in his chair with the ebony walking-stick propped against his knees.

"Well, ma'am?" Orchid asked anxiously. "What's wrong with him?"

Lady took a moment to eat some gumbo with the small wooden spoon that had come with the cup. "Let me tell you a little story," she began. "When I was a girl on the plantation, the cook's daughter—'bout thirteen

or fourteen years old, I recall—said she was talkin' to a man who lived in
Buscarole, and that was maybe seven miles from where we were. Said she
listened to him, and they talked back and forth *in her head*. Believe that
or not, but she said he was an old man and he was a carpenter, and all of
a sudden she was knowin' ever'thin' 'bout hammers and different types of
saws, and all kinds of lumber and joints and pegs and…just things she could
never have known unless somebody who *did* know was tellin' her. Now yes,
we did have a carpenter for the plantation but he was a white man with his
own family and he lived at a distance, wasn't no hanky-panky goin' on.
Ended up when Savina's carpenter friend went silent, and she figured he
must've either moved or passed away. So…I've heard of this kind of thing
since then, but let me tell you it's very *rare*. Ain't nothin' wrong with your
boy, Mrs. Mayhew. Seems to have good sense and got an older soul than
most. Seems to be a good boy. I swanee, ain't nothin' wrong. You just got
yourself a listener. Early yet, still growin', but a listener all the same."

"A *what?*"

"I *said*…your boy's a listener. Same thing I called Savina McCabe and
Ronson Newberry. Only two I ever knew, but I've heard of others 'round
and about. Like I say, they're rare."

"A listener," Orchid repeated, and Curtis saw that his mama's expression
was as dull as if she'd just been whacked in the brainpan with a mallet. "Just
what does that mean? Is he out of his head or *not?*"

"Not," said Lady. "If you can't understand what I'm tellin' you, think
of a radio. You set up the wire and it pulls in the different stations that are
sendin' out their signals. Hang me if I know the particulars, but it's plain
to hear that some stations are stronger than others. Well, your boy's kinda
like a radio. He can pull in signals from other listeners…only I'm bettin' a
lot of 'em don't know they're what they are, they just think they ought to
go to the funny farm 'cause they're gettin' thoughts that are not their own.
Or I'm reckonin' they've got mamas and daddies who figure they're sick in
the head. Your boy don't hear the sound of other listeners' voices, 'cause that
would be a real doin' there, but he's pickin' up the thoughts…the signals

comin' out that are everywhere, floatin' through the air like from the radio, but you got to have another radio to pick 'em up."

"We don't have no radio," Orchid said.

Lady sighed. She ate a few more spoonfuls of her gumbo. "Mrs. Mayhew," she said after she'd dabbed her mouth on a paper napkin Mister Moon had brought back for her from the gumbo seller, "I don't know exactly how this works. I'm figurin' nobody does. How far away can your boy hear another listener? I'm thinkin' he doesn't have any idea. How does he know if he's hearin' a man, a woman or a child? Well, he seems to know that but he can't tell me in words. Will it get stronger in time, or will it drift away and someday be gone? Can a person even *guide* somethin' like this? If so, *how*?" She let the questions rest in the air. "Can't tell you much more," she said after another moment. She made a sound with her lips like air escaping a balloon. "Sometimes I wish *we* didn't have a radio. Charles is fiddlin' with that thing and listenin' through them earpieces day and night, drives me batty. What'd you favor to hear this week?" she asked Mister Moon.

"Orchestra playin' a nice tune called *Night On Bald Mountain*," he answered in his bony voice. "Kinda gave me a shiver." Then he grinned so wide it nearly cracked his face.

"Can't hardly wait to see what they'll come up with next," Lady said, speaking again to Orchid. "Or…maybe I *can*. But 'bout Mister Curtis here, you don't have to worry. He's not out of his mind. Fact of it, he has a rarity some might envy."

"I'm sorry," Orchid replied, and she repeated it more forcefully, in her downtrodden way. "I'm *sorry*. I can't help but worry 'bout my boy! What's ahead of him, if he has such an affliction as this? Who would envy such a thing but a person out of his mind? To hear other people's *thinkin'*? It ain't natural and it ain't right and it's just more of a burden on me, and Lord knows Joe left me with a heavy heart and a heavy load on my back! So I am *sorry*, ma'am, but I can't just put this aside like it was yesterday's newspaper! Lord God, no!"

Curtis saw Lady's green eyes linger on him for a few seconds, and then she said quietly, "Take him home, Mrs. Mayhew. *Appreciate* him and the gift the Lord has chosen to give him. And start feedin' him better, put some meat on them bones and get him more like his daddy was."

At that, Orchid's spine stiffened. She seemed to draw up a couple of inches and in the ruddy lamplight her face in an instant had become a cold mask.

She said, "He'll *never* be like his daddy."

It was much later that night, as Curtis was lying in bed in his room, that the voice came—faintly, a whisper from far away...:*Hello back to ya*:.

Now, as he absorbed the memory of that encounter nine years ago, Curtis pedalled off Congo Square, stopped his bicycle and cart directly in front of a small but neatly-kept white shotgun shack on St. Ann Street, walked up two concrete steps and knocked at the door.

There was no answer.

Curtis knocked again. "Mr. Crable?" he called. Then, a little louder: "Mr. Crable? It's Curtis! You all right?"

Was there a muffled sound of movement within? A car had just gone past, so it was hard to tell.

Suddenly came from behind the door what might have once been a hard old voice from the grave of time, but now time had caught up with it and strangled it and it was a pitiful trembling thing.

"*Go away, Curtis. Please. Jus' go on away.*"

"What's wrong, sir?" He didn't slur the word. "Are you sick?"

"Go 'way."

"Can't, sir. I was sent to see about you and that's what I'm gonna do. You can stay behind that door but I'm not leavin' 'til I've seen you." Curtis waited. After a few more seconds he said, "Open the door, sir. You know it's the right thing to do."

He waited a bit longer, balled up his fist and was prepared to keep knocking until the cows came home. But then a lock was turned, the door opened, and a man who resembled Wendell Crable but who had gone gray-fleshed, sunken-eyed and sickly peered out, squinting, into the sunlight.

Ol' Crab did not look at Curtis. He cast his gaze downward and then he backed away from the door as if the light were painful. "Come on, then," he said. "Best lock that bike up, we got some people 'round here steal it in a snap."

Curtis spent a moment taking the chain and lock out of the cart and securing the bicycle around a drainpipe that came down the side of the house from the roof. He entered the dimness of the front room and was hit by the smells of burned food and stale cigarette smoke. All the blinds at the windows were drawn, but from between the slats shards of light lay on the floor like a broken mirror of golden glass. Ol' Crab continued to retreat until he eased himself down into a brown chair beside which stood a table bearing a half-empty bottle of Four Roses whiskey and a glass nearly empty. A green ceramic ashtray was piled high with the burned butts of hand-rolled cigarettes, and one was still sending up tendrils of smoke.

Curtis closed the door at his back. While his eyes fully adjusted to the gloom, he could make out that Ol' Crab was wearing a white shirt left to flag around his underdrawers, because the master of the Redcaps was wearing no trousers. On Ol' Crab's feet were ancient leather slippers, worn down by the years. His legs were stretched out before him and he was leaning back in his chair with his eyes closed, his face offered toward the ceiling.

"I think you burned somethin'," Curtis said; in truth he was shocked at this sight and didn't know what else to say, because never in his life could he ever have imagined seeing Mr. Crable in such a state as this.

"Tried to bake some cornbread." Ol' Crab opened his eyes, picked up the smoldering cigarette and drew from it. "Didn't go too well."

"Mr. Crable...what's *wrong*?"

"What's wrong," he repeated, staring at nothing. "The *world* is wrong, Curtis. It's a bad place. It just...lulls you along, day-by-day, and then... when you're figurin' ever'thin' is goin' smooth and easy and you see where you're goin' for the rest of your days...then...*then*...it hits you." The seamed face turned and the hollowed eyes took him in. The mouth smiled a shade, but it was an awful thing to witness. "I got a Western Union telegram last night. Time was seventeen minutes after eight. I never got a Western Union telegram before in my whole life. Well, I got one last night!" The weary voice cracked; he stuck the cigarette into the hideous smile and then stared up at the ceiling. "I got one," he said, very softly, and Curtis saw the tears begin to roll slowly down his cheeks.

Curtis pulled another chair over beside him and sat down. He thought it best to be quiet, and just to listen.

"Telegram!" Ol' Crab said suddenly, as if awakening with a start from a near-slumber. "Lord God...Jesus...a telegram. Gave me a number to call. Up there in Chicago." He reached for the glass of whiskey, drank a swallow and put it back on the table. Curtis noted that also on the table was the small framed photograph of a smiling little girl dressed up as if for Sunday service.

"They say it was a bumb," Ol' Crab explained, but he was holding the cigarette close before his face and it was as if he were speaking to that instead of to the other person in the room. "Timebumb in a car...parked at the curb. Up there in Chicago, yesterday mornin'. Blew up...took her as she was comin' out of the laundry. She always liked her clothes to be clean and neat. Fresh. You know? She say, 'Daddy, what good's a daisy if it's not fresh?' Her mama and me, we knew she was gonna be *somebody*. Go places. Daisy was a schoolteacher up there. You see?"

"Yes sir," Curtis said, and he had known Ol' Crab had a daughter and a wife who'd passed away with cancer some six years ago, but he'd gotten that from other people because Mr. Crable was not one to talk freely about himself.

"Took her," Ol' Crab went on. "Took four others too...hurt six or eight more, he told me. Why'd he tell me that? So I wouldn't think I was bearin' all the pain in the world? Said they think it was either gangsters, or the Unions, or them Fascism people, whatever they are. Do you reckon it really matters, Curtis?"

"No, sir."

"Damn right it don't. You know, I never got a Western Union telegram before, not in my whole life."

Curtis nodded, and Ol' Crab drank again and smoked the cigarette down to where Curtis feared for the old sinewy fingers that wrote the schedules and ran the show.

When Ol' Crab put a hand to his face and let out a moan that sounded like someone's end of the world, he trembled and began to sob, brokenly, like any child might whose trust in the fairness of life had been shattered. Curtis watched the cigarette stub fall to the rug. He picked it up and crushed it out in the ashtray. Then he started to put a hand on the old man's arm, hesitated because he didn't know if it was proper or not due to their different stations, but he decided it was right and he did it anyway.

Ol' Crab put his arms around Curtis, and he held the young man tight as he cried.

Curtis put his arms around Mr. Crable's shoulders. His heart was sorrowed. He knew he could tell Mr. Crable that the Good Father promised a wonderful afterlife in Heaven, and that all who loved each other and were separated in this world would be rejoined on the golden shore; he knew he could tell Mr. Crable that already his daughter was waiting for him, and preparing him a place in the land beyond…but he did not say any of these things because he knew also that Mr. Crable was a religious man and even so there were mysteries about the permissions of the Good Father that no human being could explain, and one of them was why on a late August morning a timebomb in Chicago had been allowed to explode and kill a woman from New Orleans who was there to help children learn and grow.

Curtis thought that Mr. Crable knew he would be seeing his Daisy again—and maybe in the next few years—but the pain of loss was a terrible thing, and it would not be denied. Therefore Curtis remained silent, as Ol' Crab sobbed some of his grief away, but from the sound of it there was a whole lot more grief to be shed.

The telephone on a little table across the room began to ring.

"No," Ol' Crab said, his voice mangled, against Curtis's shoulder. "*No.*"

"Could be them callin' from Chicago," Curtis told him.

"Said…they'd call me later in the week…after they made arrangements. *Arrangements*, they called it."

The telephone continued to ring. If it wasn't Chicago, Curtis knew who it must be. "Let me answer it, sir." When Ol' Crab made no further protest, Curtis gently pulled himself free, got up and picked up the receiver. "Crable residence."

It was who he'd suspected. "Mayhew? What's wrong there?"

"Um…well suh, Mr. Crable's feelin' poorly."

"What's wrong with him?"

"He…pardon me, suh, but I'll tell you when I get back. Can I ask a favor, suh? Since Mr. Crable is feelin' so poorly, could he have a day or two off?"

"A day or *two*?"

"Yes suh. I think he needs it. And also…a day or two off with full pay. I think that would be the right thing."

"Oh, *you* think so?" It was spoken with a bite of sarcasm around the nub of a cigar.

"I do," Curtis answered, and in his voice was the same quiet firmness with which he repaired family quarrels, hurt feelings and broken hearts when asked to not only listen, but to act.

There stretched a silence.

Then: "All right. Two days with full pay. Tell him. And tell Wendell… we need him here. We can't run this place without him."

"Thank you, suh. I will."

When he hung up the phone, Curtis sat down beside Ol' Crab again, took his hands, looked him in the face and told him he was going to go into the kitchen and cook him some food, and what might he be wanting for lunch? It took awhile for Mr. Crable to answer, but then he said he had some black bean soup left over from yesterday, and Curtis could warm that up if it wasn't too much trouble, and he could chop up some celery and a grandaddy-sized onion and put that in the pot, and if it wasn't too much trouble could Curtis stay awhile and take a bowl of soup with him?

Curtis said there was nothing he would like to do better than that. After lunch and before he returned to his work Curtis would ride the five blocks to Mr. Crable's church, which was two blocks further north than his own, and let somebody know they should come stay with him awhile.

The morning moved on. Trains came and went at Union Station, bringing people in and carrying them away. The city breathed and lived in its own way, as all cities do, while a pot of black bean soup bubbled on a stove in a small house on St. Ann Street.

Twelve.

Nope, two hundred thousand bucks was not gonna be enough.

It was Pearly's thought as he drove the Ford south along First Street with the mansions of the wealthy on either side. The sun was going down, the shadows getting longer. The time was near six-thirty, and Pearly was on his way to his engagement with the Ludenmeres. He had changed his sweat-damp white shirt for another white shirt but he still wore the dark blue suit, the tie and the fedora, his detective's getup; he had removed his shoulder-holster and in the glovebox was the .38 revolver, loaded with six slugs.

Damn! he thought. There was some big fuckin' money on this street. He was convinced that anybody who could afford such sprawling edifices as these in this country's sorry economic condition had to be doing something crooked. Had to be. He would lay odds that Ludenmere was paying somebody off under the table for that government contract, or he was blackmailing some bureaucrat, probably used his own private dick to dig up the dirt. Nobody could be clean who lived like this. He passed between castles with upraised turrets and plantation houses with columns in front as thick around as his car. The windows of the upper floors under the high roofs caught the last of the sun's glare and threw it back into Pearly's eyes. Palm trees, oaks and willows shared space on the manicured green lawns, at least the parts he could see beyond the gates because just about every house was protected by stone or brick walls seven or eight feet high, some of the walls adorned with a further dense protection of ivy vines.

Occasionally he saw a sign that said *Beware Of Dog*. The paved driveways beyond the wrought-iron gates curved away from the street into the private lap of luxury. White and yellow stone, red brick, ornamentations of enamelled squares and intricately-patterned tiles, paint jobs that Pearly was sure cost more money than he'd ever seen in his life…it was fuckin' obscene, is what it was, he thought, and for that reason two hundred thousand dollars was not going to be nearly enough.

There it was. On one of the gates, down near the bottom in small brass numerals so as to be oh-so-properly restrained in this neighborhood of gaudy showmanship: *1419*.

The moment had arrived. Pearly found himself trembling a little inside. He was sweating again under his shirt. If he screwed up any bitty-bit, they were done and he might have to fight his way out of that beautiful pile of bones, which he could see beyond the gates and through the surrounding oaks was two stories done up in the plantation-house style, all white. The front porch—*veranda*, was it called?—at the top of the stairs looked as big as a fancy hotel's ballroom.

He had to be very, very careful now; he would have to use every instinct and talent he had, and particularly be careful around Clay Hartley, the chauffeur and ex-Houston cop. The more he thought about Hartley, the more nervous he got. Would an ex-cop smell the scent of a kidnap plot? Would he be able to look with his eagle eyes at a Shreveport detective and immediately see a grifter who was holding onto his nerves by his chewed-up fingernails?

He realized he was about to learn the answers because, as he stopped the car at the gate and stepped out, a man in a black uniform, a pale blue shirt and wearing a chauffeur's cap came out from behind the white stone wall that protected the Ludenmere estate.

"Detective Parr," the man said, speaking in a gravelly voice that carried the extra dusty grit of a heavy Texas accent. "Clay Hartley. Came down to meet you, save you ringin' to get in." Hartley nodded toward a button set in the wall next to the gate. Above the button was a cradle holding an ear-cone style of telephone receiver and a metal speaker grill. It was the first Pearly had ever seen of anything like that and he knew it must've cost an enormous bundle. He felt sweat at the back of his neck. Hartley was unbolting and opening the gate. Its hinges made no noise.

"Drive on in and stop. I'll ride up to the house with you," the ex-cop said.

"Sure." Had Pearly heard his voice quaver? "Sure thing," he said, more strongly to disguise the fault, and immediately wished he had not because he didn't want to overplay. He got in the car. He could still put the Ford in reverse and take off. He could just drive to Mexico himself, find some work down there and—

No, *this* was his work. This had always been his work. He was married to this life, for better or for worse, and he'd taken a lot of shit from the bitch so now it was time for her to pay up. Which, by God, she was going to do by way of this rich sonofabitch with two ripe kids to be plucked like fruit off a low-hanging branch.

He set his teeth, put the car in forward gear, and drove through the open gate. He stopped and waited while Hartley closed and locked the soundless iron, and then the passenger side door opened and the ex-cop slid in across the gray cloth.

Pearly glanced at Hartley and got a shock. He hadn't seen it before, but the man had a long scar trailing from the corner of his left eye down almost to the line of his jaw. The left eye had a dull falsity about it; the thing stared straight ahead, even as the right eye moved in its socket. A glass eye, Pearly realized; well, he thought, don't that beat all? At least they were the same color of brown, but he bet the kiddies liked dreamin' about that fish-eye when midnight came callin'.

"Problem?" Hartley asked, because Pearly had delayed a half-second too long.

"Nope." Pearly pressed the accelerator and the Ford rolled on.

"Mr. Ludenmere told me the whole story," Hartley drawled.

The whole story. Pearly didn't think he liked the way that sounded. He forged ahead. "What do you think?"

Hartley didn't answer. In the space of two heartbeats Pearly summed up his impressions of the cowboy cop turned chauffeur. How the man could drive with one blind eye was beyond Pearly, but obviously Ludenmere thought highly enough of his skills to put the lives of his wife, children and himself in those gnarled-knuckled hands. Whoever came up with the word *rawboned* had this slimjim in mind. Pearly figured him for a tough piece of leather about fifty years old, and for sure the man's flesh had begun to resemble old leather. Hartley had a craggy face with a hooked nose and a chin that looked like it was made out of iron. The good eye and the glass imitation were both sunken down in nests of sun-dried wrinkles. Pearly glanced again at the scar. Must've had the whole side of his face ripped open at some time, he thought. Tough line of work, bein' a cop in Houston.

"Belleau Wood," Hartley suddenly said.

"Huh?"

"You're lookin' at my scar. Heard your neck crick. Battle of Belleau Wood, June 6th of 1918."

"Oh. What hit you?"

"Piece of an artillery shell, size of a dime. Laid me open real good."

Pearly had to ask it. "Your eye. I mean…does it *bother* you?"

"Nope. Doesn't bother the children, either, if that's what you're askin'. Does it bother *you*?"

"I'm fine with it."

Hartley said no more until the car had pulled up on the circular drive before the house's front steps. When Pearly cut the engine, Hartley made a grumble that must've meant he was about to speak. "What you told Mr. Ludenmere," he said. "I'm of two minds on it."

Pearly waited. The hot engine ticked…ticked…ticked.

"About tellin' the police here," Hartley went on. "Seems they could help protect the children, put a watch on the house day and night. That would be a good thing. Then again…I get what your department is thinkin', considerin' all the kidnappin' goin' on. So I say let it rest as it is, for now." He turned his head toward Pearly, who found himself not wanting to look into the glass eye but the damned cold and starey thing compelled him. "I'll tell you true," Hartley said. "Anybody touches those children on my watch, I'll kill 'em straight off, forget the courtroom and the prison. I was a Marine gunnery sergeant, won three ribbons in competition for accuracy with a pistol. And if you're wonderin'…a person compensates for what they call monocular vision."

"That's a comfort to know," said Pearly, who thought *Keep blowin' hard and I'll take out your other eye with a fuckin' icepick.*

"Pleasure," Hartley said as he opened the door and got out. "You get some time, we should talk about the work."

The work? Oh, yeah. "You were a detective in Houston?"

"Flatfoot for ten years. That was my speed." He peered up toward the house. "Here's the mister. Enjoy your meal." He nodded and tipped his cap at the man who was coming down the stairs.

"Thanks, Clay. Find the place all right, Jack?" Ludenmere looked freshly-scrubbed and was wearing a short-sleeved cream-colored shirt and brown trousers.

"Could hardly miss it." Pearly forced a smile. He got out of the car and closed the door behind him. A glance at Hartley showed the chauffeur ambling away to the right. Pearly thought everything was okay and no alarms had gone off, and he'd made sure there was nothing in the car to raise any suspicions if Hartley smelled smoke and decided to amble back and go through the Ford.

Ludenmere shook Pearly's hand. "Glad we could do this." He cast his voice a little quieter when he spoke the next. "I've told Jane the same thing I told my company lawyer…you're here to sell me on some new refrigerated shippin' containers. I don't think Victor bought it, but he won't ask any questions until I tell him he can. Come on in." Three steps up, and he asked over his shoulder, "You settled into the Lafayette?"

"I am. I didn't know that string could be pulled."

"It had to be done. No sense in you havin' a hotel room with no telephone."

Pearly stopped on the next step. It was time to throw another punch. "As a matter of fact, I got a call from Chief Arlen around four. We have a name:

Enrico Orsi. We know him. A would-be racketeer wanting to impress the Chicago bunch. Have you hired any Italians in the last couple of weeks?"

"What? Italians?" Ludenmere had stopped on the next step up, just short of the porch. His confident demeanor had been clubbed with a spiky baseball bat. His face sagged. "I don't...um...I'm not sure if we—"

"Here's our caller!" the front door had suddenly opened and a smiling, sleek and attractive woman in a summery yellow-and-green-print dress floated out onto the porch. "Jack, let Mr. Parr come on in, it's too hot to stand there and gab about business! Mr. Parr, we've got some cold iced-tea with mint in the parlor, so come on!" She motioned the men into the house. As Pearly approached her and she smiled broadly at him he thought he could throw her down and fuck her right then and there because she was a fine looker, with her pretty oval-shaped face framed by waves of chestnut-colored hair and her soft brown eyes sparkling with Old South hospitality.

But as he followed her into the house he simply allowed himself a wan smile while his imagination tore her dress and her undergarments off and he spread her open as wide as a juicy melon about to be split in two. "Thank you, Mrs. Ludenmere," he said. "I sure do like iced-tea."

Keep your mind on the job, Ginger had said when they'd talked by phone this afternoon. *When you walk into that house, you'd better be ready and you'd better be careful.*

Who do you think you're talkin' to? he'd asked. *A virgin punk? I'm not Donnie Baines, sweetheart.*

I told you already...Donnie Baines did you a good one today, babycakes. He stayed on the phone with Ludenmere for about three minutes tellin' him why it was against police policy for him to pay for your goddamned room at that hotel, and he played it as smooth as a butter salesman. So you can thank him yourself when you get back here, and anyway it's good you've got a phone in your room and we don't have to pay a cent for it.

Hi-de-ho, Pearly had said, and then hung up the telephone in Room 424 of the very exclusive and expensive Lafayette Hotel on St. Charles Avenue. The room smelled of clean linens and lime soap and it had a window that looked down upon the life and traffic of the avenue. After Pearly's meeting with Ludenmere, he'd used the payphone at the King Louis—which really was a dump, after all—to check in with Ginger and found that Ludenmere had called the fake Shreveport Police Department number, which Ginger had figured might happen so that was why she and Donnie had hung around the phone in the hallway at the Clementine for an extra half-hour.

Ludenmere had asked first to speak with Chief Bazer. "Ruth" the operator said that the Chief was in a city council meeting but would he like to speak with Captain Arlen? As Pearly understood it, the kid had done pretty trim, but then again Ginger had been standing by his side probably ready to kick him in the balls if he said anything she didn't like. Donnie in the guise of Captain Arlen had tried to talk Ludenmere out of paying for the hotel room but in the end had said he would run it by Chief Bazer after lunch. So then a message went to the King Louis's front desk from Ginger to call home, Pearly had called Ludenmere at his office in the early afternoon to thank him and say the Chief had given the okay, and that was how the little game had gone. But that card with the fake phone number on it was a danger. They had to get this job done before Ludenmere took it upon himself to call it when some other occupant of the Clementine might pick up the receiver and tell the caller he must be either drunk or out of his mind.

The trick, Ginger had said, *is to make Ludenmere believe you're the only cop he needs right now. And by-the-by, I've got a name for you to spring on him. Italian, like the big-time gangsters. That'll put a scare into him. You come up with a background.*

Whose name is it?

Some old dead painter lived about three hundred years ago, Ginger told him. *Found it in an art book at the library. So paint him up good, honeypie. He won't mind.*

"It has been so hot this summer!" said Jane Ludenmere, as she guided Pearly through the mansion's high-ceilinged foyer. Everything seemed to him to be made of light-colored wood, the floor was covered with a blue-and-gold Oriental rug and a wide staircase carpeted in blue ascended to the second floor. An ornate grandfather clock quietly ticked the time away. The air within the house smelled of sassafras and maybe the mint tea that was waiting for him. He was amazed...stunned would be more accurate; he'd never set foot in a house like this before, and now he was absolutely certain Ludenmere was a crook...*had to be*, to afford this kind of living. "I imagine it's been the same in Shreveport," Jane said, pausing before the open double doors that led into another room to the right.

"John, I told her you're from Shreveport," Ludenmere said, maybe too quickly, "but I didn't want to bore her with the business details."

"My husband thinks my mind can't hold his business details. I'd like to see him run the details of our house and keeping up with the children for a few days. Mavis, would you take our guest's hat?" A Negro maid had appeared from a hallway beyond the stairs. "John, do you want to take your coat and tie off and be comfortable? We're informal here."

Pearly gave his fedora to the maid. "I'll keep my coat and tie on, thank you." For whatever reason, he felt more comfortable fully dressed in his detective suit. "Not bein' formal," he said. "Just my way."

"Absolutely fine. Come on in here, the parlor's always been a cooler room."

It was, because a large electric fan with wooden blades turned slowly but efficiently from the pale blue ceiling. The walls were painted white and held densely-populated bookshelves. Above the white fireplace mantel was a huge gold-rimmed mirror that Pearly thought made both himself, Ludenmere, the wife and probably everybody who looked into it appear both younger and more elegant than they were; his reflection even made *him* look like he had some noble timber in there where the termites gnawed. The parlor's furniture was every bit as refined as he'd even seen in a movie where the rich folks invited the common man to the mansion on whatever twist of plot lay ahead; upon a sand-colored rug was a glass-topped coffee table, and around the table were arranged two light brown leather easychairs and a white sofa that had nearly the curve of a semi-circle in it. Pearly hankered to sink into one of those leather easies, so he took the nearest one and thought that something like this was the first thing he would buy to go in the Mexican mansion. To be able to sit in one of these and look through his window down at the blue bay, with no more worries and no more scrabbling to survive, that would fit him to a—

"Tea?" Jane had gone to a sideboard table and poured a tall glass nearly full from a silver pitcher, and now she plunked ice cubes into the glass with tongs from a silver ice bucket. "Would you have some sugar syrup?"

"I would, please. Just a dash ought to be fine." When Jane brought him the glass he said, "You have a very beautiful house."

"Thank you. We do love it." She gave her husband the second glass of tea she was carrying and returned to the sideboard to make her own.

From where he was sitting, Pearly could look through a pair of windows not at a blue Mexican bay but at the green Ludenmere lawn, the oaks and that big brute of a stone wall protecting the estate. The damned place was a fortress, no doubt about it. It was his task tonight to get in deeper, case the house, and figure out where the weak place might be. But it wasn't going to be like whoever snatched the Lindbergh kid, using a ladder to climb up to a window and take a baby out of a crib. No way. Here you had a fortress with a glass-eyed ex-Marine sharpshooter as a guard, two older kids with loud voices and that damned beast of a wall. How would you get in and out with two kids kicking and screaming under your arm?

He recalled something Ginger had said: *So we figure out how to take 'em in broad daylight, and in a way that they won't be hollerin' for Daddy.*

Good luck with that, he remembered saying.

Before Pearly had left Shreveport, Ginger had taken hold of his lapels and kissed him on the lips, peered into his face with her champagne-colored eyes and said in that way of hers both demanding and coquettish: *Come back with somethin'.*

"Good tea," he said as he sipped at it, but his mind was on the mission. "Yes, it's been hot in Shreveport, too. But that's Louisiana, isn't it?"

"John, you might know my father," Jane said as she settled herself beside Ludenmere on the curved white sofa. Pearly cautioned himself not to be caught looking at her legs. "Yeager Grandier?" she prompted. "The attorney?"

Pearly felt his face freeze. She was smiling at him, waiting for an answer. In the space of about two seconds he realized this might be someone a detective was supposed to at least have heard of—a prosecutor or a defense attorney, maybe—but damned if he knew how to reply.

Unwittingly, Ludenmere came to his rescue. "Honey, not everybody in the world or in Shreveport knows the great Grandier family," he chided. Then, to Pearly: "He's a corporate attorney for the Beecham Timber Company, no reason you would've heard of him."

"Oh. No, that's kinda out of my territory." He thought there might be a shine of sweat on his forehead, even under the fan's cool breeze. He took another drink of the tea and was grateful for its chill. *Relax*, he told himself. *There's nothin' here you can't handle.*

"John, Jack tells me you have a fiancee?" Jane asked. "Can we see a picture?"

He glanced at Ludenmere but saw that the master of the house was staring off into space with a dazed expression. Still thinkin' about Enrico Orsi, Pearly figured. When they got some private time together he would have to paint the racketeer up, as Ginger had said. Have to point out that they were not dealing with just one man, but likely with a gang of four or more, and have to point out too that the word in Shreveport was that Orsi was right now somewhere in New Orleans.

"You do have a picture?" Jane prodded. "In your wallet?"

Ludenmere came to life again. Pearly knew why: he didn't want Jane to catch any glimpse of the badge if it was in the wallet. "Jane, come on! You're interrogatin' our supper guest! John'll show us a picture when he gets good and ready! Isn't it time for food to be on the table?"

"Actually," said Pearly with a soft smile, "I had a picture but Emma didn't like that one, said it made her look too citified…and she's just a country girl at heart…nothin' uptown about her at all, and I like that. So…I took it out of my wallet, like she wanted, 'cause she knew people would be askin' to see it and that's not what she wanted to…" He paused, making a show of finding the right word when he already had it in mind. "To *present*," he finished. "She's promisin' to get me a new one this next week."

Jane nodded her approval. "Very gentlemanly of you, and *that* is a dying attribute in this day and time."

Pearly heard whispers.

They were coming from the entrance foyer. When he peered in that direction he caught sight of a small face and head quickly pulling back from the open door's edge.

"Children, come in and say hello to Mr. Parr," Jane said. There were further whispers but no movement.

"Nilla! You and Little Jack come on in here." Ludenmere's voice was more that of the stern father. "Be gracious, now," he added, in a softer tone.

She came in first, with her little brother a few steps behind.

And there they were. Pearly smiled at them, seeing one hundred thousand dollars each standing on two legs.

The ten-year-old girl was tall for her age, with a lanky frame likely taking after her basketball star daddy, but otherwise she was nearly a miniature model of her mother. She had the same shoulder-length chestnut-colored hair, the same oval-shaped face, the same finely-etched nose as her mother, but she had her daddy's light blue eyes. Just about the same color as the ceiling in this room, Pearly thought. Nilla Ludenmere was wearing a pink dress with a silk rose stitched on the right side of her lapel, and there was something uncomfortable in her expression that told Pearly she might rather be wearing overalls than that frilly getup.

The eight-year-old Little Jack resembled his father except he had his mother's brown eyes.

Pearly thought this kid looked like a rounder, the kind who sneaked lizards into the house and let them run loose just for the fun of the uproar. Pearly bet this one gave his mama triple fits. Little Jack had reddish-blonde hair a few shades lighter than his daddy's, and its thickness obviously defied a comb because it was everywhichaway on that head. It looked to Pearly like six red-tailed squirrels and a beaver or two were having a war up in there. Little Jack wore neatly-pressed gray trousers, shiny black shoes and a white short-sleeved shirt with a button-down collar, and the way he chewed on his lower lip while he stared at Pearly made Pearly think he secretly wanted to break the skin and spit blood across the room.

"Our young lady and our wild Indian," Jane said. "Say hello, children."

They did. Pearly said hello back, and kept his smile fixed in place.

He hated them.

They were everything he detested about life: the unfairness of it, the brutal and merciless wheel of fortune that doled out the good luck to the haves and the bad luck to the have nots, the false cleanliness and faked uprightness of the upper crust, when it was obvious to one and all that Ludenmere had made his money down in the mud that had mired Pearly to a state of near-poverty and certainly at times a numbing desperation. Oh no, Ludenmere wasn't clean, he thought. Far from it. And these two kids standing here smiling under this electric fan in this parlor room in this mansion fortress are going to make their daddy pay for his crimes. They're going to make *life* pay, he thought, because it is time the wheel of fortune favored a man who was thrown away as a baby and never ever had a chance to breathe air that didn't have the stink of despair in it.

Oh yes, he vowed, as he looked at the smiles and considered that they were not smiles, they were smirks because these privileged punks smelled on him the rotten peaches odor of the unwashed working-class, *everyone in this goddamned room will pay.*

"Nilla," he said easily, with all these thoughts locked in his head like lions in their cages. "That's kind of a different name, isn't it?"

"Want to tell him, honey?" Jane prompted.

The girl might have been whispering outside the room, but she wasn't shy before a stranger. She looked him in the face and said in a firm voice, "Before I was born, mama had cravings for vanilla cookies. *And*...she liked to dip them in hot pepper sauce."

"That's why she's so darn mean to me," Little Jack piped up. "Too much—" He stopped because his sister popped him on the back of the head with the flat of her hand, and his eyes shot devils at her.

"Hey!" Ludenmere said sharply. "None of that!" He gave Pearly a smile and a shrug. "They've had too long a vacation and not enough structure. Well, they start back to school on Monday, so in four days we'll be seein' some changes around here."

You bet, Pearly thought, and when he looked at the children again he saw them with their eyeholes stitched up and green tongues of money hanging out of their mouths. Suddenly an idea hit him; it was such a simple thing that it almost robbed him of his breath. He imagined he heard the wheel of fortune turning, but maybe it was only an errant noise from the fan. He asked, "They go to the same school?"

"Yep. The Harrington School."

Pearly nodded. Another glance at the kids and their faces were made of decayed meat covered with crawling flies. "How far away is that school?"

Ludenmere was slow in answering. "About three miles, give or take." He had realized what the detective from Shreveport was getting at. He drank his iced-tea and said, "*Stop that!*" when Little Jack reached out a quick hand and gave his sister a shove.

A Negro butler came in and announced that supper was served. Pearly watched the kids hop and bounce with the fierce energy of childhood on their way to the dining room.

Come back with somethin', Ginger had said.

And he thought: *Got it.*

Thirteen.

:*My name's* Dwayne. *What's yours?*:

:*Curtis.*:

:*Are you my angel or my devil?*:

:*I'm a boy. Just that.*:

:*A boy? You a white boy or a nigger?*:

:*I'm a Negro.*:

:*That beats all. Talkin' to my nigger angel. How old you be?*:

:*Eleven.*:

:*I'm six-hundred-and-sixty-six. They don't give me my letters in here. I get letters but they burn 'em. I seen 'em doin' it. Smelled the smoke, so I know it was real. Hey, I need to get out of here. You listenin'?*:

:*Yes. Where are you?*:

:*I'm in Hell right now. They burn my letters out in the cornfield.*:

:*I'm in New Orleans. Are you in Louisiana?*:

:*You're gettin' mighty feeble, I can't hardly hear you no more.*:

:*I asked if you are in Louisiana.*:

:*I'm right here, in this place they brought me to. Stafford chews tobacco but I don't chew no tobacco, it makes me fuckin' sick. Listen…Curtis…can you come get me out? I need to go home and they won't let me go home.*:

:*Where are you?*:

:*I'm here, right here. I ain't takin' no more of them damn pills, neither. Myra thought she was sooooo fuckin' cute! Wasn't nothin' a knife couldn't fix. I got to get out of here and go home, somebody's gonna steal my dog.*:

Nine years away from that mental conversation, Curtis lay on the bed in his room with the bedtable lamp shining and his copy of *Le Morte D'Arthur* lying at his side where he'd just put it when the memory of long-ago Dwayne came upon him. He listened to rain tapping at his window. In the distance thunder boomed hollowly across the river. It had been raining off and on since Sunday afternoon, and now here it was Tuesday night near ten-thirty and the boomers were still rolling in from the west. At least the heat had broken, but the steam wasn't much better.

Dwayne had answered his *hello* sent out at Lady's request that night in Congo Square.

It had dawned on the eleven-year-old Curtis, as their disjointed talks continued, that Dwayne was in a mental hospital somewhere in Louisiana but exactly how many miles away was unknown.

Curtis pieced together that the hospital was more of a prison for the mentally disturbed, and Dwayne must've been kept with the criminally insane because he talked regularly about Myra and the knife, and how the knife had been put in his hand by the dark thing that came out of the wall one night after supper.

It was strange, Curtis mused, that he had learned to hone and amplify his mental ear and voice by listening to a killer in an insane asylum. Their communication had gone on for nearly a year, until Curtis got the impression that not only was Dwayne refusing his pills but he'd started to turn violent toward the other inmates. It seemed that Dwayne thought the "dark thing" had come into the hospital and was moving from person to person with plans to kill him. Not long after that, Dwayne had gone silent. Whether someone had actually killed Dwayne or the doctors had done something to him that destroyed his telepathy, Curtis never knew; he never knew, either, what the name of the hospital was or exactly where it was.

But they were out there. Other listeners, like himself. How many of them had been driven insane by the ability, and not knowing what it was, was hard to say.

He heard his mama coughing in her bedroom. She would be asking him to fetch her a glass of water soon. It always happened. How sick she actually was, no one knew but herself. She declined all suggestions to go see a doctor. If it wasn't her back hurting, it was her stomach, or her legs, or her head aching so bad she couldn't see straight. She didn't have a head of iron like Joe Mayhew had, Curtis thought as he listened to the soft music of the rain. It was true, as he understood it, that a barrel of tar had fallen off a platform at the Harmony Street dock and hit Joe Mayhew in the head before it struck his shoulder, broke it in three places, and then crashed down upon his ribs to break two of those. The story—and he'd gotten this from people like Prince Purdy after Lady had ignited his curiosity about his daddy, because Orchid wouldn't tell a word of it—was that the doctor at the hospital had said Joe would carry a bruise on his forehead for awhile but his skull was undamaged, and right there the doc had made the remark *Must have a head like iron.* Curtis remembered his father as a large bearlike figure moving around the house, sweeping him up in a pair of mighty arms, swinging him around until he saw stars and then setting him down again, gentle as a kiss.

He recalled one Sunday summer afternoon, two months before the accident, when his daddy and mama—happy, then—took him to hear the bands play in Congo Square. They were strolling through the active market area—people selling straw hats, walking-sticks, cane chairs and the like—when Curtis looked up to see a flock of birds lifting from one of the old oaks and taking flight. His daddy suddenly put his huge hand on Curtis's shoulder and asked in his bass-voiced rumble, "What color you think your bird is?"

"Sir?"

"Your bird. That little thing flyin' 'round in you that people call a soul. What color you think it to be?"

"Joe!" Orchid—so much younger then, so much more vital—had turned a scowl upon her husband. "Stop that nonsense!"

"Wasn't no nonsense to my daddy and his daddy and every daddy that came before," Joe had said. "No, ma'am! Ever'body's soul is a bird, wantin' to fly free. Whole of life is about gettin' the wings loose from all earthly weights and ever'thing that binds you to *this*." He stomped one big boot upon the dirt, and dust puffed up.

"That's whoodoo talkin'."

"Ain't. I knew a Christian preacher said the very same thing when I was younger'n Curtis. Said our souls start out as young birds in the nest without markin's or color, and it is on us to do the markin' and colorin' so when we go on—"

"This is not proper talk in front of our boy."

"What say? About goin' *on*? Hell's bells, woman, if he ain't got that fact of life in his head by now after all the churchin', somebody has done a failure."

"Brown like me," said Curtis, who'd been thinking about it since he'd been asked, since to him it made perfect sense.

"Don't have to be your skin color," Joe answered. "Know what color I think my bird to be? Bright red with orange wings. I've painted it up real good in my years. Well...maybe it's got some dark spots there on its belly, but otherwise...yep, bright red with orange wings."

"Ree-dick-u-liss," said Orchid.

"Now 'bout your mama's bird," Joe said, and gave his son a quick wink. "Got to be gloomy gray with wings the darkest blue short of midnight, 'cept she's got a big ol' yella beak that opens and closes—*snap!*—like a beartrap."

"You are talkin' *crazy*! I'm not that!" Orchid gave that big right shoulder a punch but she was half-smiling when she did it.

"Curtis!" Joe's voice came down as a rumbly whisper that sounded like a passing freight train. "Let's you and me work on gettin' some bright red or orange or some color on your mama's bird that just 'bout shocks the eyeballs out. Deal?"

"Yes sir," Curtis had said, and when he reached up his daddy's hand was there.

The rain on Curtis's window tapped and tapped. Thunder growled, still distantly. Curtis wondered how the Knights of the Round Table got around in their shining suits of armor when it was raining; wouldn't the sound of your own tin roof drive you to distraction?

It took a long time for his daddy's body to heal, after the accident, but Joe Mayhew became a silent man to whom laughter was a stranger. Curtis thought that maybe his skull hadn't been fractured but the wings of his bird had been broken. He did go back to work, after a time, but things were never the same. Curtis later heard that Ironhead Joe could no longer do half the work he used to do, and the bossman took him off the docks and put him in the warehouse where he stacked up the lighter boxes and sacks. Joe Mayhew became a man apart from his wife and son, and apart too from the man he used to be. Curtis in later years figured that his daddy was ashamed of being diminished, made smaller than what he once was by fate and a falling barrel of tar.

Ironhead Joe took to going on long walks. One night he did not come home.

Curtis heard his mama coughing. Soon she'd be calling for him, to get that glass of water.

:*Curtis, are you awake?*:

It took him a few seconds to move his thoughts away from himself, and into the realm where he could answer. His private radio, he thought... taking in the signal, and sending out his own.

:*I am,*: he said.

:*What're you doing?*:

:*I was just lyin' here readin' and listenin' to the rain.*:

:*It's raining where I am, too,*: she said. :*What're you reading?*:

:*A book about King Arthur and the Knights of the Round Table. Do you know about that?*:

:*I've heard about it. That was a long time ago, wasn't it?*:

:*Yes,*: he said, :*it surely was.*:

She was quiet for awhile, and then she asked, :*Is Mr. Crable doing better now?*:

On Friday night, Curtis had told her about Mr. Crable's daughter being killed, simply because Ol' Crab's despair had latched into his mind and he had to put it somewhere. :*Some better,*: he answered. :*He's back to workin', but he's gonna be goin' up to Chicago day after tomorrow. They're givin' him a round-trip ticket.*:

:*That's good to hear.*:

:*Yes. Funny thing…Mr. Crable's been workin' around trains for nearly all his life but this'll just be the third time he's ever ridden on one.*:

:*Have you? Ever ridden on a train, I mean?*:

:*No,*: Curtis said, :*I never have.*:

:*We have, a few times. My family and me. We went up to New York City last year.*:

:*Oh. Likely I was carryin' your bags, then.*:

Again, there was a silence but Curtis could still feel the power of her presence, like a faint electrical buzz in his head. She said, :*Would you know me if you saw me?*:

:*Would you know me?*:

:*I don't know. Probably not.*:

:*Same here. So you passed right on through Union Station with your family and I never knew it.*:

:*This is so crazy,*: she said. :*Talking like this, and knowing somebody but not knowing them.*:

:*It's a mystery, that's for sure,*: he agreed. :*But it's our mystery, isn't it?*:

:*Yes it is.*:

Curtis heard the thunder again, a little closer this time. Was she gone? No, the presence was still there.

:*I have another mystery,*: she said. :*It's about my daddy.*:

:*What about him?*:

:*He's…*: She didn't go on for a time, as if she were deciding whether to confide this or not but Curtis knew she would because on this rainy night she needed a listener. :*He's worried about something,*: she said. :*It's something bad. I've seen him worried before…he's worried a lot, about business things… but this is different. I told Mama and she said she sees it too but she says it's because of…well…more business things. But I think this is different, Curtis. And then…there's another thing.*:

:*What is it?*:

:*We had a business friend of Daddy's over for supper last Thursday. Mr. Parr, his name is. Well…when Mr. Hartley picked us up at school today…we were drivin' past the park, and…we passed a car at the curb…and I looked over and saw it was Mr. Parr behind the wheel. Then Mr. Parr followed us all the way home. I told Mr. Hartley about it and he said I was wrong. Mistaken, is what he said exactly. Then I told my daddy about it and he said I was wrong. But I know what I saw, and I know Mr. Parr followed us all the way home from school today.*:

:*That* is *kinda strange,*: Curtis said. :*Why would that be?*:

:*I don't know…but…when I told Daddy about it, he said I was seeing things and then he got a little upset and he said that he was surprised that I hadn't seen* Curtis *following us home. He said I wasn't to be talking like this before Mama because she's already nervous about…you know…this thing.*:

:*Did your little brother see Mr. Parr too?*:

:*No, and I didn't say anything about it to him.*:

"Curtis?" It was his mama's voice, weak but in its own way demanding.

:*I'm sorry your daddy's so worried,*: Curtis said. :*Everything passes, though. He'll get through it.*:

:*I just want to know why Mr. Parr followed us home. I think Mr. Hartley and Daddy both know and they won't tell me.*:

"Curtis! I need some water!"

:*I have to go. My mama's callin'. Do you think you can get on to sleep?*:

:*I'll try…but it's in my head that something is really wrong.*:

"Curtis!" came the call, with a hint of anger in it.

:*Mama's gettin' mad,*: Curtis said. :*Gettin' her feathers all ruffled up. Really, I have to go. Don't worry yourself so much you can't sleep, you got school tomorrow. Goodnight, now.*:

:*If I can't sleep, can we talk later?*:

:*Surely,*: he answered. :*Goodnight.*:

"Curtis, have you gone deaf?"

:*Goodnight,*: she said, and added :*thank you,*: and then she was gone.

"Comin'!" Curtis called toward the wall that separated himself from his mother, and he got out of bed and went into the hallway. From behind her closed door Orchid said, "Bring me the nice glass tonight," and she coughed a few times to speed his pace.

"Yes'm," Curtis answered. He went into the small kitchen, switched on the overhead light and reached up to the high shelf where the nice glass rested on a square of dark blue velvet. It was heavy in his hand and had many diamond-like facets around the base. The pipes gave a short but high-pitched shriek when he drew water from the faucet. He took the glass of water in to his mama, who was sitting up in bed propped in her nest of pillows, the bedside lamp with its flower-print shade casting a dusty light edged with shadows.

"Took you long enough," Orchid said, with a sniffle. "Couldn't you hear me?"

He handed her the nice glass, and then he decided to say, "I was speakin' to someone."

"I didn't hear you on the telephone."

"Wasn't on the telephone."

Her hand stopped with the nice glass near her mouth. Then she drank some water and let her scarfed head fall back as if she had been struck yet another blow from the deadly foe of life.

"Mercy," she said. "Mercy, mercy on me."

"You didn't think it had gone away, did you?"

"I didn't want to know. Don't want to know *now*."

Curtis thought of telling her *She's a girl ten years old, has a businessman father and a driver named Hartley who takes herself and her brother to school so she must be rich and live somewhere in a fine house* but he did not, because that would be mean and his mama did not want to know. "Need anything else?" he asked.

"Stay with me awhile," she said. "Won't you?"

Curtis nodded. He sat down across from her bed in the tired chair that sagged under his slight weight and was colored the mottled hue of many grays.

"Still rainin'," she said.

"Yes'm."

"I get kinda sad when it rains. Seems like a lonely sound, to me."

Curtis remained silent, knowing there was more to come. He wanted to listen to her, to allow her to spill out everything she was holding within, and that was something his mama had never understood.

She took another drink of water and rolled the nice glass between her fragile hands. "Your daddy," she said quietly, "proposed marriage to me in the rain. Did you know that?" She waited for him to shake his head, *no*. "He did. We came out of a dance, and we were walkin' along the street. It started to rain, and I cuddled up next to him because he was just like... like a big *mountain* I could feel protected by. Oh, and he was a good dancer too, to be his size. But I remember...in the rain...I cuddled up close and he looked down into my face and kissed me. And right then... right then...before he asked me, I knew I was *his*. I knew I couldn't belong to no other. Then he said them words: 'Orchid, would you take me to be your husband?' Them words...a woman don't ever forget 'em. You'll get your chance to say 'em to some girl someday, by-and-by. Then...I think we can be happy again."

"Yes'm," Curtis said.

"It is a hard thing," said Orchid, "to watch somebody drift away from you. It is...a little death, I think. You try to figure out...what can you *do*, to make things right? You laugh when you feel like cryin', and when you look across the room at the man you love...you just see a ghost standin' there. Oh...hear that thunder? Just hollered right over our house, seemed like."

Curtis said, "I wish I could do somethin' to make you feel better, mama. If you'd let me take you to see—"

"No doctors," she interrupted. "Uh uh. Cost too much money. Spent all that money takin' *you* to see the doctors, and what good did that do?"

I can't help what I am, he wanted to say...but what would the noble Knights of the Round Table say to that, if they were in his shoes? They would not want to lay further hurt upon a defenseless creature like the woman who lay in the bed before him, and so he replied, "I can afford a doctor for you, mama."

"*Barely*," she said. "Lord God, we're just scrapin' by as it is, you're wantin' to throw money away on a useless doctor?"

Curtis had no answer for that, because she would hear no answer.

"I am *so* tired," she said.

"I'll let you get on to sleep, then."

"Not yet. Not just yet." Orchid drank the rest of the water from the nice glass. "Tell me this," she said after a pause. "How do you do...you know... that listenin' thing? I mean...how do you *talk* with your mind?"

Curtis had been about to get up, but now he eased back into the creaky chair because never ever had his mama asked him a question like this before. He thought about it a few seconds and formulated an answer. "At work... one of the other 'caps...we call him Brightboy...he can roll his tongue up like a rug somebody's skidded on. Three or four folds in that thing. None of the others can do it. I can't even *think* how to do it, but it's natural to him. When I was in the fifth grade...there was a boy named Noah Walcott. On the playground one day I saw him catch a wasp in his hand. Bunch of other kids saw it too, he was puttin' on a show. He clasped that wasp in his fist and he shook it like he was shakin' dice...and then he put the wasp in his mouth. But it never stung him. Opened his mouth, and out it flew. I remember...he said wasps and hornets and everythin' that stung was scared of him, and he'd never been stung and never would be.

"And then," Curtis went on, "there was that fella Beauley—we got to callin' him 'Beauty'—who worked at the station for awhile. You remember I told you about him?"

"No, I don't."

That didn't surprise Curtis, because his mama did not listen.

"Well...Beauley on his good days could tell you nearly nine times out of ten what the next person either comin' into the station from the street or from the trackside would be wearin', not to mention whether they'd be a man, woman or child. He'd say, 'Next man comin' in has got on a yellow bowtie and he's wearin' a blue shirt and two-tone shoes,' and there the man would be. Or it would be, 'Family comin' in, man in a gray coat, woman with a flowery hat, little boy wearin' white kneesocks.' There they would be, sure as tellin'. Now other days, Beauley couldn't seem to keep his own shoelaces tied and his cart on a straight line. Bossman had to fire Beauley because he started goin' into trances, just standin' there starin' at nothin'. You don't remember I told you this?"

"You didn't," Orchid said.

"I might be wrong then," he told her, but he knew he was not. "What I'm sayin' is…life is so full of mysteries that only the Good Father can answer. We can't pierce the veil. I don't know how I do what I do. It's grown on me, is all I can say."

"This other one you're speakin' to…does this person seize it or try to cast it away?"

"She seizes it. And if you're startin' to think I've found a girl, I'll tell you that she's ten years old and white. Her family's got a driver."

"Have mercy," Orchid muttered, but she was no longer listening to him. She was studying the nice glass with its gleaming of diamond-like facets around its base. "Waterford crystal," she said. "Given to my grandmother by a colored gentleman from England, that long ago. Passed on down to me as a wedding gift from my mother. You're named for this… Curtis *Waterford*. Very few like this one, I'm thinkin'. Most all the batch this came from broken and lost by now…unless they in a *museum*. I named you for this because I always thought it was such a beautiful and rare thing. You see?"

"I do," Curtis said.

"Well…white people find out you can talk to people in your mind… you're gonna wind up in a museum," Orchid said. "Gonna wind up with your head in one of them display cases, after they take your brain out and cut it to pieces to study it. That's the way of white people. Take somethin' apart to study it, and then it's broke."

"I'll stay away from museums," Curtis replied, with a wry smile.

"They'll drag you away from me, they find out 'bout this. Then I'll lose you like I lost your daddy." Orchid had finished her water; she held the nice glass out for Curtis, and he got up from his chair and took it. "Wash it up," she said. "Dry it good and put it back where it was."

"Yes'm."

"Listen here, though…I'm thinkin' we ought to go to the farm. Spend some time with Maw and Pap. Maybe move over there and be with 'em. Lord knows I hate to give up the house, but maybe the time has come."

"I think that would be a good idea, for *you*," said Curtis. "But I can't go, mama. I like my work, I can't give that up."

"Carryin' bags all day long, you can't give that up?"

"I help people," he said. "I help 'em get from here to there and back again. That's what I do."

"You make that sound like a fine thing."

"To me," he said, "it is."

Orchid let out a long sigh. "Ironheaded," she said. "Just like your daddy."

"I believe that's a compliment, and I'll take it as such."

"Go on with y'self, then. Ain't nothin' more."

He spent a moment straightening the covers around her and helping her get situated for sleep. Suddenly she grasped his free hand and pressed it to her cheek.

"I have not done right by you, son." There was a hitch in her voice. "I am sorry for that."

He let his fingers cup her cheek. "It's all right, mama," he told her gently. "Don't fret 'bout anythin'."

She held him there for a time, and he let himself be held.

When she released him, he asked, "Want me to turn out the light?"

"No," she said, in a faraway voice; she was staring at the window where the rain trickled down. "No, I'll leave the light on for awhile."

"All right, then. Goodnight."

"'Night to you." She waited until he was almost out of the room, and then she said, "I love you, son. And your daddy would be very, very proud of you."

It took Curtis a few seconds to compose himself enough to answer, because coming from her that was a powerful statement. "Thank you, mama," he said. "I love you too. And I thank you for listening to me tonight."

"Only got two ears. My head don't work like yours."

He closed the door softly, rinsed out the nice glass in the kitchen and then dried it. He returned it to its place on the upper shelf, on its square of dark blue velvet. He went back to his room and read some more about the ancient knights, while he listened for his friend to come back if she needed him. She did not—this night, at least—so at last he closed the book after reading about the death of King Harmaunce of the Red City, and he found sleep a peaceful companion.

Fourteen.

It hinged on two things: timing, and the art of the sale.

Pearly was waiting behind the wheel of the Ford, as rain pattered down upon the windshield from the slate-gray sky. He had pulled up to the curb next to the small public park a block south of the Harrington School, the exact same place he'd been on Monday and Tuesday afternoons. The Ford's engine was running and the wipers swept back and forth. Pearly checked his wristwatch. It was twelve minutes after three. Hartley should be driving past any minute now.

"Nerves?" Ginger asked from where she had slid down in the passenger seat and half-crouched on the floorboard.

"I'm fine," he answered, but he wished he had time for a cigarette; he did have some butterflies and he needed to smoke them out.

"Good for you. My back's fuckin' breakin'," said Donnie from the rear seat, where he also had contorted himself into a hidden position.

Pearly said to Ginger, "Remember about the gun in the—"

"Glovebox. Got it." She gave him a tight grin, but her eyes were narrowed and hard. "Just do your job, detective. Everything else'll be butter."

Pearly kept glancing into the left sideview mirror and then the rearview… sideview and rearview…sideview and rearview. The shining expensive cars of the wealthy families whose kids went to the Harrington School kept passing the Ford like a snooty parade, but still no sign of Hartley's long maroon-colored 1933 Oldsmobile Touring Sedan. He gripped the steering wheel with both hands, ready to swing the Ford out from the curb as soon as Hartley had passed.

Sideview...rearview...sideview...rearview.

Timing and the art of the sale. Both were up to him. In probably less than ten minutes now, it would be a done deal if it went right. It came to him that he hoped the car would hold up; he'd put a lot of miles on it, driving back to Shreveport in the middle of the night on Friday to pick up Ginger and Donnie and then turning right around and bringing them to New Orleans, plus the driving he'd done for them here and up around Lake Pontchartrain at the swamp town of Kenner. The time was ticking away now. He checked his wristwatch again, seeing that only a couple of minutes had crept past since the last time he'd looked...and then suddenly he saw the Oldsmobile's big radiator grill coming up on his left side in the sideview mirror. Hartley flashed his headlamps. The maroon car moved past at a stately pace. Did Nilla Ludenmere look back at the Ford through the rear window? Yes, she did. Was she still looking? Yes again.

Nailed me, Pearly thought. He figured she'd seen him yesterday or this morning, but no matter. It was time to roll.

"We're on," he said. He waited for Hartley to get about four car lengths ahead and then he pulled away from the curb and followed, keeping his distance. Over the weekend he had worked Ludenmere into thinking it was a real good idea for the Shreveport detective to ride backup when Hartley took the kids to and from school. There was the problem of keeping them from knowing they were being tailed—"watched over" in case the Orsi gang tried anything, as Pearly had put it to Ludenmere—so they wouldn't get the wife all nervous, so Pearly had parked a couple of blocks away from the Garden District mansion in the mornings and again a couple of blocks away from the Harrington School in the afternoons, but the girl had nailed him. That was okay; there was no more need for that pretense. Still...old Glass-Eye had to be sold, because if he got his hand on that pistol in the glovebox the snatch would be busted and somebody was likely to get drilled.

"Shit!" Donnie groaned. "I got a fuckin' crick in my leg!"

"Bite down on it." There was nothing in Ginger's voice but pure ice. "When he stops this rig you'd better be ready to move."

"Turnin' right up ahead," Pearly reported. The wipers swept back and forth across the rain-streaked glass. He sped up. "I don't want to hit any lights." He had spoken his thought aloud, and Ginger answered with a terse, "Lose him and you're my goddamned supper."

"I won't lose him. If he sees he's gettin' too far ahead he'll slow down. Did the same thing Monday and yesterday. He changed the route yesterday, but both days we went through that—*damn!*" A brown dog had just loped across the street right in front of the Ford, nearly grazing the front fender.

"What the *hell*?" Donnie yelped.

"Keep your head down," Ginger said. "You're in cotton back there compared to me."

"We're all right. Dog ran out in the street. Okay…there he is up ahead. Just saw his brake lights flash. I was sayin'…both days he went through that warehouse area, so I'm thinkin' he'll go through it again."

"Better be right, genius."

His temper flared at that one. "You'd just better be *fast*, honeypie. We'll be comin' to it in a couple of minutes, if we make this light."

His palms were damp on the wheel and his heart was pounding, but he found he wasn't afraid. He was more excited than anything. *Exhilarated* would be the right word, he thought. The toughest part of this action so far had been convincing Ludenmere in one of their phone calls that even though the word was that Orsi had come to New Orleans it still wasn't in his best interest to alert the city cops. *I've got a friend on the force, been a detective for a couple of years,* Pearly had told him. *I'll bring him to speed, he'll make some private inquiries and keep it on the low. Trust me on this.*

They had to make the move today, because Jack Ludenmere's trust could only go so far and Pearly had sensed he was running out of road.

They passed through an area of small houses and a few vacant lots, and then they entered a warehouse district of low, blocky buildings. A couple of trucks trundled by, but otherwise the only vehicles on this stretch of street were the Ford and the Oldsmobile. "This is it," Pearly said, and he pressed the accelerator down and began flashing his headlamps. Almost immediately he saw Hartley's brake lights flare. The touring sedan slowed to a crawl. Pearly said, "Ready?"

There was no answer; there didn't need to be. They were ready, and this was the moment.

Pearly passed Hartley on the left, slowed the Ford and pulled slightly to the right so the chauffeur would have to stop against the curb. As Hartley pulled up beside him and stopped, Pearly was already reaching over Ginger to roll down the window.

The chauffeur's window rolled down. "What is it?" he asked, his voice tight.

"Listen," said Pearly in an easy tone, "Nilla's already seen me, so that jig is up. But your left rear tire is goin' flat. I think I can see a nail in it."

"It feels all right."

"You might want to stop at a gas station and get it checked. Come on, take a look and see what you think." Pearly quickly got out of the car and started walking through the light rain around to the Oldsmobile's left rear side.

Hartley didn't move.

"*Shit*," Ginger whispered from her crouched position. She was listening for the chauffeur's door to open, and it wasn't happening.

"I see the nail," Pearly said, thinking he had to get that bastard out and right *now*.

"I can change the tire at the house," Hartley answered.

"Your call, Clay," Pearly said; it was the first time he'd ever used the man's name. "It'll probably hold." He cast another look at the supposedly injured tire and with a silent curse he started back around to the Ford. In about fifteen seconds Plan B was going to have to go into action, and with that gun in Hartley's glovebox and the locks on the Oldsmobile's doors Plan B was a bucketful of shit.

"You fellas got car trouble?" a man's voice called. Startled out of five years' life, Pearly saw a man in dungarees standing about twenty-five yards away beneath a metal roof that jutted out from a warehouse's loading dock. He'd been smoking a cigarette under shelter from the rain.

Pearly called back, "A little tire trouble, but we're movin' on!"

Hartley's door suddenly opened, and Pearly lost another year. Hartley left the engine running. He said wearily, "Okay, let me take a gander."

Pearly stepped back. He looked at the Oldsmobile's rear window and saw both Nilla's and Little Jack's face pressed together cheek-to-cheek watching the drama unfold. The little girl's eyes were fixed on him, and they carried the intensity he recalled from the little girl in Texas, the Jodi of the misspelled name in the Golden Edition Bible, the Jodi of the burnt-up puppies.

When Hartley came around behind the car to check the tire, Pearly reached into his suit jacket and put his hand on the grip of the shoulder holster's .38 revolver. At the same instant, Ginger opened her door and slid smoothly behind the Oldsmobile's wheel. Donnie started coming out right after her.

Pearly pulled at the revolver.

The hammer hung on something.

Donnie staggered out of the Ford's backseat and crashed against the side of the Olds.

"Damn foot's asleep!" he hollered.

Pearly saw Hartley's body tense like that of a hunting dog on the scent. Within the car, Ginger had already opened the glovebox, checked the .45 Smith and Wesson revolver's six bullet load and was offering the chauffeur's weapon to Donnie, who seemed to be struggling against gravity itself. Hartley whipped around to aim both his good eye and glass eye at Pearly; the man's face had gone gray, and then it grayed a few shades further when Pearly nearly ripped the .38 out of its holster and pressed the barrel into the man's stomach.

"Get in—" Pearly's voice cracked and he had to try it again. "Get in the back seat with the kids."

"Come on, move it!" Ginger snapped. Donnie took the offered pistol, and holding it low he limped around to get in the passenger side of the Olds.

Pearly saw Hartley lift his face toward the warehouse worker who was still smoking his cigarette and seemed oblivious to what was happening. Raindrops pattered down on the brim of the chauffeur's cap. The man's mouth quivered, wanting to open. Pearly pressed the gun deeper into Hartley's stomach and positioned himself with his back to the warehouse. "You die for nothin'," he said, his face close up to Hartley's. "We're gonna take the kids, whether you're with 'em or not."

Hartley just stared at him. The quivering mouth crimped and the voice came out, but calmly and quietly: "I'll see you in Hell for this."

"After you." Pearly motioned with a lift of his chin toward the Olds. He caught sight again of Nilla staring at him through the glass. He wished blood would start spurting from those eyes, but her expression was still placid though puzzled and she yet likely had no idea of what was going on.

Hartley turned away from Pearly. He got into the rear seat with Pearly's gun pressed against his back. Once inside, he faced his own pistol in the hand of Donnie Baines, who had positioned himself in the passenger seat so he could keep everybody under control. Pearly closed the door on Hartley and strode back to the Ford. He got behind the wheel and drove away, and Ginger followed in the Olds right behind him.

"Got 'em!" Donnie crowed. "Goddamn it, we got 'em!"

"Goin' for a nice ride, folks," said Ginger. "Settle back and relax."

Nilla and her brother were both wearing their uniforms, dark blue jackets with white blouses, a dark blue skirt for her and for him neatly-creased dark blue trousers. On the breast pocket of the jackets was the ornate stitched gold-colored badge and white HS of the Harrington School. Nilla was confused but not yet frantic, and Little Jack was open-mouthed and transfixed in watching the movements of the pistol in the young man's hand, as if he were watching a snake's head sway back and forth. "What's happening, Mr. Hartley? Who are these people?" she asked. "Why was Mr. Parr here?"

"We're gonna be all right," Hartley told her. He placed a rough hand atop her own softer one. He stared into the face of the man with the gun. "I would ask that you not curse in front of the children," he said.

Donnie seemed to have been struck dumb for an instant. Then he laughed like the braying of a mule and kept laughing until Ginger reached over and smacked him on the knee. "Keep your attention where it needs to be!" she said, and he went silent.

The two cars moved on, turning toward the northwest and the swampland that ringed Lake Pontchartrain.

THREE.

A Cabin on the Lake

Fifteen.

Curtis was carrying out onto the track area two very expensive-looking alligator-hide suitcases for a young man in a gray fedora and a tan-colored raincoat when he heard the murmur of something. Just a murmur, maybe some words mashed together but indecipherable. He wasn't sure if it had been in his head or some noise of the passengers boarding the three-forty.

The locomotive was hissing steam and metal things were banging together. Pigeons fluttered around in the metal beams of the shelter roof. He figured that as a train got up to steam, people were talking excitedly, carts were rolling across the gritty pavement and hot machinery was also speaking, there was just about every noise in the world in Union—

:*Curtis*,: it came.

Soft, it was. A touch and then gone.

Curtis listened, as his shoes took him automatically down the train toward the traveller's car, to wish him a pleasant trip—as was his custom— and hand over the cases to the baggage boy for their further passage.

He got about four more strides when it hit him.

:*CURTIS CALL MY DADDY THIS MAN IN THE CAR THIS MAN TOOK MR. HARTLEYOUTIDON'TKNOWWHEREWE'REGOING SHESAIDFORANICERIDESETTLEBACKFOLKS—*:

The power of it hitting him was like a solid punch to the forehead. His head went back and his knees buckled, he dropped the two suitcases and suddenly he was down on the concrete.

:CURTIS CURTIS HELP US CURTIS THIS MAN IN THE CAR HE'S GOT A GUN.:

"You all right? You slip on something?" the young traveller asked, but he was a white man and he kept his distance.

Curtis couldn't focus enough to answer either one of the speakers. His brain buzzed with frantic energy and his heart was pounding so hard he thought it might tear through his chest.

:CURTIS CAN YOU HEAR ME CALL MY DADDY PLEASE CALL HIM.:

His head was banging like a Mardi Gras drum, but he got out a weak *:What?:*

:I'M NILLA LUDENMERE MY DADDY IS JACK LUDENMERE SOME PEOPLE HAVE GOT ME AND MY BROTHER PLEASE CURTIS PLEASE.:

:What?: he directed outward again, stupidly. He was aware then of people around him, and Cricket was reaching down to help him up but Curtis had as much strength as a ragdoll and he couldn't even grasp Cricket's hand.

:I'M NILLA LUDENMERE,: she said again, and Curtis's own voice with Nilla's words in it was like a bomb blast in his skull. *:LITTLE JACK AND ME. THEY'RE TAKING US SOMEWHERE.:*

:Who?: he got out. *:Takin' you where?:*

The strength of her sending had ebbed, but it was still rushed and nearly garbled. *:Two men and a woman. Mr. Parr was here. I'm sitting next to Mr. Hartley. I don't know where they're taking us.:*

:You say…call your daddy? His name is Jack Ludenmere?:

:Yes Curtis yes…this man has got a gun aimed right at us.:

"Grab hold and stand up, Curtis. You okay?" Cricket was asking, and now the new man Prentiss was leaning down to give some help.

Lord God! Curtis thought. And then, to Nilla, *:You're bein' kidnapped? Is that right?:*

:Yes Curtis…call my daddy…let him know…please…:

She sounded nearly worn out from what had been several mind-searing shouts of energy, and her sending toward the end had begun to fade. Curtis said, :*I'll do it, Nilla. What's the phone number?*:

"Curtis, stand up!"

:*OR2-42...no, wait...OR2-24...I can't think, my head's hurtin'...OR2-2461...that's the number...*:

:*All right. Don't wring yourself out, now. I'll call your daddy.*:

She was quiet, likely both her energy spent and allowing him to go make the call. When he struggled up, both Ol' Crab and the new man, Prentiss, were there to help as well as Brightboy.

His falling had caused a commotion but not enough to delay any schedules; the engine was still steaming up and the passengers were still boarding. Ol' Crab said to the young traveller, "You can go on, suh, we'll take care of your bags, and thank you kindly for your aid here," and he gave the man a smile to bade him on his way.

The wide mouth in Prentiss's fleshy face opened to drawl, "Maybe I ain't no doc, but looks to me like Longlegs is feelin' poorly."

"Thank you for your professional opinion, Doc. I can take things from here."

"*Doc*," said Brightboy with a snigger, and thus was born Prentiss's new monicker.

"Gotta get to the phone, Mr. Crable," Curtis said. He felt the prickles of sweat on his face and at the back of his neck. "I'm all right, I just gotta get to the phone."

"Doc, get these bags movin'." Ol' Crab's tone of voice said it had better be done right quick. When Doc obeyed, Ol' Crab told Brightboy to go about his business too, and then he took hold of Curtis's shoulders and looked him square in the face. "Why do you have to get to the phone in such a doggone hurry?"

"I just do, sir. I can't explain it right now, but...it's real important, I swear it is."

"All right, all right, you don't have to do no swearin'. You hurt y'self when you fell?"

"No sir. Just have to get to the phone."

Ol' Crab nodded. "Go on, then," he said, and then: "You got change?"

"Yes sir, I do."

Ol' Crab released his shoulders. Curtis left the platform and hurried back into the station and to the door at the far right that led to the Redcaps' room. On the wall just beyond the lockers was the pay phone. Curtis had kept the number firmly in his mind; he put the nickel into the slot and dialed it with a shaky hand.

"Ludenmere residence," a woman answered after four rings. She had a lilt of Creole in her accent.

"I need to speak to Mr. Jack Ludenmere, please."

"Mr. Ludenmere is at his office. Would you care to leave a message?"

"Uh…is this Mrs. Ludenmere?" Curtis asked.

"I am employed by the Ludenmeres," came the reply. "Mrs. Ludenmere is at a club meetin'. Do you have a message?"

"I need the office number. Can you give that to me?"

"One moment," she replied, and in a matter of maybe fifteen seconds she came back with it. Curtis thanked her, put another nickel into the slot to dial the number, and was answered by a white woman with a businesslike voice who said, "Ludenmere shipping, how may I direct your call?"

Curtis repeated his need to speak to Jack Ludenmere and was asked if his call was expected. He said it was not, but it was about something Mr. Ludenmere needed to know. "Name, please?" she asked. He told her, and she said, "I'll connect you with Mr. Ludenmere's secretary, please hold the line."

He waited.

:*I'm tryin', Nilla, I'm tryin',*: he sent out, but she didn't respond.

Then, another white woman's rigid voice: "Mr. Ludenmere's office. Mr. Mayhew, is it?"

"Curtis Mayhew, yes'm. I need to speak to Mr. Ludenmere, real quick."

"He's out of the building. What would be the reason for your call?"

"Listen…please ma'am…is he *really* out? 'Cause this is mighty important."

There was a slight pause before she replied. "Yes, he's really out and I'm not expecting him back until another hour or so, if then. I can take any message you care to leave."

He started to tell her and it was going to come out in a rush but he stopped himself. How did he know who to trust? The secretary he was talking to might have had a hand in it. The kidnappers might be from the very office. He had to back off and think; his brain was still frazzled.

"I'll try later," he said, and hung up.

As soon as he returned the receiver to its cradle Curtis was struck with the feeling that he had to act, to do *something*, because every second wasted was another second the kidnappers were getting further away. He felt as if he could hardly breathe and his heart was still beating wildly, even danger-ously. He had to at least *try*.

He took his last nickel out of his trousers and put it into the slot. He dialed O, and when the operator answered he asked in as calm a voice as possible for the Police Department.

"Oh, Mr. Ludenmere! I wasn't expecting you back so soon!"

The master of his shipping empire had just entered the outer office, his raincoat over his arm and his gray fedora still speckled with raindrops. He gave Alice a shrug and said, "I know now why I skipped the last two triple B meetin's. Borin' as all hell. Then after the speeches came the rubber chicken *and* I got buttonholed by Cyrus Kelley in the Frenchman's Bar for another damned hour." The Better Business Bureau meetings, held once a month, had never been his favorite outings. "I thought about goin' home but I've got work to do. What're my calls?"

She tore off the sheet of paper from her pad that had the names, numbers, messages and times the calls were placed all written in her neat penmanship.

He scanned the list. All the names were known to him but the last one. "Curtis Mayhew? Who is that?"

"I don't know, sir, he didn't leave a message."

"Called at three twenty-two? Didn't leave a number either?"

"No, sir."

Ludenmere scanned the names again. Rich Buchanan up in Memphis needed to be called this afternoon…Mike O'Mara could wait, and so could Ken Sonderfeld…but who the hell was Curtis Mayhew? His attention kept being drawn to that name: *Curtis*.

That's his name, Daddy. I'm talkin' to somebody in my head, really I am, and his name is Curtis.

Coincidence, he thought. The girl had her grandmother's wild imagination, that was the root of it.

He said to Alice, "Give me about ten minutes to decompress and then get Rich Buchanan on the line." He went into his office, closed the door, hung up his raincoat, hat and suit jacket and nearly collapsed into the chair behind his desk. Usually he would swing around and look down for a moment with the pride of ownership at the docks and the warehouses that bore his name, but today he couldn't seem to gather the energy. It was this damned Orsi thing, and being wrung out worrying night and day—minute after minute—over the welfare of his children. If Parr didn't show results soon—say in the next couple of days—he was going to call Chief Bazer in Shreveport and request more men on the job. Either that, or go to the local police and to hell with the reporters, let them print whatever they—

His intercom buzzed.

"Not ten minutes yet," he answered, a little harshly.

"Sir…there's a man on the line who's asking to speak to you. He won't give his name, but he says he's calling on behalf of a Detective Parr."

For about three seconds Ludenmere sat as if frozen. He didn't like the sound of that. Then all the blood seemed to rush back into his limbs and his face and he felt as swollen as a tick in a hounddog's ear.

"Put him through," he said, and he waited five seconds and picked up the receiver. "Jack Ludenmere speakin'."

"Afternoon," came the voice. It was muffled and low-pitched, almost a raspy whisper, and instantly made the flesh crawl along Ludenmere's spine.

"We have your kids, the Shreveport dick and your chauffeur. Nice gun he kept in his glovebox."

Ludenmere could not answer. His voice was gone. Dark motes spun before his eyes and his heart hammered.

"This will be the only communication," the caller went on. "At one o'clock tomorrow mornin', you're to bring two hundred thousand dollars to the end of a fishin' pier on Sandusky Road in Kenner. It's a right turn off Sawmill Road. Bring the money in a cardboard box, closed but unsealed. Nothin' higher than fifties. You come alone. No cops, no *smell* of cops, and no weapons. We don't want anybody hurt. You play it right, then everybody goes home where they belong. Got it?"

Ludenmere, the man who had talked his way into many deals that had over the years cemented his fortune, could not for the life of him speak a word.

"*Got it?*" the eerie muffled voice demanded.

Ludenmere took a breath and forced his own voice out; it sounded weak and afraid, like no one he'd ever heard before. "Wait…*wait*. Are my children all right? Please…don't hurt them. Okay?"

"They're all right. The rest depends on you. Any cops come with you or there's anythin' we don't like, the kids die. Hear me?"

"I hear you," the weak and frightened voice replied. "But…listen…I can't raise that much money by one o'clock. The business day is almost over. I've got…I've got fifteen thousand in a safe at home. I can bring that, for a starter."

"Ha," the kidnapper said, but it was not a laugh. There was a pause, and then: "All right, we'll make it one o'clock on Friday mornin'. But listen up, mister…you're gonna add that fifteen thousand to the box for this inconvenience. Got that?"

"Yes," Ludenmere said.

"End of the pier, Sandusky Road, one o'clock Friday mornin'. Be there… no cops, no guns…box with two hundred and fifteen grand in it…everythin' smooth and easy."

Click, went the line, and the man was gone.

Ludenmere sat with the phone still pressed to his ear. The blood was roaring in his head.

Instantly he cursed himself for not telling the man—Orsi himself?—he wanted to speak to both Nilla and Little Jack, and for not clarifying when and where he would get them back. His dealmaker skills had failed him at a crucial moment, and he realized he would forever have to live with that failure. But…he had to play this right now, keep everything as much in control as possible, for a man who had lost so much control. At least he had the extra day, to get all the money together. Two hundred and fifteen thousand…two million and fifteen thousand…he would pay whatever he had to pay to get them back unharmed.

He put the phone's receiver down. How to go about getting that much cash? Victor…Victor could help him figure this out, and right now he needed a—

The intercom buzzed again.

"*Yeah?*" His voice was so strained that once more he didn't recognize it and it must have startled Alice because she didn't immediately respond. "*What is it?*" he asked, and sounded like he wanted to tear somebody's throat out by the teeth.

"Sir…um…you have a call from a police detective by the name of Albert Angenelli. Shall I put him through?"

"*What?*"

"You have a call from a police detective by the—"

"All right, all right," Ludenmere said. He felt sweat dripping under his arms and the walls of his office seemed to be moving around and around him in slow-motion. "Put him through."

"Mr. Ludenmere?" came a large and hearty voice over the telephone. "Detective Captain Angenelli over here at the Central Station. How are you today?"

"Shitty. How are you?"

"Well…I'm pretty good, myself. Sorry to hear you're havin' a problem. Business?"

"Captain, I'm a busy man. Can I help you with somethin'?"

"You can clear up a little question we have for you," Angenelli said, the smile still in his voice. "We had a caller about ten minutes ago who claimed your two children have been kidnapped this afternoon. Is that true?"

If the office walls had been moving around him before, now they stopped and began to close in on him.

His mind raced. To tell this policeman everything now, and risk the lives of his children...or not?

"Mr. Ludenmere?" Angenelli prompted, with a more serious note creeping into the sunny voice.

"Who told you that?" he asked.

"Well, it's peculiar is what it is. We got a call from a Redcap at Union Station by the name of Curtis Mayhew. I'm lookin' at the report right now. He says your children have been kidnapped by two men and a woman and one of the men has a gun...only he can't tell us how he knows this to be true. We told him to stay where he is, we'd go pick him up and bring him here. Is this on the level?"

The moment of decision was in front of him. He had to make it before his reeling brain gave out.

"Captain Angenelli," Ludenmere said, "this...is a damnable hoax. My children are at home right now with their mother."

"You're sure about that?"

"Positive. I..." Jesus, what a lie this would have to be! "I just talked to my wife. They're home safe and sound, like every afternoon after school."

"Hm. That's doubly peculiar then, don't you think?"

"What I think," said Ludenmere, and he reached up to blot with his fingers small beads of cold sweat from his forehead, "is that this Curtis Mayhew person is a lunatic, or he's wantin' some kind of attention from me. I don't know...people are hard to figure out."

"I'll say. Do you even know this fella? He's a Negro, by the way, all them Redcaps are. Is he holdin' some kind of grudge against you?"

"Never met him that I know of, never heard of him before."

"That's a downright puzzler."

Ludenmere was silent, and so was the police captain. Ludenmere's vision was going hazy. He feared that he might either scream in the next few seconds or he would just quite simply pass out.

Angenelli finally spoke after what seemed an agonizing eternity. "Then should we send a car over to pick this man up, or not? I mean to say, makin' a false claim like this could be an offense on its own. We ought to lock him up here for a while until we—"

"No, no," Ludenmere interrupted, but he'd tried to make it sound unrushed and unconcerned, "I wouldn't spend the time, the money or the energy. Let me ask this...was this colored man *drunk*? On dope or somethin'? I suspect when one of those bucks gets into the whiskey and the dope they see more than pink elephants."

"It can be a real mess, that's true."

"I'm glad you don't have to wade through it in this case, then."

There was a crackling sound. Ludenmere realized the police captain was unwrapping a stick of chewing gum, and when the man spoke again it was around the chew. "You're a mighty important man, Mr. Ludenmere," he said. "I read about that new contract you got."

"My *business* got," he corrected.

"Sure. A lot of money to be made there. I'm sure also that the story went out to a lot of other newspapers, maybe clear to California. You know, I've wanted to meet you for quite some time, shake your hand in person for the job you're doin' helpin' New Orleans and this whole country get back on its feet. Think I could come by some evenin', meet you and the family?"

"We'd be happy to have you over," Ludenmere said.

"How about tonight?" Angenelli asked, around his chewing gum.

Ludenmere's stomach lurched. "No...my wife...Jane...and I...and the children...we're all goin' out to supper tonight. It's been planned for...oh...a week, I guess."

"I see. Maybe next week, then?"

"Yes. Next week would be fine."

Angenelli chewed on, as Ludenmere thought he was about to jump out of his skin.

"Let me tell you a little about kidnappers," said Angenelli, and no longer was his voice warm and smiling. "There are some vile and desperate people out there, Mr. Ludenmere. So bad a fine man like you could never imagine it. Just about every day—somewhere—these people take another human bein' for ransom. Oh, it's the hard times, I know, but that's not the all of it. It is *very* rare that a payoff is made and the victim is returned alive. Oh yeah, the kidnappers always say to keep the cops out of it or things'll get rough, but... it gets rough anyway. Now...some of these kidnappers do it strictly for the money, sure, but there are some who do it because...well, let's just say they were born to the job. Their vileness was just searchin' for a way to spill out. They like the thrill of it, the idea that they're in charge, that they're somebody who ought to be respected, even if they have to take children off the street to do it. Then you're not dealin' with human bein's like you and me anymore, Mr. Ludenmere. You're dealin' with animals who don't have any problem about cuttin' a little girl's throat once they get their money. Or...they might do it anyway, money or not, if it suits 'em. That's the reality of things, sir." He paused for a few seconds before he spoke again, and he cracked the gum with his teeth. "Now...do you have anythin' you want to tell me?"

The world stopped.

It only lurched forward again when Ludenmere said, "No."

"Your children are at home, you say?"

"Captain Angenelli...let's be logical, all right?" Ludenmere turned around in his chair to gaze down upon the docks and the warehouses, the boats and the river and the city and none of it seemed to matter worth a damn anymore. "*Logical*," he repeated, with an effort. "How would a Redcap at Union Station *know* that my children had been kidnapped this afternoon? *How*? And he says he can't tell you, correct? So what is he...a *mind reader*? Only...he's not a mind reader, he's just a...I don't know, a troublemaker or crazy or...like I say, flyin' high on dope. How do you explain *him*?"

"A downright puzzler," said the captain.

"Know what I'm gonna do tonight?" Ludenmere pressed on before the other man could respond. "I'm gonna hug my children and kiss my wife, and we're goin' out for a nice family supper that's been too long comin'."

"Good for you. Where're you eatin'?"

"Arnaud's," Ludenmere answered quickly. "Of course."

"Heard that's a fine place. A few dollars over my budget, though. Well, then…I suppose I should let you get on back to work, shouldn't I?"

"Wednesdays are always busy here."

"Yes sir. All right then. Tell you what, let me leave you my number and when you decide on a night I might come over and meet the family, you can let me know. That suit you?"

"Yes, it does." He wrote the number down on his notepad with his black Parker but his hand was so shaky it was hardly legible.

"I guess that's it, then. Sorry to have to bring this to your attention."

"It's your job, Captain, and I appreciate that you take pride in it. Thank you for the call."

When Angenelli had hung up, Ludenmere went into action like a bullet shot from a pistol. He got up, knocked at Victor's door, opened it and found the corporate lawyer's office empty. Victor may be somewhere else in the building. On his way across the office to his own door Ludenmere staggered and had to catch himself against the wall, which made the array of framed citations and awards—including several from the Triple-B—shudder on their nails.

He composed himself and in the outer office asked Alice to cancel the call to Rich Buchanan, then to find Victor for him and have Victor come see him at once. Then he turned around, went back into his own office and shut the door. He walked into his small private bathroom, shut that door as well, opened up both faucet taps on full blast, leaned over and threw up into the toilet the remnants of rubbery chicken, mashed potatoes, string beans, okra, buttermilk biscuits and pecan pie until the blood gushed from his mouth and the fouled water beneath his gasping face turned a dull and cloudy red.

Sixteen.

"Is that a real gun?" the boy asked.

"Real enough," Donnie said.

"Prove it," came the challenge.

Donnie almost opened the cylinder to show Little Jack Ludenmere the bullets but he caught himself. Ginger wasn't going to let that happen, anyway; she'd been ready to take one hand off the Oldsmobile's steering wheel to punch him in the ribs. "Now's the chance," she said with grit in her voice, "to show you're smarter than a third-grader."

"Fourth grader!" Little Jack had nearly shouted it with indignation. "I got double-promoted!"

"Settle down," Nilla told him. She put her hand on his arm to calm him, just as Hartley had put his hand on her own. "Where're you taking us?" she asked the brown-haired woman at the wheel.

"Timbuktu. Now shut up and keep him shut."

"I'm not afraid of *you*," Little Jack sneered at Donnie, even though the pistol was pointed right at his face. "Our daddy'll find you and whip your tail!"

"You're a comical little motherfucker," Donnie said, with a crooked grin on his mouth.

"Please, sir," said Hartley. "Your language."

The pistol's barrel shifted toward Hartley. A red tinge had begun to surface on the younger man's hollow cheeks. "Don't tell me how to *talk*, squarehead. Hey, I'll bet you take that glass eye out of your face you look like you've got an asshole in there. You ever done that? Speak! I asked you a question!"

"Leave 'em alone," Ginger said. The rain had picked up and the wipers were working harder. Ahead of them the straight gray road was bordered by scrub forest and thorny thickets broken by an occasional shack that might be occupied or might be empty, it was impossible to tell. "We'll be comin' up to the place in a minute, don't antagonize 'em."

"Don't *what*?"

"Don't get 'em riled for nothin'."

"Somebody's breath stinks," said Little Jack, and he added, "I'm lookin' at *you*."

"You and me," Donnie said to the boy in what was nearly a guttural growl, "are gonna have a lot of *fun*, I can tell that right off."

"Ignore him," Ginger ordered. "I mean it. You be the grown-up."

Donnie make a noise with his lips like an explosive fart, but he said no more.

After her head had cleared from the impact of being driven off by these two and having a pistol waved in her face, Nilla Ludenmere had realized that she might have to grow up fast, if for no reason but to protect her brother. Gone, it seemed, were the days of dolls, pretty dresses and pretend tea parties; all the sunny playtime of a ten-year-old seemed as distant as her daddy and mama were right now, and she had realized also that Mr. Hartley could not protect them. That alone was a terrifying thought, but she knew it to be a fact. "What do you want with us?" she asked, though she had already reasoned it had to be about money.

"Just a short visit," the woman at the wheel said. "That's all."

Nilla pressed on. "How much money are you wanting from our daddy?"

"Nothin' he can't afford. You're a smart little girl, aren't you?"

"I know why you took us."

"So you do." Ginger was looking through the rain for an old barn coming up on the right.

About a half-mile past that was a dirt road—mud today, have to be careful not to get the tires stuck—where they were meeting Pearly after he'd made the call at the phonebooth in the Rexall Pharmacy on West Esplanade Avenue in Metairie and bought the items they needed.

They passed a wooden sign with the words printed neatly in white: Welcome to Kenner, A Town With A Future. About thirty yards beyond the sign was a second one, smaller, just a couple of boards nailed together and put up on stakes. Painted on that sign in ragged red letters was 2nd Annual Rattlesnake Rodeo, Sat. Sept. 1, Judging At Noon, Kelso Park.

"You see that?" Donnie asked Ginger. "What the fuck is a rattlesnake rodeo?"

"Bunch of redneck geeks go out in the woods to catch rattlers," she answered. "They make a contest out of it, who bags the most and the biggest. Then they cook 'em up and eat 'em."

"Really? Shit, that's ugly. You ever et snake?"

"Yep."

"What's it taste like?"

"Chicken," she said, "only snakier."

Nilla closed her eyes, the better to concentrate. What followed was always like a low level of electricity flowing through her body, and she knew what that was like because when she was five years old she'd stuck a fork in a wall socket. It wasn't that extreme, wasn't the same as the shock that had sent her to the hospital and remained vividly in her memory as a quick buzz of blasting pain, but it was there all the same. She called out to him. :*Curtis, talk to me.*:

It took him a few seconds to reply, and always when she spoke to him and he spoke back to her like this she heard in her brain a quiet crackling sound like that from the records her mama liked to play on the gramophone, that old-sounding piano music from people who sounded foreign with names that she'd first thought were Baytovin, Showpan and Moe Zart until the music teacher at the Harrington School had taught lessons on the classical pianists last year and cleared that up.

:I'm here, Nilla,: he came back, and she was glad he used her name because it made her feel he was close to her.

:We're in the town of Kenner,: she said. *:On a long road with woods on both sides. Did you call my daddy?:*

:I'm sorry, but I couldn't get him. I called the police, they said they'd tell him and they're comin' to the station to pick me up real soon.:

:All right. Just so he knows.:

:He ought to know by now. Don't be afraid, he'll get you out of this.:

:I'm not afraid,: she answered, and maybe she was but she didn't want this woman and man to see it, and Mr. Hartley's strong hand on her own was helping keep up her pretend courage. *:I want this to be over, and I'm scared for Little Jack.:*

:It'll be over soon, I'll bet.:

"Hey Vesta, I think this kid's gone to sleep!"

Nilla opened her eyes. The man with the gun was grinning at her.

Donnie glanced at Ginger and saw from the hot glare in her eyes and the slight display of bared teeth that he had awakened the demon. "He ain't here, so what does it matter?" Donnie asked. She shook her head and returned her attention to the road. Her ominous silence was enough to tell him that he would pay with his balls the next time he dared to speak her real first name.

"Here's the turn," Ginger said.

:We're turning off the main road,: Nilla sent to Curtis. *:Bumpy...muddy. Going into the woods.:*

:Okay,: he said. *:I'm here with you.:*

Ginger drove as far as she dared along the muddy road bordered by dripping forest and then stopped the car. She turned the engine off.

"Why're you stoppin'?" Little Jack asked, and this time there was a quaver in his voice.

"We're gonna take you in them woods and skin you alive," Donnie hissed. "Gonna throw your skins up in the trees and we're gonna cut your fuckin' heads off and leave 'em for the—"

"All right, all right," Ginger interrupted. "Cut that crap." To the others she said, "We're gonna sit here and wait for a little while. Should be about fifteen or twenty minutes."

:*We're waiting,*: Nilla told Curtis. :*Here in the car.*:

:*Waitin' for what?*:

"What are we waiting for?" she asked the woman.

"Listen, kid," Ginger said, and swivelled around in the seat to take stock of Nilla Ludenmere. "You need to button your lip 'cause you're startin' to bother me. Donnie…our chauffeur friend is thinkin'…just thinkin'…about reachin' for that door handle. See how he's all crouched forward, like he's gettin' ready to run a race? Hartley, you'll take a bullet before you get that door open, and out here nobody'll hear the shot."

"You're wrong," Hartley answered, his face expressionless. "I would never leave the children."

"Oh, a *hero*. Well, good for you. Bein' a hero cost you that eye and give you that scar?"

"That's *my* business."

:*Curtis,*: Nilla said, :*the man's name is Donnie and the woman's name is Vesta.*:

:*What about the other man?*:

:*The other man is—*:

She was interrupted when Donnie reached over the seat with his free hand and grabbed hold of her chin. It jarred her so much her mind tumbled and she lost the connection with Curtis.

"You're a pretty kid," Donnie said, staring fixedly into her eyes. "You favor your mama?"

At once Little Jack grasped Donnie's hand and like a spitting wildcat he thrashed about trying to dislodge the grip. When Donnie just laughed at this effort over Ginger's command to let the girl go, Little Jack's teeth went for the man's hand. At once Donnie jerked his hand back as if from a hot stove and laughed like this was the greatest comedy he'd ever seen.

"Ma'am," Hartley said quietly, as he reached around Nilla and lodged his fingers into the back of Little Jack's coat collar, "can't you control your monkey?"

In an instant Donnie's face flooded with blood; even the whites of his eyes seemed to shimmer with it. His mouth was a twisted line and all his laughing was done. He cocked the revolver's hammer, aiming the barrel straight at Hartley's face.

"Shake it off," Ginger said, as if she were telling someone to shoo a fly away from a picnic basket. "He's likin' to bait you. Hartley, I wouldn't do too much of that if I was you, it's a real dangerous game. Donnie, ease up on that hammer, now. Do it. Come on, ease up."

"Kill this one-eyed motherfucker in five seconds," Donnie vowed. His voice trembled with the passion of the idea.

"Let's don't make a mess," she told him, her voice light and seemingly carefree. "Ease that hammer in now, let's straighten ourselves up."

For all his eight-year-old bravado, Little Jack suddenly shivered, broke and began sobbing. "Want to go home…go home…want to go home…" he cried, his head buried against his sister's shoulder. All Nilla could do was stroke his hair and say the stupidest thing she thought she'd ever said in her young life, "We'll go home real soon, I promise."

Donnie eased the hammer forward. He stared daggers at Clay Hartley, whose single eye stared back impassively and whose glass eye seemed to reflect the insane savagery of killing.

Curtis had been listening for Nilla to continue and was about to call her when a man in a brown suit and a woman in a pale purple dress and a hat with a sharp-tipped black feather in it came right up to him in the station and parked their two bags at his feet. Then they looked at him as if they could see right through him and the man put his hands on his hips and said, "Well? Do you work here or not?"

"Yes suh I do, pardon me," said Curtis, and so he carried their bags about forty feet to the desk where the luggage tags were filled out, since the next train was not due to leave for nearly an hour, and got a nickel for his effort. He touched the brim of his red cap and said, "Thank you, suh," and then he heard Cricket's voice behind him say, "That there is Curtis Mayhew."

Curtis turned around. Coming toward him was a slim and distinguished-looking white man—an older fellow, maybe in his early sixties—wearing a pressed gray suit and crisp fedora, a white shirt and a black tie with small white dots. He came on with a brisk stride, while Cricket made a motion at Curtis of shrugging his shoulders before he turned away to tend to his own self.

"Curtis Mayhew," said the white man when he reached the subject of his interest, and he looked Curtis up and down from the tips of his spit-shined shoes to the peak of his crimson cap.

"Yes suh, that's me."

"I am empowered to take you out of here to meet someone who very *much* wants to meet you."

"Who would that be, suh?"

"Curtis?" Ol' Crab must've seen Cricket bring the man in, because suddenly he was right there johnny-on-the-spot, positioning himself off to one side but nearly between them. "You entertainin' a visitor? Are you a traveller today, suh?" he asked, his gaze searching for the luggage that he knew was not there.

"I need to take this boy out of here for awhile," came the answer.

"Oh, you do? Well...seein' as he's workin' and we got trains due in and out of here 'fore he gets *off* work...I don't see how that's possible."

"Hm," said the man. He made his mouth crimp with irritation. Then he pulled out a thin wallet from inside his coat and produced a bill with Alexander Hamilton's portrait on it. He held it under Ol' Crab's nose and waved it as if spreading the heady perfume of money. "I imagine you're in charge of the Redcaps," he said. "Will this set him free for the rest of the day?"

Ol' Crab didn't look at the money. He smiled politely, "*Sir*," he said, sharpening the word, "if you don't remove that little slip a' green paper from in front of my face, I might forget I'm a gentleman and you're a white man."

"Oh, you want *twenty* dollars, then?"

"Can you tell me what's goin' on here?" Ol' Crab asked Curtis, as if the other man had simply evaporated.

"No he can't," the man answered firmly.

It struck Curtis who the man must be. "Are you from the *police*?"

"That's right."

"Hey, hey, hey!" Ol' Crab wore a frown that made every line in his face appear to be a bottomless trench. "What's this 'bout the police? Curtis, you in some trouble?"

"No sir, it's not me, it's—"

"It's official business," said the man. He pushed the ten dollar bill down into the breast pocket of Ol' Crab's jacket. "Take this and *fix* things. Can you do that?"

"I...reckon I...Curtis, I'll stand for you with the bossman, but...the *police*? Can't you tell me what's—"

"No, he cannot." The man took hold of Curtis's left elbow. "Come on, I've got a car waiting."

Ol' Crab kept pace with them to the station's entrance. Beyond the doors the rain was falling steadily, puddling the sidewalk and street. "Curtis!" Ol' Crab called. "You need me, you need anythin', you call me. Got change?"

"I do," Curtis answered. "Thank you, Mr. Crable."

"All right. I'll be callin' you later on to check up on you, now! Hear?"

"I hear," said Curtis, and then the man in the pressed gray suit and crisp fedora guided him toward the right rear door of a rain-speckled but shining black automobile with white-walled tires and chrome so bright it burned the eyes even on this day of gathered clouds. The door was opened for him, he was just about pushed into the plush tan-colored backseat, and there on the left side of the car sat a lean man in his mid-forties. This new man's angular face was turned toward Curtis, and Curtis thought that something about his light blue eyes looked both hopeful and terrified. He had reddish-blonde hair that was wildly tousled and needed combing, with hints of gray showing on the sides. He wore a plain white shirt with the sleeves rolled up and dark brown trousers, no hat and no coat.

"Where to?" the driver asked when he'd gotten behind the wheel, started the engine and turned on the wipers.

"Just drive, Victor."

The fine car pulled smoothly away from Union Station and headed west on South Rampart.

"My name is Jack Ludenmere," the man sitting beside Curtis said. "Before you speak one other word, I want you to tell me one thing about my daughter that it would be *impossible* for you to know without...without talkin' to her like she claims you do."

"Like what, suh?"

"Like...what does she want to be when she grows up."

"I never asked her that before." Curtis saw the man's slow blink. Then he said, "I'll ask her now, but I can't carry on two conversations at once. That's how this is."

Ludenmere's only response was an almost imperceptible nod.

:*Nilla,*: Curtis called while looking directly at her father. :*Nilla, you hear me?*:

A few seconds passed, and then came :*I hear you, we're sitting here waiting I don't know what for but Little Jack started crying and it was awfulIdidn'tknowwhattodoIjusthadto—*:

:*Slow down,*: he said. :*You're gettin' all garbled. Take a few deep breaths, that'll likely help.*:

"When are you gonna ask her?" Ludenmere spoke up, but Curtis paid him no attention and kept his focus on the girl.

:*I'm better now, I think,*: she came back. :*That man with the gun—Donnie—he's scaring me, Curtis. It's like the woman can hardly hold him back from shooting Mr. Hartley.*:

Curtis sent out, :*Nilla, I'm with your daddy right now, and a policeman named Victor. Don't get all rushed and garbled again, but answer me this question…what do you want to be when you grow up?*:

:*What? What're you asking?*:

:*Your daddy's testin' me. Would you answer that question, please?*:

:*I…said I wanted to be a nurse, but daddy says I'm smart enough to be a doctor.*:

:*All right. I'm gonna talk to him now, so I'm…*:: What did they say on the radio when the programs were over? :*I'm signin' off for just a little while,*: he said.

:*Curtis! Curtis! Tell daddy we're all right! Tell him I love him! Tell him we're scared but we're going to get home okay, I know we will!*:

:*I'll tell him,*: Curtis said, and then he felt the power between them fade like bright radio tubes diminishing to a soft glow…not completely gone, but resting. He seemed to have a fog over his eyes for a few seconds and he had to wait for it to fade as well. Then he said, "Nilla says to tell you they're all right, that she loves you, that they're scared but she knows they're gonna get home okay. To the question, she says…she wanted to be a nurse, but you say she's smart enough to be a doctor." He let that hang, and then he added, "I'd likely agree with you there."

Jack Ludenmere didn't move for what seemed to be a long time but was likely only a half-dozen beats of Curtis's heart. Ludenmere then took both hands and ran them up the sides of his face and into the distress of his hair; he leaned forward with his face almost to his knees and Curtis thought at first that the man was going to be sick. He stayed like that for several more seconds, and over the noise of the wipers and the purr of the car's engine Curtis heard him make one awful gasp for breath and then he was silent.

When Ludenmere sat back again the area beneath his eyes was gray and his face was slack.

"Tell me," he said in a feeble voice, "*how*…you can speak to Nilla that way. Is it…I mean…I know you people dabble in voodoo and such…and I don't give a damn about that, you do as you please…but is that what *this* is…a voodoo spell that somebody cast on her?"

"No, it's not that. Far from it."

"My daughter...my Nilla...she's not crazy. There's nothin' wrong with her mind."

"No, there's not," Curtis said, sensing that Ludenmere was nearly daring him to speak otherwise. "Nothin' wrong with my mind, either. My mama thought there was, for the longest time. Made me kinda start thinkin' it, myself."

"You mean this is like...a *natural* thing? I've never heard of anything like this before!"

"I don't know how natural it is. Maybe it's *supernatural*. But there's nothin' wrong with Nilla's mind, I can tell you that."

"So..." Ludenmere struggled to put his thoughts into words. "So you hear her voice in your head? And she hears yours?"

"No sir," Curtis replied, dropping the subservient softness because he knew that here it wasn't necessary. "It's not exactly like that. I don't hear the voice, but I hear the words. The same for her with me. She's told me so."

"My *God*," Ludenmere breathed. He looked as near to passing out as any man Curtis had ever seen. "I thought...my wife and I thought...she had made you up, just to annoy us. Then when she kept on with it...and told us she was talkin' to you and you were talkin' back...we thought... maybe somethin' was really wrong with her. My God, how can somethin' like this *be*?"

"Jack?" said Victor as he drove. "Can't help but overhear. Goes with what you've told me. I'm a fan of the writer Upton Sinclair. Ever read anything by him?"

"Huh? What's he got to do with it?"

"Four years ago he wrote and self-published a book titled *Mental Radio*, about his wife's mental telepathy. The jury's still out on that one and there are lots of questions, but...it's in the ether, so to speak."

"More than in the ether, whatever that is," Curtis said. "It's *real*." He realized they seemed to be driving pointlessly around the Union Station area. "Aren't we goin' to the police station?"

"No," said Ludenmere, "we are not."

"Your driver's a policeman, isn't he?"

"No. Never mind who he is. I want to know where my son and daughter are. Has she told you?"

"Yes sir. In Kenner. They're stopped somewhere in the woods. She says they're sittin' in the car waitin'."

"Waitin' on what?"

"I don't know, sir. I don't think she knows, either." He decided not to say anything about the gun, but he did decide to tell him the names as he understood them. "There's a man named Donnie and a woman named Vesta. She says Mr. Hartley was there, and Mr. Parr."

"He's a detective from Shreveport. But didn't she say there's another man?"

"Yes sir. I didn't get his name."

"They must be waitin' for him," Ludenmere said. "He's the one who made the phone call. From there I'll bet they're gonna take the kids to whatever hideout they've dug up."

"Can I ask…why we're not goin' to the police station?"

"The phone call, that's why." Ludenmere again ran a hand across his face and up into his hair. "The sonsofbitches—the kidnappers—say that if I bring the police into this they'll kill my children. I believe they will. They want two hundred thousand dollars delivered in a cardboard box to the end of a fishin' pier at one o'clock on Friday mornin'."

"Two hundred and fifteen thousand," Victor reminded him, and he honked the horn at a slow horse cart that had crossed the lane in front of the car.

"Yeah. That. Victor's my company lawyer. He can get the money for me. And you, Curtis…you're not leavin' my sight until I get my children back, safe and sound. Mental telepathy, mental radio, whatever the hell it is… you're my only way of keepin' contact with Nilla, so you're stickin' with me."

Curtis nodded; of course it made sense, but he still had to ask, "What about my job? I'm gonna lose it if I don't—"

"How much did you make last year?"

"I did pretty good," Curtis said. "Made nearly five hundred dollars."

"I'll pay you three times five hundred. When this is over, I'll go to bat for you with whoever needs to be persuaded. That suit you?"

"Yes sir. That's a mighty lot of money. I'd appreciate bein' able to give most of that to my mama and some to Mr. Crable, the man who's in charge of the Redcaps."

"Do whatever you like with it. I just want to keep in contact with Nilla. Can you speak to her now? Tell her I'm gonna get her and Little Jack out of this and not to worry?"

"Yes sir, I will."

Ludenmere watched Curtis's face; it didn't change very much, though the expression in the eyes seemed to go a little distant. Otherwise, in communicating with Nilla he was exactly as before. It was a mystery to Ludenmere and he didn't have the time or energy to try to figure it out. The most pressing and immediate things on his plate were getting the money and somehow telling Jane what was going on, and not having her crack to pieces. He would have to do that as soon as he brought Curtis through the front door. If she was back from her charity club meeting she would already be wondering why the kids were so late at coming home from school.

"Want me to keep driving around, Jack?" Victor asked.

"No," Ludenmere said with a heavy sigh, "it's time to head home."

Victor turned the car toward the Garden District and drove on through the gray rain.

Seventeen.

Ginger was out of the Olds in a flash when Pearly pulled up in the Ford on the muddy forest road. She was just as quickly on him nearly before he could get out of the car.

"How was it?" she asked.

"Fine. He bought it all." Pearly had gotten into a phone booth at the Rexall pharmacy and pressed a handkerchief against the phone's mouthpiece to muffle his voice, plus had spoken the terms in as raspy a whisper as he could manage. "How's everythin' here?"

She ignored the question because she was ready to roll. "You got the goods?"

"Got 'em." He went around and opened the passenger door. On the seat were two paper bags, one from the Rexall holding boxes of cotton wadding and a roll of electrical tape and in the other from a market near the Rexall—

"What're all the groceries for?" Her tone had sharpened. She'd looked into the second bag and seen four cans of pork 'n' beans, three apples, a loaf of bread and some ham spread, two bottles of Coca-Cola, three boxes of Cracker Jack, a roll of toilet paper, a kitchen knife with a serrated edge and a combination bottle and can opener. "You got twice as much stuff as I told you to get."

"I decided we might need it."

"You decided," she said. Her mouth went crooked. "*You* decided."

Pearly straightened his shoulders. He was ready to let her have it with both barrels. "There was one hitch." He saw her face instantly tighten.

"Ludenmere can't bring the money until one o'clock on Friday mornin'. He said he couldn't get hold of—"

"Bullshit," Ginger interrupted, and her eyes were fierce. She leaned in so close their noses nearly touched. "Bull...*shit.*" Her teeth were clenched. "You're tellin' me you let him off the hook for an extra day?"

"It was all I could do. He—"

"Oh, fuck that! Are you fuckin' *crazy*? You let him off the hook! Goddamn it, I told you...if he poor-mouthed about not bein' able to get the dough, you strong arm him! Tell him we're gonna cut the brats' ears off at five minutes after one if he doesn't show up with every fuckin' penny on *schedule*! Oh, no...oh, no...don't tell me you've fucked this up!" She put her hands on her hips and began to walk in circles from the car through the wet weeds and back again. She kept shaking her head, staring at the ground and saying "No, no...no, no," as raindrops speckled her hair.

"Okay, it's not the end of the world," Pearly said.

She ceased her circling and suddenly came at him almost at a run, and with such a rictus of rage on her face that the sharp point of a blade of terror pricked his throat. He balled his fists up, thinking that he might have to actually fight the bitch off.

She stopped short of attacking him. The champagne-colored eyes were full of fire. "Do you think this is a summer camp?" she asked through her gritted teeth. "Do you think we're gonna sit around the fire tonight and sing songs? You fucked up, Pearly. I thought you were a professional!"

"I've never kidnapped anybody before," he said. "Have you?"

"I know better than to give anybody time to *think*! Too much time, and he's gonna be thinkin' he ought to call the cops in! And now we've gotta babysit those two for a whole day and take care of that damned chauffeur!"

Pearly said, "I sweetened the deal by fifteen thousand bucks. Doesn't that count for anythin'?"

"No, it does not." Ginger looked up at the clouds as if trying to find an answer to her frustrations in the sky. When she returned her attention to Pearly her face was cold and the rain ran down her cheeks. "You just sit in the car. Donnie and I'll take care of the rest of it. Gimme the gun and the bag. Put the knife in it." She took the .38 and the Rexall bag when Pearly offered them, and he shrugged his shoulders and got back behind the Ford's steering wheel to gladly stay out of her way.

Ginger walked back to the Oldsmobile. She opened the left rear door and aimed the pistol at Hartley. "You. Out. Donnie, come on and help me."

"Either of you two move," Donnie told Nilla and Little Jack, "and you'll wish you weren't never born. Understand?"

"We understand," Nilla answered. She had just finished hearing from Curtis that her daddy said he was going to get them out of this and not to worry. She was near tears but she was not going to let herself break down, if only to be strong for her brother. She was tired and her head throbbed; she had never talked to Curtis like this for so long and so intensely, and she felt drained.

It was a blessing to know that Curtis could be reached—and through him her father—but she thought that much depended on her too because the mind-talking could only go so far and she was running out of strength.

"We're gonna be all right," Hartley told the children before he got out of the car. He faced the two guns and the two kidnappers, and he lifted his chin in defiance and said, "What now?"

"Take your shoes off and throw 'em in the woods," Ginger said. He did. "Open your coat," she ordered. When he obeyed, she told him to take his belt off and also throw it away. "Wallet," she said, and he gave that up to Donnie. She took his wristwatch and frisked him but left the small change in his pocket. Then Ginger said behind the unwavering pistol, "Stand real still, Hartley. Donnie, go ahead."

Donnie plucked the chauffeur's cap off, exposing Hartley's close-cropped gray hair, and put it on his own head at a rakish tilt. He opened one of the boxes of cotton. "Open your mouth," he demanded, and he forced a handful of cotton in. He cut a length of electrical tape with the knife, pressed it to Hartley's lips and wound it around the man's head. Then came wads of cotton pushed into the eyesockets and more tape around the head securing them. "Hands in front of you and clasp 'em," came the following command. The tape was wrapped tightly and securely around Hartley's wrists and hands. Though his fingers did have a few inches of freedom, his thumbs were trapped. He was then guided back to the car. Next out was Nilla, who was also made to throw away her shoes, have cotton stuffed into her mouth, pressed into her eyesockets and taped up, and her wrists and hands bound as Hartley's had been.

When it came time for Little Jack's binding, the boy had to be forcefully pulled out of the car by his legs, kicking and screaming. "Take those fuckin' Buster Browns off," Donnie said as he held Little Jack by the hair, and even though he had the gun in his hand he got a kick to the left shin that rattled his teeth and drew the water of pain to his eyes. For that transgression, Donnie released Little Jack's hair quick enough to give the boy a stinging slap to the face and then jammed a fistful of cotton into his mouth to swell Little Jack's cheeks. The tape went on and then Little Jack got the eye treatment, as rough as Donnie could give it.

"Easy with him," Ginger cautioned. "Don't break the merchandise."

"I ought to break his fuckin' neck. I'm gonna have a knot on my leg for a week." Donnie grabbed a handful of the boy's hair again, violently shook Little Jack's head back and forth and hissed in a taped-up ear, "Oh yes…you and me are gonna have some real fun, kid." He nearly jerked the boy's arms out of their sockets, and Ginger held Little Jack still by the shoulders while Donnie taped the hands.

Sitting in the car next to Clay Hartley with her mouth full of cotton, her eyes blinded and her hands bound, Nilla tried as hard as she could to focus on speaking to Curtis through her terror. :*Curtis, are you there?*:

He didn't respond. :*Curtis? Please answer.*: She felt a sob rise up in her throat; the sticky black tape had gone around her head and over both ears and all she could hear at the moment was the roar of her own blood rushing through the veins.

Then, after what seemed an agonizingly long time…:*I'm here, Nilla. You're soundin' weak…real far away.*:

:I'm so tired…my head aches something awful. Are you still with my daddy?:

:Yes. He's takin' me back to your house. I'm gonna stay with him 'til you get home.:

:They've put cotton in our mouths and over our eyes. They've got us taped up, I can't see anything. Oh, Curtis…my mama…she's going to be so worried.:

:Your daddy told me so. He said he doesn't know how she's gonna take this, but he has to tell her as soon as we get there.:

:I'm about to start crying. I can't do that…I just can't. If I start…I don't know if I can stop. Tell me something good, Curtis…something good so I won't cry,: she said.

:Well…I never asked you that question, about what you wanted to be when you grow up. How come you'd like to be a nurse?:

She had to make herself swallow the sob, and it went down like a lump of coal. *:I like studying health,:* she sent to him. *:It's my best subject in school.:*

:That's a fine ambition,: Curtis replied. *:Always need good nurses, I suspect. Who knows? Maybe along the way you might decide to be a doctor.:*

:Being a doctor…seems like it would be awful hard to…OH!: she said, with an intensity that caused her head to ache even worse. *:The car door slammed! Now…they're getting in…the engine's starting. We're moving again!:*

:All right, Nilla. I'm gonna tell your daddy what's happenin'. You're soundin' kinda weak and I think it's 'cause you've got all this in your head. Just remember…I'm here and your daddy's here, and he's told me he's workin' on gettin' those people the money they want, then it'll all be over and that'll be real soon.:

:All right,: she said, and she nodded but again the storm of tears was threatening. *:All right, I'll remember.:*

"What'd you nod your head for?" It was Donnie's voice, harsh and loud. "I didn't ask you anythin'. You! Girlie! I'm talkin' to you!" She felt something hard prod her shoulder and realized it must be the gun's barrel.

"She can't answer," Ginger said quietly. And added: "*Fool.*" She was following Pearly in the Ford ahead, as they turned to the right onto the rainswept main road.

"Oh. Yeah. Well, hell…she nodded like she was…I don't know… listenin' to somethin'. Weird."

"Stop wavin' that gat around and sit tight. In about three minutes I want Hartley's head pushed down. Nobody'll see the kids. *You* listen for when I tell you, and do it quick."

"Yes, master sergeant ma'am," Donnie said, and he gave both a salute and a blast of a forced laugh that blew a flying tendril of snot out of his right nostril.

In the Ford leading the kidnap parade, Pearly was still burnt up over taking a shellacking from the enraged woman. Sure, he knew he'd given Ludenmere an extra day and that could be a dangerous thing, but the added fifteen thousand meant something…didn't it?

"Hell with it," he said, and watched the community of Kenner come up through the woods.

They were on Sawmill Road, the main road into town. Other dirt and gravel roads led off to the right going to various cabins and fishing camps. About a half-mile from where they'd pulled off to bind up the kids and Hartley—an act that Ginger had said they needed to do to assert their control over the victims and keep them docile driving through town—was a wooden board on a pole indicating Sandusky Road, and at the end of that would be the fishing pier they'd scouted out as the money-drop location.

Here and there along Sawmill Road stood rustic cabins, some so rustic they looked as if they'd been uninhabited since the Civil War. Pearly thought that Kenner might be a town with a future, as the sign back there had said, but the future was yet a long ways off. The thick pine and scrub woods gave way to a railroad siding on the left where a few worn-looking boxcars languished waiting to be called to service, followed in a hundred yards by a small gas station, then a cemetery, a white stone church, a few brick or wooden houses, and a business district of about two blocks. A couple of other cars passed and a haywagon was on the road, but other than that Kenner was asleep in the drowsy rain. Pearly passed a cafe, a hardware store, a place with a sign that said *Evie's "Everything" Shoppe*, a brick structure that was half-finished and had a wheelbarrow of bricks out front but no workers visible, a squat little building that might have served as the town hall next to a so-called park where grass was as sparse as hair on a bald head, a few more houses and that was Kenner.

Again the woods closed in. Here and there another road led off to the right, heading to more fishing cabins on the Pontchartrain. Pearly was a little more than a quarter mile from crossing over Jefferson Parish into St. Charles Parish when he slowed at a road marked only by four round and rusted cannonballs piled up and sealed together in the chickweeds. *Cannonball Road, they're gonna name it soon as they get the papers done*, the man at the rental office in Metairie had said. *Yep, the fishin' is real good out that way but the swamp's your nextdoor neighbor so keep your snakestick handy, you go out strollin'*.

We'll do that, Pearly had told the man, as Ginger and Donnie had waited in the car outside.

Hope to catch some big fish the next few days, but the point is to scout this area and look for investments. Time seems to be right to put some money down on land up in there.

Sounds like a plan. Sorry I can't rent you a cabin with indoor plumbin' and electricity. Then again...none of 'em's got any of that. If you're interested, I got a marina for sale at Boar's Head Point...took some damage in that last blow we had, but for eight hundred bucks you could clean it up and call y'self an admiral.

I'll get back to you on that, Pearly had said, wanting to finish the business of renting the cabin for two dollars a day—cash in advance, three day minimum—and get out of there as fast as possible.

He took the right turn onto Cannonball Road, drove between pine forest through several mud puddles, and pulled up alongside a cabin with wood so weathered it had turned nearly black and as shiny in the wet as fresh tar. The tin roof looked like it had barely survived a hailstorm of boulders. Weeping willow trees overhung the place and the broken remnants of scraggly pines nearer the lake showed that the last blow had indeed been a whopper. An outhouse stood behind the cabin and a path led over a four-foot-high mound of earth to the fishing pier, which Pearly had already seen had a precarious lean to the left. Beside the pier was a waist-high oak stump where the fish were cleaned, and nearby a firepit to cook up the finnies. The place was a far holler from the Lafayette Hotel and it made the King Louis look like a dreamboat...but they were alone out here in the sticks, and that was all that mattered.

Ginger pulled up in the Olds. She and Donnie got out and then began the task of herding Hartley and the children out of the car and marching them to the cabin. On the way, Little Jack fell down and Donnie jerked him up by the collar and gave him a shake before shoving him on.

As he entered the cabin with the bag of groceries, Pearly thought the fishermen who rented this dismal hole either liked punishment or were too cheap to buy a fifteen-cent French Quarter trout. The front room was furnished only with a few wicker chairs, a knife-scarred table and on the floor a worn-out brown throwrug made of coiled rope. In what passed as a kitchen there was a small wood-burning stove, a green formica-topped table and four chairs, some cabinets holding plates, cups and saucers, a tarnished coffee pot and a tray of silverware. The bare-mattressed cot and pillow that Donnie had slept on last night was beside a door at the rear of the place, which led to a screened-in porch, a screened door and a couple of wooden steps going down to the yard. Two other rooms were behind closed doors on the right and the left, both of them little more than good-sized closets. In the room on the right was a bunkbed and a small desk. The room on the left had been prepared for the new arrivals. A pair of oil lamps sat on the scarred table, along with a bull's-eye lantern and a regular flashlight. The windows were curtained with a pattern of sea anchors and leaping marlin, cutting what light there was to a gray haze. The whole place smelled to Pearly like the lake had more than once flooded over the pitiful levee and left its brackish mud between the rough floorboards, which was likely true.

"Keep movin'," Ginger said, and pushed Hartley when he stopped. "Donnie, open the door for 'em. Pearly, bring a flashlight in."

He put the grocery bag on the table and did as she asked. The room they were being herded into was completely bare except for a wooden bucket in a corner. The single window had been boarded up both inside and outside, the nails sunken deeply so no fingers however desperate and bloody could work them out.

"Take their blindfolds and gags off," she told Donnie. "Do it *easy*, don't tear anythin'. Pearly, keep that light in their eyes."

Donnie tucked the chauffeur's pistol into his waistband and went about the work, which turned out to be such a mess that after the cotton was removed the wads of tape had to be cut out of their hair with the kitchen knife, a process that made Hartley and the children stand as still as statues and Little Jack's eyes widen with terror in his mud-streaked face.

"Leave the wrist-bindin's on," Ginger directed when Donnie had finished. Then, to Hartley: "Welcome to your new home for the next couple of nights. It's not what you're used to, I'm guessin', but it's all we got. If Mr. Ludenmere is a good boy you'll be out of here soon, and we're figurin' he'll be a *real* good boy."

"It stinks in here even worse than that man's breath," said Little Jack, who had regained some of his fire. Nilla nudged him with an elbow to keep his mouth shut, but she knew that was like trying to put a cork in a beehive.

"It likely won't smell any sweeter," Ginger answered, with a soft and heartless smile. "Your bucket over there is what you get. There won't be much light in here during the day, and none after dark. You'll sleep on the floor, if you care to sleep. Hartley, you see this door?"

"I see it," he said.

"There's no lock on it. Now...we didn't expect you to stay overnight... so...we're gonna up-end that table and prop it against the door, and any little wiggle we see or skreechy noises we hear, we're not gonna like."

Hartley said, "The children are worth money. You won't hurt them."

"Well, you're right and *wrong* about that. We won't kill 'em, is what you mean to say. Now you…you're not worth a motherfuckin' dime, is what I figure. In fact, you're just dead weight already, aren't you?"

Hartley didn't reply, because he knew how true the woman's words were.

Nilla spoke up, though her heart was beating hard and she felt like she might fall down any minute and curl up into a whimpering ball. "Mr. Parr, I thought you were my daddy's friend."

It took him a few seconds to formulate an answer. "Kid, my friends are in your daddy's wallet, and I want all of 'em I can get. It won't be too long 'til I've got a load of new friends in my pockets. Then it'll all be over and you can go home."

"Sure," Ginger replied, in a voice that sounded listless. "Like he said."

"Put that light on the fucker's face," Donnie said, and he reached over to grasp Pearly's wrist and aim the flashlight's beam. "Look at how that damn eye shines! Weird…he squints with the good eye but the other one don't flinch."

"We've done enough," said Ginger. "Let's leave 'em be for now."

"Wait…wait. That damn eye gives me the fuckin' creeps. How am I gonna sleep out there tonight knowin' this thing is in here?"

"You'll just have to tough it out."

"Tough it out, my ass. I'm takin' it." Donnie drew the pistol from his waistband and took a step toward Hartley. Instantly the chauffeur retreated.

"Donnie! Come on, I said!"

"AND I SAID I'M TAKIN' IT!" the young man bellowed, and when Pearly aimed the light at Donnie he saw a face contorted with hatred and rage, the crimson blood spreading up from the thick neck in an instant to swell the cheeks and lips and put a reddish gleam in the slits of the eyes. "HEAR ME?" he challenged. There seemed to pass a long moment of terrible silence broken only by the harsh rasp of Donnie's breathing and the patter of new rain on the tin roof. Nilla pressed close against her brother and in her mind spoke not to Curtis but to God, *Help us, please help us.*

"All right, Heinz," Ginger said soothingly, as if she were trying to calm a wild beast. "All right, take it easy. Go ahead and do it, if it's what you want."

"*It is.*" With those two words he rushed upon Hartley, put the pistol to the side of the man's head and clasped his free hand to Hartley's left eye-socket. Hartley shivered, but he did not fight.

The hand worked and worked, and Pearly found himself keeping the light aimed at the drama because there was a mad sickness to it that fascinated him. It was like watching an ultimate violation, for one man to pluck the eye of another. Hartley gave a gasp, there was a damp sucking sound, and when Donnie's hand came away the wet red hole in the chauffeur's face was a ghastly sight…yet to Pearly, it was a show of power over another human being that he could not help but appreciate.

"Okay, you happy now?" Ginger asked.

"Sure am." Donnie's voice was a little giddy. He opened his fist to let the glass eye shine in the flashlight's beam. "Thing's still warm." He closed his fist around it again, held it up to his ear and shook it as if expecting it to give off a rattle.

Ginger left the room and Donnie followed with his new prize. Pearly swept his light over the fearful faces of the children and the one-eyed face of Clay Hartley. "Just settle down and don't cause us any trouble," he told them. "The quicker this is over, the better." He backed out of the room and closed the door.

A single crack of light crept between the boards in the prison room, but that was all the illumination they were going to get. Nilla was aware of Mr. Hartley just standing there motionless, and then she made out that his bound hands came up and the fingers touched gently around the gaping hole where his eye had been.

"Sorry, children." His voice was as hoarse as if he'd been shouting for an hour against hurricane winds. "That wasn't too pleasant, was it?"

"Did it hurt?" Little Jack asked.

"Not too much."

"I shoulda kicked that man harder."

"Listen to me, both of you," Hartley said sternly. "Do not aggravate these people. Do you know what that word means?"

"I do," said Nilla. And for her brother's benefit she added, "Not to get them riled up."

"Correct. We'll have to stay the night, but we'll likely get out of here soon. We'll make do, won't we?"

"Yes sir," both of them replied, Nilla more positively than Little Jack.

"It's so dark in here," Little Jack said. "And I've gotta pee somethin' awful."

"Bucket's in the corner," Hartley answered. "If you miss it, I don't think anybody'll mind."

"You mean...I've gotta pee in front of my *sister*?"

"Yep. Good thing it's so dark in here, huh?"

"Oh go on, Little Jack," said Nilla. "Don't be a baby about it."

"I'll pee on you if I've got a mind to."

"Go use the bucket," Hartley said. "Go on, it's only about three steps over there."

Little Jack went over to it with a grudging step and a sigh of resignation.

Nilla sat down on the floor in the far corner. She leaned back against the wall, closed her eyes and tried to imagine herself sitting in her room at the house, but her imagination wasn't that refined. :*Curtis?*: she sent out.

He came back almost at once. :*I'm here.*:

:*Where are you?*:

:*I'm with your daddy at the house. Never been in a place like this before, 'bout took my breath away. Your daddy's gone to talk to your mama. Where are you?*:

:*In a room in a terrible old cabin. There's no light in here. That man—Donnie—took Mr. Hartley's glass eye out. I think he's crazy. He got so mad his face went red...and the woman called him Heinz. I guess because of the ketchup.*:

Curtis did not reply.

:*You still there?*: she asked.

:*Yes. You say she called him Heinz?*:

:*Yes.*:

:*That's funny,*: Curtis said. :*Not in a laughin' way, but funny.*:

:*There's nothing to laugh about here. I feel like crying but I can't, not in front of Little Jack.*:

:*Do you have any idea where the cabin is?*:

:*I don't know if we're in Kenner or past it. After they put the cotton and tape over our eyes they drove for what seemed like another fifteen minutes, but we only made the one right turn.*:

:*So you must be on the lake side,*: he said. :*Probably past the town.*:

:*Maybe, I don't—*:

Her concentration was interrupted by a thunderous hammering on the door that caused her to catch her breath and jump so hard she hurt her back against the rough boards.

"Y'all don't get too comfortable in there," Donnie said beyond the door, and he laughed like a gunshot.

Eighteen.

Heinz, Curtis thought as he sat in an overstuffed chair in the Ludenmere's palatial parlor.

He remembered a young white man who had bumped into him at Union Station and whose face had gone ketchup-red with anger. There had been a woman and another man with him, and the woman had called the angry gent *Heinz.* The same trio who had kidnapped Nilla and Little Jack? Bad people travelled by train just as well as good people, so—

He had lost his connection with Nilla. He was about to call her again when Ludenmere came into the room, gray-faced and weary-looking, and eased himself down into a chair opposite Curtis.

"I was just speakin' to Nilla," Curtis explained. "She says they're in a cabin, maybe past Kenner but for sure on the lakeside 'cause they made a right turn off the main road."

"Doesn't help much," Ludenmere said in a tired voice. He leaned his head back and closed his eyes. "Lots of cabins and fishin' camps up in there. Even if I was to know the exact cabin…I'm not gonna do anythin' to bring harm to my children. *Our* children," he corrected.

Curtis had heard a single heart-wrenching cry from upstairs about ten minutes ago, then silence. "Was it bad?" he asked.

"Bad. She has some prescribed sedatives, so I gave her one and maybe she can sleep for awhile. Jane…keeps up appearances to outsiders, but she's fragile." His eyes opened but they looked bleary, the blue color washed out.

"Her father is a wealthy corporate attorney in Shreveport. What people don't know is that he's an alcoholic and a ragin' bully. He didn't treat Jane or her sister very well growin' up. Both of them can put on a good show… but both of them paid for the abuse and they're still payin' for it. Any issue that causes what I'd guess you'd call stress…it's doubly hard on her."

"Maybe you should call a doctor?"

"I thought about it. Maybe I should. Maybe that would be what a good husband should do…but the doctor'll be askin' questions, Jane's liable to blurt out the story, the doc goes to the police in spite of my tellin' him to stay quiet or he tells somebody else who goes to either the police or the newspaper…I can't chance that. Not right here with everythin' set for Friday mornin'. No, I've got to handle this on my own." Ludenmere turned his tortured face toward the picture window. "I was Jane's knight in shinin' armor," he said quietly. "But I guess…in time, all armor gets tarnished."

"I think you're doin' what you believe to be the best," Curtis said.

"Yeah. The thing is, if somethin' happens to our children…I'll lose Jane too. She'll drift away from me, I know. It'll be the end of…well, of everythin' I've ever found good and worthwhile in this world." He suddenly shook his head and gave a mirthless laugh. "Listen to me! Talkin' to you like I've known you all my life! Like you're a family friend and not a—" He paused, his mouth still open.

"Not a Negro?" Curtis prompted, but it was spoken calmly and with truth.

"Not a *stranger*," said Ludenmere. "I don't give a damn what color you are. You're my connection to Nilla and that's all that matters. Maybe you're *her* knight in shinin' armor."

"My armor's not too shiny," Curtis said.

"Well, bein' a *black* knight, I guess that's true."

In spite of the trials and tribulations of the day, that struck Curtis as just being doggoned funny. He couldn't suppress the laugh that spilled out. And in spite of the heaviness he was feeling—and maybe because of it—Ludenmere had to give up a genuine laugh too, and after the laugh came out and rang around the room he felt both lighter and steadier.

"What's gonna happen tomorrow," he said when the laugh had faded, "is…Victor'll bring the box of money in the early afternoon. Then you and me are gonna drive out to find Sandusky Road and that fishin' pier. I don't want to be tryin' to find it in the dark." He stood up from the chair. "I'd best go sit with Jane. Listen…you can have the guest bedroom upstairs. Mavis'll show you. It's got its own bathroom. Anythin' you want to eat…we've got a lot of food in the kitchen. Mavis is a good cook, too. Steaks, ham, bread for sandwiches…ice cream and cake…got a whole fresh—" He paused again, looking like a man who was desperately trying to avoid a step that would send him plunging off a cliff, and then he said lamely, "Melon."

"Watermelon?" Curtis asked.

"Yeah. That."

"One of my favorites," Curtis said, with a slight smile. "Haven't had but two all summer."

"Help yourself, and like I say Mavis'll cook you up whatever else you'd like."

"Thank you." Curtis motioned toward a telephone on a table across the room. "Can I use that? I'd better call my mama, she'll be worryin'."

"Sure, go ahead. Oh…would you speak to Nilla again, tell her I've got everythin' under control and it won't be long now before she and Little Jack are home?"

"I'll do it right now." Curtis was anxious to restore the connection with Nilla, since she'd been interrupted in mid-sentence before. :*Nilla,*: he sent out. :*You okay?*:

:*Yes,*: she answered. And then, :*Kind of okay, I guess.*:

Her sending was weak, fading in and out like a device with dying batteries.

Curtis said, :*You need to rest yourself. Get your strength back. Will you be able to sleep any?*:

:*No, I don't think so.*:

:*Well, try. It'll be good for you. Your daddy's here with me. He says to tell you he's got everythin' under control and it won't be long before you and Little*

Jack are home.: When she didn't respond after a few seconds he asked, :*Can you hear me?*:

:*I hear you…but I'm awful scared, Curtis. That man Donnie keeps pounding on the door every few…seems like. Maybe they don't…sleep. We're getting hungry too, we don't have any…use the bathroom in a…have to go pretty soon, I think, but at least…any light at all.*:

:*You need to rest,*: he insisted. :*Rest your body and your mind.*:

:*What? I didn't…all that.*:

This was new and disturbing, he thought. Nilla was worn out and her sending was wearing out too. If she didn't get some rest he might lose her completely, and obviously her tired brain wasn't able to pick up all his sending either. :*I'm gonna sign off now,*: he told her. :*I'll try back later, but please… please…you try to—*:

:*What? What did you say? I can't…so far away.*:

:*Your daddy says he loves you,*: Curtis said, and with that he looked up at Ludenmere, spent a few seconds refocusing on where he was and to whom he was speaking, and he said, "She says they're doin' all right. Says they're ready to come home."

"I'll get them back safe and sound. I swear to God I will."

"Yes sir," Curtis said.

"The phone's yours," Ludenmere told him. He started to leave the room but hesitated.

"I was so wrong about Nilla…about this…*gift* of hers. And yours too. I'll never understand it if I live to be a hundred and ten, but I thank you for bein' here to help, and I thank you for bein' my daughter's friend."

"I appreciate her bein' a friend to me," Curtis replied. "She's a mighty good listener."

Ludenmere nodded, turned and left the room, and Curtis sat in the chair thinking it was best he didn't know that Nilla's power was weakening, and that if she didn't sleep—or at least rest her burdened mind—it might be impossible to reach her. He figured she likely knew something was wrong, and why. It would be up to her to find the strength of will to fix it, and he thought she would just have to make herself go blank to recharge her mental energy, if she could.

He had never realized there was a limit to it. He didn't know if he liked that or not because as much as he was pleased at being called someone's knight in shining armor he was also pleased to know that there were chinks in the armor and someday it might weaken on him too. It made him feel a little more like everyone else in the world and not as much as the supernatural rarity Lady had made him out to be that night in Congo Square. He was just a young man, after all, a Redcap and proud of the work of helping people get from here to there and back again.

He got up from the chair and went across the sand-colored rug to the telephone.

Orchid answered on the fourth ring. She had trained herself to sound near dead even in her most excitable moods. "Hello?"

"Hi, Mama."

"*Curtis*! Oh my Lord, are you callin' from the jailhouse?"

He gazed around the wonderful room. "No, I'm not. I guess Mr. Crable called you?"

"Yes he did! Told me the whole tale! Who's got you messed up with the law? That Rowdy Patterson fella, that big ol' loudmouth piece a' skunk?"

"Mama," Curtis said calmly, "just listen, will you? I'm not messed up with the law. I'm—"

"When are you comin' home, then? I'm gettin' sick worryin'!"

"I'm...doin' somethin' important," he told her. "I won't be—"

"Come on home, now! Hear? I'll leave the lights on, you come on home right this minute."

"I won't be home tonight, Mama," Curtis pressed on. "Likely not tomorrow—"

"That's a fool talkin' a fool's talk! Boy can't run off from home and leave a sick mama behind, Lord God mercy no! You don't sound y'self, you're with somebody gonna get you all messed up!"

Curtis felt her swaying him, as she always did, but on this day he was rooted. "Mama, what I have to do is—"

"I don't wanna hear it, I don't wanna—"

"*Listen to me!*" he said, and the sharpness of his voice shocked him as much as it did Orchid because both of them became silent. When he'd recovered himself, he went on into her silence. "I'm not gonna explain it. It's somethin' important I have to do. I won't be home tonight or tomorrow night. This is for *me*, as much as for anybody else. Can you understand that?"

It seemed a long time before she answered.

"Come home," she whispered, in a broken voice. "Joe, come home."

"Mama," Curtis said quietly, "you need to get back into life. You have to. You're not dyin', you're not sick. You *want* to be, but you're not. You've turned away from the neighbors, and the church, and ever'body who matters. I think you have to find a new start, Mama. Put all this behind you… just let it go. Maybe it would be a good thing for you to go visit Maw and Pap. A healthy thing. Just for a few days, just to hear somebody else talkin'. And you know how Pap likes to play his guitar. I'll bet he's come up with a whole slew of new songs."

She didn't reply, but Curtis could hear her slow and shallow breathing as if she were trying to urge up a cough.

"Nobody feels sorry for you but yourself," Curtis said. "I love you, and that's why I'm tellin' you true because you've got a whole life ahead of you that you're tryin' to throw away. Joe is gone and he's not comin' back, Mama. That's the *real* of things, and that's where you need to start."

She didn't answer for so long that he had to prompt her to speech. "Hear what I'm sayin'?"

Orchid said, "I'm leavin' the lights on 'til you come home," and then she hung up the phone.

Curtis listened to the dial tone for a few seconds, as if from it he were gathering some kind of message. He figured the message was that his mama was going to go to bed the same as always and tomorrow would be the same as always and the day after that without change. How he could push her back into life, he didn't know. He replaced the receiver in its cradle, walked to the window and looked out upon the grand Ludenmere property, which to him was truly another realm and beat all to pieces the measly Gordon estate. The rain had stopped but everything was still dripping. The light was beginning to fade, the world turning a darker gray under a cloud-covered sky. He thought about trying to contact Nilla again, but dismissed it because her batteries needed a rest and maybe his did too.

Someone cleared their throat behind him. He turned around and found that the maid, Mavis, was standing at the parlor's threshold.

"Suh?" she asked, with that softness in the word designed to carry the note of subservience, "would you be havin' supper?"

"I would be. And I'm not a 'sir', I'm just plain Curtis."

She nodded but she looked confused, because obviously he was a guest in the house and, though he was a Negro and never had there been a Negro guest in this house and surely not one to sleep in the guest bedroom as Mr. Ludenmere had told her this young man was going to be doing tonight, he must be of some important status or he would not have been allowed to set foot in here.

She cast her gaze up and down his uniform and then glanced at his red cap on the table where he'd placed it. "Mind my askin', are you a soldier?"

"No'm, I'm a Redcap at the Union Station."

"I didn't hear that Mr. and Mrs. Ludenmere are takin' a trip," she said. Her own world had never included train travel. Her brow furrowed. "Mind my askin', where are the children tonight?"

Curtis figured she couldn't ask the master of the house that question without seeming to overstep her boundaries, but to him she could. "They'll be home soon," he answered, and she knew that was all she was going to get even though she'd heard Mrs. Ludenmere give a pitiful cry and something was very wrong with the orderly nature of the house, but in keeping with her place she continued what would be her usual duties by asking, "What would Mr. Curtis like for supper this evenin'?"

It was a question he had never been asked before in his life.

"You decide," he told her.

Her mouth opened and then closed again and she looked completely lost. Curtis thought that maybe no one had ever offered her the chance to make her own decision...so here they stood in the beautiful room, neither speaking, each uncomfortable in their unaccustomed freedom, both waiting on the other like shadows soon to pass.

Night had fallen, the full dark of the countryside far away from the smear of lights and the sound of cars on concrete. Around the cabin on the lake the crickets, cicadas and other insects in the woods were sending out their music of clicks and chirrups, clacks and drones. The air had turned heavy, the rain had ceased, and in the wet heat the mist rose from Lake Pontchartrain and slowly drifted through the forest leaving pieces of itself hanging in the pines and oaks like old fragments of fragile and yellowed linen.

In the total darkness of the prison room, Nilla heard the sound of the heavy table being moved from the door. Several times she had tried to sleep and had failed. Little Jack's bravado had broken again what might have been two hours ago, and he had begun to cry in the dark until she had gotten up next to him, shoulder-to-shoulder. Hartley had attempted to ease their situation by starting the game of Twenty Questions but Little Jack wouldn't play and Nilla felt so tired and listless she couldn't concentrate.

"Everybody stay still," Hartley cautioned from his sitting position on the floor across the room.

The door opened and a glare of light intruded. It was only the flame of an oil lamp, yet its brightness stung their eyes.

"Three blind mice," said Donnie as he followed the light into the room. He closed the door behind him and stood directing the lamp's glow all around the cramped little chamber. "*Now* it smells bad in here," he said. "Who had the runs?"

Nilla longed to tell the man to get out and leave them alone, but she feared even speaking to him.

"Isn't it past your bedtime?" Hartley asked.

"Naw. The others are out smokin' on the back porch, thought I'd step in and visit for awhile. Hey, how do you like *this*?" Donnie knelt down on the floor and lifted the lamp so Hartley could see the gleaming glass eye stuck to the center of his forehead with electrical tape. "Now I'm a three-eyed sonofabitch. How 'bout that?" When Hartley remained silent, Donnie said, "I asked you a question, asshole face…how 'bout that?"

"Fine," said Hartley.

"*Fine*, he said," Donnie grinned in the light at Nilla. "Ain't I pretty, little girl?"

"Yes," she answered, staring at the opposite wall.

"Damn right. *Handsome*, I should say. Got three eyes the better to see you with, Little Red Ridin' Hood. Hey, what's your daddy call you?"

"Nilla."

"I mean…like…a pet name. I'll bet he's got one for you. Like… Sugarlips, or Sweet Fanny, or—"

"Why don't you leave us alone?" Hartley said. "Isn't it enough that we're in here with no food or water, and—"

"*Shut up*," Donnie said, with a harsh rasp of dread menace in his voice. "If I want to hear you fart, I'll kick it out of you." He moved the lamp a few inches so it shone more fully on Little Jack, who had pressed up close against his sister and clenched her fingers as much as he was able with his hands bound before him. "Look at the tough guy now," said Donnie. "You been cryin', toughie?"

"*No*," the boy said, throwing the word like a poisoned dart.

"Well now, that's a damn lie, ain't it? Your eyes are all puffed up, looks like somebody's been doin' a two-step on your face. How do you like where you are, toughie? Kinda a far piece from your rich daddy's mansion. Bet you've got all the toys and games and shit you ever wanted, don't you? Bet you just have to name somethin' you want and it's handed right to you, no sweat. Huh? Ain't that so?"

"No."

"I'll bet." Donnie sat in silence for a time, as Nilla's heart continued to thud in her chest with fear of the man. "One thing your goddamned daddy has failed at, boy," Donnie went on, "is teachin' you respect for your elders. You're supposed to call me 'sir' when you speak to me."

"I won't speak to you anymore, then," said Little Jack. "Go back to your hole."

Hartley winced. Nilla thudded her shoulder against her brother's to warn him to silence, but the words were out and gone.

Donnie gave a hard laugh followed by a low whistle. He brought the lamp over closer to Nilla and Little Jack and crouched there barely two feet away, while Hartley was gathering his strength to scrabble into action if need be.

"You," said Donnie to Little Jack, "are a piece a' work. I might admire your balls if you didn't piss me off so bad. Hey, think fast!" He reached out and slapped the boy across the side of the face. "Think fast!" he said, and slapped him again on the other side.

"For God's sake," Hartley growled. "Leave the boy alone! If you want to bully somebody, come bully me!"

"Naw, that ain't no fun. Think faster!" *Smack*, went the slap. It had been a harder blow, and the sound of it made Nilla's stomach churn. She thought if she threw up on him he would leave but there was nothing in her to expel.

"Stop it!" Little Jack said, with the first glimmers of fresh tears in his eyes. "I didn't—"

Smack! And that was the hardest slap yet. In the lamplight Nilla saw her brother give a stunned blink and a thread of blood broke over his lower lip.

Hartley struggled to his feet before the next blow could be delivered. "All right," he said. "You want to fight, let's get to it. I'll knock your teeth out with my hands bound up."

"Will you, now? Huh," said Donnie, and as he came up off the floor Nilla saw his face turn red just before he drove a tremendous punch into Hartley's groin. Their chauffeur doubled over, gasping. Donnie hammered him across the back of the head with a noise like an axe hitting timber and Hartley went down face-first to the floor.

"Help!" Nilla suddenly shouted. "Help us, please!"

At once Donnie had spun around, leaned in and gripped her chin in a hand like a crushing vise. His enraged face loomed as large as an ugly planet. She felt his fingers tighten as if he were trying to crack open a walnut. Then there was a solid-sounding *thunk*, Donnie released her and staggered back, and beside Nilla Little Jack was staggering too, his eyes rolling up from the force of the headbutt he'd just delivered to the side of Donnie's skull. He fell to his knees and leaned over and Nilla saw the terrifying sight of her brother's blood drops spattering the floorboards from his busted lip.

"Fuck all, what're you tryin' to *do*?" came what was nearly a scream from the doorway. Nilla squinted into the beam of the flashlight the woman held, and behind her was the shape of the man who had betrayed her father.

"Donnie!" Ginger shrieked. "You fuckin' idiot! What have you done to 'em?"

"Fun…havin' some fun, that's all," Donnie answered. His voice sounded like he was eating a bowl of mush. "Hartley came at me, I had to put him down." He shook his head back and forth to stop the bells ringing. "Little bastard popped me in the head, I had to lay him down too."

"That's a lie!" Nilla shouted, and she felt her own face swell with the blood of anger. "All of that's a lie! That man kept slapping Little Jack!"

"Okay, okay!" Ginger held up a hand to silence everyone. Hartley was groaning and doubled up on the floor. "What'd you do to him?"

"He ain't hurt, not too bad. Hey, I'm gettin' bored just sittin' and countin' my warts."

Ginger swung the flashlight's beam into Donnie's face. The glass eye gleamed on his forehead in its nest of black tape. He gave a toothy smile though his own eyes were still dazed and the silver fang in his mouth gleamed.

"You're makin' me crazy," Ginger said.

"Well," he answered, "that wouldn't be too hard to do, would it?"

Something seemed to rush into the room. Pearly felt it, like another presence that had suddenly elbowed its way in. Even though the air in the cabin was warm and damp, he felt a chill gnawing at his bones.

Ginger kept the light aimed into Donnie's stupidly-grinning face. Her hot anger had gone away, but the cool quiet of her voice was to Pearly somehow worse when she spoke a single word, delivered with menacing power: "*Don't*."

Donnie shrugged. "Ain't nothin' to me."

Nilla was beside her brother, who was spitting blood. Little Jack gave a shudder but he did not cry or release a single sob; it seemed to her that he might never cry again, and that suddenly he was far older than his eight years of life. "I'm all right," he said, and even his voice sounded more manly. She crawled over to see about Mr. Hartley, who was trying to sit up and having a tough time of it.

She looked up at the three kidnappers who stood between her and the door. "We need some food and water," she told them. "Can't we have any?"

"Donnie," Ginger said, "go get the canteen."

"Why me?"

"Because I'm tellin' you to, that's why. Pearly, watch 'em a minute." She went out to where the grocery bag sat on the kitchen table. They'd gone through two cans of pork 'n' beans, one of the bottles of Coca-Cola and Donnie had chomped down two of the apples. She didn't feel like opening the ham spread for sandwiches or opening another can of the pork 'n' beans. She plucked out one of the boxes of Cracker Jack and took that back to the room. "Here," she said, and threw it on the floor between Nilla and Hartley. "That'll have to do." Donnie came in with a metal canteen and Ginger told him to unscrew the cap and give them all a drink. Pearly heard Donnie mutter something that was unintelligible and probably foul, but the young hellion obeyed the mistress of the house. Nilla got a drink first. When Little Jack turned his head away from the canteen, Nilla told him to take a drink in the strongest sisterly voice she could muster and he did. Hartley was up on his knees by now, and he also drank from the offered canteen without comment.

"All right," said Ginger when Donnie was done. "Daddy Ludenmere's payin' up about this time tomorrow mornin', so nobody's gonna be dyin' from thirst or starvation. Everybody happy now?" She didn't wait for the reply that would never come. "*Go*," she told Donnie, who gave a small but infuriating chuckle as he followed Pearly out of the room.

When the door was closed, Nilla heard the noise of the table being propped up again. After that, she could hear the muffled voice of the woman telling Donnie to go get a smoke or take a walk or go squat in the woods but to leave the kids alone. The woman used language that a whole crate of soap could not wash from a person's mouth.

"Help me with this," Little Jack said.

He was trying to get the Cracker Jack open. He wound up holding the box while Nilla's fingers tore at the paper. At last they got it open and they were able to tilt the box into each other's mouths to get some of the caramel-covered popcorn. "Do you want some of this, Mr. Hartley?" Nilla asked.

"No," he answered hollowly, and still in pain. "You kids eat up."

Nilla sat back, her teeth crunching the popcorn. To try to reach Curtis again? No, he needed his rest too…and the thing was, she feared that her fear was making her lose the concentration to connect, and that fear grew past fear into dread. She would try again later in the morning, and before then she would try to force herself to get some sleep if she could.

"Gimme some more," Little Jack said.

With a precarious grip by the tips of her fingers, she tilted the box again into his mouth.

"Hey, hey!" he said with his mouth full. He spat something out on the floor and when he could speak through the popcorn he said, "I got the prize!"

"Good for you." Nilla closed her eyes. It was no darker than it had been before.

"I lost it. Wait…here it is." His searching fingers had found the small paper packet next to his left knee. "What do you think it could be?"

"Glasses to see in the dark."

"Oh yeah, that'd be what we need. I'll hold it if you can tear it open."

"Jack," she said, and realized it was the first time she hadn't put the *Little* before it, "I'm trying to rest, okay?"

"Just help me."

"Let it wait."

"Why?" he asked, and it was a good question.

She sighed with resignation, opened her eyes into the darkness and reached toward him. They found each other and he guided the packet to her fingers. She then guided it to her mouth and tore it open with her teeth while her brother held it. Little Jack said, "Thanks," and she figured he would either empty it onto the floor or try to pluck it out with his fingertips.

About ten seconds passed, and then Little Jack said, "I think it's a ring. Yeah, it is…a ring…but there's somethin' else on it…kind of a…rocket ship or somethin'…wait, wait…oh yeah…I think it's a tin whistle."

From the other side of the room came Hartley's voice, still raspy with injury: "Don't blow it. You say it's tin?"

"Yes sir, I guess. Some kind of metal. I couldn't blow it anyway, not with my fat lip."

"Bring it over here. Be careful not to drop it."

"Yes sir." Nilla heard her brother crawling over to Hartley. "Here it is," Little Jack said as he put it between Hartley's fingers. There was a long pause, and then Hartley said quietly, "I've got some change in my left pocket. There's a dime in there. It'll be the thinnest coin. Will you get that out, please?"

"What're you doing, Mr. Hartley?" Nilla asked.

"Quiet," he cautioned. And then he went on, in a whisper, "This is like a miniature Buck Rogers rocket ship on a ring. It's a whistle…made of pot metal, I think. But there's a seam that's got a very small crack in it. I'm gonna try to work it open with a dime. Got it, Jack?" He too, had lost the *Little*. "Okay, good…just hold onto it for a minute, I'm gonna need your help to do this."

Nilla crawled closer to the others. "Why are you going to work it open?" she whispered.

"Gonna *try*," he corrected. "If I can use that dime to widen the crack, maybe I can peel the metal back and make a sharp edge. Then if that crazy man comes in here to hurt us again I'll have somethin' to ward him off with until the woman can calm him down."

"Is that smart?" she dared to ask. "I mean…if you cut him, won't he hurt us more?"

"What I want to do is make him think twice if he comes in here again and starts some shi…some business," Hartley said. "If I can peel the seam back enough, I'll have a blade, and I think I can get the ring part on the first joint of my little finger. It won't be much, but I'm not gonna sit and have to watch Jack take another beatin' without fightin' back. Okay?" he asked, and she realized he was wanting her permission to continue, because what he was proposing might be necessary but it was awfully dangerous too.

She wished she could ask Curtis his opinion, and through him her daddy's, but this was up to her.

She thought about it awhile longer, remembering how terrible the sound of her brother being slapped had been, and how terrible had been the sight of Mr. Hartley being hurt and falling to the floor where he lay gasping and defenseless.

This was up to her.

At last she opened her mouth, and she whispered, "Okay."

Nineteen.

Pearly thought he had found escape from what seemed an endless and humidly hot night by lying on the top bunk of the bunkbeds and fixing his mind upon Mexico. Ginger had stretched out on the bunk below after smoking another cigarette in the aftermath of the commotion caused by Donnie, and Pearly couldn't help but say to her in the glow of one of the oil lamps, "I told you he was gonna be trouble. He's a loose cannon."

"I needed a cannon, loose or not," she said. "Instead of a pop-gun like you."

Then he'd wisely shut his mouth, Ginger had said no more, and he closed his eyes and travelled to Mexico in his mind. He saw the blue ocean waves breaking foam upon the white-sand beach, he saw the winding path that led up to his mansion perched atop the green hill, he heard the songs of the wild birds in the verdant trees and smelled…money. It had a particular perfume, a wealthy scent, a smell of freedom. With his share he would never have to go out on that damned road again and sweat out the selling of inscribed Bibles, gold mine bonds, oil well deeds, letters from attorneys and banks and investment firms, all counterfeit to snag the suckers and especially the ill-educated who had caught their own heady whiff of cash.

Something for nothing. It was the engine that drove all confidence games. People thinking they were going to get something for free. And all he was ever selling was air. But this time…he had merchandise to sell, and by this time tomorrow the deal would be done. Hot damn! he thought. A box of cash and all the good things that came with it. Then to Mexico, and all that came with his dreams.

He didn't know how long he'd drifted off, but he was awakened by the sound of the door to the bunkbed room closing. The oil lamp's wick was glowing orange on the writing desk. He leaned over and saw that Ginger had left her bunk. Gone to the outhouse? Then why didn't she take the light? He checked his wristwatch and saw it was about twenty minutes past three. Well, whatever she was up to, she was a big girl and she could sure as hell take care of herself. So...back to sleep, if he could.

But he could not. He mopped sweat from his face with the sheet and in another fifteen minutes checked his watch again. She still hadn't returned. Now he was wondering what she was up to. Gone for a walk in the woods? Doubtful, not after what he'd told her about the rental agent saying they needed a snakestick. He figured the canebreak rattlers around here likely killed nine or ten people a year, probably all niggers out working the fields. So where was Miss High-And-Mighty-Loose-Cannon-Lovin' Ginger LaFrance?

He was unable to let it go. He thought she must be out on the back porch, probably smoking another fag and trying to find a breeze in the heavy heat that had descended since midnight but, again, why hadn't she taken the lamp? Something smelled funny...the rotten peaches odor of wrongness in the air.

Clad in his undershirt and trousers, he swung down from the top bunk, picked up the lamp and went out into the front room.

She was sitting in a corner, her back to the wall, in one of the wicker chairs.

Her champagne-colored eyes glinted in the lamp's light, but she did not look at either the light or him. She stared straight ahead.

She had the kitchen knife with the serrated edge clasped in a double-handed grip before her. Her cheeks and forehead were damp with sweat. As Pearly watched, she slowly lifted the knife, hung it suspended in the air for a few seconds over her head, and then brought it down so fast and hard Pearly felt the movement of air and heard the hiss of the blade.

"No, no," she whispered, her face slack and her eyes fixed upon nothing that Pearly could see. "No...told you...not that way...no, no...who are you...who are you..."

"Ginger?" Pearly asked. He stepped toward her, the light offered as a solace to whatever darkness she was fighting.

"I wouldn't do that," came a quiet voice, followed by the crunch of teeth into an apple.

Pearly turned and saw Donnie sitting not in a chair but on the floor in the opposite corner. His legs were crossed beneath him and he was bare-chested. Beads of sweat glistened at the base of his throat. Thankfully he had removed the glass eye and electrical tape from his forehead. He took another bite of the last apple and said, "You probably want to step back. She's liable to get up from that fuckin' chair and cut your heart out."

Pearly retreated toward Donnie. When his own back had nearly hit the wall, he watched Ginger lift the knife up once more in the double-handed grip, hang it suspended for a few seconds and then bring it down with fearsome speed and power. This time her face contorted with a savage expression. "Told you!" she said, but it was still just a ragged whisper. "No, no...not that way...who are you...who are you..." Then her face went slack again, the sweat gleamed on her cheeks and forehead, and with the knife clasped before her she slowly began to rock herself forward and back...forward and back...forward and back...while the dead eyes stared at nothing living.

"What's wrong with her?" Pearly asked.

"She gets like this sometimes," Donnie answered, which Pearly figured was no answer at all. "I guess it's like lettin' go of tension or somethin'."

"What? She's tense about tomorrow so she goes into a..." He didn't even know what it ought to be called. She was whispering again but it was so low and unintelligible that it could've been a foreign language. "Can she hear us?" he asked.

"Naw. I've sat when she's done this, called her every name of whore and laughed my ass off watchin' her play the knife—and it's always a knife, she can find 'em by smell I think—so I don't believe she can hear any talkin' when she's this deep in."

"*Damn*," Pearly said, more of an exhaled breath than a word.

"Yeah. Hey…she ever pull that thing on you with the gun? The single bullet and all?"

Pearly was about to reply in the affirmative when he remembered he was talking to Ginger's nephew. Or, supposedly her nephew. How the hell would he know about that, unless…? "Maybe," Pearly said.

"Bet she did. Look at her rock herself. Got that knife ready to stab the world to death. You ain't gettin' me any nearer to her, that's for damn sure." He crunched into the apple again, enjoying the show that was being played out before him.

"How long does this go on?"

"Seen it go for a couple of hours. At the end of it she quiets down, gets up, puts the knife away and goes back to wherever she's sleepin'. At light, she won't remember a thing."

Pearly eased down onto the floor a few feet away from Donnie, with the oil lamp between them. He listened to the eerie singsong rhythm of Ginger's rant, which was delivered with ferocity but still remained a whisper. "How come she doesn't want me to know her real name?" he asked.

"Don't want anybody to know it. I'm family, so I do, but…it's just the way she is, Mister Pearly. Thinks that whoever knows her real name has got some kind of power over her. Couldn't stand that, I'm thinkin'. She can't stay in one place too long, either." He took another bite of the apple and watched the knife slowly go up, hang and then come down with a strength that would drive the blade into a bone. "Changes states and towns, changes her name. Got a fever to change herself, is what my ma says. Only she can't change herself, not really, so she's always on the move. But…she's right proud of herself, comin' through what she did."

"Comin' through what?"

"Don't think she'd like me to tell that."

Pearly considered his options. Then he said, "Tell me what you can and I'll give you an extra five hundred from my share."

Donnie chewed on the apple and watched Ginger, who was still muttering and staring at nothing, though her rocking forward and back had ceased. "A thousand dollars," he said, in a voice so low it was as if he feared Ginger might hear it even though she was transfixed and deaf to the room in her own private apocalypse.

"Okay. Done."

"Ought to shake on it." He held a hand out, Pearly shook it, and Donnie said, "Now if you don't pay up I won't feel so bad 'bout killin' you."

"Fine. What's the story?"

"This is all my ma's tellin', you know, so if I don't have the facts exactly right it's on her. Well...she had a kid at sixteen. Didn't know who the daddy was, could've been three or four men is what ma says. She wanted to keep the kid. Ran off from home to do it, wound up in Alabama. Got work as a secretary but...you know...she had to do some other things to make enough money. Anyway, she lived in what my ma said was 'cross the tracks. I reckon every town's got one of those. One day...she was sleepin' in the place she was livin'...and the kid—I think he was six about then—went out to a playground couple of blocks away. Other kids played there all the time, kind of a neighborhood place I guess."

Donnie paused to chew the apple down. Ginger had begun rocking herself again, though her mutterings were silent and the knife had ceased its war against the air.

"Two rich kids stole their daddy's car," Donnie went on. "Took it joyridin', into that place across the tracks. Guess it was excitin' for 'em. Hell, I've done that, I know what it's like. So they go screamin' around with the cops on their tail and all of a sudden the kid drivin' the car loses control of the wheel and that fine rich man's car goes right into the playground. Yep. Hurt four kids playin' there, broke their bones and such. But *her* little boy...well, ma said it broke him to pieces and tore him all up inside. Ambulance took him to the hospital but it was a time before they found out who the mama was, because she'd been lyin' passed-out drunk in her bed. By the time the police straightened everythin' out and she got to the hospital her little boy was dead...but it had took two days for him to pass."

"She could've sued the family," Pearly said. "Gotten a lot of money that way."

"Yeah. Well, she got a lawyer and tried that. Pretty soon they turned it around that she was an unfit mother and it was mostly her fault for lettin' her kid go out to that playground while she was lyin' drunk in the bed. Yeah, my ma said they brought two lawyers in from Atlanta to turn everythin' on its fuckin' head. Then they fixed it so...*Ginger*...lost her job, lost everythin' else and was lookin' at jail time on charges of whorin' and usin' drugs. 'Bout then is when she cracked up, I reckon, and they sent her to that hospital."

"What hospital?"

"Bryce, in Tuscaloosa. You know. A nuthouse."

"A mental hospital? How long did she stay in there?"

"Two years, is what I heard. When they let her out, they near 'bout kicked her out of Alabama too. Right then, I think, is when she decided she wasn't gonna be who she used to be. Right then, I think, she decided that it wasn't all men who were gonna have the power and money in the world, and she was gonna get some herself however she could. Now I know that's true 'cause she's told me that directly." He crunched a final time into the apple, biting down into the core, and then spat out a seed. "There you go. That story worth a thousand bucks, Mister Pearly?"

"Yes."

"Let me tell you somethin' for free," Donnie said. "Soon as the money's been got, she's gone. I don't know if you thought you were makin' plans with her or anythin', for after, but it ain't gonna happen. So if I was you I'd pull up stakes soon as you got that cash in your hand, you head out wherever you're goin' and don't look back."

"Thanks for the advice," Pearly replied, and he meant it. "What're you plannin' on doin' with your share?"

"Raisin' hell," said Donnie. His eyebrows went up. "What else is there?"

Though Pearly didn't care much for the younger man, he thought that maybe truer words had never been spoken. He stood up, dared to walk closer to Ginger, and moved the lamp back and forth before her sightless eyes.

"Playin' with fire there," Donnie said.

Ginger showed no reaction, except when he lowered the lamp and the darkness was on her face again she started that singsong muttering once more: "Told you...told you...no, no...not that way...told you..." And then the strange question, as if directed at herself: "Who are you? Who are you?" Her voice trailed off, unanswered.

"I'm hittin' the hay," Pearly told Donnie, but he knew he would be sleeping with both eyes open and his ears to the wall. He returned to the bunkbed room, put the lamp on the desk and climbed up to the top bunk, and there he lay trying to envision the paradise of Mexico again but all he was seeing was a vast plain of thornbrush and smelling the bitter fruit of rotten peaches.

When the door opened he nearly jumped out of his skin. By the lamp's dying glow he could make out on his wristwatch that it was four forty-three. He heard her slide into the lower bunk, and then there was silence but for the hard beating of his heart.

Afraid of her? he asked himself.

Terrified, was the answer.

But it would be over in about twenty-one hours, and then he was quits with the both of them. Ginger was the one who'd brought up the idea of heading straight to Mexico, but what Donnie had told him made sense; Ginger had no destination, she was just travelling from one name and one con job to another, and that was her life.

"You're awake," she said.

He didn't reply. He breathed so shallowly he felt like it was barely keeping him alive. After awhile he heard her turn over in the sheet and then be still, and he lay sleepless as dirty light slowly crept over the windowsill and through the curtains of ship anchors and leaping gamefish struggling vainly and forever against their hooks.

FOUR.

Blood Will Tell

Twenty.

"You ready?"

"Yes sir."

"It's time."

Curtis and Ludenmere had shared that exchange nearly thirty minutes ago. Now, as the seconds ticked away toward one o'clock on Friday morning, Ludenmere guided his second car—a dark blue Pierce-Arrow sedan—through the streets of New Orleans on a northwesterly course. Curtis had the passenger seat, and behind them on the rear seat was the cardboard box holding two hundred and fifteen thousand dollars in bills not larger than fifties, the box itself lightly taped shut but not heavily sealed.

As he'd not had a change of clothes, Curtis still wore his Redcap uniform but had left the crimson cap at the Ludenmere mansion. Ludenmere had hardly slept last night and had drowsed only for an hour or so yesterday afternoon, when they'd gotten back from their trip to find the fishing pier at the end of Sandusky Road. He was dishevelled and weary and operating on the strength of nervous energy alone. He had offered the Pierce-Arrow's wheel to Curtis but that wasn't going to work since Curtis told him he'd never in his life sat behind the wheel of a car.

The streets were nearly deserted but for a few other nocturnal travellers. The day had been cloudy and heavy. To the northwest occasional streaks of lightning flared over the lake, and by their stark illumination for an instant turned the seething sky around them vivid purple. Ludenmere had brought a thermos of strong black coffee along and as he navigated the ghostly-quiet streets he drank down jolts of java one after the other.

"Tell her we're comin'," Ludenmere said, his dark-hollowed eyes fixed on the way ahead.

Curtis had already done that when they'd left the house, but he nodded and sent out, :*Nilla, he says to tell you again we're comin'. It won't be long now.*:

:*All right,*: she sent back. :*I don't think they've left yet.*:

:*But…they're bringin' you and Little Jack, aren't they?*:

:*I don't know. Like I said before, they've kept us in this room all day.*:

Curtis was relieved that her sending was stronger than it had been yesterday. She must've been able to get a little rest, enough to recharge herself. They'd been talking briefly during the day, as he hadn't wanted to run her down again, and it was during one of those talks that she'd told him they hadn't seen any of the three all day, had had nothing to eat and nothing to drink.

:*Let me know when they come for you,*: Curtis told her. :*We'll be at that pier at one on the dot.*:

:*Thank you, Curtis. Thank you so much for being here.*:

:*Well, we're gonna be* there *real soon, so there's nothin' for any of you to worry about.*:

"What's she sayin'?" Ludenmere asked, breaking Curtis's concentration.

"She says they haven't left yet."

"Yeah, I expect they'll make us wait a spell at that damned pier. But… we've got the money and that's a done deal, thanks to Victor. He wanted to come with me and hide in the back seat, but I told him if they found him—and they were bound to look—there'd be hell to pay. I'm gonna have enough trouble explainin' *you*."

"How're you gonna do that?"

Ludenmere stopped at a red light. He'd already told Curtis they weren't going to run any lights or do any speeding; being pulled over by the police was not part of the plan and would ruin the time schedule they'd figured out this afternoon. "I'll say you're my driver. They may not like it, but they won't pay much notice to you."

Curtis knew what that meant. "You mean 'cause I'm a Negro?"

"That's right, and also 'cause you're a skinny kid who doesn't look like you could threaten a snowball. Don't ask me to tiptoe through any gardens right now, Curtis. I'm not in the mood."

"Fair enough," Curtis said, without anger or resentment, because it was the reality of his world.

The light changed and Ludenmere drove on through the misty streets, where by night and the yellow-tinged streetlamps the famous old oaks and weeping willows of the city took on the shapes of gnarled dragons lurking on the roadside.

During the day, Ludenmere had shown Curtis a professionally-taken photograph in a silver frame of both the kids, smiling with their arms around each other. They were handsome children. Curtis thought Little Jack looked a lot like their father, but Nilla looked younger than he'd expected. He guessed it was because when they talked she had sometimes seemed older than ten years, surely older than he'd been at that age, and he figured it was because she—like her brother—had been blessed with the gift of not only a rich father, but the richness of an education. He thought she probably knew a lot more about the world than he did, though he tried to travel as much as he could through reading. It was a sorry thing, now, that she and Little Jack were getting such an education in how plain mean, conniving and selfish some people could be, especially about money...something he'd already been taught in his dealings with the Rowdy Pattersons and Miles Wilsons of the world.

"What I can't figure," said Ludenmere after he'd driven about another half-mile, "was how they got the kids with both Hartley and Detective Parr bein' on the alert. I swear to God, I thought Parr was smarter than that, to let themselves be waylaid between the school and the house. How the hell did that *happen*? And both of them with guns...I just can't figure it out."

Curtis said, "I doubt they wanted to do any shootin' with the children liable to get hurt."

"Yeah. Right. You know, I blame myself for this. When that detective came to me, the first thing I should've done is hire three more bodyguards. But...the way he told it...maybe I didn't want to believe it was true. I mean...he wasn't sure about it himself. Just a story from some lowlife criminal who wanted to stay out of prison. But damn it, I should've acted! Should've hired three extra bodyguards right that afternoon!" He reached for the coffee thermos again for a drink of more fuel.

"It'll be over soon," Curtis said, but it sounded more lame than helpful.

"*This* part'll be over," Ludenmere corrected. "I don't think the idea that my—our—children were kidnapped and at the mercy of three criminals for thirty-four hours is gonna be over anytime soon. Jane's hangin' on by whatever fingernails she's got left, and so am I. When we get the children back... God only knows what shape they'll be in...mentally, I mean."

"They're holdin' up."

"Ask her again if they've left yet."

The answer to that was :*No, not yet.*:

"Gonna make us wait," Ludenmere said between clenched teeth. "Goddamn bastards gonna make us wait."

Leaving the outskirts of New Orleans behind, they reached Sawmill Road that led into Kenner. Ludenmere took a left and in silence drove toward the meeting place. Through his side window Curtis watched the lightning flare over Lake Pontchartrain, sending out jagged and blazing whips from clouds to earth. The noise of thunder came to him like a muffled bass drum.

His heart was beating harder and his stomach—enriched with a ham sandwich from a rich man's kitchen—felt like it wanted to lurch and spill its contents into the fine, leathery-smelling car.

:*Curtis? Curtis, we heard the front door open and close. We think they're leaving!*:

:*They're not takin' you with 'em?*:

:*No.*:

"Nilla says she thinks they're leavin' now," Curtis reported, "but they're not takin' the kids with 'em."

"I figured they wouldn't. They'll want to see that all the money's there first," Ludenmere said. "I don't know how this is gonna work, but I want my children back *tonight*. I want 'em in this car with me when we head back home, and by God that's what's gonna happen."

Behind the wheel of the Oldsmobile, Ginger shifted uneasily in the seat. She made a noise that sounded to Pearly like a whisper of discontent.

"What's wrong?" he asked.

"Somethin' I've forgotten," she answered, as she steered the car east along Sawmill Road. "Can't remember what. Somethin'. That damned Donnie...last night...got me all out of whack."

Pearly said nothing. Between them on the seat was Hartley's .45 Smith & Wesson revolver, and Pearly carried his .38 pistol in the shoulder holster under his coat. They had also brought along the bull's-eye lantern and the flashlight. A streak of lightning across the sky to the northwest lit up the interior of the car for an instant, and the thunder that followed seemed to vibrate in Pearly's bones. His palms were damp and his shirt was sticking to his back. He had rolled down his window to let the air circulate and cool himself off, but even the moving air was thick with heat and the wet clammy noxion of the approaching storm.

"Fine night to get paid two hundred thousand bucks," said Ginger, but it was spoken with absolutely no emotion, either good or bad.

"Two hundred and fifteen," he said.

"Yeah." She swerved the car a few feet to crunch a tire over a raccoon that was sneaking across the road. "Somethin' I've forgotten," she said. "Damn if I can remember."

They would be passing through Kenner in a couple minutes more. Pearly wished he could light up a cigarette and swallow it down, but he could do that later. Mexico, Mexico, he thought.

It was not so far away now.

Again Ginger shifted uneasily, and the words were out of Pearly's mouth before he could think to stop them: "I thought you said you didn't have any kids."

"Huh? I don't."

"Never?"

"Fuck, no. I hate kids. Gettin' in the way of everythin'."

"Uh huh. Don't you mean you hate rich men's kids?"

She didn't answer that one right off. Did he see her hands tighten on the wheel? It was hard to tell. The lightning flared, sending a dozen spears into the dark, and the thunder came with a sharper edge.

They passed through Kenner, which had likely folded up and gone to sleep at eight o'clock. Two stray dogs were nosing around some trash cans, but that was all the movement in evidence.

"What're you talkin' about?" Ginger asked. Her voice was a little too light. "Gettin' crazy, the closer we get to the payoff?"

"Just thinkin' out loud, I guess." He realized he was one foot in, and he might as well put the other one in too. "Thinkin' that I hope this job is just about kidnappin', and not really about some kind of...oh, I don't know...revenge."

"Revenge? For *what*?"

"Oh...*life*, I suppose. Like I say, just thinkin' out loud."

"Stop thinkin', you're makin' me nervous. I'm doin' the talkin' when we get there. Got that?"

"Sure, whatever you say."

"Comin' up real soon," she said. "Take the safety off my gun."

"Why?"

"Because," she answered, her eyes deadset on the centerpoint of the cones of light that fell upon the road ahead, "I want you to."

They heard the scrape of the table being moved.

The door opened. Donnie came in holding an oil lamp and the pillow from his cot. Tucked into the waistband of his jeans and against the white cotton of the undershirt he wore was the handle of the kitchen knife with the serrated blade.

Beside her, Nilla felt Little Jack tremble in spite of his bravery. Across the room, Hartley slowly drew his knees up against his chest.

"Howdy, folks," said Donnie. He grinned in the yellow light. "Came to keep you company for awhile." His eyes moved toward the boy. "How you doin' there, kid?"

Ludenmere pulled the car to a stop at the end of Sandusky Road, about three hundred yards off Sawmill. Before them was thirty-five feet of fishing pier. To the right stood a pair of cabins, both dark and empty as they had been when Ludenmere and Curtis had peered through the grimy windows this afternoon, and to the left was a mass of scrub brush and woods.

Ludenmere cut the engine. He reached on the seat between them for the flashlight he'd brought. He peered into the rearview mirror. No sign of another car yet. He said tersely, "All right, let's get to it." He switched the light on and gave it to Curtis. They got out of the car as another streak of lightning flamed across the sky, and the following crack of thunder was as sharp as a whipstrike.

Ludenmere leaned into the backseat and picked up the money box. The cardboard box with that much cash in it weighed over twenty pounds, though the container itself was only a little larger than a Stetson hatbox. It held twenty-three hundred fifties, three thousand twenties and four thousand tens, the denominations stacked together and secured with thick rubber bands. Curtis followed Ludenmere out onto the pier, which they'd seen by daylight was warped downward in the middle and had a thin wooden railing. A length of rope dangled from the left side into the black water, and off on the right were broken and mollusk-encrusted pilings where an older pier must have once stood before a squall had taken it under.

Curtis kept the light aimed at their feet as they reached the end of the pier and Ludenmere set the money box down. The spaces between the boards glinted with the dark and briny-smelling lake, which was being stirred into motion by the approaching storm. Waves had begun to slap the muddy shore. Curtis felt the raw wind pushing at his back. It shrilled past his ears as he and Ludenmere faced the road. Lightning lit up the woods and flamed over the lake, and the thunder cracked and boomed to wake the sleepers in Kenner's cemetery.

They waited, watchful for the lights of another car.

"Blowin' up a rain out there," said Donnie. "Hear that thunder? Me, I kinda like storms. You like storms, kid? Or do they scare you some?"

Little Jack didn't answer; he kept his face angled toward the floor.

"When I was about your age I saw what was left of a fella got struck by lightnin', out in a cow pasture," Donnie went on, swinging the oil lamp slowly back and forth. "Turned coal black, his whole body was. Clothes blown right off. Face was burned to the skull, and he was just lyin' there with a death grin on his mouth. Know what me and my buddies did? We knocked his teeth out with a stick. He had three silvers in there. I took 'em and got some money for 'em later on, 'nuff to buy a pack of rubbers. You ever see anythin' like that, kid?"

Her cheeks burning, Nilla squinted up into the light. "Why don't you leave us alone? You're going to get what you're after soon enough."

"Just askin', sugarlips. Bet I've seen some nasty things you kids never dreamed of in your worst nightmares."

"Go scare yourself and look in a mirror," Little Jack said suddenly, with acidic heat. "*Stop it!*" he growled at Nilla when his sister shot a warning elbow into his ribs.

Donnie laughed quietly, but there was no humor in it. When his false laughter was done, he aimed the lamp at Hartley. "How you doin', ol' One Eye? You ain't sayin' much."

"Nothin' to say," came the answer.

"I reckon not. Now this kid here…he's got a mouth on him. Just lets them insults fly out like he could take 'em back if he wanted to. That's a real bad habit of yours, kid. You know that?" He swatted Little Jack in the head with the pillow, but it was only a gentle nudge. "Speak when spoken to," he said, and swatted him with the pillow again, just a little harder.

Curtis and Ludenmere saw the headlights coming. "Jesus Christ," said Ludenmere bitterly. "That's my own damned car!"

The Oldsmobile turned so that the headlights aimed down the length of the pier and directly upon the two men, all but blinding them in the glare. Then the car stopped and the engine was cut; the headlights remained on but no one got out.

"Come on, come on," Ludenmere said under his breath. He lifted both arms in recognition and to show he was holding no weapon. Curtis also lifted both arms, pointing the flashlight's beam skyward. Still there was no reaction from the car. "We've got your money!" Ludenmere shouted, but was nearly drowned out by the following roll of thunder. "It's all there!" He put a foot against the cardboard box.

The car's driver got out, followed by the passenger. Sure enough, the driver—a slim figure, maybe the woman? Curtis thought—walked to the Pierce-Arrow, turned on a flashlight and peered into the backseat. The light then went searching in the woods on the left and toward the cabins on the right. The second figure paused to shield the bull's-eye lantern from the wind with his body and touch a match to the wick. He aimed the focused and magnified beam around in a slow circle. When the two kidnappers were satisfied, they approached the pier but neither Curtis nor

Ludenmere could tell much about them in the glare. The two stopped midway out.

"You were told to come alone," the woman said. "Don't take orders too well, do you? Who's the nigger?"

"My driver."

"That's bullshit. Your driver's with us right this minute."

"My *new* driver," said Ludenmere.

"You too rich to drive your own fuckin' car? Boy, keep that light upturned! Hear?" The woman's voice had sharpened, because Curtis had started to bring his hand with the flashlight down. Her attention returned to Ludenmere. "Well, you've been a pretty good boy otherwise. We're gonna come out now and get the box. You two stay real still and this'll all be over in about five minutes."

"Hold it!" The note of command in Ludenmere's voice stopped the kidnappers in their tracks. "I want my children back *tonight*. You take the money and go to hell with it, but I'm goin' home with my children."

There was an uncertain pause. Curtis smelled ozone in the air. The lightning flashed so close that for a brief instant he and Ludenmere could nearly make out the features of the man and woman, and more importantly they saw the gleam of metal in her right hand that could only be a pistol; then the thunder crashed again with ear-cracking force.

"You're out of tune," the woman said. "No go on that one."

"When do I get them, then?"

"We'll let you know. First thing is, we count the bills and make sure you haven't shorted us."

"*Nope*," said Ludenmere.

"What?"

"I said…nope. You're takin' me to my children and handin' 'em over as soon as you put your hands on this box. I haven't shorted you. That would be pretty damn stupid, wouldn't it?"

"What's stupid," the woman said, "is you standin' there arguin' with me and Hartley's .45. Now that is *real* fuckin' stupid."

Ludenmere ignored her. Curtis felt sweat running down his sides under his arms. He could smell the rain coming; it wasn't too far away now, rolling toward them across the lake. Ludenmere said, "I want *everybody* freed tonight...my children, Hartley and Detective Parr. Hear me?"

"Ha," she replied tonelessly. "Hear him, Detective Parr?"

Curtis saw the silent man shift his weight. Then the man said, "I hear."

It took a few more seconds, but suddenly Ludenmere staggered and grabbed hold of Curtis's shoulder to keep himself from falling.

"He gets it now," the man said to the woman, with what sounded to Curtis like a smug satisfaction that was evil to the core.

Donnie had put the oil lamp down on the floor, and with the next crash of thunder he swung the pillow hard against Little Jack's head.

"Leave him alone," Hartley said, but quietly.

"I ain't botherin' him much. Am I, kid?" The following strike with the pillow made Little Jack say, "Ow! That hurt!"

"Leave us all alone!" Nilla cried out.

"Well now," Donnie answered in an easy voice, his eyes glinting in the lamplight, "there you go again, you rich kids tryin' to rob me of all my fun."

And as soon as he'd pronounced the last word, he swung the pillow with seemingly tremendous strength at Little Jack's head, and followed that up by leaping behind the pillow upon the boy. He pinned Little Jack's head and face down on the floor and put all his weight on the boy's skull. Little Jack thrashed and gave a muffled cry, his legs kicked wildly, and Nilla in her start of terror screamed out a message to her listener.

"My God," Ludenmere breathed, as the wind swept past Curtis and him and the lightning crackled through the clouds. "Oh my God...no."

"Yes indeed," the woman said. "Played you good and proper, didn't we? Now…we're comin' for that money, and you might be real used to gettin' your own way, but I'd advise you to—"

Suddenly Curtis couldn't hear her.

In his head was the frantic scream of : *Curtis! Donnie's hurting Little Jack!*:

"Little Jack!" he said urgently to Ludenmere. He didn't know how else to put it but, "Nilla says he's gettin' hurt!"

Ludenmere trembled. His face had bleached to fish-belly gray. He shouted at the kidnappers, "My boy's gettin' hurt! Goddamn you, you're takin' me to my—"

He started toward them, took two steps, and the woman shot him.

There were two quick shots. Ludenmere wheeled violently around and grabbed hold of Curtis. His momentum was carrying them both backward. A third shot sent a bullet zipping past Curtis's right ear, and then he and Ludenmere crashed through the railing and hit the black water of Lake Pontchartrain.

Twenty-One.

"You will let him up."

Hartley had spoken it calmly, as Little Jack continued to thrash and fight with his head trapped beneath the pillow and Donnie's weight; it had been spoken not with a threat or as a plea, but as a prediction and a certainty.

Donnie grinned fiercely in the lamplight. Sweat sparkled on his reddened cheeks. He said, "Make—"

He didn't get out the rest of it, because Hartley was suddenly up on his knees. Hartley's tape-bound hands swung toward Donnie's face in a blur, from right to left. The ring on his little finger, with its pot metal Buck Rogers rocket ship jimmied open at a seam to form a ragged-edged cutter two millimeters thicker than the dime Hartley had used as a tool, tore across Donnie's left cheek and that side of his nose, and from the ghastly slash in Donnie's flesh the scarlet blood spattered the far wall.

Instantly Hartley's prediction came true. Donnie gave a high shriek like a wounded animal and fell back off Little Jack, colliding with Nilla who scrabbled away from him with frantic speed. Her message sent in a scream to Curtis was still caught in her brain like a banner of fire. Little Jack rolled out from under the pillow, gasping for air. In his convulsion Donnie's elbow knocked over the lantern; its glass cracked but the oil reservoir did not break open, and the burning wick continued to throw contorted shadows upon the walls.

One of Donnie's hands went to his gashed face. The other pulled the knife out from his waistband, and just that fast Donnie caught his backward motion and propelled himself toward Hartley. Before Hartley could avoid the blade it sank into his left side, turned on a rib, then was wrenched out and stabbed again into the man's lower belly. All Hartley could see was Donnie's teeth right in his face, but Nilla saw the knife's bloody blade glint in the light. It sank into Hartley's left forearm, and then Nilla kicked into the backs of Donnie's knees with both stockinged feet as hard as she could, throwing him off balance and bringing from him a howl of pain. Hartley fell back against the wall and swung once more with the cutter at Donnie's face, but at that instant the younger man's head had begun to turn toward Nilla and so the jagged edge of the Buck Rogers rocket ship hit him on the left side of his throat under the ear. It carved across the flesh in a brutal blur, the force of the blow breaking Hartley's little finger with a noise like a snapping twig.

Donnie gave a sound that was not a shriek or a scream, but rather a gasp of surprise.

His eyes blinked as he stared at Hartley.

Then the blood sprayed out in a fan-shaped arc from the cut carotid artery, leaping higher with the beats of Donnie's heart. He dropped the knife and clutched at his throat, the fingers working as if to seal the wound with pressure alone. His eyes were wide with terror in his gory face. The blood was fountaining out. Donnie whimpered and spun around like a wild beast trying to find a way out of a trap. He tripped over Nilla and crashed against the wall, leaving there his scrawled crimson signature. In his panicked madness he had lost his bearings, though the door was only eight feet behind him. He staggered past Little Jack, who was huddled on the floor still gasping for breath. His bloody hands scrabbled at the walls as if trying to claw himself out, as he threw gruesome plumes in every direction.

As Ginger ran to the end of the pier with Pearly behind her, a streak of lightning shot past so close they could hear the air sizzle, and then with the next earth-shattering crack of thunder the heavens opened up, the rain slamming them in their faces as the storm came off the lake with a moan of wind and crash of waves against the pilings.

They were drenched in a matter of seconds. Ginger was probing the churning water around the pier's end with her light. Pearly swept the bull's-eye lantern's beam across the waves.

"There!" she shouted, and she fired a fourth bullet into the lake but Pearly couldn't see what she was shooting at. The money box was at their feet. "We've got the cash!" he shouted at her through the wind's roar, though she stood right at his side. "Let's go!"

"I hit him!" she shouted back, streams of rain running through her hair and down her face. "I know I hit that sonofabitch!"

"Okay, okay! Let's go!"

She seemed to Pearly hesitant to just take the money and leave, which made the most sense to him; she was still scanning the water with her light, the pistol outstretched to find a target. He set his lantern down atop the box and picked it up. "Ginger, let's get out of here!" he urged. "*Now!*"

At last she lowered the gun and the light. Silently she turned toward the two cars parked at the foot of the pier, and Pearly followed her through the blowing rain. At the Oldsmobile he put the box into the backseat, told her he was driving, and was surprised when she got into the passenger side without a word. He started the engine, switched on the windshield wipers, backed the car up to find a place to turn around, and then headed again toward Sawmill Road.

"Damn!" he said. "I'm wet to the bone!"

She didn't answer. She held the gun in her lap, nearly cradling it as one would hold an infant.

"Two hundred and fifteen fuckin' thousand!" Pearly crowed. "He didn't short us, I know it! He wanted the kids, he didn't give a shit about the money." He drove on for another moment without speaking, and then he had to voice something that had occurred to him when the first shot had gone off. "You wanted to shoot him, didn't you? To kill him, if you could?"

There was no answer.

"I figure…that's why you didn't just have him drop the box off and leave. You wanted him there so you could shoot him. Sure, he gave you an excuse by rushin' you, but…was that what this was really about? Shootin' a rich man whose name got in the papers? And the toppin' on that cake was that he had two kids?"

"Maybe that was part of it," she said, staring straight ahead. "But it was most about takin' the prize. And we did."

"Yeah, we sure as hell did." He frowned, because through his nearly-intoxicated elation at being rich and about to head south of the border to a new life something else had jabbed him in the brain. "I heard that nigger say somethin' about Little Jack just before Ludenmere went crazy. Did you hear what—"

"Oh…*shit!*" she said. "I remember what I forgot! The prize. In the Cracker Jack box. Donnie got me so fouled up…I forgot to take the prize out of that fuckin' box!"

"So what?"

"It could've been a little fork or scissors…somethin' metal, somethin' with a sharp edge. *Shit!*"

"Hold on, now! So what if it was? You think they can use—"

"I think Donnie's too stupid not to go in that room and taunt 'em. There's no tellin'. Hit the gas, Pearly, get us there *fast!*"

As the Olds pulled away, two figures who clung to each other staggered out of the waves and through the rain upon the muddy shore. Curtis was no master of swimming but knew enough to keep himself from drowning, even in the turbulent water and with his arm around Ludenmere; he figured it had been a blessing that the lake off the end of the pier was only about five feet deep and his long legs had found a purchase. He helped Ludenmere up into the relative shelter of the woods, and there in the pelting rain and under the windswept branches he eased the other man down against the trunk of a willow tree.

"Oh my God," Ludenmere said feebly. "Oh Jesus…oh my God."

The lightning kept flickering and by its illumination Curtis saw all the blood on the front of Ludenmere's shirt, up on the right at the collarbone. Another shot must've grazed Ludenmere's head on the right side because there was blood trickling down his forehead and, mixing with the rain, streaking out to make the man's face a tormented mask.

Curtis had to take a few breaths before he could speak. His heart was racing and he had started to shiver, not from the lake or the rain but from the terrifying experience of being shot at. He could still hear that bullet going past his head. All he could think to say was, "Are you hurt bad?"

Ludenmere gave the worst curse that Curtis had ever heard in his life. The man probed at his collarbone with his left hand and uttered a second foul oath, but he sounded nearly worn-out. "Think the bone's busted," he said. "Can't do much with my right arm. Damn it to Hell. That Parr…set me up. Bastard walked in my office and set me up."

"We've got to get on out of here," Curtis said. "Get you to a doctor."

"My children." For an instant Ludenmere's voice cracked and became almost a sob. "What happened to Little Jack? Is he all right? Please…ask her."

"I will." But Curtis found it was easier said than done. His mind was jangled and full of the noise of gunshots and the sizzle of his own hot coals of anger. He could not concentrate past the bad man's evil declaration of *He gets it now.* :*Nilla,*: Curtis sent out, but he wasn't sure if it was reaching her for all the static in his brain. :*Nilla, what happened to Little Jack?*:

There was no reply. Curtis could not feel her on the other end of the mental radio; the tubes were not glowing.

"I'm sorry, sir," he told Ludenmere. "I can't get to her right now."

"Oh Jesus…you say…you don't know how to drive?"

"No, sir, I don't." Curtis paused to wipe the rain out of his eyes. "I'll get up to the road and find help. Find a house…somebody to help us. There's *got* to be somebody livin' in one of those cabins up there."

"Right. Yeah…I don't think…I'd better move from here…damn… don't think I *can* move. Near passin' out, Curtis…"

Curtis had no idea if Ludenmere was going to die or not; he had no way of knowing how bad the injury was, but he figured the least—and maybe the *most*—he could do was go for help.

"I'll find somebody," he said. "You hang on, I'll be back directly."

When Ludenmere didn't reply, Curtis knew it was time to get going. He stood up in the driving rain and began half-running and half-staggering in his soggy Redcap's uniform and his waterlogged shoes the three-hundred-yard distance to Sawmill Road.

❦

Donnie had fallen to his knees. He was facing Nilla, Little Jack and Hartley, and even as the blood spouted from the cut artery and his wounded face began to bleach to gray the black cinders of his eyes still said he would kill them if he could. He let out a bellow that might have had words in it, or might have been a warning to the spirit realm that Donnie Baines was on his way and he could lick any phantom in the house.

He drew a tremendous breath, as if that would give him a few more seconds of life, and maybe it did. Then he shuddered like a dog that had been hit by a dump truck and he fell forward on his face with his eyes still open but staring no longer at anything of value to a corpse. He landed in the mess of his own gore, and caused it to ripple across the floor like a small tidal wave.

"Out," Hartley said. "Got to get out." His own face had grayed. The blood was filling up his shirt at the belly. "Jack...can you pick up the lamp?" The boy was in shock, staring numbly at the dead man. "*Jack!*" Hartley tried to shout, but it was more of a painful wheeze. The boy jumped; tears sprang to his eyes and a thread of saliva drooled down from his lower lip.

"I can get it," Nilla said. She got her hands under the lantern's wire handle and let it slide down to her wrists, then lifted it off the floor that way. Though the outer glass was cracked, the flame was still strong.

"Got to get out," Hartley repeated. "They come back and find this, they'll kill us." He pushed away from the wall he'd been leaning against and Nilla saw both the terrible pain and the awesome willpower in his single-eyed face. "Come on, Jack," he urged. "Steady up now, hear me?"

"Yes, sir," the boy answered, but his eyes were still swollen with shock and his voice sounded hollow.

"Lead us out of here," Hartley told Nilla.

Rain was hammering madly down on the tin roof. Nilla's light showed that Donnie had opened the back door to let the air circulate. Out on the porch they found the screened door was latched, but Hartley solved that problem by kicking the whole thing off its hinges. Then he gave a gasp and doubled over, and Nilla saw that not only was he bleeding badly from his wounds but he was also bleeding from the mouth, which she did not have to be a nurse or a doctor to figure was a very bad sign.

In the driving rain, the two steps down to the muddy earth were too many for Hartley. He took a fall that put him on his injured side and slammed from him a harsh grunt of pain. As Nilla was leaning down to try to help him, she heard something in her mind that sounded like a distant garble of words. Maybe there was a question in it, but if it was Curtis speaking he wasn't making any sense. She had neither the time nor the concentration to answer; right now the only thing she could think about was getting her brother and herself as far away from the kidnappers as possible, and she was aware that Mr. Hartley could be dying in front of her eyes.

She was unable to do anything to help him to his feet. "I can get up," he said, priming himself to try. With a supreme effort he struggled to his knees and stayed there for a moment, as lightning streaked overhead and the thunder spoke and the rain came down upon all. Then he did stand up, slowly, fighting not only his injuries but the weight of the storm. He hunched over and pressed his elbows into his belly as if to hold his insides from sliding out.

Headlights came through the rain up at the front of the cabin. The car stopped. Nilla heard two doors open and shut.

"Let's go!" Hartley said, and motioned with a lift of his chin toward the woods to the left.

"Jack!" She hit him on the shoulder with an elbow, because he was standing there open-mouthed and seemingly as dumb as a rock. "Go!" she said, and hit him again to get him moving. His first couple of steps were made like he was sludging through glue, but then he started running into the woods without care that everything was dark ahead of him, and he was gone like a jackrabbit. Nilla held the lantern up for Hartley to see his way. They hadn't gotten but about twenty feet when he fell again, even harder than before.

A flashlight shone from the cabin's back porch, searching for the runaways.

"Get!" Hartley said. "I'm finished, Nilla." Now a pair of lights were working from the porch, and when one found them the other did too.

"I can't—"

"Take care of your brother," he told her. "That's what you have to—" His gaze shifted, his eyes squinting in the glare of the two combined lights. "They're comin'. Get while you can."

She had no choice. She ran, following Little Jack into the unknown.

"Looky here," said Ginger as she walked to Hartley and put the light in his pallid face. "What I found…a one-eyed dead man."

Behind her, Pearly shone his bull's-eye lantern into the woods. In the last minute the rain had eased from a hard downpour to a steady fall, and through it he could see the light of their lantern, moving away.

"They won't get far," Ginger said, but she had not moved her attention from Hartley. "All this mud and the thicket out there…not far at all. Likely break their legs and we'll hear 'em cryin'." She knelt down a safe distance from Hartley, and it was then he saw the gun in her other hand. "You made a mess. How'd you do it?"

"Ask Donnie," said Hartley, with a grim smile that showed his bloody teeth.

"Now here's a brave man, Pearly. You say he was in the war? Oh yeah, that scar and all. Well, looks to me like he's gonna be dead here real quick. We brought you the knife you killed Donnie with. Give it here, Pearly." She put the flashlight aside, moved the pistol to her left hand and took the gory knife from Pearly's hand in her right. "Looks like he stuck you a few times, too. You used this, or did you *make* yourself a blade somehow?"

"Ginger," Pearly said. "We've got two hundred and fifteen thousand fuckin' dollars split two ways!" He had barely been able to suppress his delight at seeing the third split dead on the floor back there, at the same time realizing the chauffeur and the kids had gotten out, but now his blood-lust was up and it was all a matter of taking care of business. "Let's finish him off and cut out! We don't need the brats!"

"Yes," she answered, still staring fixedly at Hartley, "we do. Think on this, Pearly: if Bonnie and Clyde had had two kids with 'em in that car, would the lawmen have shot them to pieces? Hell, no. We're gettin' those brats and takin' 'em with us. They're gonna be our insurance policy against bein' shot up on the road."

"I get that," he said. "But we're dumpin' 'em somewhere, right? Soon as we're in the clear?"

"Oh, yeah." Ginger slowly wiped the knife's blade on Hartley's trouser leg. "We'll dump 'em...somewhere. By the by," she said to Hartley, "I think I might've killed your master. Now...I'm not gonna waste a bullet on you, 'cause I can tell you're sinkin'. We're gonna go fetch those kiddies back, and if you're not dead by the time we do...you'll wish you were." With that, she drove the knife with ferocious strength into the calf of Hartley's left leg, and she twisted the blade.

Nilla had caught up to Little Jack in the dripping woods. They both heard the ragged wail from behind them that made them stop in their tracks and stare at each other, their eyes wide and glistening in the lantern's yellow light.

Nilla broke the silence that followed. "We've got to keep moving. We'll find a road or another cabin, or somebody."

"Yeah," her brother said. Then: "What do you think they'll do to Mr. Hartley?"

"I think they've already done it. We can't help him, Jack. He would want us to keep going."

"Yeah." It was delivered gruffly, in a voice that might have belonged to their father at that age, yet in it was also a note of terrible pain that was all the father's son.

There was no time or energy to waste, and they both knew that. Nilla didn't know if those two would come after them or not, but she couldn't risk slowing down to find out.

They went on into the thicket, their feet sinking through weeds and mud as the rain continued to steadily fall, and beyond the lantern's flame was nothing but a world of dark upon dark.

Twenty-Two.

It was raining in fits and starts when Curtis found the first cabin. He had turned west on the darkened stretch of Sawmill Road and was running in the direction of town. He banged on the cabin's door…once…again, and a third time, but there were no lights and no one answered. He gave a shout of "Help me, please!" and hit the door twice again. There was still no reply from what must've been an abandoned place, and Curtis ran on.

The next cabin was about eighty yards away and on the left side of the road, and he'd almost gone past it before he'd realized it was there. Beside the cabin, nearly hidden in the brush, was the battered frame of a car sitting on cinderblocks. Curtis crossed the road, ran through the weeds and up a pair of cinderblock steps to the door. He hammered on the weathered wood and shouted, "Help me! Somebody, quick!"

Nothing.

"Please!" he tried once more. "Help me!" He balled up his fist and hammered again…and suddenly he saw a faint light moving beyond a front window. Did a face peer out from the dirty glass? He couldn't tell. He was about to shout and beat at the door a third time when he heard a bolt being thrown back.

The door came open and the double barrels of a shotgun were put in his face.

"Get on outta here, you!" hollered the old man holding the gun. He was a bony Negro, bald-headed and with a white beard, wearing a gray nightshirt. Curtis saw behind the man's right shoulder an equally-aged and

277

frail Negro woman, white-haired and with a face like a roadmap on dried parchment, lifting an oil lamp to give off a meager light.

"Please, sir!" Curtis said. "There's a man—"

"Get on outta here, I said! I don't want no damn trouble!" The shotgun was trembling and the old man's eyes were wild. He looked fearfully from side to side and then thrust the double barrels against Curtis's chest. "I'll shoot you down, you don't move off!"

Curtis thought that if he spoke one more word the fear-crazed old man might blow a hole through him, and what good would that do for Ludenmere, Nilla and Little Jack? He had no choice but to say, "I'm movin', sir, I'm movin'." He backed off the steps and away from the door, the door slammed shut and the bolt was thrown, and Curtis turned and ran back to Sawmill Road. He began to run along the center of the road in the direction of Kenner again, and in a couple of minutes the breath was rasping in his lungs. He saw another cabin but its roof had collapsed. He kept going, as the thunder boomed distantly to the southeast and the lightning was a brief flash of illumination over New Orleans. The rain had become a drizzle. Mist was rising from the wet woods on either side of the road. Still Curtis ran on, and then he saw his shadow thrown before him on the cracked pavement.

He turned around. Headlights were coming. Coming fast.

He stood in the road's center and waved his arms up and down.

Whoever it was, they weren't touching their brakes.

"Hey! Hey!" Curtis shouted, and jumped up and down in the glare of the lights for emphasis. The car wasn't slowing; it was going to run him right over.

When Curtis realized he was about to be struck, he leaped aside and the car—no, it was a beat-up pickup truck wet with rain and somebody riding in the truckbed—swept past him doing what Curtis figured was maybe fifty miles an hour. The vehicle went on another hundred feet and then its driver must've stood on the brakes because the single working tail light flared, the pickup started skidding and it looked for an instant like it was going to swerve and crash over on its side.

After that the truck just sat there, its rough engine idling.

Curtis was about to get himself in gear again and run to the truck when the vehicle suddenly was put into reverse with a grinding of gears. It came at speed toward him, but its driver couldn't keep a straight line and the vehicle ran off the road on the right side before the steering was corrected.

Then the pickup truck was there beside him, at a crooked angle.

The driver had rolled down his window. A flashlight was clicked on and shone into Curtis's eyes.

"What're you doin' out here, boy?" the driver asked.

Curtis couldn't make out the face. The voice sounded like it belonged to a young man, but it was hard and a little slurred. He was aware that the person in the truckbed had gotten down and with a staggering gait had come around to stand on his right, uncomfortably close.

"There's a man needs help," Curtis said. "He's been—"

"I think that's him," someone else said—another young, hard voice. It belonged to the pickup's passenger. "Prob'ly is."

"There's a man's been shot," Curtis went on. "I need to get him—"

"You shoot somebody, nigger?" asked the young man on Curtis's right. His voice was also slurred, and Curtis realized these three young whites had likely been out drinking their fill to overflowing of rot-gut moonshine.

"No, not me. He's—"

"No, *sir*," said the one standing up. "You say *sir* to me, boy."

"You think that's him, Monty?"

"Prob'ly is. Charlene said he was skinny."

"Please," Curtis said. "*Listen*. There's a man's been shot and he needs help."

Monty, the passenger, went on as if Curtis had not spoken. "She said she never saw him before yest'a'day. Buck prowlin' around up here lookin' for a white girl to rape."

"Yep." The driver took a swig from a clay jug that had either been in his lap or in Monty's possession, and Curtis could smell the strong liquor of a backwoods still. "Out here up to no fuckin' good," the driver said.

"Man's been *shot*!" Curtis said, near exasperation. "Can't you hear what I'm sayin'?"

"We don't care if a damn nigger's been shot," said the one standing up. "Do we, Whipper?"

"No," said the driver. "We don't." He opened his door and slid out with the jug in hand, and Curtis thought that anybody called 'Whipper' was someone he wanted to be very far away from.

But it was way too late for that.

"If you won't help me," Curtis said, "I'm movin' on."

"Movin' on, he says," said Monty.

The passenger got out of the truck. The light was still in Curtis's eyes, and all he could make out about Whipper was that he was short and stocky and had meanness in his voice. The flashlight beam by itself was used like a weapon to blind him. Curtis looked to left and right on the road, but there was nobody else coming.

He felt the violence building. These three were eager for it, and the moonshine had only primed them further. It was only a matter of seconds now before one of them made the first move.

Curtis turned away from the truck and ran.

"Get him, Fido!" Whipper shouted, and Monty let out a happy whoop.

The third one—Fido—must've been faster than the others, because he was on Curtis like a mad dog before Curtis had made ten yards toward the woods. An arm locked around Curtis's neck, and Fido's considerable weight threw him so hard to the ground the muddy earth might've been concrete. The breath burst from Curtis's lungs, and as he rolled to get away Fido fell on him with a knee to his throat.

Something crunched. Curtis felt a pain rip from his throat up the back of his skull and for a terrible instant he feared his head would explode. Fido pinned him to the ground, that knee pressing down with paralyzing force.

"He ain't goin' nowhere," Fido said. He slapped Curtis's hands away, and then he laughed like he'd done this kind of thing many times before and enjoyed it way too much. After the laugh, he drove a fist into his victim's face that burst the nose into a bloody mass and knocked Curtis senseless.

Curtis came to with the realization that he was being dragged across the pavement. He tried to get his feet under him but one of the toughs gave him a punch in the center of the chest and again knocked the breath out of him. Someone else smacked him with an open hand across the right temple, and that person said, "Ow, shit! This nigger's got a head like iron!"

"We'll fix that for him. Get 'im up in there!"

"He don't weigh nothin'."

"Ain't been eatin' his pig's feet and shitbread. Watch the bag, Monty."

Curtis was thrown over the side into the truck's bed. His right hand hit something that felt like rough burlap. There was a movement in it and then he heard not one rattlings but many.

He lay in the truckbed on his side with the bag next to him. The rattlings subsided. One of the young men—Monty?—climbed into the truckbed and shoved Curtis's legs over with a booted foot to give himself more room. The pickup's engine gave a rattle not unlike the sound from the bag, it boomed a blast of exhaust, and then Curtis felt the truck start moving, gaining speed fast.

His face was a heavy burden of pain. He could feel his eyes swelling up. His throat also seemed to be swollen tight because he could swallow only with an effort, and that effort was the most searing agony he'd ever felt in his life. He passed out and came back again, in time to hear Monty give a yell to the misty night that sounded like the battlecry of a vicious tribe that fought a war upon every Negro skin just for the pleasure of the fighting.

And the killing too, Curtis thought in his nightmare haze. He knew these men might kill him this early morning, might beat him to death and leave him hanging by the neck from a tree limb. And then...what would become of Mr. Ludenmere, and of Nilla and Little Jack? He tried to lift his head but it weighed at least two hundred pounds. Could he speak to Monty? At least say the word *Please* as somebody might try to calm a wild animal? When he tried that, the pain that ripped through his throat was almost unbearable, and his voice was not even loud enough to be a ragged moan, but was the whisper of one.

He realized, tasting the blood in his mouth, that whatever bad injury had been done to his throat by that crushing knee…he had lost the power of speech.

In his twilight Curtis heard Whipper and Fido laugh like they were going to a fine party. Then the wind of their speed tore the laughter to shreds, and the truck growled on.

⌇

"They're still comin'."

Nilla paused in her forward motion to look back over her shoulder. Her brother was right. She could see the two lights, searching for them through the trees. Had they gotten any closer since the last time she'd looked, maybe ten minutes ago? She couldn't tell.

"They're not gonna stop," Little Jack said. It had been spoken as a dry and inescapable fact, in the same way Nilla had heard her father put things many times. In the glow of the lantern that Nilla held before her by the wire handle around her wrists, Little Jack was a creature of the forest hardly recognizable as an eight-year-old boy: hollow-eyed, bloody and muddy.

"You look like some kind of monster," she said, as if teasing her brother at this awful moment could remove them from the moment itself.

"Ha ha," he replied, but tonelessly. "And you've got alligator dookey in your hair."

They both realized at the same time that this kind of talk was not going to help anything.

"There aren't any alligators around here," Nilla said, at the same time moving the light from side to side with her heart in her mouth. The way ahead was as the way behind had been, a morass of muddy earth that sucked at their feet, low thorny brush, thickets of prickly palmettos and thin pines that had been warped into grotesque shapes by the wind off the lake. The lake itself was maybe twenty or thirty yards off to the right, through the scrubs. Across its expanse night reigned supreme, not a single dot of light anywhere.

But the two lights behind them were coming, and Nilla knew her brother was right; likely the man and woman had killed Mr. Hartley, and they were not going to stop.

"We gotta keep goin'," Little Jack said. "Can't you put that light out? If you do, they can't follow us."

"I'm not walkin' in here in the full dark. Either of us break a leg and…I don't want to think about it." She had considered that already, weighed the possibilities as much as she could—including the possibility of coming upon alligators, a nest of snakes or the wild boars that her daddy had once told her roamed around near the lake—and decided the light had to stay. One thing they could do, she figured, was to turn to the left away from the lake and head in that direction, which would be sort of south or maybe southwest. That would give them a better chance of finding a road. But was there even a road up in here within miles? She had no idea.

What had gotten on her mind and stayed there the last ten minutes or so was not the man and woman following them but what had happened to her father and Curtis.

"Let's go!" Little Jack urged.

Nilla nodded, but she took a moment to try to calm her mind, to steady herself, and then she called to her listener. :*Curtis?*:

There was no reply. She didn't feel connected to him, in that usual way of feeling the energy between them like hearing the faint crackling of the records her mama played. She didn't know if she was getting through or not…or the terrible thought, that Curtis—and her father too—were either badly hurt or dead. She tried again, and a third time. :*Curtis, please,*: she said. :*Answer me.*:

But still there was no reply from her friend, and she stood hearing only the sound of the night insects after the rain, their declarations of chirrupings and clickings returning to full volume.

She looked back over her shoulder again. Now she could tell for sure that the lights were closer. She figured that the muddy earth would be just as sticky on the shoes of the man and woman behind them as it was on their own shoeless feet—maybe worse—but it was time to move.

"All right," she told her brother, and they went on.

"Okay, haul him out."

"What the fuck are we doin' *here?*"

"Got an idea, Monty. You and Fido just get him on the ground."

Fresh pain wracked Curtis as he was pushed and pulled over the truck's side. He landed in a crumpled heap on gravelled earth. The flashlight was shone into his eyes again; he could see only through the left, as the right was almost swollen shut.

"You done a job on that face," said a voice that Curtis thought was Whipper's. "Hey, boy!" A boot's toe nudged Curtis roughly in the ribs. "What you been up to tonight?"

Curtis shook his two-ton head, unable to communicate any more than that. He thought he heard something through the pain; it was a faint and garbled :*Curtazzzzz. Pliss. Ser Me.*:

"He ain't gonna talk." Was that Fido? Curtis reckoned Fido likely had no idea what damage he'd done. "Must've been up to no good or he would'a been home. What are we gonna do with him?"

"Rusty Upton and Tater Britt fixed that one they caught last week over in St. Charles."

Monty was speaking, with a measure of pride to relate a job well-done. "Kicked his teeth in and sent him runnin' through them woods naked as a blackbird."

"Tater was in on that?" Fido asked. "Shit, I talked to him couple'a days ago, he didn't say nothin' about it."

"Yeah, he was in on it. Hell, you talk to Tater...he knows some fellas swung a nigger up in St. Tammany."

"Naw! Really?"

"Really. Gimme a drink 'fore you finish the jug off, you sot."

"Whipper, we gonna fix this one? I can kick his teeth in from right here."

"We'll fix him, all right. You and Monty pick him up."

Curtis was pulled to his feet. The light seared his good eye. His heart was pumping hard and he felt the crawl of blood over his lips and chin from the broken lump of his nose.

"Nigger," Whipper said close to his face, "we don't like to get rough, but your kind just asks for it. Just begs to be knocked back in your place, 'cause you don't know what's good for you. Out here in the night, causin' shit. No, we don't like to get rough."

"Fuck it! We *are* rough!" said Fido, with a crazed cackle.

"Gimme the jug," Whipper said. Curtis could hear him chug down the 'shine. "Okay, take it," he told one of the others as he handed it back.

Then Whipper hit him in the mouth with a hard-knuckled fist.

Curtis's lower lip was split open and two front teeth on the bottom row were knocked into his mouth. Red comets streaked through his head. His legs sagged and he would've fallen if the other two weren't holding him up.

"Nice one, Whipper," Fido said. "Couldn't'a done better myself."

"Best is yet to be," Whipper said.

There was a stretch of silence, and then Curtis heard Monty quietly say, "We could swing him, if we had a mind to."

No one else spoke.

Curtis's legs were still rubbery. As if on its own accord his right hand came up to grasp at the front of Whipper's shirt, but Whipper quickly slapped it away and said, "Don't put your dirty fingers on me, boy!"

Monty said, "I think he *is* the one looked at Charlene. Skinny and all. 'Bout the same age, I figure. Yep, he's likely the one. Runnin' loose up in here at night and all...it ain't right. We could swing him, if we could get us some rope."

"Got a better idea. Gimme another swig." When Whipper had downed it, Curtis braced himself for another blow but it did not come...at least, not yet. "Strip him naked," Whipper said.

At that, Curtis tried to fight. He started thrashing for all he was worth, but he realized within a few seconds that he wasn't worth a plugged nickel.

Whipper hit him on the left cheekbone with a brutal strength born of either practice or pure animal ferocity, and probably some of both. The blow rocked Curtis's head to the side and put out the last of his fading light. He was aware of falling, aware of sharp edges of gravel pressing into his cheek, and then he knew no more until he heard one of their voices fade in, saying, "…some kind of uniform?"

"Ain't no soldier, that's for sure."

"Could be he's run away from prison? Maybe a chain gang?"

"Naw." That was Fido's drawl. "He'd be wearin' stripes."

"Well what the hell kind of uniform is it, then?" Monty asked.

"Hell if I know," said Whipper. "Movie house usher, maybe."

"Movie house usher? Niggers ain't got their own movie houses! Do they?" No one could supply an answer, so Monty went on. "And how come he's out here at night wearin' a movie house usher uniform?"

"I don't know and I don't care," Whipper told him. "All I know is, they's ways to swing him other than a rope and a tree limb. Get everythin' off, his drawers and socks too."

"I ain't touchin' his drawers."

"Well step aside then, I'll do it. You reach over there and get the bag."

"The *bag*? What for?"

"'Cause I said to. Go on, get it done!"

Curtis heard a sliding sound and a chorus of rattlings. He felt his underwear being pulled off him, then his socks, and he thought he must be lying completely naked in the gravel.

"Throw all his damn clothes in the back of the truck. Shoes too," Whipper directed. "Gimme the bag, Monty. Pick him up and drag him yonder. That boxcar over there'll do."

Curtis felt their hands under his arms, and he was being dragged where they wanted him to be. He made out the shine of the flashlight's beam on a railroad track, but the track had so many weeds around it that it was surely not near a station.

"Right here," Whipper said.

Curtis heard the sound of a boxcar's door being pushed open, the sliders shrieking from disuse.

"Get him up in there."

He was lifted again, pushed forward and onto the splintery floor.

"Drag him over there, against that wall," Whipper directed.

On the way, one of them punched Curtis in the ribs and drove a knuckle in for good measure. Then he was thrown down with his back against the boxcar's wall. The light shone on him as the three stood admiring their work.

"Okay," said Whipper. "Gimme the bag and you two get on out."

"What're you gonna do to him?"

"Well, we ain't gonna swing him...but we'll let the snakes do the job for us. Get out, I'm gonna dump the bag on the floor."

"Shit, Whipper!" Fido said. "You gonna dump all twelve of 'em? What about the rodeo? You got some prize-winners in there!"

"This right here's the prize. We'll come back and snatch 'em up again... say give it twenty-four hours. Anyway, I can always find more of 'em. Back up, now."

One of them gave a harsh laugh. "Hot damn!" said Monty. "In twenty-four hours this nigger'll be a dead dog!"

"Yep," Whipper agreed. "That's the idea."

Curtis listened then to the ominous silence. It was broken by the noise of what he took to be rattlesnakes being shaken out of the burlap bag between himself and the boxcar's door. The sound of angry rattlings made the flesh crawl at the back of Curtis's neck.

"Nighty-night, nigger," Whipper said.

"Yeah, don't let the bedbugs bite," said Fido, and then he gave that cackle again.

Curtis heard the boxcar's door slide shut. He heard the three laugh as they were striding away. The rattlings subsided. In another moment he heard the pickup truck's engine start up. The truck boomed exhaust again, and then there was the sound of the vehicle moving away...and finally, quiet.

But not absolute quiet, because over the beating of his heart Curtis could hear the slitherings of the rattlesnakes across each other and over the boxcar's floor. They were searching for a place to crawl into, and he knew it was just a matter of time before they found him.

Twelve of them, Fido had said. At least one or two were going to crawl up against his body in the next few minutes. He was going to die from the venom of a rattlesnake's fangs, and that was that.

Nilla, he thought, though he was unable to send out any kind of message; his mind was so jangled with pain that it was impossible to concentrate. Ludenmere might already be dead...but what about Nilla and Little Jack?

A fine knight in shining armor he had turned out to be, he thought. If it weren't so terrible and his face weren't so wrecked, he might have given a grim smile to the darkness, and then he might have started sobbing.

But instead, all he could do was lie there with his back against the wall and wait for the first snake to slither up against him...and then would come the warning rattling, and the sting of the bite on his unprotected flesh.

Twenty-Three.

"They're swingin' south," Pearly said. "Tryin' to find a road."

"We're gonna have to swing wider and herd 'em back in," Ginger replied. She was carrying the flashlight in her left hand and in her right was the .45 revolver. "I figured they'd give out by now. Didn't have any food all day and I doubt they got much sleep. Won't be long, though."

Pearly nodded. He kept the beam of his bull's-eye lantern low because he was more concerned about where he was stepping. Only a few minutes ago his right foot had gone into muck that had seized him up so hard it had been an effort to pull out and he'd almost left his shoe in it. The earth was softer than it had been, and pools of water rose up to fill their footprints. Nearly hidden in the knee-high weeds and brambles were patches of darker mud that he feared were as thick as glue and just as viscous.

"Got to get 'em before daylight," Ginger said, walking ahead of Pearly a few paces, but she was being careful with her footing too. "Scoop 'em up, take 'em back and hit it to Mexico."

"You sure we need 'em?" he had to ask. "Odds are they're gonna get lost out here." It had occurred to him that he and Ginger might also get themselves lost, but he didn't want to dwell on that. As long as they stayed near the lakeshore, they could find their way back. Above them the clouds were beginning to break open and a few stars were showing through the wisps but there was no sight of a moon. "You sure we need 'em?" he asked again.

"We need 'em. If Ludenmere and that driver aren't done for, we've still got trouble, but as long as we have those brats, the cops are gonna back off. Nothin' they can do to us with those kids in the car."

"Yeah," Pearly said, but he was still thinking that this whole thing had been more about Ginger's revenge on a rich man instead of the kidnapping itself. That is, if Donnie had been telling the truth about her past. He saw that Ginger had begun to change their direction, heading a few degrees more to the south to herd the kids back toward the lake. He decided to probe Donnie's story, as much as he dared. "So," he said, "you had a kid once?"

She didn't reply.

"Donnie told me," he continued. "He said you—"

"He was a liar," she interrupted. "Liked lyin' to people to stir things up."

"So you never did have a kid?"

Again, it was a time before she answered. "When did you and Donnie ever have a talk about shit like that?"

"We just did. You were asleep."

"Now I *know* that's a lie."

Pearly didn't want to explain any further about the episode with her muttering in the chair and lost in some kind of delirium. But he couldn't let this go, it seemed important to clear up. "Donnie said…after your kid got killed…you wound up in a—"

She spun on him and put the light in his face.

"Hear me *good*," she said, and her voice was like a razor at his throat. "Donnie was a goddamned liar. He deserved what he got back there because he was stupid too, and he couldn't take orders. Because of him, look where we are. Okay, you were right…I shouldn't have pulled him in but I needed a third and it needed to be a man. He was a sorry-ass liar and what happened to him had been comin' a long time. Got it?"

"Sure," Pearly said. His voice was easy but he was as tight inside as a wound-up steel spring ready to burst. "That light in my eyes is not gonna help me move any faster, darlin'."

She lowered it. "Okay," she said. "Now quit jawin'. I figure we're only a couple of hundred yards behind 'em. They're gonna be havin' as tough a time as we are walkin' through this…likely tougher. And yes, we need 'em if we want to keep our skins before we get across the border. That do you for answers?"

"It'll do," he said. *For now*, he thought. He followed her when she turned away from him and started off again. It came to his mind that he could slide the .38 out of its shoulder holster, drill her in the back of the head and be on his way to Mexico with all that money for himself, but she was right about needing the kids. He might admire Bonnie and Clyde but he didn't want to end up on a slab, riddled with holes like their corpses were. No…drastic action in that regard could wait until later. If she got down to Mexico with him, how could he trust her not to plunge a knife into his heart as he slept, her being a nuthouse case? Two hundred and fifteen thousand dollars, with only one owner…damn, that sounded nice.

If he had to put her down, it would be self-defense, wouldn't it? Taking care of himself for the future?

"Whatever's on your mind," she said without looking at him, "get it off. I can feel you thinkin', Pearly. Don't you know that by now?"

"I'm thinkin' we need to watch where we step," he answered, a little shaken by her comment.

"Yeah," she answered, "we do need to watch that, don't we?"

He erased from his mind a quick image of the bullet plowing through her skull and coming out in a dizzy line, like in the Dick Tracy comic strip. Then he stopped thinking about anything but putting his mitts on those two brats and dragging them back, maybe roughing them up some to put the fear in them. That seemed to him to be the right thing to do.

Curtis listened.

He couldn't tell if the snakes were still moving or not, but none of them were rattling. He had pulled his knees up close to his chest and pressed his arms against his sides. When and if the first touch of snake happened, he imagined himself going as cold and still as a stone…but he knew himself, and he knew he was going to shiver when that slithering thing touched him, and then he might panic when the rattling started, and he might get up and try for the door and if he did reach the door he would fall out of here bitten by poisonous fangs on his legs and feet and he would die before anybody else even knew he was here.

He figured this boxcar had been sitting on these weeded-up rails for a long time. How long would it be before anyone found his body?

His head and face together were one hot ache. He was having to breathe through his wrecked mouth because his nose was even more wrecked.

Nilla…Little Jack…Mr. Ludenmere…he had failed them all.

The haze came and went. If he closed his eyes he might fall into a stupor that would be his finish. A strange question came to his fevered brain: what would the knights of his favorite book do, in this situation? What would Sir Lancelot do, and Sir Gawain? Sir Galahad…Sir Percival… Sir Gareth…Sir Lavayne…Sir Tristram and all the others…what would they do?

One thing he knew for sure: they would not accept defeat.

Sure, but it was a fantasy…a make-believe world they lived in…maybe there had been something called chivalry at one time, but the tales of those knights were not of the real world.

Yet…if they ever did exist…they would not be crouched here waiting to be snake-bit, when two innocents were counting on them for help. No. They would gather their wits and fight their way out. Or…maybe…*think* their way out.

But he could hardly focus his mind on anything. For sure he couldn't focus enough to reach Nilla. She couldn't help him, anyway, when she was the one who needed help the most. So…what to do? And he realized he'd better get to doing whatever it was, before the first rattlesnake found him.

Curtis had another question. What else was in this boxcar with him? Was it completely empty? He hadn't been able to see when they'd thrown him in here. The three toughs wouldn't have cared…but was there anything in here that could be *used*?

There was only one way to find out, and he had to be mighty careful. When he tried to stand, his head pounded and his stomach turned over; he had to stay where he was to battle against throwing up. The sickness passed, and he slowly got to his feet. His knees were still weak. He decided to move—carefully, very carefully—to his left and go all the way to the corner.

The second step he took was met with a rattling to his right and dangerously close. Then another snake joined in the ominous warning. Curtis backed up to his original position. The rattlings stopped. He felt enveloped in the heat of his own sweat. Surely the snakes could smell that; would they crawl toward him, or away?

Curtis had no choice but to keep exploring. He moved toward the corner on his right, feeling his way along the wall. Step after step, he expected to hear the rattlings start but none of the reptiles had gotten over there yet.

His shin bumped into something that would've scared the yell out of him if he'd been able. He reached down to find out what. His fingers made out a short stack of what felt like grainsacks, maybe three or four piled up. He groped beyond the sacks into the darkness. His right hand found a sloped wooden surface. But not the boxcar's wall…the gropings of both hands told him he'd discovered a large barrel that he estimated stood about two-and-a-half feet tall. There were two others alongside it. He tried to tip one and it moved; it was empty. A second one was also empty, but the third resisted him and whatever was in it—nails, maybe—was a heavy load.

Heavy enough, Curtis realized, to crush whatever it rolled over.

He attempted to lift one of the grainsacks to throw it toward the middle of the boxcar but its weight defeated him and he decided to save his strength for the heavy barrel. He was going to have to tip it over, roll it around in front of himself and then roll it toward the door, with him walking behind it. His feet and legs were still going to be at risk from the left and right, but he hoped the barrel's weight would crush any snake in the path he took.

In this darkness he couldn't tell exactly where the door was, so that was another risk. There had to be a few snakes over near that door...had to be, and he didn't like it but to get out of here there was only one way.

He recalled hearing or reading something that rattlesnakes could still sink their fangs even if their heads were cut off. He was aware that the barrel might roll over a body, crush the midsection or the tail and leave the head snapping at whatever it could find.

It was either find the way out or stay here, curl up and die.

He went to work trying to tip the barrel. The muscles cracked in his shoulders. If he had ever moved any heavy baggage in his life, he was going to have to get this thing over. Sweat burned both eyes, the one half-swollen up and the other nearly slitted. He had a moment of despair in which he feared the monster might be cemented to the floor. He got a shoulder against it and put a foot against the wall and pushed for every fiber of muscle and willpower Ironhead Joe had given him in the blood.

The barrel tilted over, crashed down with a tremendous wallop that Curtis thought might have nearly smashed it through the boards, and the twelve snakes in the boxcar started rattling a deadly symphony. There was one that sounded too close to his left leg. He drew his leg abruptly back, imagining that he might've just missed getting struck. He got behind the barrel and turned it—again with a mighty effort that his mama would have never believed was in him—toward the door, or his best guess of where it ought to be. He didn't think there would be a grip on the inside of the door, but it ought to slide open without a lot of effort...he hoped, because he didn't want to spend but a couple of seconds trying to do it.

A problem: even though the barrel was thick around the girth, he was going to have to bend low to roll it forward with both hands. He couldn't move that thing with one foot, which he would rather have done. But... there was no other way to do it. When he bent over, his head swam and he had to straighten up again because he thought he might pass out. The rattlings had stopped; he had the sensation that the snakes were waiting for him to make his move.

He leaned over once more, took a breath into his mouth through the holes where his teeth had been, and then he put his palms against the barrel and started pushing.

Instantly there came two rattlings from his right. They were beyond the path of the barrel, so he had to ignore them and keep rolling it toward the door. In front of him, a snake started its sharp and wicked buzzing sound. There was a crunching noise as Curtis pushed the barrel onward.

The underside of the barrel rolled up damp, and suddenly his bare feet were sliding in what he could only guess was snake guts; something twisted against his right foot, which must've been part of the body in its death throes.

Another one began rattling off on the left and the barrel crunched over that snake too. Curtis stepped on wildly thrashing coils that slapped against his heel. The boxcar suddenly seemed alive with the noise of the snakes. A third was crushed beneath the barrel, and then a fourth was caught under it. Curtis's hands were wet with rattlesnake blood. Another snake squirmed away under his left foot. He felt a scream drawing his injured throat as tight as the lynching noose he had escaped this night. There was no going back; he was only a few feet away from the door now, but there had to be more snakes around it. Their rattlings had grown to a crescendo of fury. He didn't know if he'd caught anything else under the barrel because no longer could he hear the sound of the bodies being crushed.

The blood-slick barrel hit wood. He reached out...but where was the door? His fingers searched desperately for some kind of protrusion to grip hold of. Coils flailed against his left foot but whether it was a snake writhing in agony or trying for a strike he didn't know.

The index finger of his left hand found a vertical metal lip. He curled his other fingers under it, got his right hand under it too, pushed hard—harder still—and the sliders shrieked as the door came open. Then he stepped up on the barrel and jumped through the opening into the night.

ॐ

They had tried to leave the lake behind, by heading south, but Nilla had seen by the two lights that the kidnappers were trying to cut them off, and worse…the lake was following them too.

Nilla's lantern showed that the woods had fallen away, and ahead of them looked to be a plain of grass interrupted here and there by high-standing clumps of rushes. Her light gleamed off water.

"Might as well give it up!" the woman called from maybe a hundred yards away. "Go easier on you if you do!"

"Don't listen to that," Nilla said, but she stood at the edge of what appeared to be a grassy swamp of unknown depth and she did not move.

"I'm not listenin'." Little Jack sounded nearly worn-out.

Nilla was holding herself together only with the thought that they would have reached a road or found another cabin with someone in it by now. There were no other lights anywhere and even the stars seemed dim through the last fragments of the clouds.

"Nowhere to go!" the woman called. "Get you somethin' to eat, you'll feel better!"

"Aren't they nice," Nilla said bitterly. "We've got to go into *that*, Jack. Are you ready?"

"Ready," he said.

She started off, with Little Jack behind her and about two feet to the right. She had taken six steps into the muck when she sank to her hips in water. The water splashed into her face and she held her arms up to keep the lantern from being doused. With a yelp, Little Jack sank down to the middle of his chest. "Keep going, keep going," she told him, as they waded onward through what appeared to be a grassy plain but deceived the eye. The bottom was sticky mud that caught at their feet. Suddenly Little Jack gave another cry and fell into the water; it swallowed him up, and Nilla could do nothing to help him with her hands bound and guarding the light. He came up spitting and trying to get his feet under himself but without the use of his hands and arms for balance it was a hard task; Nilla realized her brother could drown right there, as she watched helplessly.

With an effort he got himself righted and steady and said urgently, "I stepped on somethin' that jumped! I hurt my leg, Nilla...my ankle's hurtin'!"

"It was probably a turtle," she said, trying to make the best of it. "That's all it was."

"I don't know...maybe...my ankle's hurt...got twisted."

She looked back again at the lights. The man and woman would have to come through his swampy area too, but they were taller and their legs were longer.

"Maybe we ought to give up," Little Jack said, with pain in his voice. "I mean...I don't think I can go on much longer...and...I mean...maybe it's better with those two than with what else is out here."

"No," she told him. "It's not better with those two."

"They're gonna catch us anyway. We can't get away from 'em!"

Nilla shook her head. She didn't want to hear that, but she was afraid that it was true. In her despair she closed her eyes against the reality of the moment. As she waded onward she focused her mind upon Curtis and called out to him. :*Curtis? Are you there?*:

She didn't expect an answer. She suspected that something bad had happened to him and to her father. Maybe even they were both—

:*Nilla.*:

It came so weakly she could almost think it was herself, speaking to her own mind because she wished an answer so badly.

:*Curtis?*: she tried again.

:*Here,*: came the reply, still very weak, but now Nilla was sure it wasn't the echo of her own wishful thinking. :*Where...you?*:

She nearly screamed out what would've been heard by him as a confused tangle and surely not able to be understood, so she made herself take a few deep breaths and speak slowly. :*After us,*: she said, and corrected herself. :*They're after us. The two of them. Donnie'sdeadandMisterHartleygothurtwe're—*: She stopped herself again, to begin anew. :*The two of them are after us. We're in a swamp at the lake. Where are you?*:

:*Near,*: Curtis sent back. :*Been havin'…trouble. Kinda…*:

:*I can hardly hear you. Curtis, where's our daddy?*:

There was no reply. Nilla opened her eyes to see the way ahead, which was the same swamp. Something that sounded heavy splashed over on the left. She couldn't allow her connection with Curtis to be broken, not just yet. :*Our daddy,*: she sent. :*Is he dead?*:

He didn't answer at once, but then came :*Shot. Not dead…goin' for help…got in…mess.*:

That jolted her, but she hung on. :*Where are you?*:

:*On…ground. Boxcar.*: Something came over that was unintelligible, as if the sending had sped up in her head and gone by too fast to catch.

:*Did they shoot you too?*: she asked.

:*…find you. Somehow. Have to…up.*:

:*I can't understand what you're saying.*:

:*Get up,*: he said. :*Have to get up.*:

:*They want us to stop,*: she said. :*They're right behind us.*:

:*No. Don't…get you. Don't let 'em. Hear?*:

:*I hear,*: she replied, lifted up by his presence; though the sending was so terribly weak, the resolve behind it was still strong.

:*Gonna find…somehow. Find you. Don't let…*:

:*We'll keep going, Curtis,*: she said to his fading connection. :*We will.*:

He didn't come back after that. Nilla thought he sounded badly hurt…and that about her father being shot…she couldn't let her mind go to something as bad as that, or tell her brother either. All they could do was to continue to stay ahead of the two lights that were steadily gaining on them.

They came out of the water onto a weedy hummock that went on for maybe twenty feet.

Nilla saw how Little Jack was limping on his twisted ankle but there was nothing to be done for him. Then they went down again into a mass of rushes and once more the water took her in up to her waist and Little Jack up to his chest.

"No use in this, kids!" That was Mister Parr, her daddy's so-called friend, shouting at them.

His voice became softer, like he was a teacher mildly scolding them for not doing their homework. "Come on, now! If you think we're mad about Donnie…we're not. He asked for it, didn't he? Shouldn't have been in that room. You think we're mad at you, Nilla?"

She didn't want to waste her breath with a reply, which is what she figured he wanted her to do.

"Little Jack!" the man called. "Hey, you must be awful tired and hungry by now, huh?"

Nilla heard her brother make a small sound of pain as he waded forward, but he didn't answer either.

"Awful tired," the man said, almost crooning it. "And awful, awful hungry."

"Don't listen to that," said Nilla.

"I got water in both ears," he told her.

She could have hugged him, if she'd been able.

They went on, side-by-side now through the water while the lantern showed nothing ahead but more of the grassy swamp and dozens of flying insects zipping back and forth through the light. Nilla was tired and hungry too, as she knew Little Jack must be, but she was determined to keep going all night if she had to…though it seemed her brother was starting to really hurt because he'd slowed down and she could not forge ahead and leave him, no matter what.

Find you, Curtis had said.

She didn't think so. He was hurt, maybe shot. She felt herself wanting to cry for her father and for Curtis and the tears were close but she had no time for that; she was her brother's protector now, a thing she would never have dreamed possible three days ago. And, as she'd learned, a whole lot could change in three days, and in three days a little girl used to dolls and tea parties and soft pillows to sleep on could get plenty damn tough—as her daddy might have said—if she had to.

She had to…and she reasoned that she was going to have to get a whole lot damn tougher before it was all said and done, and Lord help her father and Curtis, but she and Little Jack were on their own.

Twenty-Four.

Curtis thought he must've swallowed his teeth when they were knocked out. His throat hurt like they'd given him a bite on the way down. He couldn't breathe through his nose, his right eye was nearly closed and the left swollen up too, his ribs ached, the joints of his shoulders were on fire, his knees were scraped and bloody where he'd landed on the gravel in that railyard, he was unable to speak...and what else?

Oh, yes...he was walking—staggering, mostly—along the side of Sawmill Road stark naked.

He was heading toward the town of Kenner, which shouldn't be too far. He'd already passed a closed-up gas station, and there stood a cemetery just past it on the left. He felt ready for the grave. He kept looking back and forth along the road, ready to head for the bushes if anyone came along but the police...and even if the police came by, what was a naked Negro in a small town going to say to a white policeman after two o'clock in the morning? Even if the naked Negro could speak, which this one could not. He'd tried, and it had come out as the croak of a half-dead toadfrog.

It was a bad injury. He kept spitting up blood. He had no illusions that he didn't need a hospital, and probably the emergency room, but at least he had avoided being swung. And...Nilla and Little Jack were still out there, and they needed him. How on God's green earth could he help them? It had gratified him that he'd been able to hear her and speak back to her, as hurt and messed-up as he was, but what good did that do if he didn't know *exactly* where they were? *A swamp at the lake*, she'd said, but he'd lost some of what she was sending because he'd been hearing her only in fragments.

It was a big lake and likely a big swamp, he thought as he kept walking. His hands were pressed against his ribs because it felt like one or more of them was jabbing his insides like a sharp blade. He remembered speaking to Nilla when all this had started and thinking according to her impressions that the cabin the kidnappers had taken the children to was likely past town, on the lake side. For sure they'd been on the lake side, but on the other side of town? The swamp must be past the town, so that made sense... but how far it was, he had no idea.

He needed clothes and shoes. He had stepped on half-a-dozen beer bottle caps and a dead possum. At least he was not dead himself and as long as that was true he held hope he could get Nilla and Little Jack away from the kidnappers.

But...in the real world again and not the fantasy world of faithful knights in shining armor, which Curtis thought might be getting mixed up in his head due to the beating he'd taken...*how?*

He reached the two-block town. It was completely silent until a dog started barking at him, and then a second one joined in. He ignored them and leaned against a wall for support; he wanted to slide down to the ground and rest awhile, just a few minutes to ease his legs and clear from his head the haze that came and went, but he realized that time was his enemy. What was he going to do, from this point? What *could* he do?

He made out a sign on a storefront: *Evie's 'Everything' Shoppe.*

Everything? Clothes, maybe? Shoes?

He pushed himself away from the wall and approached the store. The two dogs were still barking furiously at him, but they had come no closer. He peered through the store's front window.

Without lights, he couldn't make out what was in there except right in the window was a mannequin dressed in dungarees and a straw hat, and there were three pairs of women's shoes and a couple of pocket watches on a display shelf.

Miss Evie wasn't going to like what he needed to do, but it had to be done. He looked around for something to use. Just beyond the Everything Shoppe was a structure being built, and somebody had left a wheelbarrow full of bricks sitting in the rain. He walked to the wheelbarrow, picked up two bricks, walked back to the Everything Shoppe's front window, and without further hesitation threw one brick into the glass. It made a crash that silenced the dogs. Curtis threw the second brick into part of the window that had not completely shattered, and as the dogs started their barking again he pulled jagged shards of glass out of the windowframe and crawled in over the fallen mannequin and the shelf of shoes.

Once inside, he had to pause to get a few small pieces of glass out of his feet. He had a moment where his head swam and he felt near passing out again, but he steadied himself and then took stock of where he was, as he left bloody footprints on the gray linoleum tiles.

In the gloom he could tell the Everything Shoppe was probably a place where people either brought their castoffs to be sold or where the belongings of dead folks wound up. For sale with yellow price tags were rickety-looking old chairs and tables, some bigger pieces of furniture, a roller lawnmower, a display of pots and pans, dishes and glasses, a shelf of towels and bedsheets and…there, over by the wall and deeper into the store…a shelf of what looked to be folded-up blue jeans and some other articles of clothing.

He went through the jeans and found they were all big enough to put three Curtis Mayhews into, but there were two pairs of khaki trousers and the one with green plaid patches on the knees looked like it might fit. He got into that and found the waist snug but the length was way short of his ankles. No matter; it covered him up. A rack of men's and women's shoes stood just past the jeans shelf. A pair of worn brown workboots went on his feet; they were tight, even open without laces, but he could not be a choosy beggar. There were some colorful shirts on hangers but he found a pack of three white cotton t-shirts bound up with a rubber band. He took one of the t-shirts and shrugged painfully into it, and though it flagged around him he was satisfied with it.

A child's battered red wagon caught his eye. Next to it was a good-sized dollhouse that somebody had spent a lot of time building. And beside a round table that sagged on one broken leg was a white bicycle. It was a girl's bicycle, smaller than what Curtis was used to, but on closer inspection he found it had air in the tires and the chain looked all right. Attached to the handlebars was a woven-reed basket decorated with painted-on red and blue flowers.

The dogs had given up their barking and moved on, and it was time for Curtis to get out.

He wheeled the bicycle toward the broken window in his new used clothes and his torture chamber boots. Before he reached the window he caught sight of a water fountain off to the side. Above it on the wall was a handwritten sign *This Fountain Is For Whites Only*. He approached it, stepped on the pedal that operated the flow, put his face in the water that arced up and drank what he wanted. When he was done he went to work getting himself and the bicycle out of the window onto the sidewalk.

Should he risk knocking at the doors of any of the houses around here? He was torn on that; he needed the police, but he didn't want to be either shotgunned or beaten. Not being able to speak, he wouldn't have a chance to explain himself unless he could get to a pencil and paper, and how long would that take?

He decided he would ride out past Kenner and go along every road that led to the lake, in hopes of finding a cabin where Ludenmere's car was parked. He didn't know the car's make but he figured it would be obvious it belonged to a rich man. That would at least give him a starting point. What he would do from there, he didn't know, and maybe it wasn't much of a plan but it was all he had. He got up on the bicycle and found he was almost hitting himself in the chin with his knees, though it was going to be faster than walking. He spat onto the sidewalk the blood that kept rising into his mouth, and then he started pedalling west.

Ironheaded, he remembered his mama saying. *Just like your daddy.*

And proud of it, he thought.

His long legs worked the pedals, and like a tarnished knight on a white charger he moved on in his quest.

༖

Nilla and Little Jack waded out of the grassy swamp onto a muddy beach. The lantern showed to the left a field of knee-high brush dappled with clumps of palmettos and twisted pines, and to the right was the unbroken surface of the lake. Nilla looked back at the two oncoming lights. She had the thought that they ought to head across the field; that would be more to the south, and they might find a road in that direction. "This way," she told her brother, who was starting to limp badly on his injured ankle. Again, with her hands still bound she could do nothing to help him.

They had just started toward the field, which looked to be rougher and more uneven ground than it had first appeared, when a gunshot rang out. Nilla heard the bullet sing past her, dangerously close, and she froze in her tracks.

"Nope!" the woman called out. "Not goin' that way, darlin'! Just stand right where you are!"

"Can you run?" Nilla asked Little Jack.

"I can try."

"We'll stay on the beach," she said. "Easier going on your leg, but we've got to run and I'm going to throw the lantern away so they can't follow us by the light anymore. All right?"

"Yes."

"Okay." She said, "Let's go!" and she tossed the lantern's wire handle from her wrists into the air to her left. Then she began to run through the mud as Little Jack hobbled behind her, trying his best to keep up.

"Damn!" Ginger said through gritted teeth as she watched the lantern fly up and then crash down into the brush. Smoke was still curling from the barrel of the .45 revolver in her right hand. "I thought that would do the trick. Well, at least they're stayin' along the lake. Let's keep at 'em." She started wading through the last of the swampgrass toward the shore.

Pearly followed her. "Kinda risky shootin' at our insurance policies," he said.

"I want to keep 'em right out here 'til they wear out. They think they're bein' smart, but without that light they're not goin' much further and they won't try to go inland. Mark it, they'll be givin' up soon."

"Didn't you say that half-an-hour ago?"

"Maybe." She looked up at the wide expanse of stars. "Still got more'n three hours before first light. We'll run 'em to ground and be on the road in another hour."

"Unless we miss 'em in the dark," he said. "We could go right past 'em and not know it."

"City kids," she answered as they reached the shore. "Without that lantern, they'll stay near the lake where the goin's easier. Trust me, Pearly. They're gonna give out and we'll find 'em sittin' on the ground waitin' for us real soon."

He was starting to doubt that, but he said nothing. He thought that when they got the kids he was going to beat the blood out of them for this, and in his mind he saw their faces struck with terror and plastered with the handfuls of lake mud he was going to shove into their mouths. Time was being wasted when he and Ginger should be on their way to Mexico with all that money, but she was right…they needed the brats to keep from ending up shot to pieces at a highway roadblock, because if the kids were left to go free it wouldn't be long before they found their way out of here and flagged down help, and soon after that every cop in Louisiana, Mississippi, Arkansas and Texas would be on the alert, and it was a long way from New Orleans to Brownsville. Pearly figured it could be that if Ludenmere and the nigger driver weren't dead they had already gotten to the law, which made it even more imperative to get hold of those kids. Without the brats, it could be a Bonnie and Clyde massacre all over again.

He followed behind Ginger along the muddy shore. Their lights searched the darkness ahead, as about seventy yards in front of them Nilla had had to slow down for Little Jack to keep up.

"Can't keep runnin', Nilla," her brother said. "My leg's hurtin'. I'm sorry."

"All right," she told him. "We're—" She stopped, because in front of them she could make out a shape blocking their way. In another moment, as they neared it, the shape became the wreck of a small boat turned on its side with a gaping hole torn in the hull. They went around it, through a little tangle of thicket, and there was another boat—at least the front part of it—half buried in the mud. Something else stood on the shore beyond the second boat, and in the darkness it looked like the broken remnants of an ancient castle rearing up against the stars. Pieces of splintered wood littered the ground. As they got closer to the structure, Nilla almost walked into part of a sign that had been nailed up between a pair of timbers. She could make out the lettering on the part that had not been torn away, black against white but ravaged by the elements: HEAD MARINA.

A wooden staircase with a few missing risers rose up ten feet into the ruin, which appeared to have been built upon wharf pilings. She looked back and saw the lights just coming around the first wrecked boat. It occurred to her that she and Little Jack were going to be caught before they could get past this structure, but maybe there was a place inside it that they could winnow into and hide. "Up the stairs!" she said, and she waited for Little Jack to hobble up before she came. The staircase swayed beneath them, tortured nails squealed and one of the battered risers that was rotten and as soft as butter gave way under Little Jack's feet, but then they were up on what maybe had once been a screened-in porch, the rain-soaked planks of the floor tilted to the right and the roof torn off. The black rectangle of a doorway led back into...what? A room with no floor? One more step, and they could plunge down onto jagged pieces of boards, broken glass and nails.

Nilla focused her mind on Curtis, and he might not hear her but she had to try.

:Curtis!: she sent out. :We're at a marina! It's all broken up...something Head Marina! Can you hear me?:

A few terrible seconds passed, and then he came back to her. :I hear you.:

:We're gonna try to—: She had to break off, because she could see the lights down at the bottom of the stairs and the beams swept upward.

ↄ

:Try to what?: he asked, but he got nothing back.

He was pedalling the bicycle down the second road he'd found; the first had ended at a pier and a pair of darkened cabins, no cars around. The second road was the same, another pier and another cabin…but there looked to be a little fishing boat tied up at the pier, and beside the cabin was an old car…surely not a rich man's car, but a car all the same. Was there a light in the cabin? Yes…he caught a glint of it, moving past a window. Then a door opened at the back and a figure emerged carrying a flashlight and something else, Curtis couldn't tell what. The person trudged slowly down toward the pier…an early morning fisherman, Curtis thought. Going out to fish after the rain.

Did he dare to chance this? He had to.

He pedalled forward to get between the fisherman and the pier. As soon as the bike's chain clattered in its sprockets the fisherman spun around and aimed the light at Curtis.

"Who's there?" It was a woman's voice, tense with fright.

Curtis got off the bicycle, let it fall, and lifted his hands up over his head. He started walking toward the woman. The light jabbed him in the eyes.

"Stay where you are!" she ordered. "Don't you come no closer!"

He stopped and lowered his hands. He tried to speak, but pain wrenched his throat and what came out sounded like a groan.

"Sweet Jesus!" the woman said. "Who's been dancin' on your face, boy?"

He put a hand to his throat and shook his head.

"What? You can't talk?"

Again, Curtis shook his head.

"You need a doctor! Hospital, I'm thinkin'!" She approached him, but cautiously.

"God A'mighty, how are you walkin'?" She stopped a few feet away and lowered the light.

With his good eye, Curtis could make out that she was a thin but wiry-looking Negro woman maybe up in her sixties, wearing overalls and a tobacco-brown blouse with a red-checked neckerchief. White hair boiled out around a much-worn brown cap with a badge on it that displayed a red winged horse and the words *Magnolia Petroleum*. He noted uneasily that in addition to the flashlight she was carrying in her left hand a five-foot-long shaft of wood with a sharpened iron speartip on the end. Around her waist was a leather belt that held a bone-handled knife in its sheath.

He pointed at her knife.

"What? You want that?"

He nodded.

"You crazy, or drunk?"

He shook his head and made a motion with the fingers of his right hand for her to hurry and comply.

"I ain't givin' you my knife! You're out of your damn mind!"

Curtis offered his left thumb and with the index finger of his other hand made a short cutting motion across it.

"What? You wantin' to cut your thumb off?"

Another shake of the head. He kept doing the cutting motion.

"Hell, no!" she said.

He abruptly spat blood into his left palm. It was watery, but red enough. He stretched out the tail of his t-shirt, dipped his index finger into the little bloodpool and wrote HELP ME on the white cotton.

Then she knew what he was getting at, but she said, "You been beat near crazy, boy, but I'll tell you...I can get you with my gator sticker faster'n you can stick me, so stamp that on your brainpot." She lifted the knife from its sheath and gave it to him, handle first.

Curtis did not hesitate. He clenched the teeth he had left and cut a groove across his left thumb. The pain wasn't much, compared to what he'd already endured. Red blood welled out. He gave the knife back to her and, using his index finger as a pen dipped into the gory inkpot, he began to write on the tail of his t-shirt.

HEAD MARINA?

"Head to a marina? That's what you mean?"

He shook his head and pointed at the raggedly-scrawled word HEAD. Then he aimed his bloody finger toward the west.

"Boar's Head marina?"

Curtis gave a vigorous nod. That must be the place Nilla and Little Jack had reached.

"Nothin' there but a wreck. Storm took it nearly all down couple'a summers ago."

He pointed at himself, at her, and toward the boat, which he could now see had a small outboard motor. Then he made a jabbing motion to the west again.

"You want to go to Boar's Head marina? Why?"

He squeezed blood from his thumb and underlined the HELP ME once, twice and a third time.

Then he wrote POLICE and he put a fist to his ear in emulation of a telephone.

"Call the police?"

A nod answered that question.

"Ain't got no telephone. The nearest p'lice station is back a ways toward Metairie. What you got y'self into?" She realized he was unable to answer that one. "Damn," she said quietly. She looked from him to her boat and back again. "You needin' to get there quick?"

He tried his hardest to speak. It came out as a raspy and mangled "*Kik.*"

"I know a way through the marsh, take us maybe ten, fifteen minutes. Jesus, sonny! This is some mighty strange shit right here you're askin', and me not knowin'..." She let it go. "Well," she said, "you can tell 'em at the nuthouse that this was Fay Ripp's good deed for the year. Or maybe it's a *bad* deed. Come on, then, get in the boat."

∽

"Brains before beauty," Ginger said as they played their lights up the stairs. "Go on, I got a fuckin' rock in my shoe." She bent down to take care of it.

Pearly started up. The risers were spongy underfoot. He wanted to get this done and rub lake mud in the faces of those damn brats, for all this trouble. He would remember this moment, with all the muck on his shoes, when he was lying on the beach in Mexico with a hundred and seven thousand, five hundred dollars in a box under the bed in his house up on the hill...or, at least, however much money he had left after he bought the house. Then he would be set, and never again would he hear shit like *Mama, don't give this man no—*

It happened very fast.

He'd been stretching to get over a missing step, and when he put his foot down the next riser seemed to melt away, his weight shifted and he dropped his lantern to grab for the railing and the riser he had his other foot on broke loose like a rotten tooth and he fell through, just like that.

He landed hard on a chunk of debris, broken boards, glass and the tree stump that had been there at the lake's edge since the Boar's Head marina was cobbled together. He had an instant of realizing that a section of the floor inside the place had collapsed and slid into a muddy pocket below the stairs, and then the pain in his right knee seared through his leg and he nearly bit his tongue all the way through.

"Mercy," he heard Ginger say. "I was kinda thinkin' those stairs wouldn't take much weight."

His lantern was still lit and was lying somewhere off to his left. It was shining in his face. He tried to sit up and a nail went through the flesh between his thumb and forefinger. The bull's-eye lantern's beam left his face; she had leaned down to pick it up.

"Shit!" he said, through the blood in his mouth. "Hurt my fuckin' knee."

"Ouch," she answered.

"I think I can crawl outta here. Damn, that hurts!"

"Well," she told him, "just lie there a minute and catch your breath."

"Yeah," he said. "We got those kids trapped now."

"Trapped," Ginger said. "Yep. Sure are."

He heard the easy lilt of her voice and he didn't like it. There was something terribly cold about it, and it reminded him of the way she'd spoken to Doc Honeycutt there in the woods outside Stonefield, just before—

"Help me outta here," he told her. "Come on, gimme a hand." He tried to start crawling on his own, and the pain shot through his knee on a path down to his foot. When he put his hand there where the pain was the worst, he found what he guessed was four inches of sharp-edged wood sticking out of the cloth of his trouser leg. It had gone in behind his knee like a knife's blade. He brought his hand back up and looked numbly at the blood on his fingers, which Ginger was also looking at by the lantern's beam.

"That's not good, is it?" she asked.

"I can walk, once I stand up. You gonna help me, or not?"

"Well...you probably couldn't make it back to the car, could you?"

"Hell yes, I could!" Did he hear himself whine? He did, and it shamed him.

"Come on, then. If you can crawl out on your own you ought to be able to walk."

He tried again, furiously, by pushing both legs against the tangle he was caught in, but the pain was so bad he broke into a cold sweat and he feared his knee must be broken as well as pierced by the wooden dagger. "Shit!" he said, both terrified and enraged. "All right, stop fuckin' around and help me!"

"Hm," she answered. "Pearly," she said after a few seconds of silence, "you don't know Ginger too well, do you?"

"Huh? *What?*"

"Ginger always, always, *always*...helps Ginger. Haven't you figured that out by now?"

"What shit are you spewin'?"

"You can't make it back to the car. Oh, I guess I could half-carry you, but who's gonna keep the kid from runnin' off again?"

"The *kid?* Huh?"

"Yeah," she said. "I only need one. The other one I'm gonna take care of soon as I get myself in there...and thank you for lettin' me know how weak those steps are. Figure I'm gonna have to find another way in."

"Are you *crazy*?" he asked, and instantly regretted it. "You need me! You can't just leave me here!"

"True," she said.

Pearly heard the click of the .45's hammer going back. His hand started to go for his shoulder holster but he knew he couldn't get the pistol out in time and she would shoot him dead as soon as he moved.

"Listen," he said, and his voice trembled. "Please. We've been through a lot together. I did everythin' you asked. I took care of things. I did things *right*, Ginger. Without me, you couldn't have pulled this off. You know that's the truth! Listen...I'm gonna crawl out of here on my own...I'll stand up, I'll make myself walk...we'll get the kid...whichever one you want... and we'll be on the way to Mexico. Hear me?" As he spoke, his left leg pushed at the debris but the right one had gone dead. He felt tears burn at the corners of his eyes, and he thought—and feared to think—that she'd been patiently waiting for a chance to kill him just as she'd been waiting to finish off the old doc. *You fit the bill and the time was right*, she'd said to him what seemed a very long time ago.

Now he realized he no longer fit, and his time had run out.

"Mexico, Ginger!" he whined desperately. "That's where we're goin', with all the money anybody could dream of! Mexico...out of all this shit, that's where we're goin'!"

"Here's your Mexico," she said quietly, and she pulled the trigger.

Pearly saw the flame leap from the .45's muzzle. In the instant before the brains were blown out of the back of his skull by the bullet that entered his forehead he smelled not the tang of gunpowder, but the sad odor of rotten peaches.

The woman he had known as Ginger LaFrance spent a moment crawling in under the broken stairs and retrieving the .38 from the dead man's shoulder holster. Her face with its champagne-colored eyes was without expression. She tossed the .45 away, since it was out of bullets and would just be extra weight. Then she crawled back out, stood up and with the bull's-eye lantern regarded the treacherous stairs. There was a huge hole nearly in the middle of it where the recently deceased had fallen through. She decided there must be another way in, and she backed away from the stairs and went to the left up over more timbers and sheets of tin roof that had blown off, heading around to the other side.

She had to climb up a small rise. At the top her light found a cleared-off dirt area that must've been a parking lot, but here the ground was level with the marina building. A large section of the roof had slid down nearly to the ground and hung half-suspended over the building where another door ought to be. There were two rectangular windows up toward the roofline, on either side of where the door would be, and both were glassless but too narrow for even the bodies of children to climb through. The light picked out an *Enjoy Coca-Cola* sign on the wall that had survived the blow, along with a mounted thermometer that showed the painted picture of a hooked fish jumping, and from the few dozen bullet holes it was a popular place for target practice.

She pulled aside the tin roofing, careful it didn't come sliding down on her head, and exposed an opening where a door had been. She shone the light within and saw the room was mostly still held together though the floor and walls were all buckled, black with mildew, and dripping wet from the rain that had slammed through the space where the roof used to be. Her light couldn't find the children, but she was sure they were still in the building somewhere. She imagined she could smell their fear, like the pungency of bitter wine.

Her eyes glinted above the lantern's beam. When she stepped into the room she felt the weakened and diseased boards give beneath her weight. She held her gun down at her side, but ready when she needed it.

"All right, kiddies," she said, with a tight half-smile. "Come to mama."

Twenty-Five.

"Nilla," Little Jack whispered, "there's somethin' crawlin' on my neck!"

She shushed him. Whatever it was, it could not be any worse than what had just crawled into that other room and said to come to mama.

They were hiding in a bathroom the size of a broom closet at their house. They had found the door to it when they'd carefully followed their hands along the walls of that first room they'd entered off the porch and realized that half the floor had collapsed, leaving a rim of broken planks. Part of the bathroom's ceiling had been torn open to expose the night sky and the floor was sloppy with standing water.

The door was warped but Nilla had been able to close it using the strength of her shoulder. With the tips of her fingers she had pushed the latch into its socket. Then she'd told Little Jack to sit down on the floor under the sink and she had taken a position with her back against the toilet and both feet up against the door with her knees bent.

They'd heard a single gunshot. What that meant they didn't know… but they knew the woman was in the building with them, and that was bad enough.

Nilla thought the woman must be able to hear her heartbeat, it was so loud in her own ears.

:*I'm comin',*: Curtis suddenly sent to her. :*Mizz Ripp says we'll be there in 'bout five minutes.*:

:*Who?*:

:*Mizz Ripp was goin' out to catch turtles. I'm in her boat. We're 'bout five minutes away,*: he repeated, if she hadn't understood that the first time.

:*The woman's in here,*: Nilla said. :*We're hiding in a bathroom. I don't know where Mister Parr is. They've got guns, Curtis.*:

:*All right. Stay where you are, don't move.*:

:*Did you hear me? They've got guns.*:

:*I heard,*: he answered.

Her focus on speaking to Curtis was interrupted when a wash of light sneaked under the door. Then it was gone; then it back came again, searching.

Nilla heard her brother catch and hold his breath, as if that would do any good.

The light went away.

"Where might a couple'a little mice be hidin'?" they heard the woman say. "I think, maybe...*here.*"

The bathroom's door gave a quiet creak. Nilla felt the slight tremor in her feet and figured the woman had placed a hand against the wood. The light returned, aimed at the crooked crack between the bottom of the door and the floor.

"Sign on this door here says 'Rest Room'," she told them. "You restin' in there?" By the light's glow Nilla saw the doorknob slowly turn from left to right and back again. The door creaked again, a little louder; Nilla could feel the woman pushing on it. "Oh, now," she said softly, "you locked yourselves in? That's not gonna do you a whole hell of a lot of good. Kiddies, you're gonna make me mad, havin' to go through all this. And when Ginger gets mad," she said, her voice still easy, "Ginger stops actin' like a lady. You hearin' me, Nilla honey?"

Beside Nilla, Little Jack shifted and tried to rub the back of his neck on the underside of the sink. He bumped his head on a pipe and from beneath the sink came a hollow-sounding *thrummmm.*

"Must be ghosts in there," Ginger said.

Nilla and Little Jack heard the skreek of her fingernails being drawn slowly down the wood, and maybe she was getting splinters under them or in her fingers but they didn't think she cared about that...or really, cared about much of anything except pulling them out of that bathroom.

There followed a silence in which Nilla's heartbeat was deafening.

Then Ginger threw herself against the door with a scream of rage.

It was so raw, so primal and so animalistic that it made Little Jack cry out with a bleat of terror and jam himself further under the sink. Nilla let loose her own shrill scream with the effort of keeping her feet up against the door as it bowed inward and the wood gave off the pops of pistol shots.

Ginger hit the door again, the violence of the blow shuddering up through Nilla's knees and legs. Nilla gritted her teeth...the next blow was sure to break the latch and then the woman would be on them.

But it did not come.

"*Shit*," they heard the woman mutter.

Then they heard what she must have: the distant noise of an outboard motor, coming closer.

Fay Ripp slowed the boat and cut the motor. The craft drifted toward shore. "Can't get much further in," she told Curtis, who sat at the front. "Pilin's where the wharf used to be could tear the hull open. You'll have to get out here, if you're goin'."

He nodded in the beam of the flashlight that rested on the plank seat beside his captain.

With an effort he was able to croak, "'lice."

"I'll fetch 'em. Take me some time, though. You sure you want out?"

Once more a nod affirmed his decision.

"Damn," she said. "Must be awful important." She looked toward the ruin of the Boar's Head marina. Was there the glimmer of a light somewhere up there in the wreckage? She picked up the flashlight and offered it to him. "Whatever it is you've got to do, this might help."

Curtis took the light. *They've got guns*, Nilla had said. Never in his life had he used a weapon or held anything in his hand that might cause injury to someone, but now...he needed something, though it wouldn't be much use against guns. He leaned forward and put his hand on the sharpened lance that Fay Ripp used to prod alligators away from her turtle catch. Then he looked at her, waiting for her to answer.

"Yeah," she said. "Go on and take it."

With the flashlight in one hand and the lance in the other, Curtis eased himself over the side into chest-deep water.

"Careful where you step, boy," she told him. She waited for him to move away a safe distance, then she throttled up the motor again and turned the boat in the direction they'd come.

Curtis waded in over mud, rocks and past several broken wharf pilings that stood just above the surface. When he reached the shore he stood looking at the place he had been called to reach. :*Nilla,*: he said, :*I'm here,*: but she didn't answer.

He followed the flashlight's beam a few more feet to a staircase that led up to the remnants of a porch. He saw that the stairs were too broken to be used...and then he saw the body on the ground below them, lying in a mess of debris. The man's eyes were open, fixed in death, and the face—once handsome, maybe even cherubic—had been distorted by the impact of a bullet to the forehead.

So, he thought, it was just the woman now. What had Nilla said her name was? He couldn't remember.

Whoever she was, she was deadly.

It came to him that he might fail in this. The odds were so much against him. Coming into this situation—to save his friend and her brother—with a lance might have worked for the knights of old, but against a gun...no. But he wouldn't be able to shoot anybody, even if he could get a gun; it wasn't in him to wish harm on anyone, he just wanted to get the kids back.

He realized he likely wasn't up to facing the kind of evil that might be inside that wrecked marina...but who else was there to do it?

Ironheaded. Just like your daddy.

Yes, he thought. I am.

He shone his light up the stairs again, and that was when he saw the woman standing on the porch aim her gun at his face.

"Now!" Nilla cried out, and she and Little Jack hit the woman from behind an instant before the gun went off. The bullet hissed past Curtis's head. They had come out of the bathroom even though the lantern had been left on the floor to keep them cowed, but Nilla had heard Curtis say *I'm here* and had figured the woman—and Mister Parr too?—must've gone out to see who was there.

They all fell from the porch in a tangle, as Nilla had hit Ginger LaFrance high and Little Jack had thrown himself against the backs of her knees. They came down into the mud and the lake's wavelets only a few feet away from Curtis, who backed away with a strangled noise of alarm. His light showed the three figures thrashing, trying to disentangle, and then the woman struggled up, caught Nilla by the hair and put the pistol's barrel to her head.

Her name, Curtis thought frantically. What was—

"*Vesta,*" he said, the pain tearing through his throat. "*No.*"

It had sounded like the moan of wind through a graveyard.

The woman's head swivelled toward him.

By the light that fell upon her mud-streaked face, she looked stunned. Her mouth worked but made no noise. She shivered, as if a stranger speaking her true name had been the ultimate violation, as if truth itself were her mortal enemy, as if it had reached into her soul with a clawed hand and torn open something that had long been buried, and ought to have been.

In the next instant her face became a rictus beyond rage. It contorted into a horror that could freeze the blood and cause any man to retreat before its draconic ugliness.

But the son of Orchid and Ironhead Joe stood his ground.

She lifted the pistol and fired once, shooting him in the chest. As Curtis staggered back under the bullet's impact, she walked forward and shot him again, the second bullet striking him in the left side. He lost the light and the lance and he fell. She advanced on him, the hammer clicking back for a third shot to his skull.

With an anguished cry, Nilla swung a thin piece of board she'd clenched in a deathgrip off the ground and had jammed down as far as she could between her fingertips. The three rusted nails that protruded from its end smacked into the side of Ginger LaFrance's neck. Nilla wrenched her fingers off the board and it just hung there. The woman gave a gagging sound, and when she turned toward Nilla her eyes held the fires of Hell and blood was streaming from her mouth down over her chin.

The revolver rose up like a snake's head.

A speartip tore through the woman's chest from behind.

Curtis's thrust had had the power of desperation behind it, even though he felt himself fast ebbing. Nilla and Little Jack saw the speartip dripping heart's blood. The woman looked down at it as if a strange flower had bloomed from her breast. The gun went off, its slug plowing into the mud between the children, and then it fell from her shivering hand.

The woman of many names sank down to her knees but slowly, as if defying gravity and her mortal wound. She leaned forward on both hands. Blood spooled from her mouth. Curtis had fallen again and was crawling toward Nilla and Little Jack. The woman gave a shudder. Her head moved from side to side as if seeking out the one who'd stabbed her.

Curtis saw her eyes find and fix upon him.

"Who are you?" she whispered.

And again, with a rasp of indignant anger: "Who are you? Who...are you? Who—"

Her elbows gave way and her face fell forward, her eyes and mouth still open and filling up with Lake Pontchartrain water and mud, her secrets likewise buried in the muck. The lance's shaft stuck up from her back like the pole of a victory flag.

Curtis lay on his side.

Nilla reached him first. Little Jack tried to walk but his bad ankle gave way and he just sat down, his face blanked with shock.

"Curtis!" Nilla said, and seeing his mangled face and all the blood she began to weep. "Curtis!" she said. "Curtis…oh…Curtis!" She put her head down against his, as the lake washed against them both.

:*That's my name*,: he answered, but even face-to-face like this it was a weak sending. :*Don't wear it out*.:

"Talk to me!" she begged. "Please!"

:*Am talkin'. Not so good at the other way no more*.:

"We've got to get out of here…get help…somebody…"

Curtis tried his best to speak. It was with an effort that he thought might be his last. "Comin'." And then, back to what he could do. :*Police. Mizz Ripp…gone for 'em*.:

"Nilla," Little Jack said tonelessly, "I think…somebody's lyin' over there under the steps."

:*Shot dead*,: said Curtis.

It would be Mister Parr, Nilla knew. The other gunshot they'd heard. The woman had killed him before she'd come in after them.

With a shudder and a gasping of breath through the mud in her mouth, Vesta suddenly sat up.

As Curtis, Nilla and Little Jack looked on in horror, the woman struggled to her feet. She fell again, and again fought her way up. Her back was toward them, and she did not try to turn around or disturb the lance that pierced her body or the nail-pocked piece of board in the side of her neck. She began walking into the lake, step after step, and watching her through the descent of red haze in his vision Curtis thought she might be a traveller at the Union Station, crossing the marbled tiles to catch a train for an unknown destination.

She kept going as the water rose past her knees, up her thighs, and to her waist. Very suddenly she halted her progress and stood in place against the night and the stars. She remained there for several seconds, standing perfectly still in the grip of the lake, until at last she fell backward with an almost graceful motion, one hand flying up as if to give the world a final gesture of contempt. The folds of her dress floated around her, and her body swayed upon the water like any old piece of debris torn from what had once been a life.

It was over, Curtis thought. Whatever evil engine had powered that woman…it was gone.

"Is she dead?" Little Jack called to them, a cry both frantic and dazed. "Is she dead?"

:*Won't hurt you anymore,*: Curtis told her, and she said to her brother, "The police are coming. We're going to be all right."

"Yeah…yeah…but is she *dead*?"

Neither Curtis nor Nilla could make out the body any longer. Nilla didn't want to leave Curtis, get the flashlight and look for the woman; she was terrified that she would see her shambling back to shore to drag them all to a watery grave. She said, "She's dead, Jack. Just shut up now, hear?"

"Hell with it, then," he answered, which sounded just like their father.

"Our daddy," she said to Curtis. "Is he…I mean—"

:*Alive when I left him. I just…I don't know.*:

Nilla figured that was the best answer she could get, at the moment. Someone had beaten Curtis badly, he'd been through torment, and she feared that he was dying right in front of her. She couldn't stand it, that she could do nothing to help him, that he'd come so far and done so much for both of them, and now…all she could do was offer him a listener.

"They'll be here soon," she told him. "I know they will be."

:*Soon,*: he agreed. :*Mizz Ripp…she won't let us down.*:

"Get you to a hospital," Nilla said. "Oh, Curtis…without you…what would've happened?"

:*Nothin' good to speak of,*: he answered. :*Goin' home soon. Yes, you are.*:

She was silent, and he stared up at the stars.

The pain wasn't so bad, but he was getting cold. Funny, on such a warm and humid night as this, to be feeling a chill. But it was morning, wasn't it?

What time might it be? Well, the sun would rise in a few hours, and Nilla and Little Jack were free. That was the important thing.

Curtis was not afraid. He knew the police wouldn't be there in time for him, and any hospital was too far away. No. He knew it, like he knew the schedules of the trains. He felt himself weakening; he felt himself going away, as if he were dissolving into the very earth itself.

But he had done the right thing, he thought. It seemed to him that any right thing called for a price to be paid. He was glad to pay this one, and he had no regrets about it. His life for theirs…a small price, he thought.

"Hang on," Nilla said. Her voice was choked, because she also knew. "Please hang on."

:*I'll try,*: he replied, :*but…my fingers…they're gettin' some tired.*:

"What?" she asked. "I could hardly hear."

Even that was going away.

He wondered if they would've done the same thing. Them. The knights. Sir Tristram…Sir Gawain…Sir Lancelot…Sir Dynadan…Sir Galahad…all the rest of them. Would they have done the same thing? He hoped that if they lived in some other form, in some other place, they might welcome his approach…and one of them—or their shadows or shades in that mystical place—might stand before him and say the most wonderful thing.

Enter in.

"Thank you, Curtis," said the damsel. "Thank you so much for what you've done."

His eyes were closed but he was still breathing, though shallowly, when she and Little Jack heard the siren coming. It was back a ways, on a road that connected to the parking lot behind the marina. Nilla put her fingertips against Curtis's cheek. She said, close to his ear, "The police are here! I'm going to go meet them. Hang on, Curtis. Please…they're here. Do you understand?"

She heard his reply, and she was amazed that in it he sounded as strong as what he had always been.

:*I do understand,*: he said.

She stood up. She and her brother climbed the small rise to the parking lot. Little Jack was limping badly on the injured ankle that his fall off the porch had not helped. But they were both rewarded by the sight of the oncoming red pulse of the police car's spinning light...no...there were two police cars, one following right after the other, both with sirens and lights going.

Nilla looked back toward the lake in time to see it.

Afterward, she never knew if it was the brightness of the police cars' spinners or her own exhaustion and imagination, and she never told anyone about it either, but it seemed to her that she caught a flash of almost incandescent light—a streak of it—not going directly upward but rather upward and out, like a meteor flying across the lake...but it was a strange thing, because it was so small...just a little thing...as small as a bird.

And it was gone, in a heartbeat.

FIVE.

Listening

Twenty-Six.

It was true that the Devil could be a man or a woman. That the Devil could be the hard spring in the seat of a car, a gnat in the eye or the whack of a wooden baton on the iron bars of a jail cell. True also that the Devil could get behind the wheel of that car with the hard spring in the seat, and drive crazy and wild with no regard for any human being, and cause one hundred and ten million kinds of suffering for anybody and everybody until the Devil, he drives that car right over the cliff and it smashes to pieces on the sharp rocks underneath.

"Then," said the widowed Methodist preacher who married Orchid Mayhew in the autumn of 1938, "the Devil runs for cover because the Devil, he don't clean up after he wrecks the car. Nossir! It's the Good Father who comes in and cleans up. Puts that broken engine together. New lamps in those busted headlights. New glass in the windshield. Fresh new tires, so the car that was wrecked by the Devil's hand—the Devil's bad, bad drivin'—is ready to go afresh for many, many more miles.

"Now why don't the Good Father stop that Devil from gettin' behind the wheel of that car to begin with?" he asked the congregation of the Beloved Savior Methodist Church of Ville Platte, Louisiana. "We all want to know that, don't we? *Why* is the question we ask. Well, I am human and am afflicted in the human way of not bein' able to know the true will of God, but I do know this: whatever wreckage you're facin', however bad it seems, however much it looks like your engine is broken and will never *ever* run again...the Good Father is a mighty, mighty fine mechanic. If you *let* Him be. If you give up that old car the Devil's drove off the cliff. Let the Good Father work on it, 'cause the Devil...he done run for the low country."

In October of 1934 Orchid had moved from New Orleans to her family's farm a few miles outside Ville Platte. She was able to offer her Pap the two thousand dollars she had received as a gift from Mister Jack Ludenmere, and from part of that he was able to buy a much-needed new tractor. She moved into her old bedroom at the back of the house, where she languished until her Pap and Maw said she was going to go to the church picnic this year or they were going to put her in a basket and sell her as used laundry. She went, grudgingly, and that made all the difference.

She and the Pastor Micah—Mikey, to her—had a happy home situated across the street from the church. She turned out to be a very able decorator, and some of the ladies of the church valued her eye in that way. When they visited her home, they never failed to ask about the beautiful glass with diamond-like facets around its base that sat on a little square of dark blue velvet in an alcove. "My nice glass," she told them. "I don't ever use it, but I keep it there...sort of in a place of honor. Waterford, it's called. And...I don't think there'll ever be another one quite like it. Not in the whole world yet to come."

The ladies agreed. It was indeed a very nice glass.

Wendell Crable used part of the two thousand dollars he received from Mister Jack Ludenmere to buy himself a fine radio. At night he listened to the world, and by day he kept it moving. He was seventy-two years old when he left his employment as master of the Redcaps in 1937. He saw many young men come and go, he mentored some and hurried some off, because his main concern was keeping the distress out of his house. On the day of his official retirement he was honored with a plaque for exceptional service to the Union Station and its customers, which was placed on the wall that travellers passed in their hurry to get somewhere else, and stayed in its location until the terminal was torn down in 1954 to make room for the new one just across the street.

Ol' Crab passed away in March of 1941, and was laid to rest with his wife and his daughter in St. Louis Cemetery Number 1, almost within smelling distance of the incense and gumbo of Congo Square, and the hearing distance of its strengthening drumbeats.

After his stay in the hospital, Clay Hartley got a new glass eye and continued to be a chauffeur to the Ludenmere family until the summer of 1942, when it was clear that at eighteen Nilla wanted to either drive herself or be chauffeured by her beaus, and L.J. at sixteen was gnawing his knuckles to get behind the wheel of a car. Hartley—*Mister* Hartley, the grown-up kids always called him—announced it was time to move on. He wanted to see Canada from coast to coast, and maybe while he was up that way he might head to Alaska too. It's an open road, isn't it? he'd said to his boss, and to that announcement of retirement Jack Ludenmere gave him a check for ten thousand dollars and a brand new Chrysler Town and Country station wagon with wood panels on the sides.

The pressure for L.J. Ludenmere to take over his father's business was intense. The issue was settled when L.J., as a junior at LSU in 1945, went with some classmates to Atlanta and wound up at a provocative-sounding play titled *Kiss And Tell*. The play wasn't that provocative, but one of the young actresses—Sophie Haydon by name—so enthralled L.J. that he had to meet her. He wound up making his father explode and his mother reach for her medicines when he abandoned college and trailed Miss Haydon to Hollywood. In short order he found that being a success at anything in Hollywood was a tougher challenge than following in his father's footsteps, but he refused to fall back on his family's money...mostly because his father had cut him off at the roots.

L.J. got a job in the mailroom of a public relations firm and in four years had an office with a window. He became known as a hard-charger, a guy who could curse the paint off the walls, but also a man with big, solid ideas and the ability to bring together many different viewpoints. The term "Ask L.J." became the key phrase in the firm of SBMW Associates, and when Battels retired the name was changed to SJMW Associates. In 1959 he married Amy Vee Vallant of the Texas oil Vallant family, who he met during a children's hospital fund-raising function in Dallas. They had two boys and a girl, and L.J. and the family flew back to New Orleans on occasion to see the old house and the stomping grounds, and to beat at golf the old man who could still swing for the green in his late seventies.

A little girl in Texas grew up not to be scarred by a hideous sight she came upon on a July morning in 1934, but to be both outraged and empowered by it. She threw herself fiercely into her school studies, both elementary and high school, won a math scholarship to Baylor University, and developed organizational skills that she used in what she considered to be her mission in life. At the age of 32, in 1955, Mrs. Jodi Edson Fullerton—math teacher at Roy Miller High School in Corpus Christi—was flown to New York City along with five other recipients, all who had earned awards for community service from the American Society for the Prevention of Cruelty to Animals.

Even long afterward, Nilla thought she could hear him.

She thought for sure she heard in her head the crackling sounds like that of the old classical records her mama used to play, which to her meant that their power was on, their tubes had lit up, and they were connected again. Sometimes at night she woke up hearing it, and she would send out into the dark, :*Are you there, Curtis? I'm here. I'm listening.*:

But never did he answer.

She did not ask her father if the woman's body had been found. She decided it had been, and that was all she needed. If it hadn't been found, that meant the alligators had torn it to pieces.

So there.

When she was thirteen she heard someone sending out a hello. She answered, and it turned out to be a ten-year-old girl named Denise Bishop whose family had just moved from Memphis to Gulfport, Mississippi, where her father worked on a tugboat. Denise said that before the move she'd been talking to a young man in Mountain Home, Arkansas, who had gone off last year to join the Army, and she recalled that he said he used to talk to a woman who worked at the public library in Springdale, Arkansas, so there were others like themselves out there, only it was best to keep it quiet because not a whole lot of people could understand it.

Nilla had said that, luckily for her, her parents did understand. She and Denise planned to meet, but it never happened. They communicated back and forth for nearly two years, their power turned on and the tubes glowing, and then quite suddenly Nilla started having trouble both talking and listening to Denise; it was as if her battery had simply reached its end, and though she tried to give herself time to recharge and she had short periods when everything was strong and clear, she realized there was a definite decay in the signal, and it was not going to last forever.

At the age of fifteen, Nilla heard the telepathic "voice" of Denise Bishop fade out for the last time, and it was over.

School became very important to her. That, and reading in the medical field: journals and books that were way over her head but she was bound and determined to absorb their information. She had never forgotten how helpless she felt kneeling beside Curtis that terrible night at the lake, unable to do a single thing to keep him alive; it had marked her, and now it drove her.

She took an array of Red Cross courses, including emergency life-saving. It was the beginning.

Nilla entered Tulane's Medical School at the age of 24. Eight years later, after her residency requirements were met, she became Dr. Nilla Teresa Ludenmere, and a little over three years after that she became Mrs. Robert Hobart...actually, Mrs. Doctor Robert Hobart, her groom being a physician who had waded ashore at Normandy as a young medic on D-Day.

In May of 1962, the two doctors and married couple opened a free clinic on Esplanade Avenue in the Faubourg Treme, not far from Marais Street where used to stand Prince Purdy's barbershop, and two blocks past the vacant and littered lots where laughter used to spill out from the long-gone Fancy Acre, Ten Spot, and Done Didit clubs.

In spite of the city's wanting to change its name to honor the Confederate general Pierre Beauregard, the three acres of community park continued to be known as Congo Square to the residents of the Treme. But many of the local businesses and cafes were gone to the memory of the elderly, gone to dust and rust, decaying wood and fallen bricks.

The row upon row of shotgun shacks remained.

When anyone asked who the clinic was named after, Dr. Nilla Hobart said it was a friend of hers. A person who had meant so much to her life. A person, she said, who her father had once called her knight in shining armor. And the truth was, her father—as cantankerous and foul-mouthed as ever, especially after he lost a golf game to L.J.—still called her friend that, after all these years.

And Nilla had to always add, in speaking of her friend, that he had been a very, very good listener.